THE BILLIONAIRE'S SECRET

L. STEELE

For the good girls
who love morally grey heroes
who make you weak...
I see you!

PROLOGUE

Claim your free prequel to this series HERE

I have a heart that never beats, I have a home but I never sleep. I can take a man's house and build another's, I love to play games with my many brothers. I am a king among fools. Who am I?

Answer: The King of Hearts in a deck of cards

Victoria

"Will he, or won't he?"

I turn to the man playing the role of my husband. "Who are you talking about?" I ask.

"Saint," he replies.

"Who?"

"The man glowering at you from across the garden." Adam swipes a finger under his collar, "I wonder if he'll approach you before the night is over?"

I angle my body, but he shakes his head, "Don't look there."

Right. I swallow. "Is that good?"

"It's perfect," he reassures me. "Things are on plan."

This is what I want, don't I? This is why I am here. So why is my heart pounding? Why is my stomach tying itself in knots? A trickle of sweat runs down my spine.

"Act natural." He half smiles.

I swallow, tip up my chin. *I can do this.*

"Come, dear, meet your stepdaughter," he beckons.

I step forward, and my heels sink into the lawns attached to the beautiful town house located in prime real estate in the heart of London. I smooth my palm down the golden-brown dress that comes to below my knees. Good thing I'd packed this dress near the top of my luggage; that had made it much easier to change before leaving the airport. Finding the shoes had been a different story. Our flight from LAX to London had been delayed, leaving no time to spare for a stop at our hotel.

The hair on the nape of my neck prickles. An electric shiver runs down my spine. I jerk my chin up.

Blue eyes blaze at me—cerulean, cold, never-ending whorls of cornflowers in summer time, the dark depths of a lake before the water freezes over. How could so many facets be intertwined with his gaze? I swallow; sweat beads my palm.

The words from *Happiness is a Warm Gun*, by the Beatles scroll across my mind. Heat flushes my cheeks. I have a penchant for the Beatles, but why the hell did I have to think of that particular song?

Saint glances from me to my 'husband.' His jaw tics. Anger rolls off of him, a thick black cloud that slams into my chest, sinks into my blood, hooks into me and seems to yank me toward him. *Closer, get closer.* I gasp and my fingers tremble.

Saint's gaze intensifies and I shudder. My toes curl. Why am I so affected by his presence?

Adam nudges me.

I blink, then tear my gaze away from the stranger. "Summer." I hold my hand out to my stepdaughter. "It's lovely to meet you."

She's beautiful in her wedding dress. At twenty-one, she is a year younger than me. And she has already found the man of her dreams.

Me? I am taking it one day at a time. I am trying to survive. I clutch my handbag to my side.

Summer swallows. "I didn't realize…"

"That you had a stepmother?" I ask.

"…that I had a father." She glances at the man she is meeting after fifteen years.

Adam shifts uncomfortably. "I was hoping you two could get acquainted," he mumbles.

Across from me, Saint widens his stance; his hands are clenched at his sides. Huh? Is he upset about something?

"I didn't mean for this to come as such a surprise." I force myself to focus on Summer, " I wish there had been a way I could have warned you of our coming…but…"

Summer nods, "You don't need to apologize." Her eyes narrow, "I understand how it could have been."

I glance from Summer to her new husband, Sinclair Sterling, who hovers protectively over her.

He and his six friends—often referred to as the Seven by the media —co-own 7A Investments. They are among the richest, most powerful men in the country.. and… Saint is one of them. Why the hell can't I stop thinking of him?

I clear my throat, "Perhaps, we can catch up once you are recovered from your wedding and the honeymoon—"

"There is no honeymoon," Sinclair interjects.

Summer's body tenses again.

Strange. His words are brusque. Yet he hasn't been able to look away from her, his body leaning into hers. Funny how body language conveys so much more than words.

Like the man who hasn't glanced away from me since our eyes first met. Goosebumps pop on my skin.

"Not until we've sorted out the little business between us." Sinclair nods toward Adam, "Tomorrow." He steps around us and walks off, guiding Summer along.

"I won't be more than a minute." Adam strides toward a group of men in a corner of the garden. I glance after him, wanting to ask him not to leave me alone with Saint.

Too late. He prowls closer, "Victoria, is it?"

Black coffee, crushed ice, hot chocolate sauce—the timbre of his voice coils about my waist, slithers down to the hollow between my legs.

I clench my thighs together.

That voice? What I wouldn't give to have him read aloud from a Harry Potter novel. *Oh, my god, did I think that?* Why is he insinuating himself into my every obsession? I shift my weight from foot to foot.

He tilts his head, looks me up and down. Those blue eyes pale until they resemble chips of ice. My heart begins to race.

This man? He'd not take 'no' for an answer. Never turn down a challenge.

His lips curl and he widens his stance.

The movement draws my attention to the fabric tented at his crotch. *What the—?* Is he turned on? And he's making no move to hide it either? The arrogance of the man. A warmth pools deep inside of me. A melting sensation thrums out from my core. And why am I not able to stop my response? No way, am I going to indulge his interest... Or his ego for that matter.

"Mrs. Rhodes to you." I tip up my chin, up, all the way up to peer into his beautiful face, "Are you the hired help?"

His expression falters, then a chuckle rumbles from within him.

The harsh sound grates across my skin. All of my nerve endings pop in response. Why am I so tuned into him?

He abruptly stops laughing, pretends to flick something off of his suit.

Bastard. So, he thinks he can disguise his surprise by feigning boredom? Typical.

His resting dick face is all hard angles, cut lines, a mean upper lip, patrician nose and prominent chin...spoilt by that full pouty lower lip which hints at something more—sensuous, luxurious, a personality that indulges in hedonistic pleasures, that controls and does not hesitate to take. My core clenches. I raise my hand, ready to chew on my fingernail. *Ha!* And wouldn't that be a dead giveaway of how much I am affected by his presence?

I tuck my elbows into my sides. I will not give in to the temptation. But would I give in to him?

No. No way, would I indulge this melting sensation that seems to have gripped my center. I square my shoulders, twist my fingers together in front of me.

He drops his gaze to my hands, then up to my face, "You're not wearing a wedding band." He frowns.

I cover my left hand. "Not everyone who's married wears one."

He thrusts out his chin, peruses my features. His blue gaze deepens. *Don't blink. Don't look away.* When you meet a predator, it's best to not show any fear. My heart beat ratchets up.

His nostrils flare.

Bloody hell, can he sense my uncertainty?

He tilts his head, "Your husband left you on your own?" His voice ripples up my spine. My scalp tingles.

What in the ever lovin' hell is happening to me? I brace myself, tip my chin up. "He knows he can trust me," I reply.

His lips curl, "But can *you* trust *me*?"

I blink. The hell does he mean? My fingers tingle and my palms itch. I've tried every bloody remedy to cure myself of this horrible nail-biting habit. But the events of the last few months have wiped out any progress I had made.

He holds out his hand. "Saint Jordan Killian Caldwell," he drawls.

"Did you miss a name?"

His features go blank, then his lips curl, "Very good."

"Not looking for your approval," I mutter.

"You sure?" His lips kick up in a smile that isn't one at all.

I shiver.

"I'm Saint to my friends."

I glance down at his proffered hand, then thrust mine behind my back.

"Good thing I am not one of them," I mutter.

He lowers his arm. "No, you're not." His eyes gleam, "You and I, we could never have such a bland relationship."

"No?" My belly flutters.

He shakes his head, then looks me up and down. "In fact, you don't feature on my radar at all."

Jerk. Pretentious, spoilt, rich prick who wears his privilege as if the world owes him. I firm my lips.

He flicks another invisible piece of dust from his tailored jacket. The breadth of his shoulders stretches the fabric. His biceps strain against the cloth. He widens his stance, and I can't stop myself from taking in the sculpted abs outlined through the white dress shirt that sheaths his muscles. Power surrounds him. The force of his magnetism is a tangible sensation that pours off of him, hits me in the chest. I gasp. My throat closes.

"Good bye, Victoria." He turns to leave, takes a step away, then another. His jacket stretches across his tight butt—clearly, he forgot to remove the stick when he left home. My lips quirk. He prowls forward and his slacks mold to powerful thighs. I swallow. Shit, this man wears that suit like it was stitched onto him. The muscles of those powerful thighs coil and coil, barely contained in those pants that narrow over boots. Huh? He wears faded cowboy boots that've seen far better days.

What the hell?

Is that a quirk, or another affectation? Why would he wear boots that simply don't match the rest of his £7000 suits? Only when my heel sinks into the ground do I realize that I've placed my stilettos squarely in his footstep. I bite the inside of my cheek.

Let him go; don't say it. Don't let curiosity get the better of you.

"The more you think, the more you find; what am I?" I call out.

He tenses, then swivels to face me.

"What did you say?"

Those cold blue eyes bore into me, the force of his personality pinning me in place. My heart begins to race.

"N...nothing." I wave a hand in the air, "Forget it." I turn away.

Hard fingers clutch at my wrist. I am spun around with such force that I stumble. The grasp on my arm increases in pressure, and I find my balance. He keeps my hand imprisoned behind me, his arm lined up against mine, my back curved, my breasts thrust up. The heat from his body crowds me, envelops me. Less than an inch separates us.

How would it be if he had plastered my chest to his? I flick out my tongue to wet my lips. His gaze drops to my mouth. His nostrils flare.

"Repeat what you said," he rasps.

"No."

He lowers his voice to a hush, "Do it." All other noises fade away. My mind focuses on him. I take in the creases that fan out from the edges of his eyes, the furrows on his forehead, the tendons that pop at his throat.

"A puzzle," I whisper. "The answer is a puzzle."

"Why did you ask me that question?"

"I wanted to take you by surprise." I firm my lips. "That's all."

"You expect me to believe that?" He searches my features. "That you'd ask me a riddle for the hell of it?"

"Why? Does it scare you?"

The wind blows, and a tuft of his hair falls over his forehead. I raise my hand toward it. He grabs my wrist, wrenches it behind my back, then lowers his head until his nose bumps mine, "Be afraid, Victoria. Be very afraid."

"Of you?"

"Of this game you are playing." He releases me and I slump back on my heels. My chest heaves. My heart pounds so hard I am sure it's going to tear out of my rib cage.

"Or what?" I purse my lips.

"Or get ready to get hurt." He straightens the cuff of his shirt. "For I never lose, and when you do—" he straightens, fixes me with that penetrating gaze, "—no one will be able to save you."

1

Saint

"And what if I don't?" Her low voice slices through my guts. "What if I don't want to be saved?" she whispers. Her lips tremble and her chin wobbles. Her beautiful green eyes grow impossibly large in her face. An act, all an act. She's married, for fuck's sake.

"Is that how you trapped your husband?"

She pales. Her breath catches.

A sharp pain stabs at my chest. Shit, now I am upset because I hurt her feelings. Bloody fuck, do I have my balls or what?

She turns to leave, my rib cage tightens. My lungs burn. I swoop down, grab her wrist, and pinpricks of heat crawl up my arm from the touch. *What the fuck?*

She shivers, did she feel that too? Nah. Surely, it's a figment of my imagination.

I tug at her; she angles her body half toward me, half away, her handbag a red slash of color against the brown of her dress. "People are watching," she hisses.

"The fuck I care?"

She glances at me, "What if I do?"

"Do you?" So I'm attracted to her. Shit happens. She's another man's wife, the kind of complication I've preferred to steer clear of. What is it about her that insists I stay, tug at her wrist until she turns to face me?

She shakes her head. One side of her beautiful mouth twists. "But I'm afraid my husband does."

"And you care about his feelings?" I glower.

"I care about mine." She tips up her chin. Her eyes blaze with an inner fire. "If I were looking for an affair, it wouldn't be with the likes of you."

"Oh?" I peruse her features, "And are you looking for one?"

"What?"

"A lover. Someone who could arouse you with a glance, who would kiss you until you moan, someone who would pull you aside and take you while your husband mingles with the guests." I lean in close enough for her sweet sugary scent to lace my nostrils. Damn, but she's aroused. "Is that what you want?"

"No." Her eyebrows twist.

"Good." I release her so suddenly that she stumbles. "For when I take you, there will be no space for sweettalk, no emotions involved, no reason for hesitation. I'll treat your body like it were mine."

She draws in a sharp breath.

"You scared, yet?" I drawl.

"No," she mumbles.

"You should be."

A gust of wind blows her hair across her face. I reach up to tuck it behind her ear.

She shivers.

I unbutton my jacket, shrug it off.

She frowns. "What are you doing?"

I place it about her shoulders, position my mouth next to her ear, "When I finally drive into you, you'll weep not because I'm hurting you, but because you are empty without me."

Her breath hitches.

"Because you ache for me and will do anything for my fingers in you, my tongue on yours, the squeeze of my hand on your hips, the burn between your thighs as I drink from your wetness." I lower my voice.

Her breasts heave.

"When you plead with me to hurt you, to hold you down and claim you, to put you out of your agony even as you ask to be tormented further; when you beg for me with your pretty mouth, when you yearn to be filled in any way I deem fit... Then, and only then, I might let you come..." I pause, "Or not."

She swallows.

"And when I finally take you, it will be unexpected, life-altering, mind-blowing, intense. Everything else before will fade in comparison."

Her breathing grows more ragged. Good. I step back, pull the lapels of my jacket together. My knuckles brush against her breasts and she shivers.

My groin tightens and my balls hurt. Fuck me, but this might be the first time I've talked myself into a hard-on—thanks to her.

"You want that, hmm?"

She shakes her head.

I chuckle. "If I touched you between your legs, you and I both know you'd be wet. And you are soaking, aren't you?"

She bites down on her lower lip, spots of color burning high on her cheekbones.

I lower my voice to a hush, "Answer me."

She trembles, "Yes."

"Do you want me?"

She tips up her chin, "What if I do?"

"All you have to do is ask."

"And you'll give me what I want?" Her eyebrows knit.

"I'll make sure you get everything you deserve." I look her up and down, "The time you spend with me will be the single most pleasurable time of your life."

Her lips part.

Her pupils dilate.

"You feel me?"

She nods.

"Say it."

"I... I feel you," she whispers.

"Good."

I turn to leave. Take one step, another.

"Wait," she calls out.

Bingo, I bite the inside of my cheek to keep from smiling. Give it another second, then turn to glance at her.

"Your jacket." She begins to shrug out of it.

I hold up my hand, "Keep it." I pivot and leave.

What the hell happened there?

Why did she ask me a riddle? How did she know about the ghosts that have haunted my worst nightmares since the incident when six of my friends and I had been kidnapped? And why the hell had I allowed myself to be drawn into further conversation? I'd seen the hurt in her eyes and had wanted to replace it with a twisted pleasure. A primal part of me had wanted her to wear clothes I bought for her. Had wanted to replace memories of any previous encounters with her husband with those that my words had aroused in her.

Does she enjoy it when he fucks her?

I clench my fingers at my sides. What the hell is wrong with me? She's taken, married to another. I should let her go. So why does every pore in my body insist that this is not over?

I head inside the townhouse that belongs to my friend Sinclair Sterling, aka the groom of the wedding. Striding to the bar, I lean over the counter, "Where the fuck did she come from?" I slide my fingers into my pocket, searching for the pack of cigarettes that isn't there. Shit, why did I quit again? Whose bloody idea had it been to give up smoking? I sure could do with a puff now.

Weston tops up my champagne flute. "Who are you talking about?" he asks.

"Victoria," I mutter.

"You mean the woman you've been ogling—"

I snarl.

He snickers, "—I meant 'staring at' for the last half hour."

"Fuck off." I reach for the champagne.

"She's married." Weston pours the remainder of the bubbling liquid in his glass.

"Yeah." I raise the flute to my lips.

"Isn't that off limits, even for you?" He overturns the bottle, places it in the bucket of ice.

He's right. I stay away from married women... Normally. Don't need the kind of emotional baggage that comes with them. Hell no, I prefer my hookups to be neat—swoop in, decimate, get out.

I chug down the drink, then grimace. "Isn't there any real alcohol in this place?"

"That's £20,000 you chugged down there, ol' chap."

I stare into my glass. "Could have fooled me." I survey the shelf of liquors behind the bar. "Whiskey," I growl. "Why are you bartending anyway?"

"Because Damian decided he preferred the company of one of the fairer sex than our esteemed selves."

"Right," I mutter.

Weston half turns his body, reaches for the bottle I'd have chosen myself. Good man. He places the bottle on the counter, pulls out tumblers, then proceeds to pour in a generous measure. I dunk my hand into the bucket, pull out ice-cubes that I plop into my drink.

"Classy." Weston grimaces, uses ice-cube tongs for his. "So, you interested in Summer's stepmother?"

"She's Summer's age." I glower.

"You're not seriously considering this, are you?"

"Why not?" I swirl the liquid in my glass. "Besides, something about that marriage is not right."

"You can never tell from the outside," Weston retorts. "Only those in the relationship have an inkling of what's happening."

"Come on." I jerk my chin, "Watch the two of them. You really think she has feelings for that piece of shit husband of hers?"

Weston glances past me. He takes a sip from his glass, "Didn't think you were the kind to indulge in speculation."

Me neither. I rub the back of my neck. What the hell am I doing thinking about possibilities, about could-have-beens? Hadn't the events of my past taught me to move on swiftly? To never look back, never dwell on the piece of shit hand I'd been dealt. I chug down my drink.

"You're right." I set down the glass with a thump. "I am going to find out everything about her, ex-boyfriends, what food she likes, her taste in clothes—"

"Wouldn't you rather ask her about it?" He tilts his head.

"What would the fun be in that?"

He stares at me, then nods. "True. Knowledge is power and all that."

"I am going to dig out every piece of dirt on her and why she's married to that fucker of a husband." I tighten my fingers about the bottle.

Weston pulls out his phone, moves his fingers over the screen. "I know just the person to help you."

2

What is always in front of you but can't be seen?
Answer: Your future

5 days later

Victoria

Sunlight shines off the polished casket of my husband. Adam Rhodes died 4 days ago in his home city of London of a heart attack. He was fifty-five years old.

If I sound like I am reading the words from an impersonal obituary, it's because I didn't spend much time with him. I had played the role of his wife for less than two months. Nevertheless, I should cry, shouldn't I?

I bite down on my lower lip, stare as the casket disappears out of sight into the ground. No one deserves to die that young. I hadn't spent much time with him... Yet the fact that he was breathing one second, gone the next is...a shock.

A wind blows and goosebumps dot my skin. That's London for you. One moment you are warm in the sun, then the breeze brushes over you and it's as if someone walked over your grave. Not a good comparison right now. My lips twist. I hunch my shoulders in my jacket—okay, Saint's jacket. It dwarfs me, and I had rolled up the sleeves so it would fit. Why the hell had I worn it? What the hell had I been thinking? It had seemed like a small act of defiance, one way to exert control over my life, I suppose. Had I wanted to be surrounded by his scent? I huddle into its warmth.

Next to me, Summer's shoulders shake. She clings to her sister Karma. Both girls had reconnected to their father after so long, only to lose him again. This wasn't supposed to happen. It means I am on my own.

An electric current surges up my spine. I stare past the open grave. Blue eyes bore into me. The force of his physical presence crashes into me. The impact of his dominance pulls at me. The hollow feeling in my belly intensifies. The melting sensation in my core deepens. *Shit.* My 'husband' is in his newly-dug grave, not a few feet away, and I can't stop eye-fucking the man—the almost stranger—the man who'd threatened to hurt me if I engage with him again. *What the hell is wrong with me?*

He takes a step forward, and hell, if I'm going to let him approach me here in front of my family—my dead husband's family. That makes me a widow, right? A pressure builds at my temples. This entire thing is getting out of hand. This is not what I had agreed to when I had bargained with the kidnappers for Nina's freedom.

I'd agreed to pose as wife to Adam Rhodes on this trip, and returned to my home country, as part of the plan. But Saint...? This chemistry between us...? Hell, if it isn't a complication. In that sense, Adam dying had been opportune. It means I don't have to add the role of cheating spouse to my persona.

I squeeze my eyes shut. Bloody hell. How can I be this callous? I barely knew the man who had posed as my husband, but when had I become so insensitive that I couldn't pause long enough to mourn the end of someone's life?

I turn to Summer. "I have to go," I choke on the words. I don't have to fake the confusion or the pain that I am sure is etched on my face.

She glances at me, "You okay Victoria?"

I nod.

"Why don't you come home with me and..." She glances at Sinclair and her voice trails off. So, the two of them haven't resolved whatever has been marring their relationship? I wish I could offer her some advice, but glass houses, and all that.

"You could come to our place," Karma offers. "It's a tiny apartment, but you'll have company."

"I..." I swallow. "I think it's better if I am on my own." I glance between them. "Not that I don't appreciate the offer. Honestly, you two have been more than generous, considering how much of a shock the last couple of days have been." My chin wobbles. I twist my fingers together. "I need to get my head around what's happened."

Karma opens her mouth to speak, but Summer shakes her head at her sister. Karma frowns, then subsides. Whew! Okay. I don't want to tell any more lies... I need to crawl into bed and think about how to put the next phase of this plan into action.

Summer reaches forward and hugs me. I pat her shoulder. "Thank you for accepting me," I whisper.

"You're welcome." She steps back, "We need to stick together, huh? It's the only way to get through this shit that life insists on throwing at us."

I squeeze her hand, then brush past her, and head for the black limo that had brought me here. I twist open the door handle and sink inside the vehicle.

"Move over."

Saint ducks inside, forcing me to scoot over.

He drops into the seat opposite me, slams the door shut.

"What are you doing?" I gape.

He half turns and raps on the partition that separates the chauffeur from the passengers, then straightens.

The car pulls away from the curb, leaving me trapped with

this...this man whose face I have seen only once; whose features are burned into my mind. Hell. No way, am I riding with him. Not for one second more. I grab at my handle; the door doesn't open. The hell? I slap at the barrier between the seats. The driver doesn't respond. Hit the switch that opens the communication channel with the chauffeur,

"Pull over. I want to get out."

There's no answer.

"Stop this car now, or I am going to call the police."

"Go ahead." Saint smirks.

I pull out my phone from my handbag, position my fingers over the keypad. And pause. A beat, another.

"Thought not." Saint takes the phone from me and pockets it. "I'll take that jacket now." He jerks his chin at my attire.

"What?" I gape.

"My jacket, my rules." His eyes glint.

Jerk. I undo the buttons, shrug off the jacket.

"It wasn't your color anyway," he comments.

"No?"

He shakes his head, "It accentuates the dark circles under your eyes."

"Fuck you very much." I hold out the jacket to him.

He chuckles, then jerks his chin. I follow his gaze to the coat hanger by the window on his side.

It's either maneuver around him or over him to reach it.

"Do it."

What a complete bastard.

To hell with it, I am not going to allow him to intimidate me. I half crawl over him, reach for the hook at the far side, miss, then swear aloud.

His chuckle floats from over me, his scent surrounds me, and the corded muscles of his thighs graze against my stomach. I shiver, reach up for it again. Success. I hang the damn thing up, then retreat to my side of the seat.

"You get much sleep?" His voice dips, takes on that gravelly tenor that sends a fresh surge of heat down my spine. Hell, this crazy reaction to his proximity? Clearly, I hadn't imagined it from our first meeting.

"What do you think?" I glance out through the tinted windows as the car eases onto the main road. "Where are we going?" I ask.

"Where do you think?" I hear the amusement in his voice.

A fresh burst of anger flares to life in my chest. I turn on him, "Stop this, whatever it is."

"You started it." He folds one leg over his other knee, and my gaze is drawn to the beat-up cowboy boots.

"Is that the same pair you had on the other day?"

He stiffens, then circles his ankle with his thick fingers. "Curious about me? Want to get to know me better, hmm?"

"Of course, not."

I turn away, glance at the bumper-to-bumper traffic. Who knew there was a graveyard in the middle of the city tucked away behind all those trees? That's London for you. Full of surprises. You are never too far from a park, or as it turns out in this case, a resting place reserved for the very rich.

"I am taking you to your hotel." Saint's gravelly voice chafes over my skin. I'm instantly wet... Okay, wetter. Oh, my god! If anyone can seduce with words, it is this man.

"This is my car," I turn to him, "so it stands to reason that I am the one taking you—"

His smile widens.

I snap my mouth shut. "That's not what I meant."

"Oh?" He tilts his head. "I beg to differ, but let me be absolutely clear, you won't be taking me anywhere. I'll be taking you. And I promise you, I will take you, and when I do, it will never be a meeting of equals, for..." He leans in close, "I hold the power. Never forget that."

I stare into those cold blue eyes.—the blackness that crawls in their depths, that pulls at me, calls to me, that resonates with that most intimate part of me, the one that I've never acknowledged, that wants to be taken without mercy. How dare he find out about my innermost needs when I had never acknowledged them myself? Only when my palm connects with his face, do I realize what I've done.

I gasp. My fingers tingle. I take in the reddening fingerprints on his cheek.

"I... I'm sorry," I whisper.

He peels back his lips, his teeth flashing white against his tanned skin. "Oh, you will be."

He swoops down. I cringe away, but he's too fast. He buries his fingers in my hair, tugs me forward. I strain against his hold. He applies pressure—not bruising, not punishing, but just enough for me to lean into him. The black scarf slips from around my neck.

He lowers his gaze to where the tops of my breasts are exposed from above the low-cut neckline.

His jaw tics.

"What belongs to you, but is used by others?"

His voice coils around me, slithers down into the crevasse between my lower lips, reaches deep inside, touching, stroking, molding to my contours—a living entity that wants and takes, that never stops, that will not be satisfied until I submit to him. *Submit.*

"Answer the bloody question." His tone rams through the jumbled quagmire of my mind, pulling me in, drawing me down, insisting that I focus my attention on that beautiful visage.

"You have one second to answer." He raises heavy-lidded eyelids; a flush of red suffuses his cheeks. So, he's not impervious to me either. This, whatever it is between us, affects him as well.

What does that mean? Can I use it to my advantage? Do I dare leverage it to get what I want from him?

I tip up my chin. "I… I don't know." I swallow.

"Are you sure you want to find out?" He leans in close enough for his scent to overpower me. The heat from his big body slams into my chest. His breath sears my cheeks, and our noses bump. He drops his gaze to my mouth. I part my lips, close the remaining millimeters between us. The world tilts. He grabs my shoulder, applies enough pressure that I slip off the car seat and down onto the floor on my knees.

I glance up at him, "You have some nerve."

He smirks, widens his legs.

Don't look down. Don't. I glance down at the bulge that tents his crotch, which is definitely considerably larger than what I'd noticed at the wedding. Saliva pools in my mouth. How big, how beautifully heavy he'd feel down my throat. What the hell am I thinking?

"I just buried my husband," I swallow.

"You didn't love him."

My jaw drops, "How dare you arrive at that assumption?"

"Am I wrong?" His gaze burns into me. A pulse beats at his temple. He peruses my features, "Tell me."

I shake my head.

His shoulders relax. Huh, does it mean anything to him that I had no feelings for Adam? That it was all a front to get me here? Why is it important to him that I didn't love another man?

I blink at him.

He lowers his chin, "Ask me to pull the car over and leave."

"Would you do it?" I frown.

"Nope," he chuckles, "but it sure was fun allowing you to think you had the option."

Anger twists my chest. Blood thuds at my temple. I raise my hand again.

He doesn't take his gaze from my face. "Don't," he rasps.

One word. A softly spoken command. My belly quivers. The force of his personality seems to grow until it fills the space, pushes down on my shoulders, holds me in thrall of this strange connection between us. I lower my arm

"Good girl."

A flush burns my cheeks. Why does his praise mean the world to me? Why do I want to please him with every fiber in my being? This is unnatural. I frown.

"You think too much, Gigi." He touches his finger to my forehead.

"My name's Victoria," I retort.

"Gigi suits you better."

"Why is that?"

"Short for Good Girl." He presses his knuckles below my chin, "Also you look like a Gigi." He turns my face up, "Definitely, Gigi."

I stare up at him. I've always hated my name. How the hell did he perceive that? My pulse begins to race.

"Also, the answer is 'my name,'" he drawls.

"What?" I frown. "What do you mean?"

"The answer to my earlier riddle, of course. And you're welcome."

"For what?"

"I've decided to spare you the blow job."

"What?"

He nods.

"Don't tell me you didn't think about it?"

"Of course, not." I lie.

"How about this? The more you cram into it, the wetter it grows. What is it?"

"Another riddle?" I bite the inside of my cheek.

"You started the game," he reminds me. "Think you can keep up with me?"

His lips curl in that smirk—that I am coming to hate.

"This your idea of fun?" I set my jaw.

"No, but this is."

He lowers his zipper and his cock springs free. Hard, massive, it points up at me, inviting me, mocking me. A vein pulses up the underside. The head is swollen, nearly purple— How is he this aroused? Why is it that every time I see him, he seems to be erect? Why do I care? So what if my mouth waters and a pulse flares to life between my legs? The man's seriously packing, and hell, if I don't want to wrap my fingers around that beautiful length. *No, no, no, did you call his dick beautiful? Look away, look away.* I raise my gaze to his face.

"No boxers?"

Did I say that? Why is it that there is no filter to my thoughts? I am not normally this way. I am reserved, aloof... That's what I've been told, anyway. Is it the role I'm playing that's allowing me to lower my barriers? To speak what's on my mind and damn the consequences? I mean, how much worse could it get, right?

"You prefer I wear boxers?" he asks.

"I don't prefer you at all."

"More lies." He clicks his tongue. "We'll have to work on that."

"I am not working on anything with you," I mutter.

"Oh, but you will." He grips his thick cock, swipes himself from root to head. A bead of precum appears at the top.

Saliva pools in my mouth. Why is the sight of him getting himself hot so hot? I've seen my share of porn online, researched more in preparation of this role—yeah, the nerd in me couldn't stop until I'd done a bloody thorough job of it—but this...? Saint's thick fingers wrapped around himself is...a study in eroticism.

"A hole." His voice is harsh.

I blink up at him, "Is that the answer to your last riddle?" I whisper.

"Did it turn you on when I said that?" he asks.

Heat flares low in my belly. My core pulses in agreement. My throat closes. My mouth is so dry I am sure I can't force out a word.

He jerks his chin as if he's already heard my answer, then releases me, only to scoop up the moisture from his dick. He holds out his thumb. "Open." His voice is low, hushed. The dark edge to his tone brooks no refusal. *Obey him. Do it.*

My mouth waters. Heat curls low in my belly. I lower my mouth, close it around his finger.

3

Saint

I glance down at the back of her head. Her pink tongue swirls around my finger, then she takes me in, sucks on my digit. My cock jerks. Bloody hell. She isn't supposed to affect me on such an elemental level. This yearning need that boils up inside of me, that had compelled me to glance at her across the freshly-dug grave of her husband and think: mine. What the fuck is that about?

I don't do emotions.

Nor relationships.

Definitely never allow a woman to take control. Ever. I scowl as she takes my finger deeper into her mouth. She presses the length of her tongue to my digit, and heat radiates from the contact; blood rushes to my groin.

"Fucking fuck."

She sucks in her lips, mocking the motion of what she could do to my cock. A pulse flares to life behind my eyelids, at my wrist, even in my fucking balls. She leans back, releasing my finger with a wet plop.

"Is that enough?" she snaps.

"We haven't even begun."

"This is wrong." Her lips tighten. "Whatever the relationship between Adam and me... We just buried him. It's basic human decency, that we don't—"

"Fuck?" I tilt my head. "But we aren't."

"A technicality." she insists.

"Oh, believe me, when we screw, there will be nothing technical about it."

She trembles. The limo moves forward with a muted lurch. Silence a beat, then another.

"Don't do it." She murmurs.

"You mean this?" I reach down, swipe myself from base to head.

She gulps. The black of her pupils bleeds out, leaving only a circle of green around them.

This woman... Her response is the single most erotic thing I have ever seen.

Her gaze latches onto my motions as I pump myself back-forth-back.

"Why?" she asks. Her features twist. Her gaze, though, doesn't waver. She watches with a single-minded intensity that's as much of a turn on...more so...with the anticipation that builds between us.

Because there's a strange pleasure in denying myself access to what I could so easily have. One glance and she'd be on her back, opening her legs to me...but that would be too easy. Besides, I need her to come to me; to put herself at my mercy. Until then, this will have to do.

I increase the pace of my movements.

Her breathing grows ragged. Her chest rises and falls. I watch her watch me pleasure myself, and fuck, if that isn't the most erotic sensation ever.

The tension tightens at the base of my spine. Fuck, if I don't come right now. I squeeze the base of my cock to hold myself in.

"I absolve you of responsibility, Gigi," I snap.

She jerks her chin, "What do you mean?"

"You don't have to pretend. You want to do this, but your conscience doesn't permit you. Well, blame it on me. Use me as your excuse. When we get to the other side, you can resume your role in the real world, but for now, there's only me, you, and this orgasm that's pushing for release. Allow yourself to enjoy this, Gigi."

She draws in a sharp breath, her lips part, and it's as if it's a signal.

My orgasm roars out; my balls draw up. I position my dick and come all over her face, her chest, across her arms.

Her chest rises and falls; her shoulders snap back.

"Don't you dare come, Gigi."

"What?" she gasps.

"You heard me," I admonish.

She licks her lips, her shoulders heave.

I reach across and rub my cum into her face, her neck, into the creamy skin of her arms.

Then I reach for the tissue holder, snatch up some sheets and clean myself off. I tuck myself in, help her onto the seat, making sure to keep the length of the seat between us.

"You bastard," she snarls.

"You're frustrated. I understand." I smirk. This is a new low, even for me. Shit. Why eviscerate her ego completely? Is this the only way I am able to communicate? To hide behind the façade I have so carefully built to hide from the world?

She makes a noise deep in her throat.

I shake my head. "Don't do it."

"What?"

"Whatever bodily injury you were planning." I glance at her sideways. "I'm stronger than you."

"No shit." She tosses her head.

"You don't get it now, but it's for your own good."

"What?" She throws up her hands. "You coming all over me—"

"Which you enjoyed."

She opens her mouth—

I slash my palm across the air, "Don't deny it."

She flattens her lips, "—or that you didn't let me come?"

"Ah... Now that," I tap my fingers on my chest, "is easy to fix."

"I'm sure I don't want to know this."

"Oh, but you do. All you have to do is come to me and ask me for help."

"Help?"

"From whatever situation it is that you find yourself in." I turn, scan her features. "I have power, Gigi."

"And money," she says bitterly.

"More than you can imagine." I nod. "Whatever problem you have, I can resolve it for you."

"In return for what?"

I look her up and down, "I'll think of something."

"No doubt." She turns to glance outside, her profile bleak. Her chin wobbles. That same strange heat stabs at my chest, a reaction I seem to have when I hurt her.

Fuck. This...is unacceptable.

"Or not." I straighten.

The limo pulls up to the curb in front of her hotel.

She reaches for the door.

"There's one thing more."

She pauses.

"You won't come," I command.

"What?" She turns around to stare at me. "The hell do you mean?"

I lean back, place my arm across the back of the seat. "Your every orgasm belongs to me."

"No."

"Yes," I nod, waggle a finger in the air. "No cheating, darling. You will not come until I give you permission."

"Fuck you."

She pushes open the door, flounces off. The limo pulls away, turns the corner, then stops.

I push open my door, step around, and slide into the driver's seat.

"You better know what you're doing," Weston growls from the passenger seat.

I glance over him, laugh, "The uniform suits you."

"I didn't have to wear the hat." He tosses it down between the seats.

"Aww, women love men in uniform," I snicker.

"You're envious of how I look in scrubs," he retorts.

I shoot him a sideways glance. "Still can't understand why you chose to become a doctor."

"Same reason you wear those beat up cowboy boots."

"Sentimental value." I raise my shoulders.

"Keep telling yourself that," he mutters. "Besides, considering the amount of time I'm spending to help you with your affair, I may not be a doctor for much longer."

"Not an affair," I mutter, easing the car back in traffic.

"Yeah." He scratches his jaw, "Seriously, you could have allowed the woman a little time to recover from the funeral."

"It's all a bloody act." I spot a break in traffic, step on the gas, and the limo pulls forward.

"The private investigator come through with information?"

"Some." I frown. "Enough to confirm that she's not as innocent as she'd want me to believe."

"And her marriage?"

I draw in a breath, then pull out my pack of cigarettes. I depress the button for the lighter, then toss the pack over to Weston, "Light one for me, will you?"

"Thought you quit."

"Don't fucking nag me, man."

He shoots me a sideways glance, then pulls out a cigarette. He leans forward, grabs the lighter from the dash and lights it up. He blows out smoke, before placing it between my lips. I draw in a puff, then another.

"So, her marriage is—?" he prompts.

I blow out a breath. "Couldn't find any evidence of it being legal."

Weston turns to me, "You mean...?"

I hold up my hand, "I don't think it's genuine."

"Maybe it's wishful thinking?" He drums his fingers on his thigh. "You sure that you aren't splitting straws."

And isn't that the fucking truth? Why the hell can't I simply walk away from her?

"We'll find out soon enough." I draw in a breath. "For now the scene is set."

"Scene?" He glowers at me. "Don't push it, man. You're already w-a-a-y too involved with this woman."

"Involved?" I laugh. "You know how much I love riddles. It's been a long time since I've found one that challenged me."

"Be careful, Saint." He snickers, "Some puzzles are best left unsolved."

4

What is more useful when it is broken?
Answer: An egg

Three weeks later

Victoria

"Am I intruding?" I stare across the office of the executive level of 7A investments. This is it. I couldn't put it off anymore. I have nowhere else to go in this city. After Adam's death, I'd moved out of the hotel and into a studio in Hackney.

I am playing the role the Mafia has demanded of me, but the resources I have to rely on are meagre—what I have left over from the job I'd started after graduating from UCLA. A month into it, I got the call that Nina had been kidnapped, and my entire life had changed.

"You're already here." Saint glares back. "May as well come all the way in." He drags his gaze down to my chest. A flush blooms on my cheeks.

I haven't seen him since that encounter in the limo, but his every word, the expression on his face as he'd come, the way he'd massaged his cum into my skin, marking me as his... I remember every single detail. I had masturbated every night to the image of his orgasm; and I had not come. Damn him, but I couldn't let myself climax.

It wasn't for trying, honestly, but every time I came close to the edge, I lost courage, I couldn't see it through. I felt bereft. Rudderless. Needing, wanting, searching for something...someone to lead me. To take control. Damn the man, I don't need his permission to come. I don't.

His perusal shifts to my belly, my core. Moisture pools in my center. Sweat beads my palm. The invisible connection between us crackles, tightens further. My scalp tingles. The hair on my neck rises. Is the chemistry between us more potent than I remember?

My head spins.

"Victoria, are you okay?" Summer asks from across the room.

I open my mouth to answer when a sound reaches me. I glance down to find a puppy sniffing at my ankles. Huh? Why hadn't I noticed the little fella earlier? He whines, plonks himself down on his haunches and looks up at me with melting eyes. My heart squeezes. A pressure builds at my temples. Jesus, what is wrong with me?

I bend, pet him. He licks my fingers and warmth travels up my arm.

He turns, runs to his bed, and settles there with his chew toy.

He's so cute, just a baby. A heaviness grips my chest. If only I had someone to call my own. A pet? A child? The emptiness inside of me stutters, rolls into itself, grows larger, broader, swells inside, taking on a physical shape. The visceral need to procreate is a tangible thing that claws at me, shoves out at me, pushes me to draw in a sharp breath. Oh my god, what's happening to me?

Why is the sight of a dog affecting me so much? Is it because the meeting with Nina's kidnapper has shown me how quickly everything can shift? He'd told me that the plan had changed to accommodate Adam's death. No longer is it about reporting back on the activities of the Seven. My stomach ties itself in knots; I now have to win the trust of one of them.

Specifically, I have to retrieve a crucial piece of evidence that is in Saint's grasp, and get it back to them.

And I have to do this on my own. The hairs on the nape of my neck prickle.

Can I do that? Can I use the chemistry between us to win his confidence, only to betray him? My guts clench; my core melts. Why does the thought of staying close to him turn me on? Why does the fact that I would have to turn against him feel so wrong?

There is no other route to saving Nina. I have no choice but to go through with this.

My throat closes. Specks of black dot my vision.

"Victoria?" Worry threads Summer's voice. She steps forward, but the other man in the room, who I recognize as her husband, places a hand on her shoulder.

I glance between them. Guess they've worked out whatever issues they may have had? That's good. I am pleased for Summer. She deserves every happiness she can get after what she's been through. And me? What about me? I draw in a sharp breath. *One step at a time. Don't panic. This is no time to have a breakdown.* I straighten my spine. "Everything will be fine now." As I hear my words, a strange calm grips me.

I turn to Saint, "I've been looking for you."

He smirks, "About time."

Funny he should say that. I've spent the time since I last saw him researching him. Not that it had taken much effort to unearth his business success, or his weakness for beautiful women. A little more digging had unearthed his inclination for the darker kind of pleasures. The hair on my forearms rises. He doesn't believe in hiding his tastes; more likely he doesn't care who knows about it. Good. I can use the knowledge to my advantage.

I run my clammy palm down my dress; then take a step forward.

He watches me approach. That strength of his presence beckons. Tension vibrates off of him. The potency of his personality slams into my chest. I gasp and my guts twist. My belly seems to fold in on itself; I sway.

The ground comes up to meet me, but he's already there.

"Hey." He grips my shoulders, straightens me, "You okay?"

"Help me," I gasp.

His lips move. Is he speaking to me?

I frown, raise my hand. He catches my wrist. Those dark brows knit. A vein bulges at his temple. Is he angry? Why is he angry?

The world tilts; heat surrounds me, envelops me. The hard barrier of his chest digs into my cheek. That's when I realize that he's scooped me up in his arms. What the—? Had I almost fainted? Like the heroine of a Victorian novel. Finally conforming to my blasted name. I snicker.

"What's so funny?" he asks.

I glance up at the stubble on his chin. It's only noon. Did he not shaved today? Or is he one of those men who prefers that fashionably unshaven look?

"You sure you want to know?" I mutter.

"I want to find out everything about you."

I blink. Did he say that? What does he mean?

He moves toward the door of the room.

"I can walk," I protest.

"Clearly not." His voice is hard. Anger ebbs and flows around him, encompassing me in a thick fog of awareness that grates across my nerves; it swipes over my breasts, down my belly, headed for the obvious end goal that is my quivering center. I squeeze my thighs together.

His nostrils flare.

Hell, he can't smell my arousal, can he?

A chuckle rumbles up his chest.

Bastard. All of this is amusing to him.

He reaches the door, then pauses. "I am taking my business across to my space." He turns to survey the other two, "You guys cool with that?"

"Saint," Summer's voice is resolute, "don't hurt her."

Saint's muscles tense, then he tilts his head, "I won't do anything that Victoria doesn't want me to do."

He glances down at me, "We understand each other, don't we?"

The hell does he mean by that?

I open my mouth to ask, but he's already striding out and down the corridor.

"I am not your business," I protest.

He laughs, "So why are you here?"

Well, hell. He has me there. I am the one who stumbled in and collapsed at his feet. Which had not been part of the script, by the way. What the hell happened to me? I swear I am not a damsel in distress...though that's the part I've been told to assume. Lucky for me then, that my actions corroborate my persona, huh?

He walks past two offices, then shoulders open the door to the last one. He steps into one similar in size to the one we left behind. A bookcase lines one wall; on the opposite wall is a massive painting of a question mark.

A question mark? The outline is filled in with shades of blue—jeweled, hypnotic. The more I stare at it, the more I am pulled into it. My head swims and my vision fills with spots. *Shit.* I shake my head to clear it, then drag my fingers through my hair. This has to be Saint's office. I stiffen. Apparently, conforming to stereotypes of the weaker sex has its benefits. I'd found my way into Saint's inner sanctum. *Can I accomplish my goal as quickly?*

"Let me go," I huff.

"That's not what you were saying a few minutes ago." His shoulders heave. A chuckle rumbles up his chest.

"You're an asshole," I mutter.

"So, they say."

"And a condescending prat."

"At your service," he drawls.

And I turned to him for help? Not that I had a choice; but hell, if I stay silent, he'll walk all over me.

He'll take me for granted, use the force of his personality to subdue me, no doubt about that. Men such as him are so used to getting what they want. I'd become another of his conquests. He isn't known as the most eligible bachelor in London for his good behavior, that's for sure. No, I can't simply give in to him. I have to intrigue him, hold his interest long enough to win his confidence, to get close to him so I can get ahold of the information I need so badly; but damn, if I am pandering to his already swollen ego for that.

I tip up my chin. "Release me," I demand.

He yawns, continues walking toward the far end of the room. What the hell? He ignored me?

I begin to struggle in earnest, shove my elbow in his groin. He huffs, glances down at me and his gaze widens.

Good. That'll teach him to underestimate me.

"Let go of me you prick," I snarl.

His biceps flex. The muscles of his forearms ripple against my back.

The next moment I fall through the air.

5

Saint

She bounces on the couch, her glorious dark hair falling about her face. She shakes it back, scrambles up. I place my hand on her shoulder.

I should let her know exactly what I have in mind for her. How I plan to ensure it's a long time before I let her go again. Oh, I've been receiving minute by minute reports of her movements; but nothing compares to having her in my office, on my couch, under me, as I proceed to strip her of every shred of dignity. As I bring her to the edge of orgasm and never let her come. "So, you obeyed me, huh?"

"What?" She frowns.

I lean in and sniff her neck. The sugar sweet scent of her arousal, magnified, more complex than before, fills my nostrils. "Good girl." I grin down at her. "You haven't had an orgasm since we last met."

Her mouth opens and closes. "You have a nerve." She tries to sit up. I apply enough pressure on her shoulder so she sinks back into the cushions.

"Take your hands off of me."

"No."

She blinks. "You can't just...just..."

"Command you?"

"Stop me," she grinds out.

"I can. I have." I straighten and she stays where she is this time. Good. "Have you eaten?"

She scowls.

"I'll take that as a no." I stalk over to the massive table that takes up almost the entire length of one side of the room. I snatch up the phone. "Meredith?"

"Saint?" M replies, "She there with you?"

"Yeah," I mutter.

"Do you know what you're doing?"

"Don't you trust me?" I scowl.

Her voice softens, "Be careful, Saint."

"Always." I smile. "I was going to ask for—"

"I ordered you two a late lunch," she interrupts me. "It's on its way."

There's a knock on the door.

"I think it's here already. What would we do without you?"

She chuckles. "I'm immune to your charms, but I'll accept the compliment."

I drop the phone in the cradle, stalk to the door.

A girl stands there, carrying a tray of food. Another intern? How many of them do we employ here?

I scowl at her and she pales. Her arms tremble. "Uh, may I come in?"

"No."

She gapes.

I take the tray of food from her, then shut the door in her face.

"Treat them that way and no one will want to work for you," Victoria mutters.

I turn, march over to the couch. "Pay enough money and it's surprising how much they'll put up with."

She swings her legs over, places her bag on the floor next to her. "That your personal philosophy?"

"Sure." Whatever she wants to believe.

I place the food on the coffee table next to the couch and whip off the covering. The tangy scent of soup fills the air.

Her stomach grumbles. She glances from the food to me.

"It's lentil and quinoa soup." I add, "Vegetarian, as well as filled with complex carbs."

She frowns.

I pull up a chair and seat myself opposite her, then dip a spoon into the broth. I bring it to her lips, "Open."

Her pupils dilate. Is she remembering the last time I commanded her to do so? The blood rushes to my groin.

She opens her mouth and I feed her the soup. Watch as she licks her lips. My pulse begins to thud. I feed her a few more spoonful's.

A drop clings to the edge of her mouth.

I lean in, lick it off.

She draws in a sharp breath.

"Tastes good," I murmur.

She swallows.

"The soup, I mean."

She frowns.

"What's on your mind?" I ask.

"How did you find out that I was vegetarian—?" her words trail off. "Did you have me investigated?"

"You don't think I'd let you anywhere near me without doing that, do you?"

She pales.

"I'm sure you have nothing to be worried about. After all, you are ordinary, hmm?

"Bastard," she bites out.

"Not to mention that you tend towards hypoglycemia," I mutter

She gapes at me. "You know that too?"

"Is that why you fainted?"

"Almost fainted," she scowls.

"When did you last eat? You need to keep your blood sugar levels steady."

"Why do you care?" she huffs.

"I don't." I raise my shoulders. "But I need you strong enough to answer my questions."

"Is that why you're feeding me?" Her chest heaves.

"I am doing it because it amuses me to see you lap up all the attention."

A snarl escapes her, then she raises her hand.

"Your penchant for using your palm...." I tilt my head, "I'll remind you of it, when my handprint graces your butt cheeks."

She shudders, "You won't." She curls her fingers into her fist.

I sigh, "Don't make this worse on yourself."

She hesitates, then lowers her hand into her lap.

"Good girl."

She flushes, then parts her lips for the next spoonful, and the sight of her tongue... That hunger in her eyes, fuck. I press my thumb into her mouth.

She sucks on it, and fuck, if I don't feel the tug all the way to the tip of my cock.

She lets go of my digit, then smacks her lips together, "Tastes good." She raises her chin.

"You upped the ante." I allow my lips to curve.

"You didn't think I'd simply allow you to take me for granted?"

"Trust me," I scoop up more of the soup, hold it out to her. "I much prefer a fight." I tip the spoon, the soup drips into the 'V' of her neckline.

"What the hell—?" She cries out, glances down at herself. "Did you just try to burn me?"

"If you can't stand the heat, then get out." I glare at her.

She pales.

"Well?" I replace the spoon in the bowl of soup. "What's it going to be?"

She glances from me to the door, then back at me, "What if I leave?"

My heart begins to race and sweat beads my palms. I wipe my fingers on the starched white napkin, put it aside. "You won't."

Her mouth opens and closes. She splutters, "Why you presumptuous, cocky—"

"Are you?" I frown. "Leaving?"

She purses her lips, twists her fingers together.

"Want me to take the choice out of your hands?"

She doesn't reply, peers into my face, then rubs her thighs together.

My groin tightens. My muscles harden. I lean over, lick the trickle of broth that I spilled on her neck.

She freezes.

I follow the trail down to the valley between her breasts.

She shudders. "Oh, my god," she whispers.

"Want me to touch you?"

"What? No." She straightens, "Of course, not."

I rise to my feet, pivot and head for the door.

"Wait," she calls out.

I wipe the smile off of my face, turn.

She looks at me, then away.

I tap the toe of my boot against the floor.

"You're going to make me say it, aren't you?" she says bitterly.

I pull back my cuff, check the time on my watch. "My next appointment's waiting."

"Fine." She hunches her shoulders.

"Fine what?"

"Fine, I want you to touch me."

I cross the distance between us, fit my knuckles under her chin. She glances up at me, her green eyes shining with that inner turmoil I'm beginning to recognize.

"Not so hard now, is it?"

"This is not why I came," she whispers.

"Shh!" I press my thumb to her lips.

She gulps, opens her mouth again, and I shake my head. She subsides. All of the confusion and all of the emotions she's feeling are reflected in her eyes. So fucking vulnerable, this woman, yet so sassy.

"You're not as innocent as you seem," I say.

Her gaze widens.

"But that's okay." I frame her face with my hands. "I am going to enjoy unravelling your hidden agenda."

She sits up straighter. "Takes one to know one."

"Don't make the mistake of thinking you know me, Gigi."

"Don't flatter yourself," she mutters. "You're not so special. Just another spoiled billionaire a-hole, who thinks he can use his power and influence to get anything he wants."

"Gazillionaire." I grin, then slip my palm under the heavy curtain of her hair. "And you're sitting here, aren't you?"

Color flares on her cheeks. She tries to rise, but I wrap my fingers around her nape and hold her down.

Her shoulders jerk and the pulse at her neck flutters.

"Poor, Gigi. So confused. So out of your league."

"I'm more than a match for you, rich prick." She bares her teeth.

A shudder works its way down my spine. My balls throb. I haul her up by the scruff of her neck. She gasps and her breasts push up, the nipples beaded against the black cloth of her dress.

"Fucking hate that color," I grumble. I lower my head until I can make out the little creases between her eyebrows, the flecks of gold in those green irises beckoning me. Calling me. I rake my gaze down to her mouth. Her lips part. She flutters those thick eyelashes down. "Please," the whine bleeds from her lips.

"What do you need?"

"I... I don't know," she murmurs.

"You do."

I draw in a breath and her scent grows straight to my head. A hot sensation stabs in my chest. Fucking fuck. This woman, she is too potent. Weston was right, I am way too deep into this game already.

I release her so suddenly, her rear hits the couch with a thump. Turning, I stride to the door.

"You're a real piece of work you know that?" she yells after me.

I raise my hand in the air. "Rest up, Gigi. You have until I finish this next appointment to figure out why you came. After that, the choice is out of your hands."

6

I am often mistaken for being true. What am I?
Answer: A lie

Victoria

"Help me."

I snap my eyes open, jackknife up, heart racing, pulse pounding. I try to swallow and my throat hurts. Sweat slicks my palms, slides down my back. The blood thuds at my temples and my stomach twists.

After Adam's untimely death, I'd received another call. This time with instructions that I had to get close to Saint, and get hold of the evidence he has on the Mafia. The man on the phone had also played me a recording of Nina's voice crying for help. Then he'd warned me not to breathe a word about this to anyone else, before hanging up. I drag my fingers through my hair.

I've barely slept a wink the last few nights, nervous about this encounter with Saint.

Clearly, my subconscious associates that asshole with security. Enough that, for the first time in weeks, I'd fallen into a deep sleep in the middle of the day. On his couch, in his office, no less.

A sound reaches me through the door. I stiffen, swing my legs over and a jacket falls to the floor. *Huh?* It's light gray in color, different from the one he had loaned me. He hadn't been kidding when he'd said that he hates the color black on me.

Had he come in while I slept and decided not to wake me up? Had he watched me sleep, and covered me with the jacket? I blink.

At least I hadn't drooled. Small mercies. I pick up the jacket, then bury my nose in the luxurious fabric.

The scent of him laces my nostrils—masculine, complex, layers upon layers that sink into my skin. My cheeks flush. My thighs clench. Ridiculous. I can't have such a reaction to his scent. I drop the jacket on the couch, then spring up to my feet, and walk toward the desk.

Starlight streams in from the windows. Huh? It had been late afternoon when I'd arrived. How long did I sleep? I glance at the sleek wall clock on the far side of the room. What the—? It's late—almost 9pm. Why did he let me sleep away the evening?

I sink into the massive leather chair; the scent of him deepens. My belly flutters. My throat dries. *Why the hell am I having such a strong reaction to the presence—? No.* My lips twist. *Technically, that would be his absence—of this man I barely know.*

I touch the pad of the laptop in front of me and the screen lights up. It's fingerprint locked. I'd checked it as soon as Saint had left, of course. It wouldn't have been that easy, right? I have to get into his files to get what I need, which means—my shoulders slump—I have to get close to him. No choice.

I glance at the desk, spot the riding crop on it. "What the—?" Who keeps a riding crop on his work desk, in his office? Saint does; that's who. I shake my head, reach for the top drawer. It's locked. Well hell, of course it couldn't be that simple.

I open the drawer below; there's stationery, pens, excel sheets printed with rows of numbers. I wrench open the drawer at the bottom... my breath catches. A gun? *Huh?* He keeps a gun? Another noise reaches me through the door. Shit. Where the hell is Saint?

I snatch up the revolver. The weight is reassuring. Two months ago I'd never seen a gun in my life. Now? Well, I'll take every break I get.

The one thing my experience has taught me is never to be taken by surprise. I shut the drawer, then walk across the floor. Opening the door, I step into a corridor. Strain my ears... Nothing. Scratch that... Is that a sound from down the hall? I glance down the passageway, then the other way. Right. I march down the hallway to the set of double doors, and fling them open.

Pale blue eyes cut into me; his eyebrows slash down.

I take in the breadth of his shoulders ensconced in the same white dress shirt he had on earlier. Only now, the front is unbuttoned and pulled apart to reveal his cut torso. Black hair clings to the eight pack abs that ripple and flow down to meet the waistband of his pants... His unzipped pants where a woman bobs her head. So, this was his very important appointment?

She grips his powerful pant-clad thighs, which buck and flex under her touch. He parts his legs, then clasps the back of her head. The veins on his muscled forearm flex.

A moan bleeds through the air and I'm instantly wet. My mouth waters. My scalp tingles.

Omigod, why is that the most intensely erotic thing I have ever seen? I seriously can't be thinking that now. *Get out of here, get out.* My feet seem stuck to the ground, my legs too heavy to carry me out of there. I watch, riveted, as he brings up his other hand, the veins on his forearms popping.

His shirt sleeves are rolled up to his elbows; his biceps bulge as he swipes a finger across his lower lip.

"You want to share it when you have it, but when you want it you don't have it." He rumbles, "What is it?"

His tone rams through the jumbled quagmire of my mind, pulling me in, drowning me down, insisting that I focus my attention on that beautiful visage.

His lips curl. He is laughing at me.

He knows exactly the picture he presents.

So damn arrogant. So confident.

Did he orchestrate this entire tableau for my benefit? *Nah, why should he? Bet he has a mile-long queue of women outside the door ready to suck his every appendage.* I chuckle.

His glare intensifies. "You have one second to answer."

"I… I don't know." I swallow.

"A secret," he drawls. "That's the answer." His eyelids grow hooded. "What secrets are you hiding from me, I wonder?"

"None." I swallow.

"Everyone has secrets." He chuckles.

"Even you?"

"Especially me." His grin widens.

The wet sound of flesh hitting flesh fills the room. I drop my gaze to where the woman kneels between his thighs. His forearms flex, he spreads his legs, yanks her head closer, then begins to use her mouth in earnest. Back-forth-back; her entire body shakes.

A gagging noise splits the rhythmic effect.

My head spins. My core clenches and I chafe my thighs wanting… Needing more. So much more.

His chest seems to expand further and further; his shoulders swell. His pale blue eyes glow with a strange inner light.

He lowers his chin, raises an eyebrow, and a snarl rips up my throat.

A heavy sensation stabs in my chest; my vision tunnels. *I am not jealous. I am not.* I don't want him that way. Besides *he had…left me there on the couch, while he'd indulged himself?* What a complete jerk.

My heart begins to race; adrenaline laces my blood. I raise the gun, aim it at Saint.

He stares back. His shoulders stiffens.

The woman between his legs glances around. I level the gun at her. She pales.

I wiggle the gun and she rises to her feet, only to glance at him. What the—? I have a weapon trained on her and she looks to him as if seeking permission?

Saint's lips firm. "Leave."

My toes curl, my scalp prickles… and the hair on my forearms rises. Jesus, no man should have a voice like that. My arm shakes. The woman passes me, then bolts.

Silence descends. A beat, another.

I hold Saint's gaze, tip up my chin.

Two can play this game. I will not be intimidated. Will not be coerced into breaking the silence. I stare down the barrel of my pistol, at the rat's ass of a man in my cross hairs.

He relaxes into the chair. The soft material of his pants outlines the contours of his powerful thighs. *Don't look there, don't.* I glance at his crotch, which is unzipped. His dick arrows up. Is it thicker than what I remember it to be? Nah, that must be my imagination, surely—

"My face is up here," he drawls.

I jerk my chin up. His lips curl in a smirk, and moisture instantly pools at my core. Damn the man, he knows the effect he has on me. So what? I tighten my grip on the gun. I hold the weapon. So why does it feel like the one between his legs is more lethal? *Jesus, cliché much?*

"You do need to up your game, Gigi." He tilts his head.

Anger squeezes my chest.

He is toying with me. Asshole is having fun at my expense. I'll teach him what it means to sit on that lofty, privileged perch of his and sneer down his nose at those who have to fight for every bit of help, for every shred of kindness, for every soft word, tender touch…every gaze filled with love, tears, blood… "Shut up." My voice emerges—harsh, guttural. Nothing like the sophisticate I am trying to portray. I draw in a deep breath. My hand trembles.

Walk away, right now, while you can.

I can't. I won't. I have to face him down. I have to find a way to ensure that I come out of this with some small shred of my dignity intact.

He grips his gorgeous shaft, swipes it from root to tip.

My throat dries. Heat flushes my skin and sweat beads my palm.

"Stop that," I croak.

"Don't tell me what to do." His command lashes across my skin. My fingers slip. The stuffing from the chair next to his head explodes, but he's already moving.

I hear the thud of his boots on the carpet, see a blur of movement, then the gun is knocked from my hand.

I hit the ground, face down. His heavy weight presses into me. His hardness stabs into the curve of my waist. Those solid thighs grip mine on either side. I am surrounded by him. Heat from his massive body slams into me, pins me down. Moisture dribbles out between my legs. I strain and he places his cheek next to mine, his breath raising the hair on my forehead.

"You have my attention, little Gigi."

He licks the shell of my ear.

Goosebumps pop on my skin. My vision narrows; my toes curl. "I want more than that." I shiver.

There's a pause, then his chest vibrates. "What?" He growls.

"Take me as your sub."

7

I am given with pleasure when taken by force. What am I?
Answer: A kiss

Saint

"Do you have any idea what you're asking for?" I push back and flip her on her back.

Her green eyes deepen in color, glittering emeralds that cut through me, hurt me, scoop up every last drop of humanity left in me and render me incoherent.

"Well?" I glare at her.

"Y...yes." She stutters.

I rise to my feet and she pales.

"On your knees," I growl.

She hesitates.

I lower my voice to a hush, "Now." Her shoulders stiffen, then she pushes up to kneel at my feet. It puts her face at eyelevel with my crotch. My groin hardens.

I reach down, grab my cock. Her breath hitches. She drops her gaze, watches as I massage my dick.

She licks her lips and my muscles go solid. My shaft lengthens. *Ah hell, hadn't meant for things to get out of hand so quickly…literally.*

I widen my stance to accommodate my arousal and she makes a sound deep in her throat.

"That's not for you." I smirk. "Yet."

"What?" She peers up at me from under sooty eyelashes.

"You'll have to earn it first." I allow my smile to widen.

Her eyebrows draw down, she flicks out her tongue to touch her lower lip, and my cock instantly twitches. *Hell.* This response to her is interesting. Not what I expected. Best to put her in her place right away. I tuck myself in, then stalk forward to retrieve my gun.

"What are you doing?" Her squeak fills the space.

My lips twitch. I straighten, turn to her.

Her cheeks pale. "St…stop. Don't come closer."

"Why not?"

"This…this isn't what I want." Fear vibrates off of her, bleeds into the space between us… My dick instantly lengthens.

Do you blame me? She'd hit upon my weakness, then proceeded to lay her insecurities bare to me… *Well, of course, I am going to take advantage.*

"Let me be the judge of that." I stride forward.

She jerks her chin up, "Don't come closer."

"That's not what you said earlier."

"I… I didn't think—"

"What—?" I pause in front of her. "That I'd call your bluff?"

Her chin wobbles, "Are you. Will you…?"

I lean forward.

Her shoulders rise and her throat moves as she swallows.

"Rule number one, never question me."

"And if I do…?"

The next second, I press the gun to her temple. Her gaze narrows as her eyes blaze. *Bloody hell, she has some strength, this woman.* She raises her chin, and damn, if my dick doesn't follow suit. I don't need to look down to know that my cock's saluting her impudence.

"So, tell me, Gigi, why is it that you sought me out?"

"I told you it was to—"

"Ask me to be your Dom?"

She nods.

"You think I believe that?"

"Why else would I be here?" Her gaze narrows, "It isn't for your politeness or consideration, clearly."

My lips twitch before I wipe the smile from my face. I grip her hair and tug so her head falls back, "Tell me the truth."

"Couldn't it be because I saw the man behind the asshole face you show the world? Perhaps I want to get to know you better?"

"Do you?"

Her gaze skitters away.

A hot sensation coils in my stomach, "Thought not." I wrap my fingers around her neck and her gaze widens. "Perhaps I should take you at face value, after all."

"What do you mean—?"

"Shh!" I draw the barrel of the gun over her lips and her face pales. Fear radiates from her. My pulse begins to race. *Finally.* "Let's see what you're made of, shall we?"

I yank her up to her tiptoes, until she's level with my chest.

"Such a tiny little thing, you are. Not a hair out of place, even after spending hours on the couch in my office. What would it take to mess you up, huh?" I drag the barrel of the gun down her cheek—She swallows—past that lush lower lip, to the hollow at the base of her throat. Goosebumps pop on her skin.

"Not that courageous now, are you?"

She swallows, then tips up her chin and opens her mouth. I click my tongue.

Her gaze narrows, her eyes sparking with that familiar light of defiance. *Oh, good. Now we're getting somewhere.*

I drag the pistol down, hook the barrel into the dip of her neckline. She stills, the only movement, her chest rising and falling. Her nipples pebble against the fabric of her blouse. My vision narrows and I draw the gun over the nipple.

She shudders. My shaft lengthens.

"You enjoy that, hmm?"

She shakes her head.

I glare at her, "Don't lie."

"I'm not."

"Admit it. You are aroused.'

"No." She sets her lips.

"We'll see about that, shall we?"

I toss the gun to one side, then pull her forward.

She falls into me, "What the hell? You tossed a loaded gun, you—"

"Relax, I clicked the safety on." I squeeze my fingers around her nape, my fingers meeting in the front, that's how slender the length of her neck is. "The only gun you need to be worried about is the one in my pants."

She makes a gagging noise. "Ugh, that was terrible, even for you."

"And if you want to gag, there are other ways to bring that on too."

"Keep your cheap shots to yourself." She huffs, "Why do you keep a gun anyway, and in an unlocked drawer?"

"Why were you snooping in my office?" I retort.

"I..." She swallows, "You left me on my own in your space." She raises her shoulder. "It was fair game."

"Hmm." I lean into her, "And you... little Gigi, are in my space. Does that make you fair game too?"

I tighten my grasp on her, and she trembles. Her thighs quake.

Pressing her against me, I sense her every move, every breath she takes, the trembling of her eyelids. Her lips part, her hips wriggle, and damn it, but I can't stop myself. I lower my head, close my mouth over hers. I suck on her tongue, bite down on her lower lip, shove my free hand under her skirt, finding that melting core between her legs.

I slide my fingers in between her panties and skin, drag my knuckles across her clit.

A whine bubbles up her throat; I swallow it.

I thrust a finger inside her core, and hell… The melting softness is my undoing. I add a second finger, then another. Her spine curves and her neck arches. I hook my fingers inside of her, finding that hidden center of hers. Her entire body bucks.

I tear my mouth from hers, "Don't you dare come, Gigi."

She shudders, thrusts her pelvis forward.

I release my grip around her neck, yank my fingers from her pussy. I step back and her legs give way.

I catch her, push her into the door and pin her hips with mine. A pulse beats to life against my temples, on the backs of my eyelids, even in my balls. *Jesus. Hell.* This isn't how it's supposed to be.

I am supposed to get my women off, reduce them to globs of liquid need, make them crawl to me for release… And while I'd done all that to her… I'd never before been this aroused… This need to bury myself inside of her, scratch my name into her cells, her skin, tear into her and show her how it can be between us? No. No way, am I doing that. I release her and she sags against the barrier.

Back the fuck off, before she pulls you in with those beautiful eyes, that gorgeous visage, the innocence about her which is…all a façade. A trap. One way to ensure that I forget what this entire charade is about—to get to the bottom of whoever set her up to lure me in. If she thinks it is that easy to veer me off course, to distract me from the one thing that has kept me and the Seven focused all these years, then she has another think coming.

"In which sport do winners move backward and losers move forward?" I let the words hang in the air between us.

She blinks, then asks, "Which…which one?"

"A fucking tug of war is what." I chuckle. *Bloody hell.* Why had I allowed those words to escape my lips? Why the hell am I showing her a glimmer of my vulnerability?

She makes me weak, is why. No way, am I allowing that to happen again. Not when I have a hell of a lot more at stake than some piece of pussy which doesn't mean anything to me. But she isn't just another anything… She is… Gigi. An enigma, a puzzle. A riddle I am going to solve, even if it means hurting myself in the process.

I turn, snatch up my gun and shove it into my waistband.

"Wait."

I shrug on my shirt, turn to her. She swallows.

"What about…?" Her voice trails off.

"About?" I growl.

"My proposition."

"Let me think." I drum my fingers on my chest, peruse her from head to toe.

Her cheeks flush. Her eyes glitter with that inner fight. Damn, but she has a hidden depth, a fierce perseverance that is both endearing and… *Endearing? The hell?* Since when have emotions ever featured in any relationship, huh? I take, I allow a select few to make me come… then walk away. That is it. No relationships. No entanglements. Nothing that can touch the part of me that I keep hidden away. Nothing to tempt me to cross the line that is forever etched in my memory… Until her. I crack my neck, yawn, then shake my head, "No."

"What?" She gapes.

"One touch and you were ready to throw yourself at my feet, bare yourself to me, and all but ask me to take you right there. I prefer…" I pretend to think, "…a bit more spirit, a bit more spine, a bit more oomph. Not to mention…"

I glance at her gorgeous breasts, her curvy hips, her delicate ankles. If I touch her again, I am a goner. If I look into her eyes, I'll never find myself again. No, this is the right thing to do. I have to walk away from her. "…I prefer my women to have more curves."

"You bastard."

The color leaches from her face and she sways. I take a step forward, then stop myself. Why do I care if she is hurting? That is the whole point, remember? Hurt her feelings enough that she'll never turn to me again.

"Want me to spell it out for you, Doll?" I reach her, then thrust my face into hers, "I don't want you."

8

____

Why did the two lovers end up in prison?
Answer: Because they stole each other's hearts

Victoria

I stare at my reflection in the shiny elevator door—hair mussed up, lips swollen and bare of lipstick. I look…like I was thoroughly kissed. He did more than that. He turned me down, he insulted me, and I stood there and took it. What choice did I have? I can't force him to take me as his sub, can I?

I stumble out of the office building of 7A investments, my hand bag at my side.

Was it only a few hours ago that I had torn into the building?

A gust of wind buffets me. I sway; the rain slicks my hair back, floods my sight. I step forward, my feet encounter thin air, and I pitch forward. A scream rips from my throat and I am hauled back.

"Hey, you okay?"

I turn around to encounter sharp gray eyes.

"Are you all right?" the woman asks again.

I swallow, nod. Open my mouth to thank her, but no words emerge. My heart is racing so hard that I am sure it's going to jump right out of my rib cage. She peruses my face, "Victoria?" She frowns.

I peer through the rain. She's as tall as me, wearing a raincoat cinched around her waist.

"Have me met?" I scan her features.

"You're Summer's stepmother, right?"

I wince. That is so not the identity I need to be riddled with… But yeah, no getting away from it. I nod and her face cracks into a wide grin. "I saw you at Sinclair and Summer's wedding…"

I glance at her features, then shake my head, "Sorry, I have a bad memory for names."

I glance up at her clear umbrella.

"Oh, shoot." She steps forward to hold her wide umbrella over me. The rain stops pounding my face.

"It's Amelie." She prompts.

"Amelie?"

"I'm Summer's friend?"

"Ah."

"I'm a pastry chef." She grins, all bright and happy. Christ, she makes me feel a hundred years old. Was I ever that hopeful about my future? Maybe before the Mafia had gotten to me? When I had been a student at UCLA? No, I'd always been a brooder, a thinker…some would say a dreamer, even. Look where that's gotten me. I bite my lower lip. She frowns, peers into my face,

"In fact, I was on my way to meeting her right now. Why don't you come along?'

I stare, then shake my head, "I honestly don't want to impose."

"Oh, you're not imposing, and Summer will be glad to see you.

I chew the inside of my cheek. Somehow, I don't think so.

"She's mentioned how much she wants to get to know you better."

"She has?" I tilt my head. Is she saying it to make me feel better? Or is she really trying to be friendly?

A man almost walks into us, then excuses himself to veer past us. I stare. "Did he apologize?"

She laughs. "That's London for you. It's very civilized, isn't it?"

"I'd forgotten."

"You're British, of course. I could tell from your accent. So how did you meet Summer's father?"

I tense, pull myself up straight, "I think I need to leave."

Her face crumples. "Oh, I'm sorry. I hadn't meant to be nosy. Sometimes my mouth doesn't grasp what my brain is trying to communicate. Often, I speak nonsense, and by the time I've realized what I've said, it's too late."

I draw in a breath. All that bubbliness is overwhelming.

"I said too much again, didn't I?" She grimaces, her gaze turning stricken. "Please forgive me, please."

I jerk my chin. "Don't worry about it."

She locks her arm with mine, then begins to walk. I keep pace. "It's just us girls tonight. Sinclair's allowing Summer the evening off."

"*Allowing* her the evening off?"

"He's sooo possessive about her. Honestly, that man is 100% alpha… And of course, there's the rest of the Seven. Put them all in one room, and whoa." She makes a smacking sound with her lips, "I swear my ovaries can't take it."

"There's seven of them?"

She nods, "I haven't seen the seventh, of course."

"Oh? Why's that?" Perhaps she has her uses, after all? Maybe she can shed a little more light on the man I have to find a way to get close to?

"Baron, that's the guy who's not around. He's a kind of mystery figure," she adds obligingly.

"What does he do?"

She raises her shoulders. "Don't know… Anyway, the ones who are here are more than enough to keep a girl occupied, if you know what I mean."

Ah! "So you have your eye on one of them?"

"Maybe…" she giggles.

The sound is so infectious, I can't stop my lips from curving. Maybe she isn't bad company, after all.

We reach the entrance to the tube station and I hesitate.

She turns to me, "It's only a few stops on the train to get to Summer's place."

"Her house?" I swallow, *uh,* "I really don't think that's a good idea."

She grips my arm, "Nonsense, you're soaked."

"I'll dry."

"Surely, you don't want to be alone?"

I bite my lips.

"It's a good old-fashioned stay over, which we haven't done in a while, and that's important, you know? Female friendships are ah-may-z-i-n-g!" she sing-songs.

Not always, but…okay.

"We women, we need to have each other's backs…" She rocks forward on the balls of her feet, "…especially when you need a shoulder to lean on, ya know?

I narrow my gaze.

"Not that you need anyone else…" She jostles the strap of her hand bag, "…but we'd love to have you. With Summer married…we need more single gals in our group to exchange notes about eligible men…"

I wince.

"Ouch." She hunches her shoulders, "Didn't want to remind you of your newly-single status."

I lower my chin.

"Jeez, didn't mean to imply that you had to start looking right away or anything, not so soon after your husband's death… I mean—" she makes a choking noise.

I draw myself up, pat her shoulder. "It's okay. Summer's father and I were married, but we weren't ever intimate."

Her lips open in an 'O.'

Shit, hadn't meant to reveal that to her. What the hell is wrong with me? "That's our secret, huh?"

She grins, "You betcha. See, we're already getting along so well." She steps into the tube station. "You must come with me. Summer would never forgive me if I didn't bring you along."

I wrap my arms about my waist.

She turns, "Come on, you'll enjoy it. I promise."

I shuffle me feet.

"Jeez, I'm sorry." She glances past me, then breaks into a run. "Taxi," she calls out.

A black cab pulls up to the curb.

She wrenches open the door, tumbles in, then beckons, "Coming?"

Half an hour later we draw up in front of a gorgeous townhouse in Primrose Hill. I lean forward to pay off the driver. Amelie waves me off. She hands over a few notes, then opens the door and jumps out. I follow her across the sidewalk. She opens the gate, then bounds up the path to the front door.

The taxi drives off. I glance up and down the road. The trees are bathed in the fading sun, raindrops glittering on the leaves. The hair on the nape of my neck prickles. *Is someone watching me?* I stare through the fading light…but nothing stirs.

Voices reach me and I turn to find Amelie and Summer talking in front of the open door to the house. I hesitate. *Do I want to be here? I should turn and go, but where?* To the short let in Hackney, which is all I am able to afford? No, I am better off walking in, facing the women. Learning more about the Seven. Okay, about one of them, in particular. I was handed one last opportunity to find my way out of this mess and I am going to take it. I square my shoulders, then walk down the path.

When I reach the short flight of steps leading to the door, I look up. Summer smiles at me, holds out a hand. The breath rushes out of me. I take the steps, pause when I reach her. She closes the distance between us, hugs me. "Welcome home."

Tears knock at the backs of my eyes. *Jesus, why am I getting this emotional?* Summer steps back, then tugs on my arm, "You're soaked, let me get you some fresh clothes."

Half an hour later, after having showered and pulled on the clothes that Summer had left for me in the guest bedroom, I walk into the cozy room overlooking the back garden.

Summer had offered to wash and dry my clothes in the washing machine and I had agreed.

Amelie looks up, then jumps to her feet. She walks forward and takes my hand, "Come on, we're having Margaritas and ice cream."

Thunder cracks outside, then lightning illuminates the space in front of the room. I jump, my heartbeat ratcheting up.

Amelie's hand on mine tightens. "I don't like storms either," she whispers. In that moment, I want to hug her close. She tugs me forward and I follow her, sinking down on the large circular settee that faces the large window at the back of the room.

Summer walks over, a pitcher of margaritas in her hand.

"Umm. I'm not sure if I should," I mumble.

"You absolutely should." Summer laughs.

I hesitate.

"If you don't, our hostess will be most unhappy and you don't want that do you?" Amelia leans forward, holds out an empty glass.

Summer tops it off. Amelie hands it over and I wrap my fingers around it. "Could I get a bigger glass? I'll finish this in no time."

Amelie stares at the soup bowl-sized circumference, then cackles.

Summer laughs.

The fourth girl chuckles. She comes forward holding, her own glass. "I'm Isla, by the way." She raises her glass. "What are we drinking to?"

The three look at each other, then Summer turns to me, "To having family close."

I swallow.

"To friendship," Amelie clinks hers with Summer's.

"To… Orgasms?" Isla flutters her eyelashes.

I allow my lips to twitch. "To being fucked until I can't walk straight for days," I offer.

There's silence, then the girls burst out laughing. Summer sputters, "I'll drink to that."

"As if you need to?" Isla winks at Summer, "If the sparks between Sinclair and you are any indication, that's a normal state for you."

Summer makes the sign to zip her lips, "Not saying anything."

"You never share any details," Amelie pouts.

"Not one to kiss and tell." Summer raises her glass, "To guys who love us."

"To the losers who didn't deserve to keep us," Amelie tosses her head.

"The sexy bastards who are gonna be so lucky to meet us," Isla clinks her glass.

"To…" I chew on my lower lip, "TGIF."

The three stare at me.

"Thank God it's Friday?" Amelie furrows her eyebrows.

I glance at each of their faces, "Tongue Goes in First."

Amelie hoots, "I love your step-mama, Summer."

I wince, glance at Summer, who shakes her head. Her phone pings. She picks it up, checks the screen and smiles. "Sienna says she's bummed not to be here, but the pregnancy is exhausting her. She's going to stay in."

"Sienna?" I ask.

"Jace's wife." Summer sets the phone down. "He's a friend of the Seven. They moved here from LA because Sienna's pregnant and they want to bring up the child in Jace's home country."

"That sounds wonderful. It's beautiful that they can plan for the future, a life together." A ball of emotion clogs my throat.

Where has this...hankering for becoming part of an unit come from? To have someone to call my own. A family, kids. I had hoped that I'd have it all one day, until Nina's kidnapping had turned my world upside down. It could have easily been me. Hell, sometimes I wish it had been me. I'd have gladly traded places with her.

She and I? We're... Solid.

Until I met her, I was always a background friend. I never fit in with any particular circle of friends. All through high school, I'd find these cliques. They'd be close with each other and I'd sort of latch on, but I was never permanent with them.

They wouldn't have even noticed if I wasn't with them.

All of that changed when I met Nina. With her, I didn't feel left out. It was like I had found someone who got me. Someone who recognized a kindred soul, know what I mean? She had my back.

We promised to look out for each other, to be the sister we each had always wanted and never had. And then she was gone. My throat closes. No way, could I abandon her when she needs me. I'd do everything, and more, to help her.

I take a sip of my drink. The cold liquid slides down my throat. It hits my stomach and warmth instantly tingles up my spine. "Yum." I glance down at the cocktail. "This is good."

"Isn't it?" Summer licks her lips. She glances around, then sinks down into an overstuffed cushion. "I am surprised Saint allowed you leave the office on your own."

"Oh?" I sink back into the settee while the other two sprawl out next to me. "I didn't think he wanted me there a second longer."

"I don't know." Summer levels me with a stare. "He sure seemed keen to take care of you."

My cheeks heat. "It isn't what it seems." I cringe. Ugh, is that the oldest excuse in the book, or what?

Summer frowns, "Perhaps he doesn't quite know how to share what he feels for you?"

I choke on my drink. "What he feels for me?" I set my glass down with such force that some of the drink spills. I glance around. Summer hands me a box of tissues and I pull one out, mop up the drink from the table. "He left me in his room, for a so-called important appointment." I wad the tissue into a ball, "And when I find him, it's with his —" I clamp my lips shut. Damn, I want to confide in them, but can I trust them? Will I be able to trust anyone after the events of the last few months?

"Ooh." Amelie rubs her hands together. "Did you catch him with his pants down?"

Heat flushes my cheeks. I toss the balled-up tissue onto the table, "The details don't matter."

Summer looks thoughtful, but doesn't speak.

Amelie pouts. "Aww, and I thought you were going to be fun."

"Trust me, I am the most boring person you'll meet."

Amelie, looks me up and down. "It's the quiet ones who have a sting in the tail."

"Sure," I hold up my forefingers on either side of my forehead, "and these are my horns."

She giggles.

Summer tilts her head, "At any rate, he got the color back in your cheeks."

And how.

She pulls up her knees, rests her chin on them, "Did he at least kiss you?"

"Of course, not." I scowl.

"Did he make a move on you?"

I shuffle my feet.

"Are you attracted to him?" Amelie chimes in.

"Do you like him?" Isla asks in a breathless tone. "You do, don't you?"

"Hold on." I hold up my hands, scan their expectant faces. "Yes," I exhale.

"Yes, what?" Amelie bounces on the cushions.

Whoa, is she excitable or what? I let the silence draw out, then reply, "Yes to all of that."

"I knew it." She holds up a hand, and Isla high-five's her.

"Hold on." I frown. "Did you two have a bet going?"

Amelie peers at me from the other side of the settee, "You don't mind, do you?"

I raise my shoulders. "Not as long as you'll help me with what I have in mind."

"Ooh!" Amelie takes a hefty sip, then balances the glass on the arm of the sofa. "Give."

"It's all straightforward."

Not.

"Clearly there's chemistry between Saint and me, and I want to stay in London." I say, sticking to the barebones version of the convoluted reality of my life. " I don't want to return to the US."

Summer's shoulders stiffen. "So you want to get together with Saint?"

"I saw him first at your wedding." I nod toward Summer. "There was an instant connection between us. Of course, I was married to your father then—"

"But you had no feelings for him," she says.

I glance toward her. "It's not like that. I cared about him, but...Was it that obvious?" Clearly, I'm not as good an actress as I like to think, if both Saint and Summer had seen through my charade.

She scowls, "Only because I'd been trying to figure out why the hell a beautiful woman like you would want to be with him." Her features harden. "He was all wrong for you. Besides," she looks me up and down, "you'd be good for Saint."

"I... I would?" I blink.

She nods. "He needs someone who won't put up with all that alpha bullshit."

"Like you and Sinclair?"

She smiles and her eyes gleam. "I'll tell you a secret."

"Oh?"

She leans forward, as do the other women.

"These men," she tilts her head, "the trick to managing them is to let them show you their worst side; let them rage and rant. And then, when they think they have you cornered, you pull the rug out from under their feet."

I frown. O-k-a-y.

"You get what I'm saying?" She peers into my face.

No. Yes. "I...think so."

"Good." She grins. "I think you'll be fine."

"So, you don't mind that I'm hoping to get together with someone else, so soon after your father's death?"

She slashes the air with her hand. "It's unusual, but I wasn't close to Adam. He didn't deserve to die that early, and while I forgive him for abandoning me and Karma to the foster system in the UK... Well, I do believe that he had our best interests at heart and..." her lips firm, "that's what counts."

Right.

I peruse her features, then reach over and grasp her hand, "Thank you."

"For what?"

"For welcoming me into your home, into your circle... For not being..."

"A bitch?" She chuckles.

"Yeah." *That too.*

"I leave that up to my sister Karma." Her brow furrows, "Wish she was here today."

"Where is she?"

She taps her fingers on the carpet, "Off on holiday in Sicily with some hottie she hooked up with."

"Oh?" My heart begins to race. It's only a coincidence. It doesn't mean anything. Lots of people go to Sicily on holiday with a man... "So, it's new love, huh?"

Summer flips her hair over her shoulder, "That's the thing. I've never met him. It was all so sudden. One minute she was calling me to spend the night with her—which is not Karma at all either, by the way —the next she's texting me to say she's jetting off on an Italian holiday."

"Sicilian."

"That's what I said." Summer frowns.

"Not the same thing—" I bite my lips. *Shit, shouldn't have said that.* I widen my gaze, "I'm sure she's having a great time. Everyone deserves at least one dirty holiday with an alpha male of their dreams, huh?"

"Is that why you chose Saint?"

I wince. "

"But that's not the only reason, right?" Amelie inches closer. "You want the security that Saint's money can provide, and the chemistry between the two of you makes for an interesting starting point."

"I..."

She waves a hand in the air, "Hey, I'm the last to judge. I mean, relationships have been built on far less. Besides you're one of us, and Saint clearly needs you in his life."

"He does?" My head whirls.

She nods. "He just doesn't know it yet."

Oh, man, I can't keep up.

"You do realize that he's among the most twisted of the Seven?" Amelie's gaze narrows.

Interesting. Behind that overeager, always ready to please façade, is a sharp brain. And I should be the last to judge a woman by her looks.

"I am aware that he has certain hidden proclivities," I venture.

"He's a dominant?" Isla frowns.

"They all are." Summer waves her hand in the air.

Amelie turns on her, "Even Weston?"

I glance at her features. Her lips are parted, eyes slightly dilated. Is that how I looked when I walked in on Saint?

She jerks her head to me, and I glance back at Summer.

"All of the Seven will stop at nothing to get their own way." Summer holds my gaze. "These men are bloody arresting, right?"

None more so than Saint.

I want to tame him, while simultaneously throwing myself down at his feet and begging him to take me—is what I want to say. But I'd already pushed it with the TGIF comment, and I don't want these women to think I'm weird. Besides I need them on my side... fast. I nod my head. "You can say that again." I mumble.

Summer chuckles. Isla snorts.

"You thought he wouldn't be able to say no to you, that you'd make an offer he couldn't refuse?" Amelie cuts in.

I blink. *Am I that transparent, or are these women unusually perceptive?*

"You did, didn't you?" Amelie crawls close to me, her gaze wide. I glance at her. Her cheeks flush. "Go on, give." She scans my features, her expression expectant.

"Yep."

"Wait, what did I miss?" Summer glances between us.

"I believe step-mama here asked Saint to become her dominant."

Summer laughs. "No, you didn't."

"Yes." I tuck my hair behind my ears. "Though trust me, there's no," I make air quotes, "'asking' the man for anything. He wants, he takes," I mutter. "End of story."

"You're right about that. Bet that made for an interesting conversation, huh?" Isla nods.

"You have no idea." I reach for my drink.

"He turned you down?" Amelia wiggles her legs, her gaze arrested. My shoulders sag.

"How dare he?" Summer grabs a cushion and punches it.

"Yeah." Isla sits up. "We need to teach him a lesson. You're beautiful...gorgeous. You're exactly the kind of challenge he needs."

"Bet he knows it too." Summer looks me up and down. "Maybe that's why he did an about-turn? He knew if he took you on, he risked getting involved."

I shake my head. "You should have seen him, when I walked in on him. He was…"

"Angry?"

"Turned on?"

"Ready to throw you down and shag you?"

I circle the rim of my glass with my forefinger, "Distracted."

"What?" Amelie frowns.

"He was busy," I reply.

"All an act." She huffs.

Summer raises an eyebrow, then nods. "I think I'm familiar with that act. He didn't want you to see how much you affect him." Her lips curve, "Trust me. I saw the way he was eating you up with his eyes at my wedding."

"Perhaps he was interested, but he sure as hell disguised it well," I mutter.

"Only one way to find out." Amelie taps her finger to her cheek.

I glance at her warily. "Why do I have the feeling you are the last one I should be taking advice from?"

"Aww… Come on, V," she pouts, "you don't mean that."

I draw in a breath, "I guess not. After all, I get by with a little help from my friends."

"Did you quote The Beatles?" Summer chuckles.

I redden, "Old habit."

"It's delightful. You're delightful. In fact," she scowls, "you are not what I expected."

"Oh?" I meet her gaze, "What did you think I was?"

"Cold," Isla interjects.

"Hard," Amelie adds.

Summer wriggles around and makes herself comfortable, "You know… You turned up unannounced at my wedding as my father's wife, someone I never knew existed. And you were perfectly turned out, designer clothes and all."

"I prefer to be well-dressed. What's wrong with that?" I scowl.

"Not a thing." Summer looks me up and down. "Bet, that's what turns Saint on. Bet he wants to mess you up."

I flush, "Maybe." I glance between them, "What are you guys thinking?"

"I think," Amelie sits up on her knees, "you're going about this all wrong."

"I am?"

"You went in and asked him outright. Guys don't respond well to that."

"And what do you know about that?" Isla teases. "You, who haven't had a steady boyfriend in forever."

Amelie doesn't miss a beat, "I am not the one in question here… Also, I've observed human behavior up close."

"You're a pastry chef," Isla snorts.

"Exactly." Amelie's lips curve. "I've seen humans naked and vulnerable. Not literally," she hastens to add, "but you ever observe people enjoying their dessert? They let their guards down, and tune in to their baser instincts. You can tell a lot about a man by the way he eats his pudding."

Isla makes a gagging sound. "PJ. PJ," she singsongs.

"PJ?" I frown.

"Poor joke," she clarifies.

Amelie reddens. "Uh, that's not what I mean."

Summer chuckles. "Sure, you did."

"Okay so it came out all wrong, but you get me, right?" Amelie waves a hand in the air.

I take in her scarlet features. A smile trembles on my lips.

"Anyway, don't mock it until you try it." Amelie turns to me, "As I was saying…"

"Yes?"

"I think you should make Saint jealous." Her eyes gleam, "Very jealous."

9

---

*I am an odd number. Take away a letter and I become even. What number
am I?*
Answer: Seven

Saint

The music reverberates from the walls of the nightclub. The blonde
leans in and shoves her ample bosom into my face.

I glance down her neckline, yawn.

She grabs a cushion from the next chair, slaps it to the floor between
my legs, then drops to her knees. She lowers the zipper on my pants
and my dick springs free.

I shove a hand into the pocket of my slacks. I could do with a
fucking cigarette about now.

She bends and takes me into her mouth.

The blood thuds at my temples; my balls shrivel. *Hell, I don't want her.* I grip her hair, she moans—the sound too exaggerated, too theatrical... Nothing like the soft breathy cries, the whines, the keening groans from Gigi. *Why am I thinking of her again?*

I yank the blonde's head back. She glances up, a frown between her eyebrows.

"Leave."

She scowls.

Guess I owe her an explanation? Not. "It's not you…" I crack my neck, "it's me."

Her lips turn down, then she stiffens, springs up. "You're a jerk, you know that?" She pivots, then flounces off toward the exit.

"What happened?" A male voice snickers. "No lead in the old pencil?"

"Shut the fuck up, Weston." I glance over to where he's sprawled on a settee—a woman between his legs. Her head bobs as she blows him.

Not a muscle moves in his face. His features are deadpan. He's not enjoying that so much as tolerating it. Yeah, when you hop from one blow job to the next, it happens. Things leave you bored. *Flashing eyes, moist lips, the scent of her arousal in the air.* My cock is instantly erect. *The hell?* Just thinking of her seems to have the most bizarre effect on my libido. Unacceptable. No-one, not even one of the Seven, are allowed to get close. So why is it that I can't get the images of our encounter out of my head? "Clearly, I don't like her."

No fucking riddle there to solve.

"Who are you talking to?" Weston peers past me.

The fuck? Did I say that aloud? I scowl, "None of your bloody business."

"The man doth protest too much."

"Focus on your own asinine problems."

"Of which, I'll have you know, I have none." He taps the head of the woman whose face is stuck to his groin. She obediently increases her pace, raising and lowering her head at double the speed. He glances at the one on his right and she thrusts out her chest, squeezes her breasts, moaning in what is clearly fake desire. He frowns, "Less noise, more action." The woman subsides, her entire body gyrating with the effort of her ministrations on herself.

"I don't know, from where I am, you seem…"

"Occupied?" He smirks.

"Stupefied."

"At least I am getting some satisfaction… You, however…" he looks me up and down, "…are a sorry state of affairs."

I tense. "Fuck off, douchebag."

"Oh, I intend to." He widens his stance. The blonde between his knees peers up, he frowns, and she goes back to the services she's providing him.

"So, it's come down to this, huh? Just two of the Seven trading insults." I tuck myself back in, then jump to my feet, begin to pace.

"Well, Sinner's too infatuated with his new wife, Edward's out… Priest and all that, Damian's off doing whatever it is that rock stars do, Arpad's island-hopping in the Baltics, and Baron…"

"Fucking Baron." I drum my fingers on my chest, "Bet he's laughing at us from whichever corner of the world he is in."

"Of all the Seven of us, he took the incident the worst."

I stiffen.

"Not that it hasn't affected all of us in different ways. It's a bit much for twelve-year-old boys to have been subjected to what we were—"

"Stop." I grimace.

Weston's shoulders tense. Then he grips the hair of the woman in between his thigh. He tugs and she moans. He yanks her head back and forth, using her mouth to get himself off. His mouth firms, then he pulls her off of him. He snaps his fingers and all three women in the room rise to their feet. Turning, they fade toward the exit.

"Well trained." I smirk.

He grabs hold of a napkin from the side table, wipes himself then tucks himself inside of his pants.

"Bet they didn't pose much of a challenge to you, hmm?" I ask.

"Is that what you are looking for?" He tosses the cloth aside, then fixes himself and stands to his feet.

Is it? I raise my shoulders. "I'm cool, ol' chap. Easy come, easy go."

"That's what Sinner used to say." He mutters, "Then look what happened to him…"

"Sinner's a fucking fool, letting his emotions getting entangled with a woman. Not that I have anything against Summer."

He chuckles, "Of course, not."

"I am not going to make the same mistake." I crack my neck.

"You trying to convince me or yourself?" He asks.

"Neither." I shuffle my feet. "Mind you, of all us, Jace and Sinner are the happiest right now."

"No doubt ensconced with their women." He shudders.

"Tying themselves to one woman for the rest of their lives." A hot feeling stabs at my chest. *Whoa. I'm not jealous. I'm not.* Burying myself in the same pussy every night, waking up with the scent of her in my nostrils, her moans echoing in my ears, the thrum of her cunt vibrating at my fingertips… Nah. My groin hardens; blood drains to my cock. Clearly, I need a diversion. I did the right thing, turning her down. I am never going to give in to the temptation her body affords me. Nope.

Shouts reach me from the theatre below. Turning, I prowl over to the floor-to-ceiling window that overlooks the stage.

Weston joins me.

I gaze down at where a woman hangs in a graceful split from the pole in the center. The shouting dies down. She stays motionless, a long statue of grace. Her leg muscles are coiled, her calves seem to be carved out of stone. Surely, her ankles are too delicate to bear the weight of her body? Then the strains of a familiar song crash over the space. Is it The Beatles?

Who the fuck strip teases to a song by the bloody Beatles?

She arches her arm at a right angle to her body. A ripple runs through the crowd. I freeze.

Victoria does, and damn, does she give the song a whole new meaning.

She leans into the move, her hip jutting out…the silvery strip of nothing digging into the crease between her legs, stretching to outline what would be pink, juicy, pussy lips. A shimmer of lust crawls up my spine. The hair on the back of my nape rises. The music pumps up…

I stare as she twirls around once, then again. Bends one leg, thrusts out the other, then lets go, to stay poised on one arm for a second—the crowd gasps—then she wraps her arm up and around her leg, thrusts

out her breasts. Her nipples are outlined against the shimmery top…
that hugs every curve of her body, baring her creamy shoulders. The
arch of her neck, the sweat that beads that beautiful skin, clings to the
regal arch of her brow, slides down her temples, across that soft curve
of her cheek. She throws her head back, lips parted, spine arched in the
simulation of the first throes of an orgasm.

The lyrics crescendo. She's dancing to *Come Together* by The Beatles.
Jesus H Christ. Come together, indeed.

Her eyelids snap open. Familiar green eyes, stare up at me. *Her eyes.*
I glare. Under the harsh spotlights, her skin glows—white, transparent,
so fragile. *All mine.* A growl rips from me.

"How dare she?"

10

Victoria

His pale, blue eyes glitter, and even from across the space that separates us, they resemble chips of ice. Hard. Mean. His nostrils flare. Is he angry?

His jaw tics; his shoulders seem to grow in size.

No, he's not angry; he's livid. I gulp and all of my nerve-endings seem to flare. His chest heaves and the shirt stretches across the planes, outlining every single ripped muscle. No one should look that gorgeous, that lethal. My belly clenches.

I unfurl my body, coil my legs around the pole, twirl—once, twice, thrice—flatten out my body parallel to the floor in a flat line…

Stay… Stay… My biceps flex, my triceps stretch, all of my muscles coil, then I lower my legs until I'm parallel again, this time to the pole, lower my legs, until my toes touch the pole. Let go of the pole, to drop down to a crouch, then spring up, arch my back, my neck, snap out my head, search the window above. It's empty.

What the hell—? My stomach bottoms out. My arms and legs tremble.

The lyrics of my preferred song to dance to thump against my breast bone. So close, I had been so close. I could have sworn I'd caught his attention… I should have known better.

Just because he is interested in me—Oh, I'd caught the flicker of curiosity in his gaze from the moment he'd laid eyes on me—so what? He met many men and women, a billionaire like him who has the freakin' world at his feet. What does he know about being helpless, at the mercy of those who could change your life in an instant?

If I don't manage to intrigue him, I'll never be able to break Nina free of the Mafia's clutches.

Goddam him. I grab the pole with my arms, pull myself in, then scissor my legs wide apart, in a 'V' swirl, once, twice… It's thanks to Nina that I'd taken classes in pole dancing. She'd enjoyed it and had nagged me until I'd gone along with her. She thought it would help me gain confidence in myself, and help me come out of my shell. And truth is, I'd found it liberating.

On the pole I can let go of all of my inhibitions, forget I am a nerd who doesn't fit in anywhere. I can let the music get to me, allow the lyrics to twist my insides, slam against my temples, my chest, between my legs. I twirl around the pole, faster, faster—the world spins, lights flash behind my eyes. I loosen my grip, my body flies through the air, muscles loose, shoulders coiled, and I land on a roll. The audience gasps, I spring up to my knees, lower my head. Sweat drips down my temples, from my chin, splatters onto the floor.

The music rises to a crescendo, then switches off.

The cheering from the crowd smashes into me. I open my eyes, and notice the worn cowboy boots in my line of sight. The hair on the nape of my neck rises. I run my gaze up the tailor-made slacks that mold to powerful thighs and cup the bulge between the legs. I gulp. Snap my head back.

"Get up."

His lips move. I hear him above the hoots and whistles of the crowd.

I glide up to my feet, the audience cheers. "Victoria!"

"Victoria… Show your tits."

A snarl rolls up his chest. His biceps bulge. Anger strums off of him and my nerve endings spark. I've seen Saint laid back, bored, cruel intent writ in his every expression. But this…? Saint …. Livid, every muscle in his body taut, layer upon layer of muscle vibrating with surprised tension…? My thighs spasm and liquid heat curls in my belly.

"Victoria, take it all off…" Another scream from the audience rips between us.

He growls, takes a step forward, "Do it."

I blink.

"Take off your clothes."

"H…here?"

"Isn't that why you're here? To show off your assets? To cash in what you have for money? He shoves his hand into his pocket, pulls out his wallet. He holds up a credit card. The light flashes off of it, blinding me for a second. "This is what you want, right?"

I swallow, then tip up my chin. "Of course." A cold sensation stabs at my chest. My fingers and toes turn to ice. I fold all of my emotions into that tiny space deep inside. Raising one shoulder, I shrug off my scanty sparkly top, then shrug down the other side.

The fabric catches on my hard nipples, stays poised a second. One more breath and it will fall. Another hoot from the audience, "You're blocking the view, you asshole."

I wince.

Saint holds up a hand and the audience quietens.

He moves in closer, closer, until his chest brushes my half naked torso. Goosebumps flare on my skin. He swoops out his arm. I wince. He digs his fingers into my hair, tugs. I arch my head, bare the column of my neck for his perusal.

A bead of sweat runs down my temple. He drops his head and licks it up. I shudder. All of my pores pop.

"That was a terrible song to strip to, by the way."

I blink. Of all the insignificant things to say… "Not a Beatles fan, huh?"

"Hate them."

"Oh, goody." I flutter my eyelashes. "I'll make sure to strip to only them from now on."

His gaze narrows and his blue eyes lighten until they resemble water swirling under ice—deep, dangerous. He's lethal…a man who'll never let go once his interest is aroused. I gulp. My heart begins to race.

"Say that again…" His voice lowers to a hush.

"I'll make sure to…"

His hand swoops out, then he tears off the strip of cloth from over my middle. I am instantly wet. *Damn him, why do I find this hot?* It isn't. He wants to belt me, teach me a lesson for what I did. I'd dared to throw down the challenge and he had risen to it—I drop my gaze to where his arousal tents his crotch—in more ways than one.

"Do it." My voice trembles, and I... I hate that. I will not allow him to see how scared I am. Worried that my body will enjoy what he is going to do to me. Find that I want it, welcome it. Ask him to ravish me right here in front of everyone. "Lost your courage?" I tip up my chin and his features twist. He bends his knees, grabs me by my thighs, then pushes me down on the padded platform.

I stare up at him, raise my torso. He covers my body with his, plants his hips between my legs, his hardness stabbing at the hollow between my legs. His gaze bores into me. My heart begins to race, adrenaline lacing my blood. Fear claws in my gut. I raise my hand and my palm connects with his face. His head snaps back.

He straightens and my fingerprints are outlined on his cheek. *Oh, dear! That's not good, is it?*

I gulp and he bares his teeth.

I raise my hand again and he catches it, then brings up my other arm. He yanks my palms up and above my head, shackles my wrists with his fingers. Then thrusts his hand between us. I hear the click of his belt buckle, the rustle of his zipper, then his dick nudges my entrance.

"You want this, don't you? This is why you've been haunting me since I saw you. This is why you came to me for help. Admit it. You want what only I can give you."

I nod.

"Say it." He scowls, "I want to hear you.""

"You. Only you," I gasp. My insides twist and my core aches, even as moisture laces my cunt. "I need you."

Not like this.

Not like this.

"Like this," he hisses. "You want me on this stage. You want me to take you in front of everyone. You're an exhibitionist."

I freeze. How did he guess that?

"You want to be taken and broken, until you are set free. You want me to paint your insides with my cum, to rub my name into every pore of your body, say it…"

Yes.

Yes.

"You pushed me until I crossed the line, until there was no going back." His features twist. The blue in his eyes deepens until they seem almost black. "Say you want me to punish you, you want me to fuck your past right out of you," he snarls.

Goddam him for laying my soul bare in front of the world. My chin wobbles. My scalp itches. *Why is this happening? Why did it have to turn out like this? I'm only doing what is needed to save myself and my friend… So why can't he get on with it?*

"Do it."

My voice emerges as if from far away. I wrap my legs around his waist, thrust my hips up.

11

Saint

Her wet heat sears up my shaft; my groin hardens and my spine tingles. My thighs flex, grow rigid. "Jesus, fuck." The growl rips out of me. I balance my weight on my elbows, peer into her eyes.

Angry green sears through me. Emerald, jade and all the fucking precious jewels in the world couldn't compare to the brilliance in her eyes... *And now what? I am waxing poetic?*

"What are you waiting for?" Tears glitter in her eyes.

For me? For her? My heart squeezes. *The hell?* Why do I want to find out what's making her come onto me, haunt my every step, force herself on me.? Almost as if she is under duress. I stiffen, my shoulder muscles tensing. *Is that what this is? Is she trying to trap me somehow? But why? It doesn't make any sense.*

"This is what you want, right?" she seethes, her features a hard mask. "Me at your disposal. Well, here I am, so why don't you take what I am offering and be done with it? Why don't you—?"

I shake my head.

She blinks.

"Not like this." I pull back, everything in my body protesting. My pelvis jerks—wanting, needing to be inside of her. *Not yet.*

Her mouth opens and closes. "Wh…what are you doing?"

I lock my muscles, push up and off of her. "You can't top from the bottom, sweetheart."

She scowls, then glances away.

I pinch her chin. She peers up at me from under her eyelashes.

"Guess what the masochist told the sadist?" I scan her features.

"What?" She swallows.

"Hurt me."

Her pupils dilate and her breathing grows ragged.

I peel back my lips, "And what did the sadist reply with?" I ask.

She tilts her head, "I…I don't know."

"Exactly."

She frowns.

"He said 'No,' Sweetheart."

She pales.

"To everyone else, you may be a fragile beauty, but your façade doesn't fool me."

She swallows, then tosses her head, "I have no idea what you mean."

"I can see the cracks in your perfection, the need that eats away at you."

Her breath hitches, "You don't know what you're talking about."

"Don't you?" I allow my lips to curl, "I plan to break you, and when I am done with you, you'll regret ever having caught my interest."

Her lips part, and the scent of her—lilies with a dash of pepper—teases my nostrils. My dick twitches. My fingers tremble. They fucking tremble. I let go of her and she sags back.

I thrust out my chest, then tuck myself in my pants. "We do this my way." I say.

"What's that?"

"Thirty days Victoria. If you can survive for thirty days without breaking, I'll take you as my sub."

She frowns. "That's…too long," she splutters.

"Twenty-four seven."

"What?" Her cheeks pale. She sits up. Her breasts jiggle and her nipples perking up to salute me… So does my dick. *Fuck.*

"You'll work with me and warm my bed…but you can't give in to me."

"The hell? Do you have any idea how twisted that sounds? It's impossible. How the hell am I supposed to put up with your arrogance?"

"Your choice. Take it or leave it."

She twists her fingers in front of her, "Saint."

"You don't get to call me that."

"But—"

"You don't question me either."

"How?"

I make a zipping motion with my fingers over my mouth.

She squeezes her lips shut.

Thank fuck. Another word from her and I'd have tossed that stupid fucking agreement that I pulled out of my ass into the horseshit pile where it belongs. "Yes or no?"

Footsteps head toward us and shouts slice through the fog in my head, "Saint."

I shove the noise away, focus on her. Her face pales, then she jerks her chin. I slide up to my feet. Rake a last glance across those creamy breasts, her concave stomach, the slit between her pussy lips. My cock jerks and my balls thrum. I squeeze my fists at my sides. *Walk away before you do something you regret.*

A new voice calls out, "Saint!"

I jerk my chin up. Weston glowers at me. Behind him, three other men—the bouncers from the club— stand shoulder to shoulder, forming a wall between him and the crowd that's busy turning the place upside down. Too fucking bad.

We own the joint. We can do what we want with it, and that includes the possessions in it… Except her… She belongs to me. Mine to do with as I chose.

I glance down and she opens her mouth.

"Nod for yes, shake your head for no."

She stares.

"You can do that, hmm?"

She glowers. I smirk.

"Well?"

I angle my body to leave and she brings her fingers to her mouth, bites her nails. *Huh?* Who'd have thought the perfectly turned out Victoria would turn out to be, not only an accomplished stripper—but also has the gross-as-fuck habit of biting her nails? She's nervous. *Good.* Time things fall into the form I prefer them to be.

I tilt my head.

She nods, a jerk of her chin. My muscles relax. *Thank fuck. No, I hadn't been tense, or on edge... Of course, she was going to a accept my proposal. She had to.* She'd dogged my footsteps, crawled into my gut... Time I show her who is the master of her. There can be only one man who commands her every waking moment, her every second at night, her dreams, her nightmares, her innermost fears, her deepest desires... All of it belongs to me... Temporarily. It buys me time to take her apart, piece by piece.

To figure out what the hell she wants from me...and why? And if I use that time to coax her into my model of a willing sub... Well, that is my prerogative. She tips up her head so her gaze collides with mine. I shrug out of my shirt, hand it to her.

"Get dressed." I turn to leave.

"Wait," she calls out.

I glare at her over my shoulder.

She pales, then shrugs into my shirt, which hits her mid-thigh. The sleeves cover her arms completely. I frown. She darts her fingers to the front and begins to thread the buttons through the holes. *Good.* She gets me. Finally.

"When..." she swallows. "...when do we start?"

"You'll find out soon enough." I turn back, take another step toward Weston. A man behind him breaks through the chain of bodyguards.

He barrels forward, tries to brush past me, his gaze set on Victoria.

I swing and my fist connects with his jaw. He crumples to the ground. Silence descends. The mob behind stills.

I scan their faces, "Anyone, else?"

12

———————

What did the baseball glove say to the ball?
Answer: Catch you later

Victoria

"Why hasn't he called yet?" I chew on my fingernails. I haven't heard from the asshole in an entire seven days.

Well, except for the call from one of his assistants—not Meredith—directing me to a private clinic in Hampstead Heath. The doctor—a woman—had given me a complete physical and drawn enough blood for a series of blood tests. *Jesus, the brute is thorough.* He's probably having me tested for every STD under the sun.

The doc had wanted to administer the contraceptive injection, but I'd opted for birth control pills. I'd been surprised when she hadn't insisted otherwise.

The acrid taste of nail polish laces my tongue. I hold up my fingers and groan. Every one of my finger nails is bitten down to the quick. Ugh. This definitely doesn't go along with the sophisticated image I try to portray. I fist my fingers at my sides, glance around the tiny flat. Amelie had invited me to move in with her and I had agreed.

Truthfully, it had been a weight off my shoulders. No way, could I afford the rent at a studio. Hotels or long-term rentals were out of the question… Besides, I'm not planning on being broke that long. Just for a few days, until I get my feet under me. Until I manage to lure in one gazillionaire with the worst attitude ever. I have to get him to… what… fall in love with me?

Get me pregnant with his child? I shake my head. Not that, much as I want one. This is not the right time to bring a baby into this world. Really, I just need to get him to trust me enough so I can get close to him

I'd been stupid to think my charms, such as they are, would work…

I'd danced at that club, hoping to catch his attention. At least, it had worked. Maybe too well…? There had been a strange light in his eyes when he'd directed me on how exactly he wanted me to speak to him… Which is to say, hold my silence. A thrill tickles my spine… It had been hot. The way he'd taken charge, even as everything inside of me had insisted that I stand up to him—not give in, not yet. I had held my own…and that…had seemed to seal the deal… It had been a risk to coerce him to lose control. He'd taken the bait, come for me, and I'd been sure he was going to fuck me right there. The fact that it had taken place before the entire assembled audience… That had only turned me on even more. Damn him, but I'd wanted him to claim me then. Couldn't resist the strength of his body which had covered me, held me down, helpless in his hold.

I'd known he wouldn't let anything hurt me… No, he is saving that pleasure for himself. I thrust my forefinger into my mouth, chew on my fingernail… My teeth dig into the soft pad of my finger… "Ow." I shake it out.

"Have you tried coating your fingertips with salt?" Amelie flounces into the room… "Or better still, chilies." She holds a tray with two cups of steaming tea. In between them is a green chili.

I stare at it, then fold my arms behind my back. "No way, am I rubbing that on my fingertips. Knowing my luck, I'd probably touch it to my eyes instead."

She places the tray on the center table, then sinks into a sofa. "So… the plan didn't work?"

I purse my lips, shift my weight between my feet.

"It did work?"

"I… I'm not sure."

She frowns. "Explain."

I twist my fingers together in front of myself, "He, uh, asked me to wait for his message."

She sits up, "That's good, right?"

"He hasn't called."

"He will." She leans forward and picks up her Kindle.

"You sound sure," I huff.

She shoots me a glance. "You don't sound convinced."

I raise my shoulders.

She holds up her Kindle. "Trust me, I have firsthand knowledge of how to play a man and reel him in."

"Huh?"

"Romance novels, baby.'

"Oh." I blink. "You…you're joking right?"

Her eyes gleam. "Haven't you read *Fifty Shades of Grey*?"

I shake my head.

Her mouth drops open. "No way."

I walk over, sink into the overstuffed armchair next to her.

"You could have fooled me." She studies me from toe to head.

"What?"

She waves her hand in the air, "You're so graceful... You practically ooze sex appeal."

"I do not." I fold my arms around my waist.

"Sure do. In fact," she scowls, "every movement of yours seems to be choreographed. Even wearing this outfit."

I glance down at my simple knee length sweaterdress; I'd bought it at a charity shop to keep me warm in the London weather.

"You're so well put together." She says.

I bite my lips. "My ma loved black and white movies from old Hollywood. I watched them all with her. I loved the old-world glamour, how beautiful and powerful the heroines seemed. I guess I internalized their mannerisms—how they walked, talked…flirted," I lower my gaze, "seduced."

"Ah, now that makes sense."

"It does?"

"You have an old-world allure about you." She places her Kindle on the settee next to her. "An air that suggests you are a challenge."

"Does it now?"

"Bet that's why Saint can't help but be intrigued."

"Enough to keep me waiting, huh?"

"He likes to play games… All the Seven do."

"And you know them well?"

"I've only met them a couple of times, thanks to Summer, but they are all men at the top of their game, and you've set your sights on the most intriguing of them."

I bite my lips. "Saint confuses me."

"How?"

"He saw me dancing, came barreling down from where he was. He marched up to me, and I swear, I thought he was going to go all caveman and drag me out of there."

"But he didn't?"

I shake my head, pull my feet up under me. "He seemed to change his mind, and decided to humiliate me right there…."

"Then?"

I swipe my hair back from my face. "Then he stepped back, almost as if he was recalibrating his strategy. He accepted my offer."

She blinks, then whoops, "So that's good right?"

"Maybe." I shift around in the chair, "I may have overdone things. He seemed to get all jealous. So much so that he beat up a man who charged up to me."

She sits up straight, "He did?"

I nod. "It was…"

"Dramatic?" She asks.

"A surprise." I shiver. "Guess I simply knew what to say to intrigue him."

She tilts her head, "He has a hidden side, huh?"

"I researched him before approaching him."

"You did?"

I nod, "There are enough pictures of him leaving well-known BDSM clubs."

"Are you worried that you're out of your depth?" She purses her lips. "You think you'll be able to handle the lifestyle?"

I shuffle my feet... "Um," I glance at her, then away. *Shit, I revealed too much.*

How many times does a person lie, before the lie becomes the truth?

Too many.

And now I am asking riddles and answering them, as if I learned the technique at the feet of the alphahole himself. *Shit. Get a grip.*

"I've, uh, always been drawn to it." I tip up my chin, "I've never practiced it before... I hadn't seriously thought of dipping my toes into it, until Saint." That much is true, at least.

"So, you chose him because you were curious? I mean, he's not the only one of the Seven who has a hankering for that stuff, you know?"

I twist a strand of hair around my fingers, "I chose him because..."

"Because?" She asks.

It's so tempting to spill my plan...the part that really matters. If I could get it off my chest to even one person, it would help me feel lighter... I open my mouth, then shake my head. I can't. This part of my plan? It's the part that counts. It's also the one thing I dare not speak openly about. Call me superstitious, but I don't want to spoil my chances by revealing too much...too soon... "Doesn't matter," I cut the air with my hand.

Her lips draw down, "Aww, and it was getting interesting, too."

"I'll let you know when there's something to talk about."

"Promise?"

"On the existence of a fifth Beatle." I hold up my hand.

She scowls. "There wasn't one."

"I know." A smile twists my lip.

"Not fair, V."

I chuckle, "Let's say, if he doesn't call me, I am—"

My phone pings. I glance at it and freeze. Amelie jumps to her feet, crosses the floor to me. "It's him, isn't it?"

I show her the text.

Alphahole: Come down.

Jesus, is there a shortage of words in his vocabulary, or what?

"Alphahole?" She chuckles. "Quite complimentary of you to call him that."

"Not me," I choke out. "That's the rat's ass of a jerk keying his phone and ID into my phone."

"He did that?"

I throw up my hands. "I know, stalkerish much?"

A horn sounds from below and she darts to the window. "There's a car there…all dark and shiny… OMG." She turns. "He's here, waiting by the car for you." Her voice is breathless, "This is exciting. This is what you wanted, right?"

My fingers tremble. I swallow. *Is it? Is this what I'd been hoping for?* He's opened the door. I only have to step through now. I firm my lips, look up at her, "I never keyed in his name…" I purse my lips.

The only time my purse had been out of my sight was when I had fallen asleep in his office. Had he hacked into it then? I wouldn't put it past him. He's infringed on my privacy… Which, is a positive sign, right? It means he is interested. I force my fingers to un-clutch from around the phone.

Walking to the center table, I pick up my mug of tea, then sink into my arm chair. My phone pings again. I glance down.

Alphahole: Don't keep me waiting.

•　•　•

I set my jaw. The arrogance of the man. Of course, I'd had an inkling he'd want to get his own way, but this... Expecting me to drop everything and jump to his demands? No way.

My phone buzzes.

Alphahole: I know what you're doing and it won't work.
     Alphahole: You sure you want to go down this path?
     Alphahole: Don't make me come up there. You'll regret it.

My heart beat ratchets up. My pulse begins to race. *Don't give in to him. Don't.*
     There's a banging on the door. I jump.

13

Saint

The door opens. I glance down, then past the blonde who stands there, to the dark-haired woman who's captured my imagination.

I tilt my head and she juts out her lower lip. Oh, I'd like to bite down on that glistening flesh and teach her who exactly calls the shots around here. I jerk my chin and she crosses arms.

"Saint."

I look down at the blonde haired woman, "How are you, Amelie?"

She looks me up and down, "you here for Victoria?"

I try to move past her, she plants an arm either side of the door frame. I pause, glance down at her, "Is there a problem?"

She frowns, "you tell me." She taps her foot on the floor, "Is there, Saint?"

Huh? "What do you mean?" I scowl.

"You treat her good." She lowers her voice. "You hear me?"

I meet her gaze, allow my features to take on an expression of sincerity. "Always." I raise my hand, "you can trust me to do what's right for her." I say honestly.

"Amelie." Victoria springs to her feet, then crosses the room. "You were leaving, weren't you?"

"Was I?" Amelie frowns, then turns around.

Victoria nods, "Yes, you were."

Amelia takes in a breath, Victoria's gaze widens, and Amelie tosses her head. "Fine, be like that, V, but you owe me."

Victoria's mouth curves in a smile. Her features light up. I blink. She's fucking beautiful. I want her to smile like that at me. The hell am I thinking? I draw myself up to my full height.

Her green eyes twinkle, "I promise I'll make it up to you." She says.

Amelie nods. She marches to the crowded table in the center of the room, and picks up a handbag. Turning, she moves toward me. "You better not hurt her."

"Amelie!" Victoria's mouth falls open.

I chuckle, "I won't do anything to her…"

Amelie frowns, then jerks her chin.

"I promise." I glance down at Amelie.

"I'll hold you to that." She scowls, then brushes past me.

I straighten, "Nothing that she doesn't want me to, that is."

Victoria stiffens. "What was that?"

I saunter inside, "Oh, you heard me all right, so don't pretend otherwise." The door closes behind me with a snick.

Victoria pales.

I prowl forward; she takes another step back.

I reach her and she stumbles to put space between us; her hip grazes the window sill. She stiffens.

"You afraid?"

She raises her head, "No."

I swoop down, grab her waist, and twirl her so she faces the window pane. She squeaks.

I lean in, slap my hands on either side of her, "I hate liars."

"I'm…" her breath hitches, "not lying."

I step back, so quickly she flinches. Then turn my body, so I am at right angles with her. "Last chance."

Her spine stiffens and she shoots me a glance. "Told you, I'm not."

My palm connects with her butt with such force that her body jolts forward and she braces herself on the window. Her cheeks turn fiery. "How…how dare you?"

"Don't challenge me."

She opens her mouth and I bring my hand down on her arse again. Her shoulders jerk; her breathing grows ragged.

My dick is instantly hard.

She turns around, bites her lips, then her gaze narrows with intensity. She makes a low sound deep in her throat. Her fingers flex. Every part of her tenses, until she's fairly vibrating with anger.

I chuckle.

"It's not funny."

"You're right." I draw my gaze from her hair messed about her shoulders, down to the turn of her dainty ankles. "What it is, is fucking arousing."

She pulls back her shoulders, "This is all a joke to you, isn't it?"

"On the contrary," I flex my fingers.

She swallows.

I crack my neck.

Her pupils dilate.

"I take disciplining you seriously."

She raises her nose, "Forget it, it's off, it's…"

"Turn around, face the window."

She scowls.

"Do it."

She firms her lips.

"Now."

She swivels to face forward.

I plant my feet between her legs, shove them apart. Her spine arches and her shoulders knot. I wait…wait… A gust of wind blows through the open window. Her hair flows about her face. She half turns. "Why the hell don't you—?"

I raise my hand and spank her arse. She huffs. And again. Her knuckles whiten and her face falls forward. "Stop."

"Shut up."

I slap her rounded flesh again and a low moan bleeds from her lips.

All the blood drains to my groin, my cock lengthens, and my balls grow heavy. *Jesus, fuck.* I've barely touched her, and I already want to be inside of her. I need to get ahold of myself. Need to stop her little cries from coiling in my belly, from affecting my presence of mind… *Focus, focus, on her. Her needs. What she desires. Only her.*

I spank her again and her entire body trembles.

Once more. Her legs buckle. She straightens, then draws herself up to her full height.

"Don't ever question me again."

She stays silent.

"Get me?"

She jerks her head.

"Say it."

"Yes."

"Yes what?"

"Yes… Sir."

"Good girl."

Her pupils dilate. *Shit, she liked that.* I hadn't meant to compliment her yet. She has to work for it. I have to make this challenging on her, else she'll see right through me.

"Let's get out of here."

I pivot, stalk to the door.

"Wait."

I keep walking.

"Wait, please… Sir."

I pause. "What is it?"

"You are aware that you need to get to know me first, right?"

I shoot her a glance. "What does that mean?"

She locks her fingers together, "As a Dom… You need to understand me as a person before you…"

"Before I start training you?"

She nods.

"Too bad, this is how I do it."

She frowns, tucks her elbows into her sides.

"You know you're acting like a selfish prick, don't you?"

"Took you this long to figure that out, Sweetheart?"

She brings her fingers up to her mouth, then tucks them behind her back, "So now what? I follow you?"

"Yes."

"What about my clothes, my things?"

"Leave them."

"What?"

I yawn, "Did you forget that you're mine for the next 30 days?

"I don't get it, what do we do for this much time?"

I smirk.

She flushes.

"My, my, what a filthy mind you have, my little Gigi."

She draws herself up to her full height, "Don't call me that."

I plant my hands on my hips, "I'll call you what I want, when I want, and you'll answer to it."

She bites her lower lip and my gaze drops to the pulsing flesh. A growl rips from me, "Any more questions?"

She tips up her chin, "I'm not leaving without proper footwear."

Before I can say anything, she marches over to the shoe rack by the door, and exchanges her ballet pumps for stilettos. Images of taking her from behind when she's dressed in nothing but those heels fill my mind. Fuck.

She turns to me.

"Well?" I tilt my head.

She glances to the side, then back at me.

I draw in a breath. *Patience, patience.* "Out with it."

"My phone."

I follow her gaze to the device on the armrest of the only chair in the room. "What are you waiting for? Take it with you, will you?"

Half an hour later, I ease my car up to the curb in front of Selfridges.

"Wow, the place hasn't changed at all." She peers up through the window.

"Why should it? It's a hundred-year-old department store; tradition is what it's all about."

"Is that what you like?" She turns to me, "Tradition?"

"Money." I turn off the engine. "And everything it can buy. That's what I like."

"Can't fault your taste in vehicles." She runs her fingers over the dash and my cock instantly twitches.

Fuck, this reaction to her every move is crazy. I reach for the car door, "You like my chariot?"

"Chariot?" She shakes her head. "Whatever. Please don't answer that. And what's not to like?" She opens the car door on her side, "It's a macho car."

"I'm a macho man."

She blows out a breath. "I should have seen that coming." She steps out. I follow suit, zap the doors locked, then walk around to her.

"You prefer to drive yourself?" she asks.

"Always." I glance down at her. "I never trust another man with my possessions."

She brings her fingers up to her mouth, chews on a fingernail. The way her mouth sucks on her digit... *Fuck me.* The blood drains to my groin. *How the hell do I get her to stop that, huh?*

I swoop out my hand and grab her wrist. "Bad habit," I growl.

"So are you." She tosses her head.

I chuckle. "We agree on something there." I bring her hand to my lips, suck on the very same fingertip that she had placed inside her mouth.

She swallows, "Uh, can I have my hand back?"

"Never." I lower her hand, weave my fingers through hers because... Why the hell not? Then stalk into the department store.

Once inside, I release my hold on her, instantly missing how her small hand felt in mine. Soft, fragile; to be treasured and protected. Ridiculous. I prowl forward, leaving her to dawdle behind.

She glances around the aisles, the displays, then pauses. "Saint?"

I continue on.

"This is ridiculous," she mumbles.

"What did you say?" I growl.

"I meant... uh! Sir?"

My dick instantly twitches.

"You may speak."

"Where is everyone?"

"Gone."

I increase my pace.

Her footsteps speed up.

"What do you mean, gone? It's the weekend, not to mention the first week of December. The busiest time of the year for shoppers…"

"So?" I pause and she almost stumbles into my back. My fingers twitch to help her, so I tuck my arms in my sides. She scowls, then draws herself up to her full height.

"So where are the customers, the salespeople?"

"I told them I was coming."

"Ah!" Her gulp is audible. "So…so they cleared out the place?"

"Yep."

She stares, "What about the business they'll lose?"

"What about the business they'll gain from me and the rest of the Seven?"

"Right."

She marches ahead.

"Victoria."

She doesn't turn back.

"Gigi."

Her shoulders stiffen, and I can't stop my lips from quirking. So fucking prickly.

"Stop or you'll regret it."

She tosses her head, "I am regretting ever coming to you."

"Admit it. You're secretly looking forward to what I am going to do to you."

"Yeah, sure, I spend all my days and nights wondering only about that."

"I knew it."

She jerks her head around to stare at me, "Do you believe everything that feeds your ego?"

"Always."

Her gaze widens, "It's useless having a conversation with you."

I prowl toward her. "Poor Victoria, always so in control, always knows her mind and what she wants…. Or so she thinks."

She tips her head back, all the way back, "I don't think, I know."

"What you are, is too damn uptight."

She grits her teeth.

"See, that's what I mean." I whisper my knuckles over her jaw and her breath hitches. "You're too focused on containing all of that passion inside of you. You think you want to direct the course of your actions, when all along, you've been waiting for someone to come along who can force you to relinquish control."

"And I suppose you think that someone is you?"

"I don't think so." I drop my head until my lips are poised above hers. "I know so." I close my mouth over hers.

14

Victoria

Step away, turn away. Break this stupid sham of an arrangement or whatever the hell it is and run the hell away from him. His lips meet mine, fuse, clasp. I will not give in, will not open to him. He swipes his tongue across my mouth and goosebumps flare on my skin. He tilts his head, nibbles on my lower lip. Heat flashes low in my belly. The heat from his body swoops around me, curls into me, draws me closer, closer. He opens his mouth, sucking on mine, asking, demanding, insisting… A groan bleeds from me. I part my lips and he deepens the kiss. He simply takes. His tongue tangles with mine; he drinks from me. Fills my senses with his dark edgy scent, the hardness of his body a shield against the world. The dominance of his posture pushes down on my shoulders, holds me in place. A growl rumbles up his chest, and my nipples pebble into painful tips. My sex clenches; my toes curl. I raise my hands to his shoulders, dig my fingertips into those corded muscles—seeking, wanting. He tears his mouth from mine and steps back. Cool air assails my face, the flushed skin of my neck.

"So, I was right."

I lower my hands to my side, blink, sway. "What do you mean?"

"Your control will be mine, Victoria, " He brushes past me and I shake my head to clear it. By the time I turn around, he's striding away and toward the elevator. He stabs the button and the doors glide open. Of course, even the cage doors would obey him.

But I won't. Not if it's the last thing I do.

He steps inside, then turns, "Coming?"

As I approach him, the doors slide toward each other.

"What the hell?" My jaw drops open.

He jerks his chin up, "See you on the third floor. Don't keep me waiting."

The doors close, leaving me behind. *Asshole shut the escalator doors in my face? I can't even... How dare he?* Anger pulses in my veins and adrenaline laces my blood. I curl my fingers into fists... He did it. Purposely. To rile me. To get under my skin. I will not let him unnerve me. Will not allow him to break through the barriers I've put up against the world. Self-preservation. Holding onto what is mine. I won't let him in. Will never allow him to see the real me.

Oh, two can play this game. He can push. And I can pretend...to give in to him. Enough to get what I want from him: Nina's freedom, and mine. And a little bit more. A piece of myself that only belongs to me. That I'll never share with him. Yes, that is only right.

I intend to walk away from this mess with a tangible result; one that I can stake a claim on. One which no-one else—not the Mafia, not Saint—can take away from me. That is the way out. The ultimate control over my future and his, and I'll own it.

I'll have the last laugh.

I pivot, walk toward the escalators. When I reach the third floor, the same eerie emptiness greets me. Beautiful displays, mannequins with gorgeous dresses. The scent of expensive perfume lingers in the air. Jasmine, roses, and a more seductive note... Pinewood maybe? ...With a darker edge of... Chocolate? I glance around and realize that I have followed the scent up the corridor.

Counters on each side display designer clothes, sun wear, formal clothes. I reach a double door at the end, and when I touch one of the handles, the door slides open. My heart begins to race. I stop at the rack of dresses, drag my finger down the array: green, blue, pink... all colors except black. I reach the end, fingers poised over a vermillion sheath. I hesitate.

"Try it on."

I spin around and watch as the man I've come to resent steps through the door. It snicks shut behind him. The hair on my nape rises.

"Go on. It's all for you."

"For me?" My voice trembles. Hell, I hate that he has this effect on me. And after what he did earlier... Allowing the elevator doors to close in my face... I should simply leave. But what is the point? He'll simply track me down. No doubt about it. No, best not to show how much he upset me with that gesture, and I'm not sure why. It's not the worst thing he's done to me, but maybe I'd expected more from him? Maybe a more gentlemanly approach? Right. Saint may have been brought up in wealth. He may have gone to the best schools. But underneath that cultivated man-of-the-world façade, he is a rake, a man who doesn't care about worldly pretenses. He takes what he wants. No apologies. Is that what attracted me to him? Not only... It's the Mafia's mandate, of course, that I win him over. Although, I'm not sure that's going to be possible. But I can keep him occupied, take his mind off his work, his business interests, try to keep him close. And this uncomfortable friction between us can only help, right?

He crosses the floor to drop into an armchair positioned at the far end of the room.

"Don't keep me waiting, Gigi."

A shiver runs down my spine. It's the first time anyone has had a nickname for me. I've always been Victoria before this... Had insisted people call me by my full name. Saint... He'd smoothly transitioned to calling me by a completely different name and somehow it felt... *Right? Doesn't matter.* This is all temporary, until I have what I want. For now, I'll give the devil what he wants... *Pretend; that's all you need to do.*

He nods toward the space in front of him. I stiffen my spine. Head toward it.

"With the dress."

I draw in a breath, turn and snatch the beautiful material off the hanger. Soft, smooth, the dress whispers between my fingers. I dig my fingertips into the cloth, then pivot and march to the center.

I face the mirror, meet his gaze in the reflection.

His blue eyes flare. He leans back, folds one leg over the other.

"Strip."

"What?"

He grabs his ankle, holding his leg in place. "You heard me."

"You want me to take off my clothes?"

He glares at me and a frisson of anticipation grips me. He lowers his brows and my fingers tremble. I draw in a breath, hold his gaze.

"Unless you want me to…" He places his feet on the ground.

"No, I… I'll do it." I glance around for a space to put the dress.

"Drop it."

I let the fabric whisper from between my fingers. It pools in shimmering layers of crimson at my feet. I straighten. *He's seen most of you already, so what does this matter?* That was…in front of a crowd. This… Alone with him in a room… It feels…more intimate. Like I am putting on a show for him, which I am. Which is daunting, and damn him, also more arousing… Which is what he intended me to feel, no doubt. Asshole. He probably knows exactly how it will make me feel. Doing one more thing out of my comfort zone. One step closer to the edge… Closer to the deep darkness that laps at my mind, calls to me, pulls at me, tugs on me.

"Don't keep me waiting." His voice lowers to a hush and my nerve-endings pop. I reach for the button on the back of the dress, undo it. Tug at the zipper, which slithers down, baring the skin between the two halves.

Goosebumps flare on my skin. I sense his gaze following my gestures, as I tug one sleeve down my shoulder, then the other. The dress slithers down to pool around my ankles. I kick it out of the way.

Don't look up, don't. I glance up at the mirror and our gazes clash. His eyes are darker, deeper, like pools of desire locked in droplets of ice. His nostrils flare; his chest rises and falls. Ah! So, he isn't as impervious as I'd thought him to be either.

Holding his gaze, I reach for the straps of my bra, undo them. They whisper down my breasts, catch on my nipples. I draw in a breath and my breasts heave. The nylon slides down my arms, baring my torso completely. His fingers clench around his ankle. His jaw tics.

He jerks his chin toward my panties.

What the—! I don't need to remove them to try on the dress.

He glares at me and I shiver.

He tilts his head, I dip my fingers into the waistband of my panties, watch as his shoulders tense.

I lower the scrap of fabric down my thighs, to my ankles.

The blue in his eyes deepens until it seems black. Color flushes his skin. "Stay there."

I freeze, watch him in the mirror as he rises to his feet, approaches me. He pauses behind me. His gaze holds mine in the mirror. His big body dwarfs mine—me bent over, fingers entangled in my panties.

"Hold your ankles."

I swallow and my breathing deepens. He hasn't touched me, but he peruses my position—open, bare, my most intimate parts on display.

One side of his lips curls, "You do not want to challenge me, not now." Damn the man, and his ability to reduce me to a quivering mess.

"Do it, Gigi."

His voice slips into my skin, warms my blood, coils in those deepest, most secret places of mine, where I've never allowed anyone else. Not him either. *Never.* I steel my spine, curve my fingers around my ankles.

He drags a knuckle down my spine and I shudder. My knees almost give way. I must have moaned or made some incoherent cry, for he stills.

"Shh." He grips my hip to steady me. "You're doing so well, don't spoil it."

A fire lights somewhere inside of me. He praised me and insulted me in the same breath. Only Saint could do that. Simultaneous push-me and pull-me, irritate me and pleasure me.

I tip up my chin, open my mouth to speak. He dips a finger in my pussy.

I gasp. *What the—?* "You could have warned me, you—"

He slides his finger inside my channel. I huff. He adds two more digits. Too much, too full, he has to stop, he can't do this, he…he twists his fingers, hitting that spot deep inside. My toes curl; my scalp tingles. My entire body seems to lengthen, my hips arching up, enveloping even more of his wicked fingers.

He pulls out, only to stuff his fingers back in. A groan bubbles up my throat. I lower my head, my hair falls around my face, and I tighten my grip around my ankles. I cannot give in, cannot. He rubs his thumb on my clit and a trembling zips up my legs.

"Please…" I mumble. *What am I begging for? Why am I asking him for more? Keep quiet, don't show him how much this is affecting you. How could he have found his way right through to the secret core of me?* "Saint, please."

"How many?" His voice shoves through the noise in my head.

"What?"

"How many men have you had?"

I crack open my heavy eyelids, try to peer through the heavy blanket of my hair.

"Tell me, Victoria. How many have fucked you here?"

Anger flares inside, then crashes with the desire. "What's it to you?"

His muscles stiffen, tension shimmers off of his frame. "Everything about you is my business. Tell me, or so help me, I am going to pull out my fingers and—leave you aching and wanting."

I hesitate.

His fingers leave me.

My pussy spasms, needing, hurting. Empty, so empty. I cry out. "Three…you bastard. Three. Is that enough?"

"Including your husband?"

Tears prick the backs of my eyes. Fucking Saint. He had to ask that question, didn't he?

"Answer me."

"What do you think?

"I think Adam Rhodes didn't give a bloody fuck about you," he growls.

A chuckle trembles from my lips.

"So, I'm right?" he asks.

I nod.

His gaze intensifies, "But he fucked you?"

"He…did his husbandly duties, if that's what you're asking."

His fingers tighten on my waist.

"Did you love him?" His voice is impersonal as if he's interrogating a business prospect. Cut. Dry.

Everything is so fucking black and white for him. If he only knew the choices I'd had to face.

"Did you?"

"No."

I hear him release a breath. *Why should it matter to him if I'd wanted someone before him? Not that I want him either. Of course, not.*

"Thank you for sharing that."

What the—? Is be being polite?

"I gave you what you wanted." The words tumble from my lips. "Are you satisfied?"

"Not yet." He brushes his knuckles past my slit.

Pinpricks of pleasure dart up my spine.

Damn him and his touch. Why is my body so damned responsive to him? Why did it have to be him who could elicit this reaction from me when no one else can?

He teases his finger into my back hole and everything inside of me tenses.

No.

No.

"Yes," he growls. "Here… How many have had you here, my impudent little wannabe sub?"

"Ah!" I stutter.

"Tell me, or I swear I'm leaving." The heat from his body recedes again.

I gasp. "Stop. I'll tell you." I sense him still.

Wait.

Wait.

I swallow. My fingers spasm. My thigh muscles bunch. If I do this, I am giving away one more part of myself. Another secret that will no longer belong to me.

Another thing he can hold over me.

Another weapon he can use against me.

"Now, Victoria."

I gulp, then squeeze my eyes shut. "No one," I whisper. "You… You'll be the first."

15

Saint

The first. The only? The fuck am I thinking? Why does it mean so much to me to mark her in a way that no one has before? I've had my share of women, certainly never expected any one of my partners to come to me untouched… *So why am I asking something of her that seems so out of character?* It's her. She is shattering my control. I told her that I would break her down; I hadn't counted on the impact she'd have on me. I have to get back in the lead, have to wrest back my hard-earned self-restraint. Only one way to do it.

I drop to my knees. Her entire body freezes. I lick her from her swollen nub all the way up to her star-shaped opening.

Her shoulders shake. She moans and her knees seem to give way. I swoop down, wrap my fingers around her thighs. "Hold on."

I drag my tongue up her clit, retrace the path to her back hole. A whine spills from her lips and it's my undoing. I thrust my tongue inside her channel, lick her, flick my tongue in and out of her.

Her entire body shudders and her breathing grows ragged. A trembling grips her, swoops up her legs. I don't stop. I angle my head, haul her even closer until she's riding my face. Her body tenses, her pussy clenches, and moisture beads her cunt. So fucking sweet, so soft. My dick lengthens; my groin hardens. I need to be inside her. I must. I fondle the curve of her hip, insert a thumb into her back hole.

She shudders, her thigh muscles spasm, and I recognize the give-away sigh. She's close. So close. I curl my tongue inside her and a low keening cry emerges from her lips. My vision tunnels and my muscles bunch. Close, I am so close. I drag my mouth from her, scramble up to my feet. Pivoting, I stalk away.

"What the fuck?" Her startled exclamation follows me.

I reach the exit, shove open the door.

"Where are you going, you asshole?"

I pause, "I think it's your arsehole that's pushing you to speak now."

"You filthy, horrible, monster."

The hair on my horrible neck bristles. I swerve and a wind disturbs my suit sleeve as a vase sails by. It crashes onto the floor, shatters.

I turn, sweep a wary gaze over the disheveled woman, who's walking toward me. She's managed to pull up her panties in double-quick time—impressive. Other than that, she's naked. Her tits bounce, her hips wiggle, and her dark hair flies around her face. She holds up the twin of the vase that she'd thrown earlier. I duck again…but am not that quick. The heavy artifact grazes my shoulder, before crashing to the ground.

I stumble, then right myself. I brush my sleeve. "Are you quite done?" I drawl.

She clenches her tiny fingers into fists. "I am going to kill you."

"Join the queue. You'll have a long wait, by the way."

She bares her teeth and a snarl emerges from the controlled, always put together sophisticate she'd once been. This side of Gigi… I frown… It's innervating, energizing… It's fucking sexy.

"Wanna fight?" My lips curl.

"Fuck you, Saint."

I can't stop the grin that splits my face.

She snarls.

I raise my hand, "Now, now, Tory, we can work this out."

"I hate being called Tory, fucking hate it."

O-k-a-y. "Victoria."

"I loathe my name. Stupid, prissy, old-fashioned." She walks forward, fists in front. "Are you aware of the number of stupid Posh Spice references I have had to endure?"

I blink, glance around the room. What can I use as a shield? The table… Too heavy. Besides, it would hurt her if I held it up. Come to think of it…better not move from here, best to hold my stance, look her in the eyes. Her pupils are so black they seem to have expanded, until only a circle of stormy green remains.

"It doesn't help that I look like this."

I risk a quick glance down to her perky breasts, the tiny waist, the flare of her hips and that juicy, sexy, core of hers. The pink cleft between her lower lips would be glistening, from her cum. *Fuck.*

My cock thickens, my belly coils… *Fuck, fuck, fuck, look up, look away, before you reveal how much her presence affects you.*

I squeeze the bridge of my nose, and she snarls, "You can't stand to look at me, can you?"

I snap my eyelids open, "Now, that's not what this is about."

"You fucking hate my body," she huffs.

I tilt my head, "Not true."

"My tits are too big.

My fingers clench. "They're gorgeous," I growl.

"My waist is too tiny." She pouts.

"It's fucking beautiful." I furrow my brow.

"My hips are too large," she wails.

I pretend to study her curves, then scratch my chin, "Now that you mention it…"

She opens and shuts her jaw, then charges at me, "Why you jackass, you rotten excuse for a man…you."

She flings herself at me, and I take the full impact of her weight. She throws her fists, catches me in the side, against my rib cage. She peppers me with her blows. I don't react. I brace myself, allow her to hit me. "I hate you." Slam. "Bloody loathe you." She snaps her forehead into my chest. I wince…on her behalf. That had to hurt. She raises her arm again, then drops it to her side. "You're dreadful. How could you do that to me? How could you...?" Her shoulders shudder and her tiny body sways. Wetness blots my shirt. I glance down at the back of her head.

"Gigi?"

She shakes her head, her crying intensifying. A hot sensation stabs at my chest. I scoop her up, cuddle her against my body. She's so fucking light, so perfectly formed. Why the fuck hadn't I noticed that before? Because I'd been too focused on myself. On what I wanted from her, on trying to figure out why the hell she'd come to me with that crazy proposition of hers... And I will find out... But meanwhile, I am going to hold her, until this storm she's found herself in blows over.

Her sobs increase in strength.

Shit, the fuck am I supposed to do now?

I've had women cry out in passion, weep when I've brought them to orgasm, wail when I've fucked the hell out of them. But this...weeping woman... One I've begun to appreciate more than any other female in my life... *Holdonabloody second.* I've barely spent any time with her, so why does she affect me so much?

Do I understand her better than anyone else outside of the Seven?

Yes.

Fuck, what does that mean?

Nothing. I can have girlfriends... No, not like that... I mean, girls who are my friends. Yeah... No, she isn't a friend. *She is... Something... Somebody I am going to take on as a sub, remember? Yeah, got it.* I cuddle her close and she wraps her arm around me. I stalk over to the chair I'd vacated earlier. Sit down with her in my lap.

I rock her and pat her hair, but her crying only seems to grow louder.

Shit, shit, shit.

The band around my heart squeezes. Gotta do something. What does one do to quieten someone who's crying? I rock her back and forth, back and forth. She digs her fingers into my shirt, her nails digging through, into my skin. She's still weeping...but it's not as intense as earlier, right?

I continue to rock her, hum under my breath. She sniffles. Her crying lessens. I hum again…then croon the song.

She hiccups, then falls silent.

"Your pitch is off-key, by the way." She sniffles.

"I'm tone deaf," I reply cheerfully. But at least she's stopped the waterworks. Man, that was close.

She peers up at me from under her eyelashes, "Did you sing—"

"While my Guitar Gently Weeps by The Beatles?" I crack my neck. "Seems that way."

"Why?" She asks.

"It worked, didn't it?" I scowl, "Couldn't stand by and watch you have a bloody meltdown."

She huffs, "I meant, why The Beatles?"

"Why not The Beatles?"

"You hate The Beatles."

"I hate tears even more, besides, when a naked woman—"

"—Almost-naked," she protests.

I chuckle, "*Almost naked* woman throws herself at me… I had to catch you. I couldn't have you hurting yourself."

Her gaze flickers.

I fit my knuckles under her chin, so she has no choice but to glance at me.

"Only I am allowed to do that, Gigi."

She swallows.

"No one else can hurt you, except me," I lower my chin, "you feel me?"

Her pupils dilate. Her chest heaves, then she nods. "I understand… Sir."

My dick hardens at that. *Shit, what am I doing, cuddling her? I fucking hummed a song for her? Bloody-fucking-hell!*

I lean forward and she presses a hand into her chest, "It's okay, Saint, I won't tell."

I frown.

"I won't tell the Seven or anyone else. It's our secret."

"What the fuck you talking about?"

She darts me a look from under those sooty eyelashes, "That you secretly have a thing for The Beatles."

"I don't have a 'thing' for those knobheads."

"Yet you knew the words to their song."

"Who doesn't?"

She stares at me.

"What?" I scowl.

"Not everyone knows the correct words to that particular song."

Shit, is it getting hot in here?

"Admit it." She sits up in my lap.

"No."

"You secretly like them… You think it's 'uncool'—" she makes air quotes with her fingers. "—to say so."

I set my jaw, "I don't."

"It won't take away from your macho, hotter-than-hell image."

I lean back in the seat. "You think I'm macho?"

"Umm." She shuffles her feet.

"Answer me."

"Maybe…" She chews on her lower lip and my gaze traces the action. Bare lips with all the lipstick bitten off. Mascara trails down her cheeks, her eyelashes are spiky from the tears she'd shed, she's not wearing clothes… And yet, she's trying to coerce me into revealing something more about myself. It's not a big deal…but…if it means so much to her, hell if I'm going to give it to her so easily….

"Yes or no, Gigi?"

She throws up her hands. "Fine, yes, you're macho as hell, fucking sexy, the most virile man I've ever met."

"Don't forget overpoweringly charismatic."

She draws in a breath.

"And an asshole."

"You mean, alphahole?" I smirk.

She tosses her head.

"And dominant."

"Your ego is so large that—"

"It's bigger than Beatlemania at its height?" I smirk.

She blinks, "See?" She stabs a finger in my chest. "So, you admit they were a phenomenon?"

"So were *The Stones*, and they had a fuck-ton more attitude."

She raises her shoulders, "Too rebellious."

"Too conformist." I lower my chin. "Goody-goody on the outside and bitchy, on the inside."

"Over the top, bad boys, too much sex, too much fast living, too much everything."

"Exactly what you secretly covet."

She scoffs.

"Admit it. What you need to loosen up, is a whole lotta fucking." I raise an eyebrow.

"Speak for yourself." She gathers her hair to one side. Her tits jiggle again, and my dick instantly perks up. Shit, is there a direct connection between her sensual actions and a particular part of my anatomy?

I adjust her position so she's straddling me. "Tell me what you feel for me," I say, "and if I'm satisfied, I might let on what I think about that old-fashioned, overrated, ridiculous boy band."

"Boy band?" She splutters. "You called them a boy band?"

"I changed my mind." I stab my tongue in my cheek, "They were a bunch of dicks who hated each other…"

Her shoulders stiffen.

"Oh, and Lennon was especially a douche-dick."

She clutches her fingers at her sides as twin spots of color appear on her cheeks.

Hell, this is more fun than sitting in a business meeting negotiating the crap out of my opposing party.

"And The Beatles copied The Stones."

"The Beatles copied them? The Beatles?" She sputters, "Your time-lines are all warped."

I lean in close enough for our breaths to mingle, "Are you aware that you get this cute little line between your eyebrows when you go all maniac?"

"I'm not bloody Flashdance," she huffs.

I laugh.

"Nice one, Rhodes."

"That's not my surname." She slaps a palm over her mouth.

I frown, 'What's that supposed to mean?"

"N…nothing." She tries to scramble off my lap, and I grab her shoulders to hold her in place.

"Explain."

"There's nothing to explain."

"Yes, there is, what you said—"

"Was a slip of the tongue." She tips up her chin.

"You're a bad liar."

"Not lying."

"You've been heaping on the bullshit from the moment we met."

"What?" She frowns, "What do you mean?"

"You went out of your way to catch my attention, you led me on, capitalized on the chemistry between us. You made me an offer you knew would pique my interest."

"Not my fault you found me a challenge," she huffs.

"You're more than that for me."

She freezes.

Shit, shit, shit, hadn't meant to say that. Talk about a slip of the tongue, huh?

She swallows, lowers her head, "You're not making sense."

"It's simple. You wanted to become my submissive, but I've changed my mind."

She pales… "B…but we had an arrangement."

"Consider that void."

"You can't."

"I can."

"So what…does that mean?" She glances around her, "All this, bringing me on a shopping trip and stuff… Wh…why did you do it?"

"Felt like the thing."

"You wanted to catch me off balance?"

I peruse her features. She's quick, all right. Not that I had expected anything less… Not after the way she'd maneuvered herself under my skin in such a short period of time.

She wriggles around on my lap. My cock jerks in my pants.

Her breath catches. Her pupils dilate.

I smirk. "No denying that our bodies communicate with each other on a completely different level."

"That's the cause of all this…this mess." She holds herself rigid, not moving an inch. Her shoulders knot; her eyebrows twist together. "I think it's time to put an end to this…stupid arrangement. Don't you think?"

"I agree."

She opens and shuts her mouth. "You…you do?"

I nod, "I have a completely different arrangement in mind."

I peel back my lips.

She pales. Her throat moves as she swallows.

"What?" Her voice quakes… "What is it?"

"Marry me."

16

What did the female giraffe ask the handsome male giraffe?
Answer: Wanna neck with me?

Victoria

After that pronouncement he'd shoved me off his lap... Literally. I'd fallen on my arse again. It was getting to be a habit around him, that. When he wasn't spanking me, I seemed to be constantly swept off of my feet—pun intended. I can't remember the last time I'd gotten this physical so many times in a day and I'm not talking about down and dirty sex... Not that I'd had any of that either.

He'd brought me to the edge again, so close, so near to exploding all over that wicked tongue of his, and then he'd pulled back. He'd denied me the orgasm. He'd left me angry, frustrated, horny as hell... and I'd lost it. I'd wanted him like a bitch in heat... An addict who craved one last teeny tiny hit... He'd known exactly how to throw me off kilter. I'd lost my equilibrium. I had stumbled and made a mistake and he had pounced.

Marriage?

I'd assumed he'd meant a fake marriage...but he'd clarified it would be real, all right. I'd be tied to him, unable to escape him. Bound to him. I couldn't divorce him...not for a year. And during that time... he'd train me as his sub. At his convenience. "Of course," I snort. Everything is about him. About what he wants. How he decided to change the tone of our relationship with a flick of those thick, elegant fingers. I huff. Straighten my shirtdress down my hips.

It's crumpled, but hell, not like there is anyone in this entire godforsaken building to notice.

I could refuse him, of course. I haven't accepted his proposal yet. I could turn him down. *You won't. You can't.*

This entire arrangement suits my needs even more. It is a bondage from hell. I squeeze my fingers at my sides. Don't have a choice, but to go through with it. Besides... I want it. I want to be a real wife. I want to belong to someone, to have someone to call mine... Soon...very soon, I'll have the real thing. Until then... If I have to make do with Saint... Face it, it isn't a hardship, the things he does to me. The response he elicits from every pore of my traitorous body...is everything. It is what I have always hoped to have one day... If I can get even a small portion of this crazy, weird chemistry that traps us and turns everything about us to ashes? So be it. I will burn.

But I'll ensure he shatters too.

I may be going down, but I'll be taking Saint with me.

He changed the rules completely, but if he thinks I am going to back off now? He has another think coming.

He doesn't know me.

I swipe the hair back from my face, survey my flushed features. Hell, I don't know myself anymore.

I am losing perspective. Everything I had fought for, what I had thought I'd held dear to me, all of it gone... Thanks to one overbearing, over-the-top, Beatles-hating, complete wanker of an alpha male. My insides clench and sweat beads my forehead. What am I going to do? What *can* I do? My heart begins to race. I need to get out of here and into the open air. I march to the door, out into the corridor. My footsteps echo. I glance around at the brightly lit aisles, the racks of clothes, the displays. All bloody creepy, without the sales people.

The asshole didn't even wait for me. He'd merely told me to take my time to adjust my appearance and he'd left. That's it… No word, no explanation about when we'll meet next. Nothing.

I walk up the corridor toward the escalators. The hair on my forearms rises. I am alone, aren't I?

I glance around. Nothing…except the bright lights, the rows upon rows of designer wear. I hurry my pace. Footsteps sound nearby. *What the—?* I break into a run, reach the escalator, race down it. My heart begins to thud. Adrenaline laces my blood. *Who could it be? I have time to deliver on my part of the deal. I am doing everything I can about it.* I reach the second floor, the first. By the time I reach the ground floor, sweat beads my forehead. I clutch my bag close, reach for my phone and pull it out… *Who should I call? Amelie? Summer…? Saint… No…not him.* He'd simply gloat about how helpless I am. I am just scaring myself; it happens. Especially after everything I've been through over the last few weeks.

I reach the exit doors, push them and burst onto the sidewalk. A man passing by eyes me curiously. I glance away, stagger toward the bench on the sidewalk. I need to catch my breath, consider my options. I sink down onto the platform, hunch my shoulders. *Think, think.* I can deliver my end of the bargain. By marrying Saint, I'll be even closer to my target. All I have to do is go through it, pretend… No… No pretense here. I feel something for him… I have from the moment I'd first seen him. Something primal, something that makes me feel alive. And I want more of it. I want to luxuriate in it. I wanted to rip out my soul, fill myself with him… Use him for my own selfish needs, before the inevitable happens, and I have to walk away from him. I sigh. I have no choice in that… I simply have to make the most of the cards I've been dealt.

I straighten my shoulders. Pluck my compact out of my purse, snap it open. *That's it, Victoria… Calm, composed. A survivor. You can do this. You can.* I pull out a tube of my favorite lipstick, twist, and raise it to my lips.

A hand touches my shoulder. I jerk and the lipstick smears. I glance to the side, "Wha—?"

"Victoria?" The elderly woman smiles at me. Her greying hair is pulled back in a sleek chignon; creases fan out from the sides of her eyes. "Are you okay, my dear?"

"What? Yes." I frown, "Do I know you?"

"I'm Meredith, I'm…"

"Assistant to the Seven?"

Her features light up. "Indeed. We met when you came to the 7A offices?"

"Of course. I remember you now." I glance past her at the pedestrians. Pinpricks of awareness dot my neck. "What are you doing here?"

"I was passing by and saw you."

"Right." I glance back at my reflection in the compact mirror, then scrounge around in my bag.

"Here." She offers me a tissue.

"Thanks." I use it to fix my face, then snap the compact shut.

"So, you happened to be here the same time as me?"

"Coincidences." She raises her shoulder. "People think London is a big city, but really, it's a village."

"Hmm." I slip my compact into my bag. "I'm afraid I need to be somewhere else."

"I'm afraid I can't let you leave yet, Victoria." She smiles, her eyes twinkling up at me.

I frown. "Why is it that all of you seem to speak in such riddles?"

"Us?"

"Saint, and everyone connected with him."

"Perhaps you're finding hidden meanings because you're playing in them yourself?"

I pale and the world tilts around me.

"Victoria, what's wrong?"

Her voice seems to come from far away. There's a roaring in my ears. My vision tunnels. *Games. Playing. Hidden meanings. Not what it seems.*

"Victoria?" A hand grips my fingers. "My dear, you're freezing."

My teeth chatter. "It's just… The weather… It's gone cold suddenly."

"That's London for you, my dear. Still, I like it best when it's raining." She rubs my freezing hand between her warmer ones. Her flesh is smooth, unmarked. No calluses. Such well-preserved skin. Wonder what hand cream she uses. A chuckle rolls up my throat. *Am I getting hysterical?* I bite the inside of my cheek, swallow down the bile that laces my tongue.

"Better?" She peers into my face.

"Y…yes." I meet her gaze. "Thank you."

"Come on, let's get some food into you. Have you had lunch?"

"N…no."

"There's a lovely spot around the corner, that serves the best afternoon tea.

"But."

"No buts. Saint would never forgive me, if I left you here, on your own."

I twist my lips. "Oh, I don't think Saint would care either way."

"I think you'd be surprised, my dear." Her eyes gleam.

I frown, "What are you not telling me?"

She laughs. "I'm not hiding anything from you, I promise."

Where have I heard that before?

"You're right to be this cautious, but I am not the enemy. In fact," she rises to her feet, "I am on your side."

"You are?'

She holds out her hand, I take it and she pulls me up. "Most definitely." She begins to walk. I keep pace.

"Anyone who'll bring Saint to heel gets my vote… And when it happens to be the right kind of woman who can stand up to him, then trust me, I'll do anything in my power to ensure that the two of you are happy."

I stumble over a crack in the pavement.

She grabs my arm, "You all right?"

"Of course." I glance up at her, "But you have the wrong idea here."

"Do I?"

I nod, "Most definitely."

We take the zebra crossing across Oxford Street, then turn right.

"It's not like that between me and Saint."

"Then how is it?"

I peer sideways at her. Is she making fun of me? Maybe having a laugh at my expense. She meets my gaze, her own clear. Her features are composed into an expression which seems to portray… Curiosity…? A slight concern, perhaps. Can I trust her? I raise my shoulders. Does it matter? I have nothing to lose… I have come this far… I only have to see things through, and if she can help me, well, then why not?

"He asked me to marry him."

Her gaze doesn't falter. No surprise on her face.

"You knew?"

She turns her head, navigates us around a couple loaded with shopping bags. "I had hoped, though I have to admit, I hadn't thought Saint would have the balls to pop the question."

I choke.

She chuckles. "I'm a plain talking kind of gal."

"I can see that."

"Get it from my mama. She raised eight of us, and she suffered no fools."

"Right."

"Comes in handy when you have to herd the Seven and their friends along in the right direction. Know what I mean?"

I snort, "I am getting an idea who actually wears the pants in 7A."

She leans in close, "Let's keep that to ourselves, huh? Our secret."

A warmth spreads in my chest. "You bet."

"So, back to you and Saint," she pauses, then turns right and away from the bustling High Street. "You were saying?"

I wasn't…but fine…if she wants to know what my answer was. "I haven't said yes…yet."

"Are you going to?"

"Should I?"

"Are you asking my opinion?"

I turn to her, "I am."

"I think you should take your time about it."

I jerk my head toward her, "You mean…?"

She nods, "He needs you more than you realize."

"He doesn't depend on anyone." I bite the inside of my cheek.

"He wants you in his life."

"His asking me to marry him…? It's a trap," I insist.

She pauses, turns to me, "Is he trapping you or himself?"

"I don't know."

"Saint doesn't do anything unless he's completely sure of it."

"He's doing this to get revenge."

"For what?"

"For…" *Should I tell her? Should I?* "For crawling under his skin, for distracting him… I don't know." I rake my fingers through my hair. "He wants to punish me."

"And would that be so bad?"

I blink. "Are you implying what I think you are?"

"Don't let my age and gray hair distract you."

My mouth opens and closes… "You mean…you are…into the same lifestyle as the Seven?"

"I've known them since they were boys. They've been through a lot, each of them… They've each found their ways to cope. And while I don't necessarily condone it… I realize it's one way of coming to terms, to find balance in their lives."

"That doesn't answer my question."

"Which was?"

"Uh… Are you into the S&M stuff as well?"

"Maybe I am…" She raises her shoulder. "Maybe I am not. What difference does it make? After all, it's not me who has a marriage proposal from someone who means more to me than I am letting on."

She strolls forward.

I turn, follow in her wake. *Jeez… What the hell was that all about? What does she even mean? Is she that privy to the private lives of the Seven… and their friends? Does she know their associates? Business partners…? Their enemies?* I swallow and my heart begins to race. *Was I wrong to confide her? Maybe Saint didn't want me to tell anyone about his proposal. But then, he hadn't mentioned otherwise. Why would he even want to marry me? What does he get out of it? A willing slave…yes…but there are so many other women out there who would be more than happy to oblige. Why me?*

She comes to a stop in front of a beautiful heritage building. I glance up to find the elegant lettering that states, Claridge's.

She walks up it, "You coming?"

"This is what you meant by an elegant little spot?" I blink. It's only one of the most iconic hotels in the world.

"Oh, they have the best tea and sandwiches, and after the morning you've had, it's only fair I treat you, right?"

I follow her up and into the plush reception area. The liveried man by the door does a double take. "Meredith!"

"Dorian, how are you?"

Dorian walks forward, takes Meredith's hand and kisses her knuckles.

"Fit as a fiddle, my dear. And who is this charming young woman?" the built-like-a-tank man asks. Doorman, my foot. Clearly, he's there to take care of any trouble that erupts. *Is there going to be trouble?* My heart begins to race.

"This is Victoria."

Dorian tilts his head. "Ah! Good to meet you." He shakes my hand, with a half bow, then I am treated to the hand-kissing as well. He steps back, beckons us to proceed. "Your guests are waiting, Meredith. Best seat in the house for you ladies."

I trail after Meredith, "Guests? Did he say guests?"

She waves a hand in the air, "It was time to call in the reinforcements. Such devious planning to take on one of the Seven needs strong English Breakfast Tea, girlfriends, and of course, cake. Lots of cake."

Half an hour later, I lean back, "I'm stuffed." I pat my lips with my napkin.

Amelie pushes the tiered cake stand toward me. "But you haven't had the scones yet."

I stare at the shortcake-like baked goodies. A groan wells up my throat, "But—"

"You must." Summer plops one of the rectangular delights onto my plate.

"I can't."

"You can do this." Amelia's lips quirk.

Jace's wife, Sienna leans forward, pats me on the shoulder. "It's good for you."

I glance around at the faces of the women I've come to count as family. I've known them for only a few weeks, and yet, each of them has gone out of her way to make me feel welcome here. They had accepted me into their little circle…no questions asked. How rare is that?

"If you insist…"

"We do." Meredith nods.

"If Karma were here, she'd say 'if you *incest*.'" Amelie snickers.

Summer chuckles, "That girl has a sense of humor that would be more in keeping with the sensibilities of a teenage boy."

"Such non-sequiturs." Amelie tosses her head. "Honestly, she is going to get into trouble for it someday."

Summer's features firm, "What the hell is she doing in Sicily anyway? Why can't she come back? I can't help but get the feeling that she's not telling the entire truth."

My pulse thuds at my temples. "But she is fine, right?" I pat some clotted cream and strawberry jam onto my plate.

Summer's forehead furrows. "She's been messaging me, but…"

"But?"

"The messages are not like her. I mean, she tells me that she's okay, and that, in itself is weird. No jokes, no puns, no sarcasm." She looks around the table. "Have you ever known Karma to speak without resorting to some underhanded acerbic quote?"

The others shake their head.

"Maybe… Uh, it's the man she's with?" I slice the scone, then lather some of the cream onto the flaky surface, followed by a dab of jam. "Perhaps he's changing her?" I bite into the scone.

Amelie quirks her eyebrow, "Is Saint changing you?"

The bite of scone goes down the wrong way. I cough.

Summer hands me a glass of water and I down it.

"So, what's the latest between the two of you?" Isla pipes up.

I place the glass back on the table, then reach for the rest of the scone. "These are good."

"Don't change the topic," Amelie pouts.

"Let the girl have some tea." Meredith pours me a cup. "Milk?"

"I like it black."

She hands me the cup. I sip from it and the slightly acrid, bitter yet sensual taste of tea fills my senses. Almost as potent as his scent. The man who has turned my world upside down. I glance up, to find five faces turned in my direction. "What?"

"You're falling for him, huh?" Summer's brow furrows.

"No." I place the high-grade china carefully back in the saucer. Then survey the features of my friends. "I am already in love with him."

"Oh," Amelie's jaw slackens. Then she snaps her mouth shut, leans forward. "He'll hurt you, girl."

My shoulders slump. Correction. He's already wounded me in a way he'll never know. Just not as much as I am going to hurt him. But I have no choice. I peer up at her. *Should I tell her?* I take in the assembled women.

"You can trust us with anything. You know that, right?" Meredith's soft voice interrupts my thoughts.

I glance at her, then look away.

I scan their faces, "Why is it that all of you are so welcoming? You don't even know me."

"Oh, but I do." Summer's lips kick up in a smile. "It wasn't long ago that I was in your position. You see me and Sinclair and you think it was all roses and shit from day one?"

I shuffle my feet, "Guess not. I mean when I saw the two of you at the wedding, the tension between the two of you was palpable. But then you both seemed to have worked things out."

"We did." She chuckles. "It wasn't easy."

"I'm sure."

"I was lucky I had the support of these wonderful women." She looks around at the group. "It's tough doing this on your own. You haven't had it easy, V."

Tell me about it.

"I want to extend our support to you... If you'll take it." She touches my shoulder.

"We'd love to help you." Amelie takes my hand.

"You bet," Isla adds.

"We have a vested interest in this. There can be no better woman than you to deliver Saint his comeuppance," Meredith says.

A lump of emotion blocks my throat. *Tell them, tell them everything. Come clean. This could be your last chance.*

It'll put your life in danger.

It could save Saint from ruin.

I open my mouth, but I'm stopped by a familiar voice, "Why, Victoria, what a surprise to see you here."

I turn. My face pales. "You?" I swallow down the bile that laces my throat.

The tall man comes to a stop on the other side of the group. His gaze bores into me, in his eyes a warning.

"Who're you?" Amelie glowers at him.

He tilts his head, "Hello Tory." He smiles.

Fuck, fuck, fuck. My vision narrows, the band around my chest tightening. This can't be happening. Not here, not now. Not when I had been so close to finding a way out.

I shake my head, try to speak, but the words die.

"Victoria, you okay?" Summer whispers.

Meredith glances at the man, then back at me. My breathing catches while my hands and legs seem to grow numb. I can't move, can't say anything.

Can't do anything but watch as she rises to her feet. "You must be a friend of Victoria's..."

"Indeed." Antonio's smile widens. "You don't mind if I borrow her for a second do you?"

17

Look in my face, I am somebody; Look at my back, I am nobody. What am I?
Answer: A mirror

Saint

"Hit me, motherfucker." I swing with my gloved fist. Arpad ducks. I stumble. Straighten, then pivot and rush toward him. He sidesteps me. I rush forward, slamming into the ropes that demarcate the boxing ring. Using the elasticity to brace myself, I turn, shake my head.

"Wanker," I growl.

Arpad snickers. "Speak for yourself."

He slams one gloved fist into the other. "Tired already? Heard you had trouble with your performance with some woman the other day. You losing your touch, motherfucker?"

I bare my lips. First, that slip of a woman had made me lose control completely. Now, this tosser actually thinks he can defeat me? "I've never lost a fight with you before."

"Always a first time." He hunches his shoulders, takes his stance. "You going to attack or are you going to yammer all day like a pussy?"

"The fuck?" Anger claws my insides. It's not at my douchebag of a friend, who's grinning like the joke's on me...which it is... I mean, I am not that far up my own arse that I don't see the signs. Coming undone around a woman while trying to figure out what the hell her game is and drawing a blank every single time? Not advisable. Especially when, clearly, she doesn't share the same feelings I have for her... Hold on. Hold... The fuck... On... *Feelings?*

Who the fuck talks about feelings?

There is none of that here. This is pure and simple, a challenge I took on... And purely because she intrigues me. And yeah, she had belonged to the motherfucker who had ruined our lives... And he is dead... But so what? Doesn't mean I can't make him pay by owning the woman who had been his wife. Possession is 9/10ths of the law , or what-fucking-ever that means. There. I have admitted it to myself. It's a chance to get some retribution for what was done to me and the rest of the Seven. That is the only reason I had embarked on this crazy mission. That's all.

"You okay, Saint?" Arpad frowns.

"The fuck you going on about, dickhead?"

"Just," he rolls his shoulders, "you were mumbling to yourself."

"I wasn't."

"Yep." He nods, "So, it's true then."

"Do I even want to know what you are yodeling on about?"

"You tell me."

"Nothing to confess... And PS, the last time I checked, you weren't the priest among us."

"But I am the best to forgive your sins, considering nothing you say or do could ever shock me." He leans forward on the balls of his feet. "After all, with Jace and Sinclair out of the picture, you and I head up the list of most-wanted felons of the carnal kind."

"When it comes to pleasures of the flesh, I'm ahead of both of you," a new voice chimes in.

I jerk my head as Weston enters the room.

"Too bad you don't fight," I rub the back of my neck, "else it would have been satisfying taking you both on at the same time."

"You know I can't get in the ring. Have to save my fingers," he flexes his digits, "for important procedures."

I smirk, "Is that the operation theater or the theater of operations you're talking about?"

"Both," he chuckles. "So you have some of your faculties left about you?"

I throw up my hands, "What the hell are you two nattering on like gossiping women about? I—"

My neck snaps back. "Fuck." I reel back from Arpad's blow. The world tilts. I glance up from my prone position on the floor of the ring, to meet Arpad's snickering expression.

I spit out blood, "Fucker."

"My pleasure." He holds out his arm and when I take it, he hauls me to my feet. My ears ring; pain fills the cavity behind my eyes. I shake my head to clear it. "Asshole." I train my gaze between the two grinning idiots.

"Now that we have that out of the way..." Arpad uses his teeth to undo the straps on the gloves.

"So..." He turns to me, "What's gotten your knickers in such a twist, that you went down in the first round?"

"None of your business." I strip off my own gloves, drop them to my feet.

"Oh, but it is." Weston steps into the ring.

I glance up as they close in on me.

"What's this?" I scowl, "An intervention?"

"You bet." Damian hangs over the ropes.

"The fuck you doing here, rockstar?"

"Heard you were having a moment." He grins.

I crack my neck. "So what, you flew in to gloat?"

"Of course." The light glints off Damian's golden blonde hair. "I was between concerts. What better way to use my down time, than to be around to witness another epic fall?" He waggles his eyebrows.

I roll my shoulders, "Sorry to disappoint, ol' chap, but you were misinformed."

"Oh?"

"You mean you didn't shut down all of Selfridges to pick out the wardrobe for your woman."

I choke.

"Personally," Damian snickers.

"By the way, while you were at it, did you choose a ring?" Weston trains a glance in my direction, his countenance all serious-like.

"Do you guys have nothing better to do than trade gossip?"

"When it comes to you," Sinclair prowls forward, "there's nothing better."

I scowl at him. "The fuck are you doing here?"

"Edward's been delayed," Sinclair drawls. "The Father had to tend to an emergency with his flock, but he's here in spirit."

"Shit, that's a terrible pun, Sin."

He laughs, "It's the environment." He glances around the space, "Why you can't use the gym at one of your fancy hotels, I don't understand. For a man who loves rare £400,000 smoke sticks, your choice of venue to get the shit beaten out of you, sucks."

"What's wrong with it?" I glance around the shabby-chic environment.

Jace had bought the building next to the Claridge's, then left the run-down gym as-is.

I like it because, well… Occasionally, it's an interesting experience to slum it. Also, it's the one place I can count on finding someone who can hold their own against me. Men who have their own devils to defeat.

"It has character, you gotta admit," Arpad grins. "Besides, it's growing on me."

"Don't laugh too soon, dipshit. It's a fluke that you won today."

"The first of many, no doubt."

"Wanna go another round?"

"Only after Saint confesses." Weston claps me on the shoulder, "Come on, man. I have too much invested in this."

"The fuck you talking about?"

"We may have bet a million," he chuckles.

"Or two." Arpad folds his arms over his chest. "You did it then? You took her on as your sub?"

"Nope." I glance around at their faces. "I asked her to marry me."

Silence, then Sinner doubles over in laughter. "And you made fun of me for doing the same?" He chuckles, then laughs louder.

Weston holds out a hand.

Arpad glowers, "Don't have a check book, nor a pen..."

"You don't need either." Weston pulls out his phone from his pocket, swipes the screen, then hands it over to Arpad. "Key in your password, ol'chap."

Arpad punches in his numbers.

"Jesus F'ing Christ. I can't believe this shit." I stalk over to the opposite side of the ring. "That's it, I am outta here."

"Hold on, Saint," Arpad smirks.

"Don't leave us hanging now," Sinner chortles.

"Can't believe you're being such a pussy," Weston's voice stops me. "I mean, if you're afraid of the woman..."

I turn.

Weston raises his hands, "If you're in love or some shit, you can tell us."

I scowl, "Back the fuck up."

"Enlighten us then?" Weston grins.

"You remember when Sin here decided to fake a marriage with Summer?"

Sinclair scowls, "That was to lure her father out into the open."

I motion with my hand.

"The father who had a connection to the Mafia..." Weston rubs the back of his neck. "After whose death... Sinclair realized his true feelings."

"He married Summer, they lived happily after." Arpad drawls, as he removes his boxing gloves. "The fucking end."

"And blah-fucking-blah, yes; but what about the Mafia?" I undo the Velcro strip on one boxing glove, and take it off, then the other.

"We're tracking them down." Weston leans forward, "The only clue we have is the name Adam Rhodes offered before he died."

"Which we aren't sure is a lead or the mumblings of a man doped out on painkillers." Arpad rocks back on his heels.

"He was on his deathbed, so one would think there was some significance to what he said," Sinclair muses, stroking his chin.

"He mentioned a Byron and a Capo," Damian glances around the group.

I grunt, "Then, Sinclair and I got messages from an anonymous source who knew our phone numbers, and quoted Byron. There's something else."

Sinclair stiffens. Weston drums his fingers on his chest.

"I received a USB with a video. It was dropped off in an unsigned envelope to my office."

All of them turn to me.

"When?" Weston scowls.

"Right after Sterling's wedding." I rub the back of my neck.

"Why didn't you tell us about this before?" Sinner growls.

"I am telling you now," I grunt.

"And?" Damian asks, "What did it contain?"

I step through the ropes, snatch up my phone, then straighten.

The guys crowd around and I play the video I'd downloaded from the USB.

Arpad swears, "That's the first evidence we have of that bastard."

"Considering we were blindfolded all through the incident—" Weston's voice tails off.

"Fucking, fuck." Damian growls.

I stare at the back of the man—the one whose voice has haunted my nightmares for so long. My pulse rate ratchets up.

"This is... significant." Weston drums his fingers on his chest. "It could help us make real headway in tracking down those bastards."

"Which is why I engaged a private detective to run with it." I widen my stance.

"The same one who's checking up on Victoria?" Weston straightens.

"About that...." I roll my shoulders. "There's a connection between her and the Mafia."

"No." Arpad frowns.

"Yep," A headache drums at my temples. "She was sent with Rhodes for the explicit purpose getting close to us."

"And…?" Weston growls.

"And," I glance around the men, "that's all I know so far."

Sinclair swears. Damian lowers his chin.

Weston and Arpad watch me with varying expressions of incredulity.

"Clearly, you need a better investigator," Arpad growls.

"You happen to know her, by the way." I tilt my head.

Arpad stiffens, "Is it…? It can't be…"

"Karina," I nod. "Weston recommended her, and she's a trusted friend of Jace's."

He swears under his breath, "A bloody nuisance is what she is."

I lower my chin, "She's trustworthy. That's what matters."

"You're evading the issue at hand again." Weston moves toward me. "If I didn't know better, I'd think you're worried that you are in over your head."

I toss my phone at Sinner who snatches it up from the air.

I turn to Weston, "Pick up the gloves if you dare, Doc." I beckon at him. "Happy to go another round."

"You know I don't fight with my hands," Weston frowns. "I need to protect them."

"Maybe you're afraid I'd beat you?" I step back into the ring.

"I'm a surgeon, man." He blinks. "It's not a bloody excuse. And I can whip your arse with my hands tied behind my back."

"Oh?" I bounce on the balls of my feet, "Less talking, more fighting."

"Oh, I'll be doing more than that, you bloody twit." Weston steps into the ring, "I'm going to dislocate your jaw, finish what Arpad started." He folds his arms behind his back. "And without using my fists."

"Living dangerously, Doc?" I smirk.

He bends his head and rushes me.

I duck, then sweep his legs out from under him. He goes down, rolls, then springs up and rushes me. I evade him, dance over to the other side. "Come on, Doc. Show me what you've got."

Weston growls, takes a step forward, when a whistle pierces the air.

I jerk my head around. "Edward?"

The Father crosses the floor to the ring, then jumps up onto the platform. "Getting a little tired of refereeing the brawls between you boys." He frowns. "What are you guys, ten?"

"Hold on." I crack my neck, "Not my fault the wanker here decided to challenge me."

"Bet you were the one to push him into throwing the first hit, when you know that, as a surgeon, he holds back from getting involved in fights of any kind," Edward retorts.

"Yeah," I blow out a breath.

"And Weston, you should know better than indulging this spoilt brat here."

"Spoilt brat…?" I scowl. "Hold on there."

Edward glares at me and I firm my lips.

Of the Seven of us, Edward is the one who'd gone all the way to the dark side…then found light… Hell, if he turns any more pious, I'll hear angels singing whenever he walks in, which isn't to say I don't see the halo around his head right now. My point being… Oh, yeah, when the Father speaks, all of us Seven, and many of our friends and associates, listen.

"Sorry," I hold up a hand.

"Not me you should be apologizing to."

"Right." I turn to Weston, "Apologies and all that, no offense meant."

Weston drags his fingers through his hair, "None taken, you piece of shit."

"Twat," I smirk.

"Jerkhole," he grins.

"Get a room, you two," Arpad spreads his arms along the ropes.

"Nah," Weston lowers his chin, "What would Victoria say to that?"

"None of your business," I turn on him.

"Shit, you were right, Arpad." He shakes his head, "The boy's in love."

"I'm not, you twerps." I crack my neck, "I am going to say this only once, so you all had better listen up.

"Of course, it had to happen to Saint next," Sinclair teases.

I glower at him.

He raises his hands, "Go on, Saint, what's your plan then?"

I scan the faces of the others. My friends…as close as I'll get to having brothers…not that there's any blood connection between us… Well, if you don't count the blood that was spilt during the time we'd been kidnapped and held together. The longest days of my life… And when you go through an experience like that together… Well, it changes you. It unites you in ways you don't need to always elaborate with words.

It is for my friends—the dipshits I often love to hate—and also for myself, that I need to go through with the fake wedding.

Also, I need an excuse to keep the woman, who has unearthed feelings I'd thought dead since the incident, near me.

"My plan's simple. Keep her close, and the Mafia will follow."

Weston tilts his head, "You don't need to marry her for that."

"It's simpler that way."

"How?"

"It's foolproof in the short term. Victoria, I happen to find out, is old-fashioned enough that she'll respect the wedding vows."

"That's why she'd marry you so quickly after burying her first husband?"

I growl.

Weston doesn't back down, "Go on, tell us your reasoning, Saint Killian."

"Don't use that bloody name"

"It is your middle name, isn't it?"

"Among others."

"Well, then?"

"I should be able to coerce her into tying the knot sooner than not."

"Meanwhile, you get information about the Mafia from her?"

"Exactly," I prop my hands on my hips.

Weston smirks, "And during this time, of course, you make full use of your marital privileges?"

"Hey," I frown, "don't go there."

Weston blinks, "Wow, possessive about her too."

"What's it to you?" I lower my chin.

He turns to Sinclair, "Sound familiar to you?"

Sinclair chuckles, "All too much, and you know the funniest part of this?"

"No, tell me," Weston jokes.

"He has no idea that he's already well and truly fucked."

"Hook, line and sinker," Weston rubs his hands together.

"Hey, I'm here, you wankers," I growl.

"Barely," Arpad snickers. "Your mind has been elsewhere all this time."

"Yeah, I've been focused on how to take down the bastards who fucked up our lives."

"Is that what this is about? This elaborate plan of yours to keep her close?" Weston asks.

"What else can it be?" I glower.

"Clearly, you can't see what's right there in front of you." He scratches his jaw.

"Which is—?"

"Saint?" Sinner holds up my phone. "Call for you." He reaches over the ropes, "It's Meredith. She says it's urgent."

Shit! My heart begins to race. *It can't be about her, can it?* I did ask Meredith to check in on her after I'd left her in Selfridges. *She has to be fine. Has to be.*

I close the distance between us, then grab the phone from him.

"Meredith, is she okay?"

Anger twists my guts as I listen to her reply.

"I'm coming."

18

Victoria

"What do you want?" I tuck my elbows into my sides. *Don't lose it, not now. You're in a public place, there's nothing that he can do to you. You're safe. Safe?* Ha, when was the last time I'd gone to bed without waking up in the throes of a nightmare? When had I last walked down a street without looking nervously over my shoulder? Just because I am in the middle of a hotel, next to a crowded room packed with people, doesn't mean I am safe from the man who'd kidnapped Nina. I will not let him scare me – for Nina's sake.

I tip up my chin, hold his gaze. "Well?" I ask.

"You're taking too long." Antonio stares at me with those dark eyes, so lifeless.

The first and only time I'd met him was when he'd informed me about Nina's situation. It had been the singular, most scary event of my life. I'd stared into the face of darkness and realized how lucky I was not to be in his grasp. Unlike Nina. Shit. "Is she okay?"

His forehead crinkles. Those dark eyes seem to reflect some kind of inner turmoil. Before I can process what I think I've seen, he schools his features into a mask. "Do you have what I need?"

A chill runs down my back. "I'm trying my best," I reply.

"It's not good enough."

"He's a billionaire." I clench my fists at my side. "Are you aware how many women seek him out? I can't throw myself at him; that would be counterproductive—"

"You're playing too hard to get." He frowns.

"I'm being true to character."

"We are running out of time." His jaw hardens. "You've lost a month already."

"I… I had no choice. Adam's death—"

"Was unfortunate." He lowers his eyebrows. "I should have known better than to entrust such an important mission to him. He was weak. It's not a surprise that his heart gave out, at the most inopportune time."

"How can you talk badly about someone who is dead?"

He widens his stance. "If you don't deliver what I need, it will be Nina's turn."

"Please," I beg him, "don't hurt her."

His eyes shift away from mine. Then, he straightens his shoulders, "Two weeks. I'll give you two more weeks to get me the information."

"You can't be serious," I cry out. "I'm not a miracle worker, I need at least another month to win his trust, enough for him to give me access to his confidential information, I—"

"Three." He widens his stance. "Three weeks. Not a second more."

"That's very little time." I wring my fingers.

"Time you put your body to good use, hmm?"

The color fades from my cheeks.

He scrutinizes my features, "You didn't expect to get away from this without fucking him, now did you?"

I swallow. "No…but…"

"What is it? Tell me quickly." He looks at the expensive watch on his wrist. "I'm running out of time, Victoria."

"I… I…" I am not stupid. Of course, I knew I'd have to go to bed with Saint… But that was before… I'd realized how much he affects me. Perhaps a part of me had hoped that I'd somehow manage to get away without being hurt. Who am I kidding? I had taken on this role knowing I'm likely to lose everything.

"It's fine," I pull myself up to my full height, "I'll find a way to do it."

He jerks his chin, "Good."

"And Nina?"

I can't interpret the look that comes into his eyes. "You don't need to worry about her." He rolls his shoulders. "Stay focused on your task. The faster you get the USB from him, the sooner you can go free."

He looks past me, "In fact, I'll help you along in this charade."

His arm snakes out and he grips my shoulder.

"What… What are you doing?"

The hair on the nape of my neck prickles and an electric current runs up my spine. *Oh! God, no. It can't be. Saint's here; he's watching.* "Let me go."

Antonio yanks me to him with such force that I stumble into him. He lowers his head and his breath mingles with mine.

The next moment he's yanked away from me. Antonio's body arches through the air. He hits the ground with a thud.

I open my mouth to scream, then clap a hand over it. I take a step forward.

"Leave, Victoria," Saint's hard voice whips through my mind.

"But..."

He jerks his head around, and his blue eyes lighten until they resemble chips of ice. Did he overhear any of that conversation? No, he couldn't have. I have to hope for that, at least. So why is he staring at me as if he wants to wrap his fingers around my neck and choke me… as he fucks me? As he buries himself inside of me, covers my body with his, merges his scent with mine, his lips over mine, those hard pecs cutting into the soft curves of my breasts as he fucks me, takes me, paints his essence on me and wipes out everything I have seen and heard and experienced—"Victoria."

I flinch.

"Go," he jerks his chin.

My gaze darts around him to Antonio, who jumps up to his feet.

Saint turns around, deflects a blow from Antonio, who steps back, knees slightly bent, fists balled. A trickle of blood drips from his nose.

"Not bad for a spoilt playboy," he snickers.

Saint steps forward, until his chest slams into Antonio' "If I see you anywhere near her again… I'll—"

"You'll?"

"I'll beat the fuck out of you."

Antonio chuckles. "I'll have to take you up on your challenge one of these days, knowing fully well that you won't be able to win."

Saint snarls. He raises his arm. I jump forward and grab his shoulder, "Let him go," I pant. "He's baiting you. Can't you see that?"

Saint shrugs off my hold, "I gave you a simple command. If you don't obey it—"

"What are you going to do?"

His jaw tics, a nerve throbs at his temple, and his entire body goes rigid. Anger thrums off of him, mixed with…an intensity that had not been there before. If I'd thought Saint had been upset earlier…that was nothing… Nothing compared to how every muscle in his body is wound up, tightened, coiled into a mass of lethal fury that could plough down anything that gets in his way. He could kill Antonio; I have no doubt about it. There is no way I am going to let him do it. I won't let him get into trouble because of me… *And yet, you are going to sell him out. I don't have a choice about that. I have too much at stake.* But I could buy him a little more time…a few more days of freedom. For myself…for him.

"Tell me what you'll do to me if I don't follow your orders, Saint."

His gaze flicks to me, "I'll make you regret this."

"Without giving me a chance to say 'yes'?"

"What did you say?"

"I said 'yes.'"

Saint frowns.

Antonio steps back, "I'm sorry."

Saint turns to him, as if I hadn't accepted his proposal. Maybe he doesn't understand what I am alluding to? Perhaps he already regrets asking me to marry him? Either way, this lack of surprise or any kind of response from him is…strange, to say the least.

"Didn't realize the lady was taken," Antonio raises his hands. "I never meant to trespass on what's yours."

The two men exchange a glance.

Saint wraps his arm around me and pulls me close. The heat of his body slams into me, his big frame dwarfing me. I melt into him, and for a second pretend that I am his. That he belongs to me, that I am a woman who agreed to marry a man who in a few short days had stripped back the layers I've shown to the world. Who'd known how to arouse me with a look, a touch, a spanking across my backside. My nerve endings crackle and my scalp tingles. I swallow, force myself to stay where I am.

"No hard feelings, ol'chap?" Antonio holds out his hand.

Saint sets his jaw, "Leave before I have you thrown out."

Antonio chuckles. "It won't come to that." He glances down at me, and Saint's hold tightens, until I can barely breathe.

"Good luck, my dear, though by the looks of it, it will be your man who'll be needing it."

He brushes past us.

Saint stiffens. I peer up at him to find the pulse racing at the hollow of his neck. I lift my fingers to touch the skin, and he releases me. My knees threaten to give way. I put out a hand and brace myself against him.

"Who was he?" Saint asks.

"No one." I retract my arm, press my elbows into my side. "He was no one."

"He didn't seem like nobody. You guys seemed to be engaged in intimate conversation when I arrived."

"How did you find us?" I ask.

"Meredith called me."

"Right," I shuffle my feet. "Did you hear what I said earlier?"

He frowns.

"About my saying 'yes,' I mean."

"Your agreeing to marry me?"

I nod.

"I didn't expect otherwise."

I glower, "Very sure of yourself."

"Always." He widens his stance. "Unlike you."

"What's that supposed to mean?"

"You can't lie to save yourself… Tory."

"Don't call me that. I told you I don't like it."

"So I can't, but he can?"

The blood rushes from my face. "How…how much did you hear?"

"Enough."

"It…it's not what it seems, Saint."

He chuckles, "You can do better than that."

"No, really," I grip his arm.

He shakes it off, "Don't come near me."

My heart begins to thud and sweat beads my palms. This is not good. I can't afford to have Saint angry with me. Can't have him put distance between us—not when I am so close to getting everything I want.

"I'll do it, Saint."

He regards me from under those thick eyelashes.

"I'll do anything you want."

"What does that mean, exactly?"

"I'll marry you. I'll obey you. I'll give you anything you need from me."

He drums his fingers on his chest, "You'll agree to everything I ask?"

I nod.

He walks a slow circle around me. I stare ahead. Allow him to take his measure of my body, my curves, welcome his heated gaze that flows over my waist, down the cleft between my arsecheeks, around my thighs to the front, where he pauses, his gaze fixed on the triangle between my legs.

"You'll strip for me?"

"Of course."

"Let me slap your pussy?" His voice lowers to a hush.

I shudder. Squeeze my thighs together.

"Answer me."

"Yes," I snap out.

He tilts his head to the left, then the right.

"I'll take your arse, of course," he assures me.

My sex clenches and my heart begins to race.

"Of course," I tip up my chin.

His lips curl. "Wasn't asking you for your permission."

I draw in a sharp breath.

"In fact, I won't be giving you much of a heads-up on anything I have in mind. Suffice to say, Gigi, by the time I'm done with you, you won't be able to remember your name, let alone how you deceived me."

"D...deceived you?"

He doesn't know. No way. He can't know the true reason for my having approached him in the first place. "Wh...what do you mean?" I whisper.

He jerks his chin to the side, "Why him... Your former lover, who you invited here to meet you publicly, and all because you wanted to make me jealous, hmm?"

I blink. Is that what he thinks this is? That I am cheating on him? If only it were that simple. I chuckle.

"What's so funny?"

"N...nothing." A giggle bubbles up, I try to swallow it, choke. I press my lips together, can't stop the cough that breaks free. "Excuse me." I bring my hands up to cover my mouth, end up snorting. Tears roll down my cheeks. I sway. Shit, am I having some kind of a nervous breakdown? Is this a bout of hysteria? Didn't Freud cure hysteria by orgasms? Is that what I need? I wheeze, draw in a breath, then double over, my shoulders shaking.

"Victoria, what the fuck?"

Saint's boots appear in my line of sight—those same cowboy boots he's been wearing since the day I met him. For someone who's a gazillionaire, his taste in footwear is definitely eccentric.

I resist the urge to shuffle my feet, to squeeze my thighs together. It is a test, all a test. It won't be as bad as he's implying it's going to be. It can't be. He's just trying to intimidate me. I can take anything Saint throws at me and rise above it. I can.

"I...I'm sorry," I gasp, then straighten and drag the back of my hand across my face. "It's just you... I..." Another bout of giggles bubbles up.

I hunch my shoulders, try to tamp down on the laughter. More tears spill down my cheeks. "Saint… I…" The words catch in my throat. I try to get them out, but end up snorting again. What the hell is wrong with me? I am making a bloody spectacle of myself in front of this man who I am supposed to seduce. I am supposed to take on an unapproachable persona; as close to my Posh Spice alter ego as possible. Instead, I am having a complete breakdown, Kardashian style.

I laugh so hard that my knees sway. Saint grabs my shoulders, steadies me.

"Look at me."

I shake my head, glance to the right, the left, anywhere else but at him. If I do, I'll… I'll lose what little composure I own right now. Correction, I have zero self-possession left. I am drained, empty, alone… Always alone. I had Nina, but even that was taken away from me. This feels so hopeless.

"Saint," my voice seems to come from far away.

"Victoria, the fuck is wrong with you?"

I raise my head, glance up into those blue eyes. Burning bright. Sparks flare in their depths. Hot, he is so hot. Alive. Vital. Everything I am not.

"You're so beautiful." I raise my hand and he catches my wrist. His fingers dig into my skin. Real. Reassuring. Solid. He'll protect me. He'll hurt me. He'll ground me, show me how to stay in the present. "Saint, please…" My lips grow numb. I can't feel my arms and legs anymore.

"Don't you fucking faint on me."

I chuckle, "I never faint."

"Liar."

He's right, of course.

The world tilts and darkness pulls me under.

19

Saint

I pace back and forth in front of the bed... My bed. She is here, in my room, in my suite. Wrapped up in my sheets... My heart begins to thud. I've never brought any woman here. Prefer to restrict my liaisons to an impersonal hotel room that is permanently booked for me a few floors below in the hotel.

So why her? Why is she the first woman I've brought to this suite?

Maybe it's because she's going to be my wife.

Or maybe it is because of how pale she'd gone right before she'd crumpled. Her legs had gone out from under her and she'd collapsed. A dead weight. If I hadn't been there to catch her, she'd have hurt herself. And I can't have that. Not while I still have so much to unravel about this woman who'd appeared out of nowhere and entranced me. It's only because I don't know much about her...except for what I have uncovered, which has only fueled my fascination with her.

Thankfully she'd woken up enough for me to get some juice and crackers smeared with peanut butter into her. She'd refused everything else, preferring instead to sleep.

When was the last time I had taken care of anyone like this? *Never.* That's the answer. I ball my fingers into fists.

"What the hell are you doing to me, Gigi?" I hear my words and realize I spoke them out loud. That's what she's reduced me to. I am mumbling to myself as I fret about the health of a woman I don't give two fucks about. I don't… I don't have any emotions for her; no feelings. Nothing that could expose the person I once was…before… the kidnapping, before my mother died. *Fuck.* I shove my hand into my pocket.

Why did the submissive cross the road?

Because her master asked her to.

My heartbeat slows.

It runs and runs but can never flee… What is it? I snap my fingers. *You know the answer, you know it.*

Time. That's it.

Present in the sun, but not in rain.

Doing no harm, and feeling no pain.

What is it?

My breathing evens out.

A shadow.

I had been a shadow of my former self… Until I met her.

I'm not going to let her get away, not until I have resolved the puzzle that she is. I walk closer and stand over her.

Sweat beads her forehead. She thrashes her head from side to side; her chest heaves. Her fingers dig into the sheets at her side. She moans and my heart squeezes. I cup her cheek and her eyes snap open. "No," she wheezes. "Don't do it."

"Do what?" I frown.

She knocks my hand away, rolls over, then scuttles up against the head board.

"Gigi?"

She swallows. "Don't…don't come near me."

"Victoria?"

Her chin wobbles.

I switch on the lamp and light floods the room. She blinks at me. "Who…who are you?"

"Victoria, it's me, Saint."

She draws in a breath. "Saint?"

I nod, walk around to stand at the foot of the bed.

She stares at me, her eyes wide in her face. Her cheeks are too fucking pale. I stalk around to where she huddles and she freezes. Her muscles seem to lock, then she hunches into herself, making herself smaller.

I reach for the bottle of water on the bed-stand and she winces.

"Easy," I keep my tone firm, pour a glass of water and offer it to her.

She eyes it warily.

"Take it."

She hesitates. I take a sip from it. "See?" I tilt my head, "It's safe to drink."

She takes the glass from me, brings it to her lips, and drains it. Some of the liquid runs down her chin. I reach out, wipe away the wetness with my thumb.

She stays silent. I drag my finger across her lower lip. Her mouth opens. I slide my digit inside and she sucks on it. She sinks her teeth in, and fuck me, but I feel the tug all the way to the tip of my dick.

I reach for the now empty glass, pry it from her fingers. She swallows. I place the glass on the nightstand. The slight thump breaks the silence.

She shudders.

I push down with my thumb and she opens her mouth wider. I slide in my forefinger, my middle finger. She swipes her tongue across them. My shaft lengthens in my pants; the blood thuds at my temples. I pull away from her and she stiffens, watches me from under hooded eyes as I take a step back.

"What are you not telling me?" I scowl down at her.

"What do you mean?" She frowns back at me.

"Why did you have that nightmare?"

"Th...that?" She shoves her hair back from her face. "It was...nothing."

"I came in to find you thrashing on the bed, begging someone not to come near you," I growl.

"So?"

"Did he hurt you?"

"Who?"

"Don't pretend you don't know who I mean."

She tilts up her chin. "N...no." She swallows.

"Lying to me again?"

"Of course, not."

I bend down, peer into her eyes, "Tell me. What's got you terrified, Gigi?" I search her pale features. "Why are you trembling so much that you can barely sit upright?"

"Maybe it's your nearness?" Her lips twist.

"Is it?" I scowl.

"Or maybe it's the thought that you are going to own your dominance and show me what you are made of?" She looks me up and down. Her chin wobbles.

Something hot stabs at my chest.

Fuck, is this an act she's putting on? When she's hurting and unsure, and yet she's taunting me to get the better of my control.

"What are you hiding from me?" I rub the back of my neck. "Why can't you tell me what's got you so fearful that you had to come to me with a proposition that is so unlike your personality?"

"You mean someone as proper as me? Someone who seems so conservative? I couldn't know my tastes, could I?"

"Do you?" I lower my hands to my sides, "Do you know what you're asking of me? Are you ready for everything I am going to demand from you?"

Her chest rises and falls, she firms her lips. "I could ask you the same thing." She reaches forward.

"Gigi... No..."

She grabs my crotch, squeezes my erection.

A groan rips out of me. The blood thuds at my temples. "What are you doing?"

"What does it seem like?" She brings up her other hand to massage my balls and my vision tunnels. "Gigi," I warn her.

"Saint." She peers up at me from under her sooty eyelashes. "I've seen enough porn online to know what turns me on. I've spent my life trying to fit in, trying to be something I am not. I need you to set me free, want you to let me embrace my fantasies, I want this Saint, I—"

"Take your hands off of me," I snap.

She blinks.

"Now."

She pulls back, her face, pale. "I... I'm sorry."

"Show me."

"What?" She drops her hands in her lap.

"Show me you understand what you're asking for."

"But I... I meant it." She blinks rapidly. "I...do want you."

"You don't get to set the pace." I prop my hands on my hips. "You feel me?"

"B...but." She wrings her hands together. "I—"

"On your knees."

She draws in a breath.

"Now."

She scrambles to the floor, fingers twisted in front, head bowed, her dark hair flowing about her shoulders.

"Beautiful."

A visible shiver runs up her spine.

I unhook my belt, lower my zipper, a moan bleeds from her, and fuck me, but I can't wait any more.

I wrap her hair around my palm, yank. Her head falls back, her gaze wide. Color flushes her cheeks.

"Open," I demand.

Her lips part.

Fuck, the way she looks right now? My heart begins to race.

"I'm going to fuck your mouth, now."

Her gaze widens and she draws in a breath as if to say something. I don't wait. I thrust my dick between her lips.

Warmth, heat. Goosebumps explode on my skin. "Fuck," I grit my teeth and sweat beads my forehead. "Fuck, Gigi."

She swallows, and the suction sweeps up my spine. My groin hardens and my thigh muscles spasm. I tighten my grip on her hair.

"Do you have any idea what you do to my control?"

Her nostrils flare, she tips her chin up, and her eyes dart green fire.

"I'm going to use your mouth and you're going to take it, and when I come, you are going to swallow every last drop."

Her chest rises and falls; the pulse races at the base of her neck. The sweet scent of her arousal envelops me and my balls tighten. My vision narrows, my chest hurts, and fuck her, but I can't hold back any more.

I pull her forward; my dick slides down her throat. I yank her back and her teeth graze the soft skin of my shaft. Tendrils of fire race up my spine.

I use her mouth, repeat the motion, again and again, then once more. Spit gathers at the corner of her lips, overflows down her chin.

She sucks in her cheeks and my balls draw up. "Jesus, fuck, I'm coming."

I wrap the fingers of my other hand around her neck, then drag her forward. The sight of my dick disappearing in between her wet swollen lips, combined with the vibration of my cock down her throat… Bloody hell, it's the most erotic thing ever.

My scalp tingles, my knees tremble, and the coiled tension from my groin explodes out. I come, shooting my spunk down her throat.

"Swallow it," I snarl, "Do it, Gigi."

Her throat moves and tears roll down her cheeks, as I keep coming. She swallows down my cum. The sticky liquid spills over the edges of her mouth. Her breathing roughens, her fingers curled into fists at her sides.

I pull out, and the white streams of cum spray across her face, her clothes.

She licks her lips, back straight, shoulders squared. Her hair sticks to her forehead. I grab her under her arms, yank her to her tiptoes, and close my mouth over hers.

The taste of myself combined with her sweet breath, the honeyed taste of her lips, the complex notes of our joined-up essences… All of it sinks into me. Something stirs in my chest. *No, no. I will not be drawn to her. Will not allow myself to feel for her. Will not allow her to reach though the carefully cultivated layers to find the part of me I have guarded for so long.* I tear my lips from hers, scan her flushed features.

I tilt my head, "I hate you."

20

———————

Victoria

With those few words he shatters the peace that I'd found in his arms. When I'd opened up to him, and asked him to set me free... I'd meant it. Until that moment I hadn't realized how much I'd wanted to let go of my inhibitions, to not worry about what the world thought of me, to revel in what turned me on and own it... if this was the chance to do it, then I was going to embrace it. Then he'd gone and said those three words.

"What?" I tilt my head, "Why would you say that?"

"Because... I can?" He lets go of me so quickly, that I stumble.

The backs of my knees hit the bed and I sit down with a thump. "I... I don't understand."

He zips up his pants, then yanks off the belt. The leather whips through the air and I eye it warily. If he thinks I am going to be afraid of his implied threat, he has another think coming.

"Is this another one of your games, Saint?"

He bares his teeth, "Is that what you think it is, Victoria?"

I squeeze my melting pussy together, "I… I don't know what to think."

"Good." He folds the strip of leather, then jerks his chin towards the settee in the room.

"What?" I frown.

"Lean over it."

"You must be joking."

He glares at me and the blood rushes from my cheeks. Guess not. I rise to my feet. *Move. Do it.* I force myself to take a step toward it, then stop, "Give me one reason I should agree to your stupid ideas?"

The belt whips out, catches me across my breasts. I cry out, stare at him. My nipples harden. He glances at my chest, and his lips twitch. "That's what I thought. You like it, don't you?" He reaches out and pinches one of my rigid nipples.

I yell, "Jesus."

He laughs.

"Your ego is so big that I wonder you haven't been crushed by the weight of it yet," I snarl.

"That's what I think every time I look at my—" He looks down at his crotch.

"Seriously?"

He jerks his chin toward the settee, "Go on."

I swallow. He raises his belt; I head toward the blasted settee.

I hear the whine through the air a second before pain grips my backside. I stutter, speed up my pace. When I reach the settee, I pause.

I hear his footsteps behind me. *Shit.* I fall forward until I am draped over the arm. Butt in the air.

Bloody hell, what have I gotten myself into? Had I known he had this streak of meanness running through him from the beginning? Had I sensed it? Wanted it, even? Wanted him to strip me of all dignity, to tear down the pretense I had clung to, that I was in control? Because I'm not. I haven't been. Not since the day Nina disappeared. I didn't know what had happened to her and I allowed my mind to go to all of the usual places, picturing her lying in a ditch somewhere next to an overturned car, crying for help. I allowed my fears to create a story that couldn't possibly be true.

Only to find out the truth was much worse than I could have ever imagined.

They'd taken her. And then...because I just wouldn't give up and kept looking for her, insisting the police do their job...they took me. My entire life had unraveled around me. And I had watched, helpless, unable to save her or myself. A part of me had fought back and clung to something indistinct, had wanted to hope that I was still there, hidden inside. The girl who was a fighter, who had never backed down from a challenge.

The part I cling to now when he jerks my skirt up my legs. Air hits my exposed back side.

A beat. Another. He hasn't moved from his position behind me. I sense his presence though. Hard. Heavy. Throbbing. That immovable dominance that vibrates off of him and pins me in place. Waiting... waiting. I squeeze my thighs together, hear the whine of the belt as he snaps it.

I cringe, clench my buttcheeks. He laughs, "Fooled you, hmm?"

"Asshole."

"What was that?"

"Nothing," I mutter.

"So much sass, Gigi?"

Hate the name… No, I lie. It does strange things to me when he calls me that. I've always been Victoria. I'd hated being called Tory, especially by them. And no one bothered to find a nickname for me… before him.

I sense his gaze on my back, down the crease between my buttcheeks where my panties are bunched up. I reach behind to pull it out and he clicks his tongue.

I redden. *Shit, I hate that.* Hate it when he demeans me. Treats me like I am his toy, his slut. *His.* I squeeze my eyes shut. Where did that thought come from? My sex clenches; my belly quivers. Why do I find that a turn on? I am sick in the head, no doubt about it. Is that why I am here, doing what he wants…waiting… Waiting for him to take the next step. To do something…anything…whatever he wants to me.

I swallow, "Saint."

"Shh!"

His whisper comes from somewhere above me. I turn my head to find him staring at my butt. "You're fucking beautiful, you know that?" His voice is contemplative. There's an intensity to it that sends a shudder down my spine. My stomach flip flops and goosebumps rise on my skin.

"Saint…" I clear my throat. "Please…"

"Hmm." He rolls his neck and his joints pop. I wince. It's like a declaration of what is to come. The calm before the storm. The silence before the tsunami hits the shore. *Do it, do it. Don't delay.*

"I know what you want, Gigi."

"You do?"

He nods, "And I'll give it to you. Every single experience that you ache for, I promise you'll have it… And some you don't dare even think about, though in your heart you want it. Know what I mean?"

I open my mouth to speak, but the words dry up. My entire body braces… My muscles wind up, toes digging into the carpet. My clit pulses and my pussy squeezes down, wanting…needing him. His cock. His fingers. His thick thighs between mine as he tears into me with his cock. Moisture flows from between my legs and I can't stop the whine that spills from me.

"Good girl," he growls.

I shudder.

"I promise you'll get what you deserve…but first…"

I swallow.

"First, answer this riddle."

I snarl at the back of my throat. Enough with the stupid riddles already.

"Did you say something, pet?"

I shake my head, bite down on my lower lip and turn away. Fuck him, and his ability to reduce me to a trembling mass of need. My skin feels too tight for the rest of my body. My scalp feels like it's on fire. I rub my thighs together and he laughs, "Look at you. So impatient, hmm?"

Get on with it already.

"About that riddle."

Fuck off.

"Soon, but first tell me... The more you take, the more you leave behind. What is it?"

I frown. Of course, my mind goes straight to that one thing. *Could it be? Is it?*

"You dirty girl," he chuckles. "I know what you're thinking, but it's not that. It's so easy, Gigi. Go on, take a shot."

"Um," I try to form the word, but my throat is too dry. *It is, is it…?*

"Footsteps, of course."

I sag onto the couch. *Jerk.*

"One more, one more." He comes around, brushes aside my hair. "You ready, Gigi?"

I glare at him. He smirks, "Oh, but you're getting there, aren't you?"

I shoot him a glance meant to convey exactly where he can take his dick and stuff it… Up my arse. *Hell.* I squeeze my eyes shut. *Why, why is it that I am empty and hollow and aching inside, even as every part of me wants to slap his stupid, handsome face?* Right before I throw myself at his feet and ask him to lick me up, eat me up, slap my cunt, drink from it… "Ohhh."

I hear my whine, so pathetic.

"You're gorgeous, sweet thing."

I crack my eyelids open. Beseech him with my gaze. *Please, please.*

He straightens, "Not yet."

I can't stop the snarl that rips from me then.

"My god," I hear him breathe from above me. "So much spirit, so much beauty, so much everything you are, Gigi. You'll be the death of me."

I swallow. Is he aware of the likely truth in his words? No one's ever focused their complete attention on me, made me the cynosure of their ministration in this manner before.

A tear squeezes out of the corner of my eye. He bends down, scoops it up. He sucks on his finger and my heart stutters. *Why is that so damn intimate?*

"About that riddle, then."

I blow out a breath.

"It's easy, I promise."

Famous last words… *Whatever. Can you get over it already?*

"I am what you saw, but not what you see. What am I?" He asks.

A shadow. A mirage. An emotion from the end of time. *It's you, Saint, you.*

He nods, "A memory, Gigi." His features twist. "And I am going to leave you with so many that it will drown out everything and everyone that came before me, I promise."

I hear him move, sense him bend, the heat of his body intensifying a second before he tears off my panties.

What the—?

I hear the whip of the belt, then the fire explodes across my butt, up my spine. I cry out. He doesn't stop. He goes at it—one butt cheek, the other, back to the first— I scream again. The next—I shriek.

Each time he hits me, my body jolts forward. My sex clenches. A trembling builds from my toes. He spanks me so hard that my body pushes up to my tip toes. My clit rubs against the hard edge of the settee, and omigod! A quivering sweeps up from my toes. It can't be. There's no way he has brought me to the verge of orgasm so quickly, right? He leans back and the cool air grazes my butt. He dips his fingers into my exposed pussy. I shudder.

"You're fucking wet for me."

I ball my fingers into fists.

"You want my dick inside you. Don't you, you little slut?"

I shudder. *How dare he call me that?* My sex clenches around his finger. *Why do I like it so much?*

He adds a second finger inside and my trembling intensifies.

"Say it, Gigi."

"No."

He adds a third, a fourth, the emptiness at my core growing bigger, wider. *I want more. I want his fat cock inside of me. I do.* A sob wells up.

"Admit you want to be taken in every way possible. You want me to debase you, to show you exactly what it means for a woman to be open and vulnerable and completely broken down by her man."

Is he my man? Is he?

"Tell me, Gigi. Tell me you need this, to be split wide open for all of your hurts to pour out, for your insecurities to be drawn out of you, for your every nightmare to be exposed, your spirit broken and yearning...for me."

No.

"Tell me you want me to remove every evidence of other men and replace it with pain, and more pain; to gouge out every thought, every emotion, every feeling you've ever carried for anyone else but me. Tell me you want me to fuck your past out of you."

"No."

"Liar."

The heat at my back escalates. He stabs his tongue in between my arsecheeks and the climax propels up my thighs. My vision narrows and my heart stutters. *No, how can he? Why is he doing this? Why is he insisting on barreling into my deepest, darkest, most intimate of spaces?* He laves my most forbidden place and I throw back my head. The orgasm coils in my belly; my thighs clench.

He pulls away and it recedes.

What the—? My eyelids—which I hadn't realized I'd shut—fly open. I turn around to find him tugging on his shirt sleeves. He flicks a spot of invisible dust from his shoulders, and a hot molten wave of anger explodes inside me.

"How dare you...?" I sputter.

He licks his lower lip and heat sweeps up my front from throat to hair line. *Is he recalling my taste? Showing me what I could have, and withholding it from me purposely for... What? To put me in my place? To show me what I can't have?*

The anger thrums close to my heart and my chest tightens. "Why?" I snarl "Why are you doing this?"

"You don't get to ask the questions."

"I am tired of your treating me like...like..."

He angles his head. "Go on, complete that statement."

I open my mouth and he raises a finger, "But remember, one wrong word and I'll walk away. And we both know you can't afford that."

My heart begins to race. *What does he know? How much has he guessed? Why does he always remind me of everything I have to lose if this arrangement goes wrong?* I stare at him and he chuckles, "Wise choice, little Gigi."

"I hate that name."

"Lying again?" He clicks his tongue.

"What are you going to do?" I jut out my chin.

His nostrils flare as he rakes his gaze over my semi-naked body. A flush heats my skin, but I refuse to move. I will not give him the benefit of discovering how much he's unnerving me. I grit my teeth. *Stay, stay.*

He cracks his knuckles and my belly clenches.

He takes a step forward. Everything in me waits...waits. *Close the distance, you bastard. Do it… Do it, now.*

He raises his hand. The buzzing of a cellphone cuts through the thick silence. My nerve endings pop.

He slides his phone out of the pocket of his slacks. "This had better be important." His eyebrows furrow as he listens. He drags his gaze down to my bare butt cheeks. His pupils darken. *Does he want me that much? If I'm so affected by his presence, surely, he is too. Isn't that why he's strung me along so far?* He hasn't allowed me to get close, but he hasn't pushed me away either. He's toying with me. Not that it surprises me at all. I didn't expect more from this...this beast. *But why is he putting himself through the same kind of torture that I am experiencing? Why can't he take me and be done with it? Why drag this out until neither of us can bear it?*

He raises his hand, and I am sure he's going to palm my butt, to resume where he left off.

"They did what?" he snaps into the phone.

Color pops on his cheeks. His jaw tics. *What the—? What could it be that has gotten that kind of reaction— hell, any kind of reaction—from him?*

He straightens so quickly that I wince. "I'm coming…"

I splutter.

He slides the phone into his pocket, pivots, turns to go, and I jump to my feet, "You can't do this."

He takes another step forward.

My heart hammers so fast, I am sure it's going to jump out of my ribcage. I race around him, plant myself in his path, "You can't leave me like this."

He surveys me from head to toe, then bends.

I stumble back.

He straightens, tosses a scrap of fabric in my direction. My panties flop against my chest. "You'll come when I let you, and not before."

He saunters past me to the door.

Bastard.

He reaches the door and my pulse rate ratchets up. Surely, he is not going to walk away, while I am hungry and aching and wanting... wanting. My skin feels too tight for the rest of my body. His massive shoulders fill the doorway. I take in his narrow waist, the tight fit of his pants cross his gorgeous arse... My sex clenches. I inch my fingers toward my clit. He raises his hand over his shoulder, "Don't you dare, Gigi."

"What?"

"You will not bring yourself to orgasm. Have you forgotten about that?"

"The hell?"

"Hell is when I bring you to the edge of coming a few more times, when you walk around throbbing for my dick to fill you up, for my lips on you, my fingers inside your arsehole, for every part of me teasing you up the slope only to..."

"To," I breathe.

"To leave you unfulfilled, of course."

He shoulders open the door. I walk my fingers toward my center once more.

"If you disobey me... I'll..."

I swallow. "What? What will you do?"

"I'll punish you and the spankings you've received so far will seem like I've been teasing you all along."

"As if you'd know," I scoff.

He turns to survey me, "Oh, trust me, I will. Your every orgasm belongs to me from now on. Do you understand?"

21

Saint

"Fuck, fuck, fuck." I swear as I swipe myself from root to head. My dick lengthens and my balls throb. I slap my other hand against the wall of the restroom on the ground floor of the hotel. Pathetic.

I'd walked out of my suite, commanding her not to come. The call could not be put off; so I had made it out, completed my errand, and returned to the hotel, in record time.

But damn if I am heading back to my room. I do not need her. I am not dependent on her. No way am I going to allow her to see how vulnerable I am with her.

Which means I'm left me with balls the size of all the number one hits of The Beatles put together… *Fuck, had I thought that?* The woman's affliction for those losers is getting to me.

I have to fuck her out of my system… Or at least, jerk her out, to get relief.

So, I'd walked into the men's restroom and locked the door behind me. I blow out a breath, then scan my reflection in the mirror—dilated pupils, irregular breathing, a sheen of sweat dampening my brow... *Fuck.* What a dumb idea it had been to think I could get through this unscathed. I'd thought I was in control... How wrong I had been. I'd thought I could keep her close, so I could steer the proceedings, slow the pace when needed.

Fuck, fucking fuck. I squeeze my cock and pain grips my groin. I massage myself once again. The blood thrums through my veins and my pulse rate ratchets up. The scent of her—sweet and sexy, warm and giving, and opening to me—clings to my nostrils, percolates into my skin, winds its way down to coil in my groin. My thighs spasm and my balls draw up. Her green eyes—beseeching, half-drugged with lust, stormy with anger. The sound of wet flesh closing around my fingers. Her mouth around my dick, sucking on me, dragging her teeth up the underside of my swollen shaft. Her slickness, her little moans, her head thrown back as she'd verged on the edge of climax.

The tension in my belly twists in on itself. I squeeze the base of my cock harder. *Fuck me, but I am going to come, I am going to—*

A banging on the door filters into my consciousness. I ignore it, focus on my own pleasure—how I am going to thrust forward into her sweet cunt, rip into her melting pussy and— "Saint, open up this second, you asshole."

I whip my head around, stare at the closed door, "Fuck off."

"If you don't open it, I am going to kick this door down."

"It's an antique door, you tosser." Not that I fucking care about the money. I could replace it, of course, but damn, if I don't have a soft spot for history and heritage...and all that emo shit... And beautiful women who hurt from the inside out, who pretend to be strong when they are already broken. *Since when had I given in to the urge to collect wounded things to my collection?*

There's another bang and the entire door frame shudders. "I swear, I'll take it out of your share of the profits, wanker."

"You're the wanker, beating yourself in there into your hand like a pathetic pussy."

"Bitch," I swear aloud.

"I heard that, you tosser."

Fucking Weston. I tuck my erect dick inside my pants and zip myself up. Then stalk over to the door and fling it open.

Weston brushes past me and glides inside, looking for all the world like he's stepped out of a fucking photo shoot. "Jesus, do you have to deck yourself out like a peacock every time you step out?"

He leans a hip against one of the basin's, "Unlike you," he glances down pointedly at my worn-in boots, "I prefer to be prepared."

"I happen to have interesting taste."

"Including in women?"

"Don't talk about her," I snarl.

He smirks, "That why you're diddling yourself in secret?"

The back of my neck heats, "I wasn't." *Fucking fuck, now I sound—what?—about fifteen? When I had to beat myself off to sleep most nights.*

Weston chuckles, then sniffs the air, "I don't know... Smells like sex in here...the self-gratifying kind, I mean." He makes a rude gesture with his hand. "Didn't know you had to resort to that to get some these days."

I glower at him, "I told you I wasn't."

"So why did you lock the door?"

"Because…" I pull myself up to my full height, "the last I checked, I own this hotel."

"Which you're going to run into the ground by the looks of it," a new voice sounds. I groan. I don't need to turn to know it's Arpad who's walked in.

"The hell are you doing here?"

Arpad saunters in, "Weston seemed to think he'd need back-up."

"And that's you?" I smirk.

"No, that's us," Damian moseys in.

I scowl. "Why'd you have to bring him along?"

I jerk my chin toward Edward, who strolls in. He kicks the door shut, then leans his shoulder against him.

"What?" I take in their faces, then fold my arms over my chest. "Whatever it is, the answer is 'no.'"

"I didn't ask a question," Arpad grins. "Any of you hear a question?"

The others chime in.

"Nope."

"Nah."

"Naw."

I tap the toes of my boot on the ground. "Well? Say your piece, you dickheads. I have an appointment to keep."

"Correction, you ran out of the earlier meeting before we could discuss FOK Media, so we decided to move the venue," Edward says.

"To a restroom... And here I thought this was an intervention."

"Nothing like a public toilet to remind us of the kind of shit we've faced since the fuckers changed our lives in the incident and..." Weston stalks over to one of the urinals, "we're not done with the intervention." He lowers his zipper, then the tinkle of piss hitting porcelain fills the room.

"Jesus Fucking Christ," I growl.

"Don't take the Lord's name in conjunction with a profanity," Edward admonishes.

"Sorry, Father. How many Hail Mary's should I say to repent?"

"None, this time," Edward looks down his nose at me, "but you can tell us what's got you all aflutter."

"Aflutter?" I choke.

Damian laughs. The others snicker.

Weston flushes the urinal, then walks over to wash his hands, "How else do you explain your running out on us earlier, only to surface locked up in a restroom, jerking off?"

The room explodes in laughter.

"You walked in on this wanker wanking himself off?" Arpad chortles.

"Fuck, that's funny." Damian smirks.

"You caught him diddling?" Weston chuckles.

"Stop. Shut your fucking traps!" I roar.

Silence descends.

Then Edward snorts, "Ever seen Saint lose his shit?"

"Shut up, Father, before I tell them how I saved you from humiliation in a public loo on the wrong side of the tracks."

Edward pales.

The others fall quiet.

"You never did know your limits did you, Saint?" Weston growls.

"Shit, I'm sorry." I dig my fingers into my hair and tug on it. "I didn't mean for it to come out that way. Can you guys forget I blurted that out?"

"No need to apologize," Edward squares his shoulders, his stance rigid. "No big secret. After the incident, I went through a phase of trying to rediscover my sexuality. Let's just say, I didn't make the smartest of choices and Saint here, saved my arse."

"It's nothing." I roll my shoulders, "Yeah, I found him in a compromising position, but hell, we've all been there. We were all in some fucked-up space after the incident, and hell, if we each didn't make mistakes in trying to figure out our shit."

"Is that what she is? Your mistake?" Weston's voice is calm.

I squeeze the bridge of my nose, "No." I lower my arm, then scan over the faces of the men who are my brothers by dint of the blood we'd spilt together. "And therein lies the problem."

"What's the problem?" Damian drums his finger on his chest, "You like the chick? You keep her."

"I can't."

"And I thought I had problems," Edward snickers. The priest, the one among us who is the kindest, who'd never stoop to the level of the others, takes a dig at me.

"I deserve that," I rub the back of my neck, then begin to pace.

"I thought the fake marriage was the way to keep tabs on her whereabouts, except..."

"Except?"

"The danger is closer than I expected. I ran into her with a man whose reputation is bad news, to say the least."

"That was the emergency?" Weston asks.

I nod.

"Who was he?"

"I had my PI run a check on him and guess what...?"

"He drew a blank?" Arpad fills in.

I nod, "So I called in a favor with a buddy of mine at Scotland Yard and..."

"He's a wanted criminal?"

"Worse, he's suspected of being the member of an international crime organization."

"Fuck," Edward swears.

"Yeah."

It's serious enough for the Father to swear, and worrying enough for none of the others to rib him about it.

I begin to pace, "So you see, I don't think it's right to put off marrying her."

"How is marriage going to protect her?" Arpad scowls.

"I can keep her close to me. It will make it clear to the world that she's under my protection."

"And that will stop the Mafia?" Edward places the tips of his fingers together.

"Maybe not...but it'll make sure I am there to stop them if they try to hurt her."

Arpad scans my features, "You're serious about this, huh?"

"What have I been trying to tell you all this time?" I scowl

"So, do it now," Weston interjects.

"Now?" I frown.

Weston straightens, "Sure, Father here will marry you two, while I make some calls and have the paperwork rushed through for you guys."

"Hold on, hold on! I should marry her right away?"

"Today. In the next," he glances at his watch, "hour or so, tops."

"Ah," I run a finger around my collar, "a bit too soon, isn't it?"

"You've proposed to her. Explain you can't wait."

"Don't preach to me about how to handle a woman—Sorry," I jerk my chin toward Edward, "Didn't mean it that way."

"Hey, you can insult me any way you want. It will be worth it to see you tie the knot." Edward tilts his head.

He seems too calm. "I'd, uh, hoped for something quick at the town hall."

"— which I plan to preside over to ensure it's all done in the right way." Edward's lips kick up in a smile.

"You're getting back at me, is that it?" I mutter bitterly.

"You know your earlier faux paus of blurting out how you saved my ass?"

I glower at Edward.

"This is how you can make up for it," he says.

"By tying the bloody knot?"

"By getting chained up for real."

"I'll be divorcing her soon anyway. It's all a fucking farce, until I get to the bottom of this entire situation."

"You sure?" Weston scowls, "I mean, there's something between you two, isn't there?"

"All a farce," I snicker. "I know how to be convincing enough that she bought it completely. She's not my type. Besides, I don't plan to shackle myself to anyone for the rest of my life."

"Thought it was kids you're against," Damian pipes in.

"That too. Marriage, children, the whole shebang." I cut the air with my hand. "Not for me, and definitely not with her."

There's a noise at the doorway. I stiffen. Glance past Edward, who's already stepping away from the door. He wrenches it open.

The scent of lily and pepper tickles my nose. "Shit." I spot the back of a woman running, her red handbag clutched to her side. It's her. *Fucking fuck.*

I race past Edward, who grabs my arm. "Get her back, Saint," he urges.

"I plan to."

"Apologize to her."

"Fuck," I clench my fingers.

He scowls, "Don't be an asshole."

"Right."

"We'll be waiting for you in the ballroom." He releases me.

"Fuck, bloody fuck." I race out the door and after her.

22

Why was the broom late?
Answer: It overswept

Victoria

Fuck him. Fuck him. I hate him. Tears stream down my face as I race for the exit of the hotel. I should have stayed in the suite and licked my wounds, but truthfully? I had been horny for him. I had positioned my fingers over my clit and wanted to rub myself, wanted to shove my fingers inside of my pussy and bring myself to orgasm… Except, it wouldn't have helped. I would have been empty and aching… Okay, emptier than before. Now that I know what it feels like to have his fingers inside of me, his lips on me, his tongue stabbing into my deepest most intimate of spaces… *Fuck!* Besides he'd told me not to come…and… Fuck me, but I couldn't defy him. I had obeyed him. Like an idiot. I had paced the floor of the suite, until I had driven myself crazy with the thoughts whirling around in my head. Where could he have gone? Why had he left me so suddenly?

Was there someone else?

Why not, though? He asked me to marry him. Doesn't mean he is going to be exclusive. Of course, not. He has some—make that many—women lined up and waiting for him…this entire time. It's not like he is going to stop that when we are married. Married? Ha. The entire thing is a bloody charade. A stupid game to please his ego… He'd chosen me because he could. Clearly, that's the answer I'd get if I asked him, so why bother? And from what I had overheard…? Fuck the man. Did he have to declare the status of our relationship out loud to his friends? Is nothing about our relationship a secret from the rest of the world? There is so much he isn't telling me…so much unsaid stuff between us. What a pitiful turn of events this is.

I race toward the main doors of the hotel.

"Stop her!" his voice growls from somewhere behind me. I increase my pace. The doorman steps in my path.

"Get out of my way."

"I'm sorry, I can't."

I race around him, reach the doors, and another liveried man plants his body between me and my exit.

Fuck, fuck, fuck.

"I have to get out of here."

"Sorry Ma'am," he shifts his weight from foot to foot but doesn't move.

I feint right, but he moves with me. I brush past, make to step out from under his arm. Another man steps up from outside.

Fuck, I have no way out.

I grit my teeth, "Get out of my way."

He looks up, and past me. His throat moves as he swallows, "Please accept my apologies, but he pays my wages, you understand."

"Of course, he does," I swallow down angry tears, pull out my cell phone, "and if you don't let me through, I'm calling the police."

"You're not."

His voice sounds so near, so close. If I turn, I'll find him at my heels, behind me, close enough for me to lean back and allow my head to fall back against his shoulder...for him to lower his cheek next to mine, wrap his arm around my waist, pull me up against him and—I raise the phone, begin to punch in the numbers. He snatches it from me.

"Hey," I pivot around, and he holds it up and out of my reach.

"Give that back," I scowl.

"Take it, if you can reach it."

I stand up on my tiptoes, swoop up my arms. My fingertips reach halfway up his biceps.

"You'll have to do better than that," he chuckles.

I twist my lips together. *Ridiculous.* I am not indulging in this kind of childish behavior. All of this may be a laugh for him, but for me, it is the veritable end of the bloody line. I fold my arms over my chest, draw myself up to my full height. "Don't toy with me, Saint."

"Oh?" He tosses the phone to his other hand. "Come and get it."

I frown. The only way to get my phone is if I find a way to climb him.

He smirks.

Oh, no, I am not falling for that. "You want my phone? Fine, keep it then."

I turn and march toward the exit.

This time, no one stops me. I stalk out of the hotel and the cold air assails me. Goosebumps pop on my skin. I hunch my shoulders against the wind, walk up the sidewalk. Where am I going? What am I going to do? That jerk was my last hope, and surely, I have blown any chance of having any kind of relationship with him. *Why did I have to eavesdrop on that conversation of his? More worryingly, why did it hurt to hear him dismiss me?* So, he doesn't want marriage or kids, and definitely not with me. Tears push at the backs of my eyes. *I will not cry, will not.* I knew all of this... Nothing is a surprise. Not after how he'd treated me—

He'd treated my body with scant regard, he'd used me for his pleasure, then he'd brought me to the edge, over and over again...until every part of me yearns for his touch. For the rough caress of his fingers between my thighs, inside my cunt, pinching, tugging on my sensitive nipples. I shudder, and it's not from the cold. My belly aches, and it's not only because I can't remember when I last ate. My sex clenches and it's because… *I hate him, I do; and yet, every time he treats me like I am nothing, each time he shows me how little I mean to him…it turns me on. How sick is that? Why do I have to be this attracted to him? Why is it that the more he ignores me…the more I want to throw myself at his feet and ask him to take me…to not give me a choice? Bloody hell.* I squeeze my fingers at my sides. Tears fill my eyes, blocking out my sight again. The heel of my stilettos catches on the pavement. I trip forward. The stony surface races up to meet me…then halts.

I'm pulled back and around.

Heat slams into my chest and my nipples are flattened against a hard surface—not the ground where I was headed… No, this is…much worse. I look up and into the burning blue eyes of the man who holds my life in his hands…and who isn't aware of it. "Saint," his name tumbles from my lips like a prayer… Or a plea for help. How strange.

How could one man be both my worst enemy and the only one I'd trust to have my back, literally?

"For a sophisticated woman of the world, you sure can't see where you're going," his voice sounds from above me.

"For a billionaire with many business interests, you sure spend too much time stalking me."

His jaw tics; his left eyelid throbs. He releases me so quickly that I stumble back. He shoves my phone into my chest. Before I can reach for it, he's withdrawn his hand. The device slides down my body; I snatch it up. "Asshole."

He chuckles, "I much prefer, alphahole."

Anger sears my chest and the band around my ribcage tightens. My vision narrows and something inside of me snaps. I hook my leg around his, tug. His gaze widens, then his body arcs back.

23

Saint

"Fuck." My back hits the sidewalk, my head connecting with the concrete.

Stars flash behind my eyes and spots of black crowd my vision. I lay there winded, stare up at the gray London skies. That, at least, is predictable. Shades of darkness envelop this city in wintertime. It's what I like best about it. Shrouded in mysterious light, it always appears in mourning or about to regret the actions of its past, exactly like my life. I blink and the thought dissipates. Fucking hell, the knock to my head clearly impacted more than my thinking process. It seems to have shaken loose emotions I hadn't realized I have.

Huge green eyes fill my line of sight, "Saint?"

I scan her gorgeous features—her pale cheeks, the bitten lips that only enhance her fragility. Except she isn't. It is all an act, this vulnerability that she wears around herself like a cloak, to mask the deviousness that lies inside.

"I know."

Only when I hear the words do I realize that I have spoken aloud. "Wh…what do you mean?"

"I know why you asked to become my sub."

She purses her lips, adopts an expression of disinterest.

"Don't you want to know why, Gigi?"

She shakes her head.

"Come on, aren't you a little bit curious?"

She glances away, "I think you should get up from the ground." She looks around her, "It's dirty."

"But so are you…"

"What?" She whips her head around.

"Is that why I am attracted to you?" I glare at her.

She trembles. "You…you don't know what you're saying."

"Perhaps, for the first time, I do." I hold out my arm.

She stares at my proffered hand, "What…what are you doing?"

"You felled me, you can help me up, hmm?"

She swallows.

"Go on, Gigi, I don't bite." *And I always speak the truth…not.* "Don't keep me waiting."

Footsteps approach us.

She flinches.

"Do it before they get here and I'll forget this happened."

She looks up at my face, reaches for my hand.

I grab it, then pull back.

She loses her balance. The next second she falls onto me. "The hell?" She sputters, "You tricked me."

"No more than you're trying to trick me with the lies you're spinning around me, sweetheart." I bury my fingers in her hair, yank her close. "I am going to show you what happens when you poke the lion in its den."

"Saint, no—"

I smash my mouth to hers, thrust my tongue in between her lips. I devour her, suck on her with such force that our teeth clash. I hold her in place and consume her. Swipe my tongue across the roof of her mouth. I am going to punish her for what she's doing to me. For weaving a spell around me from the first time I'd met her. Enticing me, luring me into her trap. If she thinks I am going into this blindfolded, she is so fucking wrong. I am going to give her a taste of how it will be from now on. Me—the marauder, the destroyer… And she—she'll bloody well accept everything I give her, and more. I tighten my grip until my fingertips dig into her scalp, and I fucking mouth fuck her.

Her body slackens, then she kisses me back in earnest. She sucks on my tongue, pushes her lips into mine, opens her mouth completely, allowing me to take and take and… My chest lurches; my groin hardens. Blood drains to my cock so fast and so hard that my head spins. *Fucking hell.*

I tilt my head and she mirrors my action in the opposite way. The yin to my yang. The bloody darkness to everything that is wrong in me. The tempest to my storm. The turbulence to the raging intensity that roils in me, that shoves at my ribcage, that urges me to lean up, until her upper body is curved in sync with mine. We're not in resonance though. Nothing about us matches. Everything about this is wrong, which is why I must show her exactly how she is going to pay. I tear my mouth from hers, then push up to my feet, taking her with me.

I release her, and she stumbles, then rights herself.

Her features are frozen, her mouth slightly parted, those beautiful lips swollen and throbbing. Only when my breath raises the hair of her forehead, do I realize that I have leaned into her.

I jerk back. Then, pulling out the handkerchief from my breast pocket, I pat at my lips, "Your technique sucks, doll."

She whitens. The hollows under her cheeks throw her features into sharp relief.

"Jerk," she snarls.

I laugh, "I'm just getting started." I pocket the piece of linen, then yawn, "You'd better come in. You don't want to keep my friends waiting."

She blinks, "Friends? What do you mean?"

"Oh, didn't I tell you? We're getting married in…" I look at the watch on my wrist, "…precisely half an hour."

I turn to the hotel as my guards from the hotel arrive. "Are you okay, Sir?" one of them asks.

"I'm fine." I run my fingers through my hair.

The other guard walks past me, "You all right, Ma'am?" he asks Victoria.

She nods, takes a step forward and seems to lose her footing. He steadies her, and something inside of me explodes, "Get away from her!" The next second, I find my hands twisted in his collar. I plant myself between him and Gigi, "Don't you fucking touch her."

He raises his hands, "Uh, sorry, Sir, I was trying to help—"

"Well she doesn't need your help, so back the fuck off."

"Of course, Sir." He glances toward Victoria and my vision tunnels. I haul him by his collar and—

"Saint."

I raise my fist; she wraps her fingers around my bicep. "Saint, stop."

Her touch sinks in through the fabric of my tailormade suit. Her touch is more precious… *The fuck am I thinking?* I shake off her hand, release the man's collar. He lurches back, then squares his shoulders.

"Leave us," I snarl.

He pivots and walks back to the hotel.

I turn on Victoria, "Never stop me again in public, do you understand?"

She stiffens, then draws herself up to her full height, which puts her at eye level with my chest. *Shit,* she is tinier than the mental image I have of her. Perhaps it is her resilience, her feistiness, the layers of prickliness that cover her like a second skin, that contribute to her larger-than-life image, huh? *And the fuck am I thinking, waxing lyrical about this woman, huh?*

"Answer me," I growl.

She opens her mouth, when a voice interrupts us.

"Sometimes we are less unhappy in being deceived by those we love than in being undeceived by them…"

"The fuck?" I angle to the side, spot the owner of the voice, a man sprawled against the wall of the hotel.

He's dressed in a worn shirt and pants which have seen better days. His matted hair flows to his shoulders. He holds up a sign, that reads,

•   •   •

"And thou art dead, as young and fair..."

"Why didn't you complete the fucking poem?" I growl.

He appraises my features. The expression on his face is neither happy, nor sad. He's content. *Yeah, fucking imagine that? Bloody blissful motherfucker. This is what not having money can buy you, huh? Peace.* I laugh. Then unhook the bloody watch on my wrist. I drop it into his upturned hat.

A sharp inhalation of breath draws my attention. I glance over my shoulder to find Victoria's gaze fixed on the piece of jewelry I'd dropped.

"Why did you do that?"

"Why not?" I rub the back of my neck. "Why should I be the only one to suffer excesses?"

"That was what, £5000?"

"£30,000."

Her jaw drops open. "You didn't..."

"I can do anything I want, Victoria."

She wrings her fingers in front her, her gaze roaming over my face, then flicking back to Homeless Guy.

I turn to the man. "Fucking Byron, I hate him."

The man grins, his teeth bright against his lips. Huh? For someone who lives on the streets, he sure has perfect teeth.

"Have a cigarette, mate?" He glances between us.

I glare at him, then pull out the pack of cigarettes in my pocket and hand a cigarette over.

"You smoke?" She scowls. "I didn't know that."

"Lots you don't know about me."

She walks up to stand next to me, grabs the packet from my hand.

"Hey," I protest.

"These things will kill you," she scoffs, then drops the entire pack in his lap.

"You worried about me?" I frown

"Of course, not." Her face flushes.

Homeless guy looks between us. "Lighter?" he asks.

"Jesus, fuck. Get your own bloody light."

"Don't swear," she scolds me.

"I'll do whatever the bloody fuck I want." I dig out my lighter and hand it over to Homeless Guy, who promptly pulls out a cigarette and lights up.

24

What flowers are kissable?
Answer: Tulips

Victoria

I did. I had said 'yes' to him. *Oh, hell.*

I stare at my reflection in the mirrored surface of the elevator doors. Saint towers next to me, his frame dwarfing mine, his shoulders taking up too much space, his presence drawing in all of the oxygen in the enclosed space. I take a breath and my nose fills with his scent—dark, edgy, packed with pheromones that find their way unerringly to the source of my emptiness… My empty core. *Hell.*

"Is that a 'No'?" he asks.

I should say the word. Tell him it's all off. That I don't care what he's found out, that I don't give a damn about the Mafia and their hold on me. I should escape from this trap that's closing in on me, leave everything and everyone behind... Take on a new name, move to another city, another country... But where could I go?

I don't have a passport. The Mafia took that from me after I reached England. Even the possessions I left behind in his suite belong to this character that I am playing.

If it were only me, I wouldn't hesitate to leave, but Nina's life is at stake. She is in their clutches. If I do anything wrong, she'll pay the price. How could I bear that? I can't let anything happen to her.

I have to find a way out of this... Have to do what is needed without giving away the last bit of my pride.

"No."

"Excuse me?"

I turn to him. "You heard me. The answer is 'No.'"

He stares at me, then spots of color burn on his face. His jaw tics. A nerve pops at his temple. "Say that again."

I angle my body, plant my feet firmly into the floor and face him. I look him in the eye and repeat, "I wouldn't marry you if you were the last man on this earth."

His eyes gleam and he peels back his lips. A dense cloud of anger rolls off of him. It slams me in the chest and I gasp, take a step back.

He lowers his chin. My nerve endings crackle.

Shit, shit, shit. What have I done? I am fighting something inevitable here... I mean, I only meant to show him I'm not a pushover. It's the only way to hold onto his respect... Not that he has much of that. Not for much of the world, and definitely not for me. The only person he seems to have an ounce of caring for...is the person who calls him at the most inopportune times, the one for whom he seems to drop everything and run. Is it a woman?

What do I care who it is? What matters is that he is here, trying to steamroll me into doing what he wants and... I am not going to be taken for granted. Not like this and not by him. So I need his help...but damn it, I hadn't imagined the attraction between us either. He wants me, if for no other reason than to fuck me... As long as I manage to foster a smidgeon of that interest, I'll be able to reel him in... I hope.

The strap of my bag slides off my shoulder before it thumps to the floor between us.

He kicks it aside.

"Hey, that's the only one I have."

"Fuck that, I'll buy you a shopful of bags," he leans in close, "and fuck you for what you do to me, Gigi."

He drops his head until his lips are positioned a millimeter from mine. Close enough that I can make out the lines radiating from the edges of his eyes. Close enough that I can see the little scar that nicked the edge of his left eyebrow—why hadn't I noticed that before? Close enough that—he swipes out his hand. I flinch. The next second the elevator lurches to a stop.

"What was that?"

"What do you think?"

I turn to find the stop button blinking. My eyes bug out… "You… you *The hell did I say?..*"

"Paused the elevator? The least I could do to convince my errant bride, hmm?"

"Not your bride."

"That's right." He twines a lock of my hair around his fingers, then brings it up to his nose to smell it. "But you will be."

"No."

"Yes."

"Make me."

Satisfaction is etched into every hard line of his face.

"I… I…didn't…mean..."

He raises one eyebrow, "Oh, I think you did mean..." I start to shake my head, but he places a finger across my mouth, "Shh." The warmth seeps into my skin, the scent of him crowds me, and his dominance pushes down on my shoulders, holds me in place.

I draw in a breath and my chest heaves.

He presses down on my lower lip. I open my mouth.

He eases his finger inside and I curl my tongue around the tip.

His blue eyes deepen into an aquamarine. Flecks of silver burst to life deep inside. An answering tremor coils in my belly. My toes curl. My scalp tingles. And all this when he isn't doing anything more than touching me with his fingertip.

"I know what you need," his hard voice chafes my skin. My sex clenches, the emptiness inside of me roaring to life.

I want to speak to tell him, this isn't fair. He can't simply overpower me without trying too hard.

"I…"

He shakes his head.

I frown, open my mouth. He clicks his tongue. Goosebumps dot my skin. *Shit, he didn't do that, did he? Treat me like I am his property?* Like all he has to do is say kneel and I'll…do it. Hell, I'd keep my mouth open and willing until he'd stuffed his fat cock inside, while he'd shoved his fingers inside my pussy and commanded me to come… And damn him, I'd do it too. That's how much power he has over me.

I clench my fingers at my sides, force myself to not move a muscle, not a breath, not a twitch of my eyelashes, nothing to show how completely, utterly defenseless I am in front of him.

He swipes his finger along the inside of my mouth, then pulls it out and sucks on it. I'm instantly wet. He lowers his palm between my legs and cups my pussy through my skirt.

A whine bleeds from my lips and I arch into his touch.

"You were saying?" he drawls.

"I… I…" He squeezes my tender core and a shot of lust spirals upward. I bang my head back against the elevator wall.

He grinds the heel of his palm into my pussy and my eyes roll back in my head. "Saint… Please."

"I know what you need, Gigi."

"You…you do?"

"Absolutely, sweet thing. You want to be treated like the traitor you are."

"What?" I jerk my gaze to him. "What…did you say?"

"You think I don't know the identity of the man you were with earlier?"

The blood drains from my face. My heart seems to stop beating. I can't feel my hands or legs. "You…" my voice cracks. I clear my throat, "You know?"

"Your identity?" His lips twist. "I've suspected it since I spotted you at Sinclair's wedding. Imagine my not-so-surprised face when it turned out that little Miss, or should I say Mrs., Standoff here is a spy for my enemy."

"It...isn't what it seems."

He chuckles, "At least try a new line."

"It's true, I—"

He pushes up into my center with such pressure that all my nerve-endings pop. More moisture pools between my legs and my thighs spasm. I grab his forearm and he shoves my hand aside. "You don't get to touch me."

"Saint, don't—"

"That's 'Sir' to you."

I swallow.

"Say it."

I shake my head. Not like this. I didn't want things to go so wrong between us. Can't stand the hatred that flares in his eyes. The narrowness of his gaze, the cold edge of his anger that slices into my heart, rips through my guts, freezes my blood until I can't breathe. Can't speak. Can't do anything but stare at him, with a silent plea in my eyes.

Sweat beads his forehead. He meets my gaze head on. The skin is drawn over his cheeks as if this entire proceeding is not easy for him either. No, I don't believe that. He holds all of the cards right now. Hell, he holds my cunt in his hand. One word and my entire world could come crashing down around me. What's left of it, that is. And poor Nina— She'll be lost to the murky depths of the world that Antonio has her trapped in. All because this asshole of a gazillionaire, with an ego bigger than the entire city of London put together, can't bear to lose.

"You know what your problem is?" I stare into his face, "You can't stand to be vulnerable."

He frowns. "What do you mean?"

"You were attracted to me. You wanted me. Hell, you were all set to bed me, no strings attached. Then you realized someone had beat you to it... No..." I shake my hair back from my face, "You realized that I, a woman, had run circles around you and your uppity friends and none of you had any idea." I widen my smile. "None."

"Oh?"

"Yeah," I nod. "In fact, if you hadn't seen me with Antonio—"

"Don't mention his fucking name."

"Ah! So that's it?"

"What?" His eyebrows knit.

"You're jealous."

"You're wrong." He leans forward until his nose brushes mine. His chest expands, then expands some more. His shoulders seem to grow even wider. His left eyelid twitches. *Shit, that isn't a good sign at all, is it?*

"You're missing something, little Victoria," he growls.

"What?"

"I am not the one with everything to lose. You are."

Anger sweeps up my spine. I draw back my shoulders, then squeeze my thighs together, locking his hand between my legs. "The only thing I have to lose here is the fact that you haven't fucked me, so why don't you, and be done with it, hmm? Then we can bury this chemistry and get on with our lives. In fact," I bring my hand up and grip the tent at his crotch, "I'll help you along. That's what you want, isn't it? To fuck me out of your system? To have me until you get tired of me? So why don't you do it and cast me aside? That way, we don't have to go through this sham of a wedding or the arrangement of you becoming my Dom. Why pretend there is any relationship possible between us, when really, we hate each other? Fuck me already, and we can call it quits."

Don't say yes. Don't. Don't let me walk away. Please don't.

He hauls me up by his grip on my pussy so I am perched on tip toe. His nostrils flare as he surveys my face, "No."

I blink. "No?"

He nods, "I have a better idea."

"What?"

"I'll quiz you about The Beatles. If you get every answer right, I'll let you leave. If you get even one wrong… I…" He massages my clit through my clothes. My sex shudders and a tingling emanates from his touch, sweeping aside the cold, heating my blood, leaving a fiery, tangled, throbbing need in its wake. *Shit. Say it, damn it. Complete your sentence.*

He twists his hand with the right torque that his heel slams into the swollen bud of my clit. A trembling sweeps up my legs, past my waist, and my nipples pebble until I can't stand it anymore. I am one yearning mass of need, waiting to be filled by him. His cock. His fingers. His tongue. "Please," the word bleeds from my lips.

A fierce satisfaction grips his features.

Then he releases me so quickly that I fall back against the wall.

The climax instantly ebbs. "No," I gasp. "Not again. You can't do this."

He lifts one eyebrow. "You bet I can."

He ambles back, until he's propped up against the opposite end of the cage. His big body takes up almost the entire breadth of the constricted space. *Shit.* I flatten my back into the barrier behind me.

"What now?"

"Now, I ask the questions. Remember Gigi, one wrong answer." His grin widens, "One mistake and you lose all say in what's going to happen to you."

"For…how long?"

"For as long as I deem necessary to tame you, of course."

"You're crazy."

"Are you ready?"

No.

No.

I square myself holders. "Fine. Go ahead."

He nods.

" John Lennon and Paul McCartney sang backing vocals on which Rolling Stones single??"

"It was called." I frown. "We Love You."

"Correct." He smirks. "Next question," he pins me with his gaze "The Beatles couldn't read music. True or false?"

"True," I reply.

"What's your favorite color?"

"Blue," I blink.

He clicks his tongue, "Don't lie to me. Tell me the truth and I won't catapult you off a cliff."

"You're a Monty Python fan as well?" I can't stop the smile that curves my lips.

"I ask the questions," he smirks, then waggles a finger at me, "and you haven't answered the last one."

I throw up my hands, "Fine, red. My favorite color is red." I stiffen, "And did you just trick me into revealing something personal about myself?"

"Only I get to ask the questions, remember?" He angles his head. "How long did it take The Beatles to record their first album?"

"24 hours." I wring my fingers together. *What's he getting at? Why is he sneaking in questions about my personal preferences in between?*

"What's the make of your favorite car?"

"Maserati." I scowl, "Not fair, why do you even care what—?"

"What was the name of the last album by The Beatles?"

"Abbey Road."

"Your favorite flower?"

"Lilies." I purse my lips, "Honestly, you could have asked, I'd have—"

"John Lennon changed his middle name from Winston to Ono after marrying Yoko Ono. True or false?"

"True."

"Not bad, I have one last question for you." He grins something fierce and it feels like a cold hand touches my heart. He's trying to throw me off kilter, trying to ruin my concentration. *That's all it is. Focus Victoria. Don't let him get to you. Don't—*

"When is Beatles Day celebrated?" He tilts his head.

"Umm.." I chew on the inside of my cheek, "It's celebrated on June 25th?"

"Ehhhhh!" He makes the irritating sound of a gameshow buzzer and says "Wrong."

"What?" My jaw drops.

"You got that wrong."

"Can't be." I stiffen.

"It is."

"You're messing with me," I snarl.

"I'm not."

"I don't believe you."

"Check the answer on your phone."

I bend, pull the phone from my bag, "I don't have a signal."

"I do." He hands me his phone, which I notice is logged into the hotel Wi-Fi. *Why the hell hadn't I thought of that?*

I pull up the search engine on his phone, then tap in my question. The screen fills with links. I open the first one, read it. Beatles Day is celebrated on 10th July, not to be confused with Global Beatles Day.

He grabs his phone from my hand, shoves it in his pocket.

My heart begins to thud. "No," I swallow. "It can't be."

"It's true, Gigi. You lost."

"Piss off," I snarl at him. My guts churn and my breathing goes shallow. This can't be happening. How could I have lost to him, and on a Beatles' quiz? "Hangonasecond," I frown. "How did you know all that?"

"All what?"

"Don't try to be obtuse; you know what I mean." I stab a finger in his direction, "How did you pick up all those facts about my favorite band?"

He blinks, then cuts the air with his hand. "Everyone knows the answers to those questions."

"No," I shake my head, "They don't."

"It's all there in the public domain."

"So you read up on them?"

He raises his shoulders.

My pulse begins to race. I take a step forward, "Admit it, you did."

"Nah."

"Don't lie to me, Saint."

"Okay…" He tugs at his collar, "Maybe a little."

"Ha!" I clap my hands, "I knew it."

"Only so I could use my knowledge at the appropriate time."

"When you could take me down?" I grimace.

"Exactly." He taps his foot on the ground, "Doesn't change the fact that you lost."

My stomach flutters. *What does it mean? What's going to happen now that he's beat me at my own game?* He has all the bloody cards, leaving me exposed. With nowhere to hide, I glance sideways at the alarm button.

"There's no need for that."

"No?"

He shakes his head, "We're done here."

"We are?" Shit, why am I echoing his words? This entire encounter has a bit of the surreal attached to it. I bend my knees, grab my purse. It feels solid, familiar; I slip the strap over my shoulder.

"What now?"

"Now? We get married."

25

———————

Saint

I had revealed my hand. *Shit!* I hadn't meant to tell her I knew about her, had planned to keep that piece of information to myself. But when she'd almost completely shattered, when her gorgeous lips had parted, her pussy clamping down, reaching for the relief only I could provide, when her sugary scent had deepened, fuck, if the blood hadn't left my head permanently to park itself in my dick. Reaching down, I adjust myself, then snatch up my phone and shoot off a text message, before following her.

She walks ahead of me, thank fuck, so she can't see the evidence of exactly how she affected me in there. I'd trapped both of us in the elevator. Because, yeah, cliché much? Couldn't pass up the opportunity to try to subjugate her, let her know that I hold the power… I sure hadn't bloody intended to hand it over to her.

She pulls the rug from under my feet… When she isn't keeping me on my toes, that is. Does she know that?

She pauses at the end of the corridor, where the double doors open into the ball room. We're on the floor below my penthouse suite on the top floor of Claridge's. I couldn't have chosen the venue better; guess the Seven have their uses…sometimes. Allowing me to get married and afford a quick getaway after the ceremony with my—hold on there.

I halt so quickly that my heels dig into the plush carpet below.

Marriage.

Bride.

This isn't real. It's a quick ceremony to seal the deal. Like it's something I do every day—not. Treat it like a painful meeting, one in which you're surrounded by opponents looking to tear you down. I rub the back of my neck; right now, I'd take that over this mock wedding.

She turns to glance at me.

"Go on, open the door," I growl.

She frowns. "This really is unnecessary. You know that, right?"

"Is it now?" I draw up next to her. "I think it's the one thing that will bind you to me, prevent you from running away and spilling everything you've seen and heard to your handler."

She flinches. "It…it isn't like that."

"Oh?" I scrutinize her features. "Enlighten me, then."

She wrings her fingers together, "I... I can't tell you."

"Why not?"

She wraps her arms around her waist, glances away.

Anger shoots through my veins. Damn her, what is she hiding from me? Why did it have to be her to entrance me so? If only I could erase thoughts of her from my mind and return to my life as it had been. I wrap my fingers around her throat.

Her gaze widens. Her pupils dilate. I scan her flushed features, the way she's arched into my hold on the balls of her feet, handbag dangling at her shoulder, yet every part of her ready, in sync with my needs, her face upturned, her breathing ragged.

"Shit, you like it when I'm rough, don't you?"

She swallows.

"Is breath play your thing, Gigi? Does it get you off?"

She nods.

"Who else has touched you like this?"

"Nobody else," she whispers.

Could that be true?

"Am I your first dominant? Were you telling the truth when you said your arse is untouched? Tell me Gigi, tell me."

She opens her mouth. "Yes," she chokes out, "it's true."

"What is?"

"All of it. You're my first... Dom." She hiccups, "And no-one else has taken me there."

"Your arse belongs to me, Gigi."

She stares.

I tighten my grip. Color blooms on her skin and she rubs her thighs together, her gaze fixed on my face as she stalks my features, trying to read my intentions, what my next move is going to be. I pull her close enough that her breasts almost touch my chest. Almost. "Say it," I growl.

"Yours," she whispers.

"What is?"

"My arse is yours."

"And your pussy?" I bring down my other hand to cup the warmth between her legs, knowing she'll be wet. "Fuck, I can feel the stickiness of your cum through your clothes, you know that?"

She gulps; her chest rises and falls.

"Answer me, Gigi. Who does your cunt belong to?"

"You, Sir."

"And your breasts?" I release her core to pinch her nipple through her dress.

She moans.

"Tell me, Gigi."

"You, they belong to you."

"And your hungry gaze, with which you watch me as I come, who does that belong to?"

"You."

"Your hair, your skin, the nails on your toes, the eyelashes that frame those gorgeous eyes... Whose are they?"

"Yours."

"And you. Who do you belong to, Gigi?"

"You, Sir. I belong to you."

"Damn fucking right." My cock hardens impossibly and my balls tighten. The doors open. I yank her close, press my lips to hers. "Don't fucking let me down now," I whisper against her mouth. "You feel me, Gigi?"

She nods.

"Saint... Victoria, why is it that you two can't keep your hands off each other for the few minutes that's needed from you to seal this holy union?"

Victoria tries to pull away. I release her neck, only to wind my arm around her waist and pull her close. She resists, but I tug with enough force that she falls into me. I keep her there, pressed from thigh to hip, tuck her under my arm. *Good.* I have her where I can finally keep an eye—and other parts of my body—tuned into her.

I glance at Edward, "Perhaps because there isn't an unholier couple in history who've attempted to make a go at this bloody ceremony?"

"Saint," Edward admonishes me, "language."

"Fuck, Father. Seriously?"

Edward frowns, then steps back. We walk through, and come to a halt. I glance around the assembled faces.

"The fuck?" I glower. "What's this, a circus?"

"You're getting married, ol' chap, couldn't pass up the opportunity to invite our friends to witness your downfall," Weston ambles forward.

Amelie breaks away from his side and darts forward.

She embraces Victoria, "Oh my God!" she whisper-screams, "You're doing this? You're actually gonna go through with this, V?"

Victoria pats the woman on her shoulder as her eyes meet mine.

I glare at her. She swallows, something in her gaze pleading with me, beseeching me... For what? Reassurance? Asking me to tell her that it will all be okay? Perhaps a promise that all the bad stuff will go away and we'll live happily ever after? Not. She's not getting anything of the sort from me.

I turn away, crack my neck. "The fuck is it so hot in here?"

Weston blinks. He peers into my face, then chuckles. "You nervous, man?"

"Of course, not," I frown.

"You should be." He grins, "Not every day that one of the most confirmed bachelors in town decides to walk down the aisle."

"It's a fake wedding, dickwad," I growl.

He laughs, "You sure about that?"

"Of course, I am… I mean, it's real to begin, but I plan to walk away from her when—" I twist my lips.

"When?"

"When all of this is over, of course," I wave a hand in the air.

"What is over?" He folds his arms over his chest, "Explain it to me, Sherlock."

"When we've tracked down the members of the Mafia who did this to us, make sure they are locked away, or better still, six feet under. And when she is safe, when—" my voice tapers off. *Shit, do I mean that? No. I don't mean that.* Did I propose a marriage to tie her to me? Of course, I did, but only so I can keep my property safe. Because she is the key to unlocking the door, to leading us to those who turned our lives upside down.

"You gonna complete your sentence anytime soon?" Weston smirks.

"No," I growl, then drag my fingers through my hair. "You don't have to seem so pleased with yourself. You wait until it's your time."

"My time?" He cups his chin, "I'm not the one who proposed a wedding to get close to an asset."

"She's more than that," I frown.

"Of course, she is…to you." He slaps my shoulder. "It's what landed you in this mess."

"Fuck." My heart begins to race. Sweat beads my palms. "You're talking as if my life is over…"

"In a way, it is… Beginning of a journey, and all that bullshit…"

"Don't you have a procedure to attend to? You're supposed to be a hot-shot doctor—"

"Who wouldn't pass up the chance to be there for one of his closest friends."

"Ha," I snort. "What a crock of bull-fucking-shit. You're here to ensure I am tied up so you can capitalize on the assets of 7A Investments and FOK Media."

"Now would I do that?" He raises his hands. "After all, everything is spelled out in black and white. No way, can I go against the split of profits."

"There are other ways to go behind our backs and take what's not due to you."

"Especially when it's money that should have come to you." He nods, "Now, I am not saying it hadn't crossed my mind." He grins. "Not my fault if I pull it off either, given you and Sinner—" he jabs a thumb over his shoulder, "are occupied with matters of the heart, and all that."

"This isn't a matter of the heart," I growl.

"You're right, again." He slaps my shoulder. "It's your dick that's leading you on, man. You should've fucked her and gotten it out of your system—"

I redden.

"What?" He opens and closes his mouth, "No."

"Shut up," I mutter.

He takes me by my shoulders. "Look into my eyes, my child. Tell me it's not what I suspect it is."

"Back the fuck off, wanker."

He searches my features, "It is, isn't it?"

"What is?" a familiar voice sounds behind him.

I groan, "No, no, no. Enough of this asinine chitchat."

Arpad saunters up, "The man doth protest too much."

"Why the fuck aren't you on your watch already?"

"Because," he opens his arm wide, "I had to see you safely married first."

I glare at him, "You seem in a rare, fine mood, ass wipe."

"Temper, ol' chap. Gotta watch that old ticker, now that you're getting into a different phase of your life. You're going to have your hands full, as it is, dealing with the wife… The kids."

"What?" I gape. "No kids," I cut the air with my hand, "no way."

"No patter of little feet in your living room then?" Damian prowls over, his golden locks glinting in the light from the chandelier above. "You mean, you don't want the little devils waking you up early in the mornings?"

"Nope."

"But...but, you'll have so much fun teaching them to play Cricket. Oh, wait, the potty training comes before that. That could be fun; you'd be a natural at it."

I stare at him in growing horror," Jesus, I have no idea what you're talking about. I will never have kids as long as I live, okay?" Why is my voice rising, making it sound like I'm panicking?.

Victoria glances across the room at me. I meet her gaze, my features rigid. *Did she hear what I said?* Well, best that she knows. Not that it matters. I don't intend to get into any situation where that is a likely problem between us.

"What do you have against children?" Weston frowns.

"Nothing, so long as they aren't mine."

How can I explain that I don't want my DNA to be propagated? Not after I'd realized exactly how out of control I could get. Not after the time I'd almost killed the man who'd tortured me, who'd hurt me like no one else ever had. The only way to forget those images was to lock them away deep inside, along with my ability to feel. If I can't feel, I won't feel that burning anguish that came from my body physically breaking down—when my mind couldn't steer my responses, when I had lost all ability to be in command. I'll never lose control again. Never.

I widen my stance. "I won't hear another word on this topic from any of you." I survey their faces. "Ever again."

"These guys getting to you, huh?" Sinclair ambles over. He seems rested, his suit impeccable, as always. Fucker looks about ready to walk the ramp, while I?

I raise my arm and sniff myself. "Shit! I think I forgot to shower after the gym."

"No time for that now," he grins.

"We can push this back by an hour..." I shuffle my feet, "Maybe two?"

"Now come on, you got us all here. Hell, I had to put off taking Summer Christmas shopping, so we could attend your nuptials. The least you could do is give me the satisfaction of going through with it."

"Because, of course, that's a good enough reason to get married, huh?" I glower.

"As good a reason as any, considering you aren't acknowledging the real reasons why you're doing it," Sinclair snorts.

"And you know that, how?"

"Because I was in your place."

"Don't listen to Sterling," Weston leans forward on the balls of his feet. "He's not in any position to give you advice, considering he's got the old ball and chain firmly attached to his ankle."

Sinclair bares his teeth, "Watch what you say, Kincaid."

"Not saying anything wrong."

"Maybe not, but it's not as bad as it's cut out to be either.'

"Isn't it?" Weston drums his fingers on his chest, "That's what the pussy-whipped ones always say."

"I'm not—"

"Sin, darling."

Sinclair whips his head around.

Summer waves at him from the corner, where she's huddled with her friends. "Come over, babe. You gotta hear this."

Sinclair's face lights up. He pivots, moves toward them.

"Pussy-whipped." Weston shakes his head, "The man who couldn't stand to be among people, now willingly allows himself to be drawn into the midst of a crowd." He makes a gagging sound.

"I heard you," Sinclair glowers at him over his shoulder. "I'll get back at you for this, tosser."

"Too fucking late," Weston mutters. "He's sinking, man, and he isn't even aware of it.'

I watch as Sinclair stalks over to Summer. He wraps his arm around the tiny woman, draws her into his side. She literally melts into him and he nuzzles her hair.

A waitress materializes next to Damian. "God help us. I need a drink." He takes the glass of champagne, glances at the hem of her skirt, which barely reaches mid-thigh.

"When do you get off?"

She bats her eyelids, "Anytime you want."

He downs his drink in one shot. Then hands the empty glass to me.

"The fuck?" I frown, "What are you up to?"

He takes the tray with the remaining drink glasses from her, and thrusts it at Weston, who grunts, "Don't make too much noise, will ya?"

Damian smirks at the girl, "You heard that. I am going to make you scream like you never have before."

Her chest heaves. "I can't wait," she breathes.

He jerks his chin, then stalks to the exit.

"The fuck is he going?"

"I think he's cutting his losses." Weston reaches for a flute.

I take it from him, replacing it with Damian's empty one. "Thanks." I toss it back. The champagne goes down smoothly. "I'll be billing you guys for the expenses of this rush job, of course."

"You're a real piece of shit, you know that?" Weston drawls. "The least you could do is pay for your own wedding."

"Wasn't my idea to have it here in this hotel, losing business for the time we have to shut it down for the ceremony."

His jaw drops. "You serious?"

"Of course." I grab another flute of Champagne from a passing waitress.

"There wasn't anything else scheduled for this room a couple of hours ago, you cheap (insert insult of your choice). Were you expecting a last-minute booking?"

I shrug, "Maybe."

He hands the half-filled tray over to the woman, then grabs two glasses for himself.

The waitress hesitates, then glances at me, "Congratulations, Sir."

"Fuck off," I growl.

She pales, then scurries off.

"Take it easy, man," Weston cautions.

"What-fucking-ever." I glance around the room, filled with the Seven who are in town…and Summer and her girlfriends.

Victoria glances up at me, her face pale. Her gaze flicks to the door, then she looks away. *Fuck.* I can see the hollows under her cheekbones. Has she eaten anything at all?

"Perhaps it's time to get this shit-show on the road, huh?"

"We're waiting for Jace and Sienna," Weston takes a sip of the champagne. "You stock good stuff, at least. I'll give you that."

"Enjoy it, asshole. You're paying for it, after all."

Weston makes a tsk'ing sound, "Someone's nervous."

"Bitch!" I grumble, "I can't wait for it to be your turn. I'll fucking gloat."

"Sure. Considering I am not about to fall into the trap anytime soon."

A laugh peals out. He glowers across the room. I follow the direction of his gaze to where Amelie is talking with the other women. Amelie gesticulates excitedly, then props a hand on her hip. She tosses her hair, thrusts out a hand, in what I assume is a punchline in her joke. Summer and Isla laugh.

"That woman, she's bloody annoying."

"Who?" I ask, taking in Victoria's erect figure as she stands silent, her lips curved in the makings of a smile.

"Amelie," he snorts, "she talks too much, laughs too much, and have you noticed what she's wearing?"

"Huh?" I glance at her dress, "What's wrong with it?"

"Too much skin." He looks her up and down, "Her legs are too long for her dress. And her hair... Why is she wearing it up? And those fuck me heels? Seriously, you'd think she was trying to attract every male in the vicinity."

"You're attracted to her?"

He laughs, "Not bloody likely." He continues to watch her. "She's not my type."

Amelie turns her head, catches his eye. She draws herself up to her full height and flips him the bird, then turns her back on him.

"What the fuck—?" he sputters.

I laugh, "Yep, she's definitely not your type."

"What do you mean?"

"She has too much spirit for you."

"Hmm." He strokes his chin. "Maybe, maybe not."

Amelie whispers in Victoria's ear and Victoria's smile broadens.

Her features light up. My breath catches. She's beautiful, the woman I'm about to marry.

I roll my shoulders.

Married? I am fucking getting married. Had it been a moment of insanity when I'd told her to get hitched to me? Or… I can't stop my gaze from wandering over her curves. At least, she's not wearing black. Red. That's her color. Her dress is conservatively cut, but it clings to her body, highlighting those high perky breasts, the swell of her hips, those long, long legs that I want wrapped around my waist...my head—No, not yet. First, I am going to bend her over and take her from behind as I've promised myself. Sheath myself in her virgin hole… *Fuck.* My dick lengthens. I've never cared before about being any woman's first in any way...but with Gigi… Something about her makes me want to claim every new experience of hers. She is mine to own. To break. To possess. To use in getting to my final goal.

I pull out my phone, cue it up, then hand it over to Weston.

"What's that?"

"Ask the staff to cue it up over the speakers in the room, will you?"

"Now?"

"Right away."

He snatches up the phone and walks off.

My heart begins to race. Sweat beads my temples. I curl my hands at my sides, then glance over again.

Victoria tips up her head. Our gazes clash—green, emerald seas, stormy with a hint of wariness, fortified with that strength I am coming to associate with her.

She swallows and her lips tremble. I take in her features—her flushed cheeks, the straight set of her shoulders, her stiff spine. She is ready to take on the world, to face anything. The woman has a resilience that belies her delicate build.

I hold out my hand. She draws in a breath. I hold her gaze, jerk my chin. She draws herself up to her full height, hesitates.

She twists her fingers in front of her. Under the skirt of her dress, her thighs move. Is she turned on? Can she sense the imprint of my fingers inside of her, my tongue licking her clit, my mouth biting down on her pussy as I take her to the edge, only to draw back, leaving her waiting, wanting, needing.

The opening notes of *All You Need is Love* by The Beatles fill the room. The crowd quietens. Her gaze widens.

Come. I curl my fingers.

She takes a step toward me, and another.

I stay where I am, brace my feet against the plush carpets, hand outstretched, stalking her as she closes the distance between us.

When she reaches me, she pauses, glances down at my hand, then back at my face.

I allow a smirk to curl my lips. *Make a dash for it. Try to escape. Do it.*

She places her hand in mine.

I blink.

The warmth of her fingers bleeds into my skin. Her touch is soft, like the petals of a flower, waiting to be torn from its stem. Her palm trembles and she draws back, but I shackle her wrist with my fingers.

She shudders.

I draw her close, weave my fingers with hers. Stare down into her eyes, drinking from that glimmer of anticipation, of surprise, of… Something more I can't quite define. Her scent crowds my nostrils— subtle lilies, a dash of pepper, laced with that sweetness that tells me she's aroused. My groin hardens and my cock thickens. I squeeze her fingers.

"You chose a song from The Beatles," she whispers.

"This is your day." I nod toward the front of the room. "Ready, Gigi?"

26

What did the hamburger buy his sweetheart?
Answer: An onion ring

Victoria

No, I'm not ready. I'll never be ready. He walks forward and I follow. Not that I have a choice. Not that I am going to resist. It doesn't matter what transpired before this. I am here… With him now… Next to him, as he moves toward where Edward, the same minister who married Sinclair and Summer, waits for us.

"What about the paperwork for the wedding?" I whisper.

"It's taken care of."

"But how…?"

He angles an eyebrow, "Does it matter? I am the third richest man in the country. Do you think something like paperwork would get in the way of me from getting what I want?"

Right. Of course. Anything can be bought with money…except me. He probably thinks that's why I'm standing here in this sham of a ceremony, tying myself to him for as long as he intends to have me? I stiffen my shoulders. I've got this. I'll let him think what he wants. I can get through this. I've made it this far… I'm approaching the last mile. This will make it easier for me to keep an eye on him. Surely, the proximity will ensure I can wrangle my way into his affairs.

I lean into him, "What were the results of the blood tests?"

"You're clean. So am I." He angles his head, "Not that we needed to know in advance of tonight."

Huh? I furrow my brows. *Does that mean…?* He doesn't intend to fuck me on our wedding night? And it would be fucking, make no mistake. He's told me, in no uncertain terms, that he means to have me… Or perhaps he's not the bare back kind…? A hollowness grips my stomach.

"Funny," I whisper back, "I would have thought you'd be the kind who wouldn't let a rubber come between you and your wife."

"You're right," his lips twist.

"I am?"

He nods. "If you had been my wife, I'd have taken your cunt with nothing except our skin separating us. I'd have shagged you raw, until we melded into each other… But then… You're not my wife, are you…? Not really."

My heart twists. A pressure builds behind my eyes, "You're a piece of shit, you know that?"

"Takes one to know one, dear Gigi."

"I fucking hate you." I try to pull away.

His grip tightens and he holds me in place. "Hang onto that sentiment. You'll need it for what I have planned for us tonight."

The song dies away.

That he'd remembered to choose a song…for this event. What does it mean? Does he have feelings for me, despite his tendency to retreat into his douchebag extraordinaire persona?

My head spins.

My belly lurches and my pulse begins to thud. His cryptic comments are getting to me. Hell. What am I doing? Why am I here? Had I actually thought I'd get through this and find a way to rescue Nina?

I glance around the space. Amelie's gaze meets mine. She smiles, holds up crossed fingers, then pushes the tips against her forehead and mimics a gun firing off. A chuckle wells up, even as a tear trails down my cheek.

I will not cry. Will not. I swallow down the lump that blocks my throat. *Just get through this. One step at a time. I can do this. I can.*

Next to Amelie, Summer catches my eye. Her features are pinched. She looks from me to Saint, then back to me. Her forehead creases. I read the question on her face. How I wish I could confide in her. We aren't related by blood, but I'd trusted Summer on sight.

Just like I'd been attracted to Saint right away. And see where that got me? I force my lips to curve into a smile. Then lean into Saint. He stiffens. Then he brings my fingers up to his lips and kisses my knuckles.

Isla sighs.

Amelie's gaze widens.

Even Summer's features relax at that.

Of course, these women are Summer's friends, and she's married to Sinclair, one of the Seven and among Saint's closest friends. Clearly, they would believe him. They have no reason to doubt his tactics. I have no one here on my side. It is me against all of them. Me and my wits. We are well-acquainted with this situation. I turn forward as Saint comes to a stop.

He releases my hand.

The doors to the room open behind us. I hear whispers, then footsteps sound. Amelie appears next to me holding a posy of flowers.

She thrusts it at me, and I take it.

"How?"

She smiles, "Saint messaged me to get them from the flower shop in the lobby."

"He did?"

I glance at the bouquet of delicate blood red lilies. Is that why he'd asked me what my favorite flower was? My head whirls. This makes no sense. Though it's a relief to have something in my hands to hold onto, instead of wringing them in front of me.

Silence descends on the crowd. Edward looks between us. "In what is becoming a practice for quick weddings among the Seven, I am pleased to welcome all of you here today to celebrate the union of Saint Jordan Killian Caldwell with Victoria."

Behind me, I hear the sound of whispering, a small commotion. Edward looks over our heads, "Late but you're in time… Jace and Sienna."

"Sorry, Father… We rushed over as soon as we heard." Jace grins.

"You're forgiven, considering…" Edward nods at someone I can't see.

"We're here now," Sienna's voice interrupts. "Didn't mean to steal the attention from the bride."

I glance sideways in time to see Sienna walk up to take her place in one of the chairs. She places one hand on her belly, waves at me. "I'm sorry," she mouths.

I shake my head. My gaze slips back to her belly. I can't stop a smile from curving my features. How would it be to be pregnant? To swell with a child? Saint's child. A girl with his dark hair and blue eyes, that nervous energy coiled in her as she beams at boys and reduces them to mush.

Jace dips his head and places his hand over Sienna's. He kisses her forehead. They smile at each other in that secret way couples who love each other have. Something that I won't.

Tears prick the backs of my eyes again. *Jesus, the hell is wrong with me?*

More waterworks. Must be the prospect of getting married for the first time that is doing me in. It seems…to mean something. Despite the fact that it is meant to be a sham; standing next to Saint, facing the minister, seems to signify a start. A change of circumstances. Something important.

Saint shifts next to me. Heat from his body flows around me, warms my chilled skin. Goosebumps flare on my arms.

Edward turns to Saint, "Do you, Saint Jordan Killian Caldwell take Victoria…" He turns to me.

"Just Victoria," I mumble.

"Take Just Victoria," Edward smiles, "to be your lawfully-wedded wife?"

Behind me, a chuckle runs through the crowd.

This is happening, really happening. I swallow hard. My palms begin to sweat and the bouquet slips from my hands.

Saint swoops down so fast, I blink. He straightens, holding the bouquet, then turns and shoves it at Damian, who takes it from him. He glances past Damian, who's lips curve in a genuine smile.

Saint makes a noise in his throat. A warning? Nah, it can't be. He has no reason to be jealous anyway. When Saint is in the room, everyone else recedes into the background.

"Saint?" Edward prompts.

Saint squares his shoulders. I hear him take in a breath. *Huh. Is he as nervous as I am?* I peek a glance at his profile—patrician nose, square jaw, the hint of a cleft in his chin. His mouth tightens. His jaw tics… He is feeling something, all right. Perhaps this entire situation is as strange for him as it is for me? Of course, he's the one who proposed it, so why does he seem so unsure?

He shuffles his feet and his shoulders flex.

"Saint?" Edward asks, his brow furrowed.

"Ask me again," he growls.

Edward wipes all expression from his face. "Do you, Saint Jordan Killian Caldwell take Victoria to be your lawfully wedded wife, to have and to hold, to cherish and protect, 'til death do you part?"

Saint's throat moves as his swallows. The skin of his knuckles is stretched tight. He's...under pressure, all right. Nervous energy emanates from him. The force of his dominance pins me in place; it's mixed with something else—anger, frustration, the usual edginess, but multiplied.

He rakes his fingers through his hair. It's the first time I've seen Saint uncertain…unsure. My heart twists. A hot sensation stabs at my chest. I reach over and run my finger over the back of his palm.

He stiffens. Then catches my hand, threads his fingers with mine.

A murmur runs through his friends. Edward shoots them a glance. It dies down.

Saint straightens, grips my hand. He stares ahead. "I do." His voice is hard, confident. I swallow. If I closed my eyes and focused on his voice, I'd think he means it. If I bring my attention to where we are joined... Where his hand encloses mine, where he holds my hand firmly, his much bigger palm engulfing mine, I will have no doubt that he means every word of his promise.

I swallow. Heat flushes my skin. The blood thuds at my temples, my pulse pounding. This...this is so right... That surely, it is all wrong. This, whatever is between us, cannot survive. There is no space for it. We are two people colliding at the wrong place, wrong time... Nothing good can come of this... Unless I find a way to make this right. I have to hold on to the time I've been given with him, show him the real me. Love him, open myself up to him, and hope and pray that when I leave, he will not hate me. That he'll realize I had no choice but to do what I did.

I draw in a breath, focus on Edward's words.

"Do you Victoria take Saint Jordan Killian Caldwell, to be your lawfully wedded husband, to have and to hold, in sickness and in health, 'til death do you part?"

"I do." As soon as the words are out of my mouth, I know that I mean it. Something inside of me seems to settle. A calmness washes over me. It's as if my entire life, I've been headed in this direction. Everything I've done and experienced, all of it has brought me here, to stand next to Saint, holding his hand in mine as he turns to face me.

"I suppose it was too much of a rush to get rings so—"

"I have a ring," Saint replies.

"What?" I open and close my mouth.

A murmur runs through the assembled group.

"You do?" Edward frowns, then jerks his chin, "Okay, then."

Saint pats his breast pocket, his forehead crinkling. "Uh, maybe I forgot it..."

"Saint!" Edward admonishes him.

He releases my hand to feel his left pocket. "Oh, shit," he grimaces. "I can't believe I left it behind."

"Come on, Saint," Arpad calls out.

"Get with the program, you tosser," Damian smirks.

"You losing your touch, old sport?" Weston chuckles.

Edward holds his forefinger and thumb to his lips and blows. A piercing whistle echoes through the space.

The group settles.

"Right, now that you grownups, who prefer to behave like children, have settled down..." He trains a stern gaze on Saint. "Stop dicking around, will you?" Edward scolds him.

Laugher breaks out from the crowd.

Saint pats the right-hand pocket of his slacks, pulls out a ring. "Here it is."

He reaches for my left hand, slips it on my ring finger. An emerald, set in a simple platinum setting, gleams in the light from above.

"It belonged to my mother," he says.

I shoot him a surprised glance.

"Don't read anything into it." His features harden, "It happened to be at hand."

Right.

"You may kiss the bride," Edward grins at us.

"No, wait—" I begin to protest, but Saint hauls me close, bends me at the waist, then he kisses me. It's not hard, not punishing, nothing like his previous kisses. He nibbles on my lower lip, and when I open my mouth, he licks his tongue across my upper lip, tracing the curve of my cupid's bow. He wraps one arm around my shoulders, curls the other around my waist. He pulls me so close that his warmth surrounds me, his body shields me, and his shoulder blocks out the sight of everything else. I close my eyes, sink into the warm, trembling, buttery sensations that melt my insides. My toes curl and my scalp tingles. All the pores on my body pop. He tilts his head, deepens the kiss, tangles his tongue with mine. His taste is enticing, with that dark edge that calls to me, pulls me in, tugs me in, shudders down my spine, coils in the pit of my belly, slides warmth between my thighs. Liquid heat bleeds through my veins, turning me into a mass of quivering, burning, aching goo. An aching hollowness that wants, needs, demands— He breaks the kiss.

I open my eyes, gaze into those burning cerulean depths of his. His features wear an expression of shock...surprise...lust... His nostrils flare. His gaze drops to my mouth. "Gigi, I—"

A burst of applause rings out. I shudder. He firms his lips. A nerve throbs at his temple. He straightens, pulling me up with him.

The clapping intensifies.

He smiles down at me. The expression on his face is open, carefree. So damn happy. In that second, he's a man, I'm a woman. We have our lives together in front of us. United. Never alone. I have him. He is mine. For now. For this second. My lips curve. His smile widens, white teeth sparkling against his tanned skin. He winds his arm around my waist, pulls me into his side as he turns.

"Bravo."

"Beautiful."

"Congratulations."

"Well done!"

Confetti rains down on us. I blink, "Oh."

"Surprised?" he whispers.

"I wasn't expecting…" What? Nothing. Anything. I try to find the words to explain, but my brain cells have all turned to mush. "I… I don't know what to say."

"Enjoy it." He brings me in closer, and I can't stop myself from melting into his side. "Today is your day, Gigi."

He flattens his big hand over my hip. His grasp is warm, possessive. When he's like this... I can almost believe he means the tender words he's just said.

"You...you confuse me, Saint." I turn to him. "One moment, you're the most heartless bastard I've ever met... The next..." I shake my head.

"The next?" He prompts.

"You seem human, almost vulnerable." I search his features. "I think you hate yourself for not being able to conceal your feelings from me."

"Do you?" His gaze falters... Those blue eyes lighten, and for an instant I am sure I can see right through that façade he loves to wear like armor.

"You don't fool me," I declare.

"Good." His lips curve in a smile that's genuine, and predatory, and so... Saint. Filled with secrets, as if he senses what I am thinking, as if he knows what I want before I do... As if he can anticipate my every move before I make it.

"That will make the upcoming days more of a challenge."

"What?" I squint up at him.

"Enjoy it, dear wife," his features harden, "for things are about to change."

I stiffen, peer into his face.

He's wearing the same smile... But already, that hint of sensitivity that I'd spotted is gone. He jerks his chin, nods toward his friends, his expression still open, his handsome profile every bit as gorgeous, as genuine as he'd seemed a moment ago. But his eyes... Those blue eyes are dark...almost black. Was everything he'd done today an act? Had he been leading me on? And I'd wanted to believe him. For a few minutes there, I had dared to hope.

His lips curl.

He'd taken me to the edge, pretended to care, then he'd pushed me over and watched me fall.

"You bastard," I try to pull away.

His hand around my waist is solid though. He keeps me pinned to his side. He lowers his chin, nuzzles my temple, "Keep that smile, Gigi. You don't want them to know that something is wrong, do you?"

I swallow.

"Do you, pet?"

"No... No."

"Good." He kisses my temple, his breath hot like a lover's touch, "Store up the happy memories, for soon you'll wish that you never set eyes on me."

"Newsflash, asshole," I keep the smile plastered to my face, "I already wish I'd never met you, that I had never agreed to come to England, that I'd never posed as Adam's wife, that—" I stop to take a breath.

He grins down at me, "Go on, don't let me stop you."

I grit my teeth, hold his burning gaze. How had I thought there was passion in his eyes? It's a need to get even. To get revenge. That's all this is about. Retribution. I am a pawn caught between two opposing forces, and by the time this charade is over, there may be nothing left of me—nothing but this burning need to avenge myself. With Saint. With the Mafia. With Antonio... With everyone who has taken advantage of me. I've had enough of being backed into a corner, of being underestimated. I am going to make sure this brute realizes it too, by the time I am done.

I direct my next words at him with deadly intent, "I wish that I had asked someone else to be my Dom."

His gaze sharpens and his fingers dig into the curve of my hip.

"You dare say that to my face?" His nostrils flare. Color sears his cheeks, and damn it, but my sex clenches instantly. Goosebumps flare on my skin and a shiver runs down my back. This...this is what I want. Saint—angry, blinded with jealousy, coming for me, taking me with no quarter. This language I understand. This passion is what we have in common and I am going to make the most of it.

"Why, worried you won't measure up to Adam Rhodes?'

A vein pops at his temple. "You know how to push me over the edge, don't you?"

"Maybe I should have asked one of your friends." I glance past him to where Damian is watching us. He raises the bouquet of flowers. I smile, shake my head, "Yeah, who better than a rock star god to take my virgin ass?"

"You cunt," he bares his teeth, and a little thrill shudders down my spine. This is it. I've done it now. I've broken through his control. What is he going to do next?

Saint doesn't disappoint.

He bends his knees, peers into my eyes, "I think it's time we consummated this marriage, don't you?"

27

Saint

"Turn around and hug the post."

She tips up her head and glares at me.

I'd rushed her up here to my suite in the penthouse of the hotel, without bothering to say goodbye to my friends. If they thought I was in a hurry to get her alone in a room, well, that's too bad. I don't give a fuck what kind of impression I left behind. All that matters is getting her to obey. To bend her to my will, to lean her over the bed and teach her a lesson. But first— "Do it," I growl from my position near the doorway.

She hesitates, twists her fingers. The emerald of her ring catches the light from above and sparkles. *Fucking hell.* I'd given her the ring that had belonged to my mother. The one she had given to me before she'd left me and my father.

I'd held onto it, the last reminder of the only parent who had loved me. Why had I given it to her? Why had I carried it around with me since I'd met her? Had I subconsciously known that the occasion would present itself, and had wanted to be prepared? No matter. It is done. No going back now. Not that it means anything, of course. An empty gesture. It had been the most convenient solution to send a message to the Mafia that this is serious. They'll believe I've swallowed their bait. They'll see me as a sitting patsy, ready to be reeled in by them. Really, it's a way to lure them into reveal their next hand… Meanwhile I have more pressing matters. Namely, a wife who insists on baiting me, throwing her past in my face, daring me to do the one thing I swore I wouldn't—fuck her like I mean it.

Do I want to go through with it? Am I so taken in by her that I'll throw all caution to the wind and transform this into a real wedding night?

She draws herself up to her full height.

I jerk my chin in the direction of the massive four-poster bed. The best money can buy, of course. I had it flown in from Russia. It belonged to some fucking Czar or the other… The fuck I care? I'd seen it at Christie's and wanted it. The only piece of furniture in the entire suite that I had chosen. All with an eye for my relaxation, of course. I smirk.

The pillars are made of solid oak and wide enough for the purpose I have in mind.

I hadn't meant to sleep with her tonight, but she had eviscerated my carefully calculated control, something she is surprisingly skilled at doing. Too bad. She'll have to cope with the fall-out. She is going to need all that gutsiness she's shown so far to get her through the night.

"Don't keep me waiting," I snarl.

She pales, then marches across the room to the closest post.

"Lean in, Gigi. Wrap your arms around it."

She does.

I approach her and she stiffens.

I press my palm into the small of her back and her entire body trembles. I apply enough pressure for her breasts to flatten against the surface of the post.

"Stay there," I growl.

She stands motionless.

I step toward the walk-in closet, choose a couple of ties, then turn and stalk toward her.

"What are you doing?" She half turns.

"Don't," I command.

She pauses, then faces forward.

I cup the back of her head, turn her face, until her cheek is pressed into the wood.

"Like that. Don't want to hurt you now, do we?"

"You're concerned about me?"

"Only because you're my property. You serve a purpose."

"And what's that?"

"Haven't you figured it out, Gigi?"

I reach over her, twist one tie around her wrists. She stiffens. "Why are you—?"

"No questions," I snap.

She purses her lips together, gazes up at me as I test the knots. Good. There's enough leverage for her to move her wrists, so the blood circulation will not get cut off. At the same time, it's secure enough that she can't escape.

I step back, then twist the other around her eyes. "No, Saint—"

"Any more talking and I'll stuff your panties in your mouth."

She wheezes. "B…but."

"Take what's coming to you. Don't you want to show me how good a submissive you can be?"

"You're supposed to be taking care of my needs, you asshole."

I slap her butt.

"What the fuck—?" she howls.

"Language Gigi."

"What?"

"If you want to curse, I prefer alphahole, I've told you that. I won't repeat myself again. And taking care of your desires is exactly what I'm doing."

"Not," she huffs.

"Don't mock it 'til you try it, darling."

She firms her lips.

I step back, then survey my handiwork. Her back is stiff, her shoulders straight. Good. I want her to fight this. Need her to resist this. Hope she understands that this is the only way. For her? For me? Of course, I am being selfish. I get off on her pain, on how I'll feel when I have her broken and begging and trusting only me to take care of her needs. That there is no going back now. I am her salvation. Her only hope. She has to give up her secrets to me, has to tell me why she is here. That is the only way for me to accept her… And *I want that.* I drag my fingers through my hair. *More than anything else.*

Turning, I march to the desk by the window, rummage around in the drawer, until I find what I am looking for. Clasping the pair of scissors, I walk back to stand behind her.

"Wha…what are you going to do?"

"Shh," I lean forward and lick her lips. "Trust me."

"Why…why are you saying that?" She swallows.

"You'll see." I squat down, then take the scissors to the hem of her dress. I drag the blades upward, cutting through the fabric. I straighten, snipping away at the cloth and it parts all the way to the neckline. A final snip and the dress parts.

"If this is some warped way of punishing me—"

I laugh. "Punishing? I haven't even started, my lovely wife."

She swallows. "Don't…don't call me that."

"Why not?" I switch the scissors to my other hand, then drag my knuckles across her ring.

Her fingers tremble.

"We were just married."

"I was there, you…you brute."

"Finally, your vocabulary is expanding."

I step back, then cut through the sleeves. The dress pools around her feet. Another snip, and her bra drops off. I return the scissors to the drawer, then turn back to her. The long slender column of her back meets the flare of her hips. Her long, toned legs end in those fuck-me stilettos she so favors.

I move closer. "The first time I saw you, I swore I'd have you naked and begging for my touch."

"Fuck you."

"You bet, but first—" I reach down, tear off her panties.

She screams. Her entire body curves. Her butt trembles. Her thigh muscles coil. I kick her legs apart and she wheezes, "Untie me, you scoundrel."

I chuckle, "If those are the extent of your insults, I fear there's much I have to teach you."

"Bastard."

"Technically, I am not. Though my father would have wished otherwise."

"I don't want to hear your sob story."

"But I want your sobs, little Gigi." I drop to my haunches in between her parted thighs, lower my head and swipe my tongue up between her pussy lips.

She cries out.

My breath catches, "Fuck, you're soaking."

"I…it's a mistake."

"Tell that to your body. You want me, Gigi. You know how that makes me feel?"

I wrap my fingers around her thighs, then thrust my tongue inside her soaking channel.

"Oh, my god," she moans.

My dick lengthens. My groin hardens. I tilt my face, then thrust my tongue inside her cunt again and again. I lick up her pussy juice, swipe my tongue all the way up into the valley between her arsecheeks. I curl my tongue inside her puckered hole and she whines. "Oh, Saint, please…"

"Like that, Gigi," I mutter against the most forbidden part of her. "Tell me what you want."

"You…" she gasps. "I want you…"

I rise to my feet, unzip my pants; shove my hand down my boxers and take out my cock. My blood throbs at my temples, in my balls. "Where…" I clear my throat, "where do you want me?"

She bites on her lower lip.

"Where Gigi?"

"I … I.." she stutters.

My vision tunnels. I swipe my throbbing cock across the valley between her arsecheeks. She shudders.

"Do you want me here?"

She nods.

"Say it aloud."

"Take me, Saint. Please."

Thank Fuck. I draw back, then insert my thumb inside her puckered hole. She groans. I ease my finger inside. She bangs her forehead against the pillar. With my remaining fingers I scoop up some more of the moisture from her pussy, then add a finger to my thumb.

"Oh." Her shoulders hunch. "It's… it's…"

What?"

"Different," she huffs.

"No shit." I set my jaw, "I am going to ensure you never forget our first time."

I dip my other palm between her thighs. I cup her pussy, shove three fingers inside her soaking channel, and her entire body bucks. She throws her head back, her hair rippling about her shoulders. "Ohmigod," she gasps. "Saint… I… I…" A trembling sweeps up her legs. Her breathing goes shallow. A whine spills from her lips. "I'm… going to come—" she gasps.

The doorbell sounds and I pull out my fingers.

"No!" Her body jerks as if she's unable to stop herself. She whips her head in my direction. "Don't you dare leave me—"

The bell sounds again.

"Sorry, sweetheart, no choice."

I take a step back, lose my footing and stumble. *Shit*. I'm as off balance as she is. Truth be told… If the doorbell hadn't rung—as I'd planned for it to—I'd have taken her right then, in the arse, then proceeded to tear into her pussy too. Good thing I don't trust myself around her anymore. *Since when have I needed checks and balances around another person, huh?*

Since I met her.

Since she'd flipped the entire situation by proposing the one thing I've wanted more than anything—to take her as mine, to make her submit, to bend her will to mine, have her shatter around me. *Fuck*. I drag my fingers through my hair. Who is breaking whom here? I'm no longer sure.

The bell rings again. She straightens, "Saint...?"

I don't reply. I pivot on my heels, push my dick back into my pants as I walk out of the bedroom, past the living room, and wrench the door open.

A room service attendant straightens. Her face pales. On the cart in front of her is a bottle of Champagne, a bowl of strawberries, and a variety of cheeses and dips.

"Should I wheel this in?" Her voice trembles.

"No," I growl.

"Ah...compliments of the—"

"Leave," I pull the cart into the room.

"The staff and the management wish you—"

"Fuck off—"

"But... Damian wanted me to tell you—"

I glower at her.

She pales, opens her mouth again.

"The fuck?" I jerk my chin over her head. "You tell that motherfucker to stay away from me and my wife and one more thing—"

"Wh...what?"

Sweat beads her upper lip. *Good god, isn't there anyone who can talk to me without looking like they are about to have a coronary? Yeah, that's where the Seven come in.* Fuckers can be counted on taking me down a notch at any time. And her, of course. She can go toe to toe with me. I frown. *How dare she?* She is going to be taught a lesson, all right.

"Uh... Mr. Caldwell," the waitress stutters.

"Make sure I'm not disturbed again."

I slam the door in her ashen face. *Good, no one should be happy today.* This wedding isn't a cause for celebration. It is...a fucking massacre. Mine...and hers. I am sinking into a maelstrom of emotions, caught in a quicksand that threatens to overwhelm me. Soon, I will be in over my head. Only thing? I am taking her down with me.

I shove the cart into the bedroom.

"Saint?" Victoria gasps, "Who...was that?"

"Not your concern."

"Why do you sound angry?" she scowls.

"I'm not angry."

"Are you hungry?"

"Are you?"

"So, you're hungry." She nods.

"I'm not, and I told you to keep your mouth shut, didn't I?"

"Definitely hangry."

"I'm not a fucking child," I scowl.

"You're acting like one." Her lips curve. The glistening flesh calls to me. I could forget all this. I could walk over, kiss her, untie her, throw her on the bed, climb on top of the bed and bury my aching cock inside her soft, gorgeous, heated pussy. I could—

"Saint."

"What?" I growl, shaking my head. *Jesus, being this close to her is doing weird things to my head. Maybe she's right. Maybe I am hungry. Is that why I am feeling lightheaded?*

She shuffles her feet, "Did you order us something to eat."

I sneer, "I ordered something all right."

28

Victoria

He prowls closer, his footsteps muffled by the carpet as he approaches. The creaking of wheels gets louder—he definitely ordered something. That is a food cart, isn't it? The clank of silverware, of plates being moved around, reaches me.

I sense him shift his weight. There's silence then a pop. I jump. "What the—?"

"Relax," he laughs. "Thought the occasion called for some bubbles, don't you think?"

I worry my lower lip. *Should I agree?* I swallow and my throat protests. Cold, bubbly champagne. I hadn't managed to nick a glass at the wedding— at my own wedding. I worry the ring on my left ring finger. The weight is already familiar. *Damn, that's not good. I won't be wearing it for much longer, after all.*

The sound of liquid hitting a glass reaches me. My tongue swells. I lick my lips.

"Want a sip, darlin'?"

It's fine. It won't hurt. Besides I could do with some Dutch courage about now. "Yes, please."

"You're forgetting something."

Am I? What… Oh! "Yes, please, Sir!"

"That's my girl."

I flush. *Shit, why does that make me so happy? I'm not going to pander to the ego of this over-the-top, tyrannical, motherfucker of a guy who is…my husband. Bloody hell.* "Can I get that champagne?" I whisper.

"Of course."

His footsteps grow closer. Something cool touches my lips. The cold liquid fills my mouth. Bubbles break on my tongue. *Yum.* I swallow it down, open my mouth again. More of the bubbles flow in, overflow my chin. Coldness hits my chest.

"Oops."

More liquid slides down my skin. I shiver.

"Sorry, babe."

"No, you're not." I lick the remaining liquid from my lower lip.

"Do that again and I won't be responsible for what happens next."

"Oh," I swallow.

"Not that either," he groans. "When you form your mouth into that shape, all I can think of is having it wrapped around my cock."

Wetness pools between my legs...and it's not from the champagne. My nipples pebble and my sex clenches. I chafe my thighs, try to hold in the ache. *Shit, this is crazy.* Perhaps it's the forced not-being-able-to-climax thing that has me wound so tightly. I am on the edge of the precipice. One more touch, one more caress of those fingers in the most intimate of my places, one more kiss, one more nip on my clit, a tug on my nipples and I'll shatter.

"Saint," I whine.

"I know."

A wetness curls around my nipple. I gasp, "What are you doing?"

"What does it feel like?" He licks the cold champagne off the curve of my breast.

I whimper.

He swipes his way down the underside of my breast. His large palms descend on either side of my hips. He holds me down as I mentally follow the progress of his tongue, down my belly, to my navel. He dips his tongue inside my belly button. My pussy seems to fold in on itself.

"Damn you," I huff.

He nips on the sensitive skin above my pussy. I jump.

"You're forgetting something again, babe."

Right.

He presses a kiss to the top of my aching, throbbing, trembling core.

"Say it. Go on."

"Damn you, *Sir,*" I snarl.

"Good girl." He drags his chin across my clit. I shudder. *Omigod.* That was… That is… Oh! He rubs his whiskered skin straight down my lower lips. My thighs spasm and my scalp tingles. Goosebumps pop across my skin. "Please, Saint."

"You've got a choice now."

"I do?"

I sense him nod against my core. "You answer my questions correctly and I'll let you come. Get them wrong and… Well… You'll have to find out what happens then." He nips on my clit, I moan. *Hell, this… This is torture. This is heaven.* This, with his face between my thighs as he presses a soft kiss to my dripping cunt. As he licks up my cum from the inside of my thigh, then straightens to press his lips to mine. "Open."

I oblige, and he slides his tongue inside my mouth. The taste of me, of him, of the lingering tang of the champagne, goes straight to my head.

When he tears his mouth from mine, I sway toward him, seeking more, wanting more.

"Saint," I huff, "Please, Sir, please."

He laughs. "Do you hear yourself, little Gigi? You're too greedy."

"I'm not."

"Yep, you are." The heat of his body recedes and a cry escapes my lips. I strain against my restrains. Reach out with my leg, feeling for him, searching for him.

"Now. Now." He clicks his tongue. "I promised to take care of you, didn't I?"

I nod.

"I'll give you what you're aching for, but first you need to answer a few questions."

"What the fuck, Saint?" I cry out. "Another bloody riddle?"

"You know I can't live without them."

"I thought you weren't dependent on anything or anyone," I pout.

"Indulge me on this one."

"Like I have a choice?" I toss my head.

"You do. Of course, you do."

Not. He knows it. I know it. So why the bloody hell is he pretending otherwise?

"Ask your stupid questions," I mumble.

"You hungry?"

"Is that the question?"

"Yes."

I pause, tilt my head. "Is this a trick? So help me, Saint, if it is—"

He pops a cracker, topped with something savory, into my mouth. I crunch down. Flavors explode on my tongue. *Yum.* I crunch down the food. Then open my lips. "More."

"First tell me what that was."

"That's what you want to know?"

I sense him nod.

Silence stretches. I run my tongue over my teeth, suck down the taste, "That was…hummus?"

"Well done, Gigi."

His footsteps thump on the carpet. Then another cracker is placed on my tongue. This one is slathered with something pungent, sharp, salty. The taste overwhelms me. I gulp it down, then scrunch up my face, "Ugh…" I grimace. "Was that…blue cheese?"

"You didn't like it?"

"I hate aged cheese. It tastes like old shoe."

"You've tasted old shoe?" I hear the smirk in his voice.

"It smells like old socks. They're similar in taste, right?"

"Don't know," he chuckles. "I've never tasted it myself. Open," he commands.

I part my lips and he places another cracker in my mouth. "And this?"

Complex textures—buttery, soft, creamy… I crunch down on the cracker and fresh taste envelops my taste buds. I swallow, smack my lips. "Burrata," I exclaim.

"You weren't kidding. You do prefer fresh cheeses, hmm?"

"I never lie when food is concerned," I sniff.

"No, only when it's real life."

My shoulders droop; my face heats. "Damn you, Saint."

"Yeah."

There's silence a beat, then another. I can't hear him. *Where is he? What is he doing?*

Something brushes against my lips; I open my mouth again, crunch down on what I assume is a cracker. Fire erupts on my tongue. "What the—?" I splutter. My eyes water. My mouth feels like it's been doused in flames.

"Here."

The cool edge of glass is placed against my mouth. He holds the back of my head in place. "Drink up."

I hesitate.

"It's water, Gigi. I am not completely insensitive."

Right. I chug down the icy liquid and the edge of the searing pain recedes.

"What was that?" I gasp.

"You tell me."

I shake my head, "I barely tasted the food, you jerk."

He chuckles. "Go on, bet you can take a guess."

I set my jaw.

He caresses my pussy, which instantly clenches. *Hell, what am I doing?* I hate him, yet I need him. I can't stop my body from leaning into his touch. Push my pelvis forward, so more of his skin connects with mine. *Bloody. Hell.* "Why are you doing this?" I snarl. "Why can't you simply fuck me and be done with it."

He leans in close enough for his nose to bump mine. "Because that's not what you want."

"And you know what I want?"

I sense him nod. "Of course. Why do you think I accepted your offer?"

"Because you want to humiliate me?"

"You mistake my intent." He clicks his tongue, "This was so you could find out more about your tastes."

"That's what you think this is?" I scoff. "You having my best interests at heart?"

"Not really." He pauses. "I'm using you to get back at the men who changed my life and those of the Seven."

"Has it occurred to you that they're using me too?"

Silence.

"What…what did they do to you Saint?"

He stiffens. Anger radiates off of him. I flinch.

What the hell am I doing? Why did I ask him that? Is it because my eyes are bound? Is it because I can't see him, that I am so tuned into him that I can discern the imperceptible edge of fear—helplessness even—that bleeds from him? Nah, that's my imagination. There is not an ounce of weakness about this man. Not only am I unable to see, but my remaining senses have been fooled by him as well.

"It's fine," I swallow. "Don't tell me. I don't want to know."

"You giving up so easily?" His hard voice whips through my head.

I straighten. "Giving up?" I allow a smile to curve my lips. "I haven't made it this far by losing hope. It's the only thing I have to cling to." *And you? What about you? Why do I want to lean on you?* What insanity is this, that even bound and blindfolded, knowing he can do anything to me, I trust him…to play with my body any which way he wants?

That's all this is—a carnal need for him to possess me, break me, show me how it can be between a woman and a man. So what, if there aren't any emotions involved? It'll make it easier for me to lure him to whatever… Whatever it is that the Mafia has planned for him. I don't care what happens after that. I don't. As long as they free my friend. That's all this is about. It doesn't matter that my heart will be shattered by the end. I'll find a way to go on. I always do. I tip up my chin, "Chili pepper."

"What?" He sounds surprised.

"That was a five-spice sauce."

"You're right."

He pauses, then tears the blindfold from my eyes. I blink. His face comes into focus. "So…you'll untie me now?"

He scratches his chin.

I frown. "The deal was, if I got the answers right you would—"

"I would…?"

An understanding sinks into my mind. "You… You…"

"I'll…?" he prompts.

"You'll let me come?" I train my gaze on his face. *Please. Please say, yes. Please.*

He shakes his head.

I stare.

"I changed my mind," he smirks.

"What?" That familiar anger thrums up my spine. My blood thuds at my temples and my heartbeat ratchets up.

He steps to the cart, scoops up some of that last spicy dip onto his cracker, then pops it in his mouth. Color sears his cheeks, then he reaches for more of the Champagne and washes it down. "Whew, you weren't kidding there. It is hot."

"You…you horrible man."

He chuckles.

"You can't do this to me."

He cuts off a slice of cheese—not the blue cheese, something else that looks like cheddar?—and bites into it. His jaws move. He tips the bottle of Champagne up, then chugs down more liquid. The strong column of his throat flexes as he swallows it down. *Why the hell does he have to look sexy, doing something as simple as eating?* He reaches for a strawberry, is about to pop it into his mouth then stops.

"Do you like strawberries, Gigi?"

"What?"

He frowns, "Answer the question."

Class-A wanker. That's what he is. A douchebag of the first order. A bloody, horrendous brute of a man who...hides a hurt that is eating away at him from the inside. I blink. *Shit, I don't need flashes of insight about his character... That will only elicit empathy for him. Am I looking for a spark of redemption in this guy? No, that would only make what I have to do to him so much worse.*

I purse my lips and he scowls, "Yes or No?"

Shit, nothing is simple with this guy, is it? He is so...so...complicated.

He glares at me and I shiver. My scalp tingles and my toes curl. *Oh, shit, this...is not going to end well. Not at all.* "Yes," I croak. "I... I love strawberries."

"So do I." His eyes twinkle , "Especially when they're soaked in your cum." He steps around, then drops to his knees between my still-parted legs.

29

Saint

I press the fruit into the opening of her pussy. She inhales. I drag the strawberry up her dripping cunt, then bring it to my mouth. I bite into the fruit and the tart, tangy, fruity taste bursts on my tongue. Laced with it, is the sugary sweet taste of her cum. My dick tents my pants and my vision tunnels. *Fuck. I need more.* Much more. More of this, more of her essence. I swallow the rest of the fruit, toss away the stem, then reach for another strawberry. They are now my favorite fruit ever. I fit the fruit in the opening of her channel. Her entire body shudders. "Saint," she breathes.

Yeah, I know exactly how she's feeling.

I scoop up more of her juices, bite off the entire fruit. The tastes fill my senses, go to my head. The world tilts. *Fuck. What is she doing to me?* Dropping the stem, I snatch up another of the berries. I slide it into her wet pussy.

She groans.

"How does it feel?" my voice cracks. I swallow. *Shit, this entire expe-*

rience is getting to me. I set out to show her I could have my way with her; turns out, I am the one at her mercy. Starved for her taste, addicted to her scent. Needing to wallow in her gorgeous essence, mark her with my cum. Stake my claim on her before this—whatever it is between us— comes to an end.

"Tell me, Gigi." I press the berry deeper into her sweet cunt.

"It… it," her voice shakes, "It makes me want more. So much more. I want to taste it." She gulps, "Please… Sir."

Her words sink into my blood, race straight to my belly and coil in my gut. *Fuck this.* I slip the strawberry out, then rise up to my feet and offer it to her, "Eat it."

She takes a bite, chews and swallows. Her gaze grows heavy. Her cheeks flush.

"Well?" I frown. "How does it taste?"

"Sexy." Her blush deepens. "I mean…it…tastes like nothing I've ever eaten before."

I crunch on the rest of the fruit, toss away the stem. "Want more?"

She nods.

I scoop up another. Reaching between us, I roll the fruit in the cum that trails down her inner thigh. I bite on it, offer her the rest. Take another strawberry, stroke it up her pussy.

Her legs buckle. I grip her shoulder to support her. Offer the fruit to her, then eat the rest. I repeat it with another berry, then another. My breathing deepens and sweat beads my spine. My mouth waters; my dick lengthens. I reach for the next berry, but when I press it to her cunt, she groans, "I can't… I want..." She arches her spine, pushes the back of her head into my chest.

She parts her lips and I pop the strawberry in. She tears off half of it. I bite down on the other half, chew and swallow, then go in for seconds. I press my lips to hers, lick up the tangy taste of the berry, the sweetness of her mouth, the complex notes of her cum. My dick throbs and a pulse beats to life on my eyelids, at my temples, even in my fucking balls. I toe off my shoes, then reach down, shove down my zipper, then my pants and my briefs; kick them aside. I grab my dick, position it between her arsecheeks. The head of my weeping cock, nudges against her back hole.

I bring my fingers around to the front, slip them inside her cunt. Her pussy clamps down on me. I groan, "Fuck, you're so ready for me. Can you feel that?"

"Saint." She turns her head, licks the side of my jaw. Another ripple of pleasure tears down my spine. A pressure builds in my groin. I push forward, until my dick is inside her puckered hole. A whine slips from her lips. "It's too much," she gasps.

"Not enough." I bring my other hand around, insert my thumb into her mouth. She bites down on my digit, and I feel the pull all the way down to my shaft.

"Gigi, fuck," I groan, "I need to be inside of you."

"Then do it." She nuzzles my cheek. "Take me. Come inside me."

"What?"

"Do it the right way," she whispers.

"It has to be this way." I growl.

"It doesn't have to be like this," she pleads.

"You worried that it will hurt?" My thighs spasm and my cock lengthens inside of her.

She gasps, a bead of sweat running down her temple, "Not me, but I think you're not ready to face whatever is between us."

I frown. "And what's that, exactly?"

"You pretend not to feel anything, but the fact is..." she peers up at me from under her sooty eyelashes, "...fact is that you sense the connection, how attracted you are to me, and it worries you."

"Me?" I snort. "Sweetheart, the only thing you should be worried about is how much of me you can take inside of you." I angle my hips and my shaft slips in through her tight ring.

She gasps. A growl rips from me. I grit my teeth, stay where I am. *Stay. Stay.* I set my jaw so hard, pain shoots up my face. "Fuck," I snarl. "You're fucking beautiful."

"And you're a fucking coward."

The drumming at my temple intensifies. A tightness pushes down on my ribcage. Sweat pours down my spine until my shirt sticks to my back. Fucking with her is primal, angry, visceral...a messy coalescence of our combined body fluids, of lust and caution, a need to subdue and suppress, a primal urge to own, to mate. To push myself and her to the edge where nothing else remains. Not our pasts, not her betrayal, not the way I have to use her for my own selfish ends. Not the sensual way she rubs against me, the curve of her hips pressed into the hard bones of my pelvis. Not how she strains against her restraints, her face buried into my neck as she licks the sweat that clings to my skin, as I pull out of her so suddenly that she whines.

"Fuck me, Saint, please."

"I am going to slap your pussy until you cry, spank your arse so my fingerprints are etched into your memory, choke you while you suck on my dick." I search her features, "Do you want that?"

She nods.

"I'll plug your mouth with my tongue, as my fingers cram your spasming back hole, and crush you under the weight of my intention. Then I'll screw you until you scream my name and ask me to let you come, and even then, I will not. Not until every part of you has been stamped with my essence, my name written on every cell of your body... until your breath is mine, your heartbeat mirroring my urgency as I thrust into you again and again... Until you beg for release."

Her breath hitches.

"And even then, I won't let you come... You willing to play this game with me, Gigi?

She nods

"Good girl."

Reaching up, I untie her restraints. She pulls back her arms. I flip her around, hook my hands under her thighs, lift her up and into the pillar. She winds her long legs around my waist

I bend my knees, peer into her eyes. "You sure?" I growl.

"You having second thoughts?" she huffs.

I twist my lips, "You on birth control?"

"You think I'm lying?"

She meets my gaze, green eyes clear, the smooth, unfurled calm of the surface of a lake, just before I dive into the depths. Cool, peaceful, everything I've searched for. Every damn slice of heaven I've wanted. I am going to hell, and I am taking her with me.

Her pupils dilate until the black seems to bleed out, leaving only a circle of green at the edges.

"I dare you." She smiles, a beautiful curve of her lips that punches me straight in the gut.

"Fuck you, Gigi."

I piston my hips forward and drive inside her.

She screams, "No, no, no," and throws her head back against the pillar.

"What the actual fuck?" I look down to where we are connected.

Her pussy clenches down on my cock, even as she digs her fingernails into my shoulders. *It can't be. Can it?* The world ebbs and flows around me. My leg muscles spasm and my fingers grow numb. I glare at her face, "Tell me it's not fucking true, Victoria."

"I am...was a virgin," She swallows, her face pale, then tips up her chin. "So what? It was an inconvenience."

"You used me?" I begin to pull out.

She snarls, buries her heels into the backs of my hips. "Don't you dare!" she cries out.

"Don't tell me what to do," I glare at her.

She throws her arms around my shoulders, leans in close. "You're a coward," she whispers in my ears.

"It won't work," I laugh. "You're trying to goad me on, hoping to make me lose control, I—

She bites the side of my neck. Buries her teeth until she breaks skin. Goosebumps pop on my skin. The pain thrums across my nerve endings and my cock hardens even further inside her. "Jesus," I swear. "You're a hellion."

She pulls back, a drop of blood—my blood—glistening on her lips.

"And it turns you on." Her eyes gleam.

I snarl, grip her thighs so hard that she winces. But she doesn't back down. I'm marking her. She'll have marks where I held her—so? This is what I set out to do, didn't I? Claim her?

"Damn right, it does. You're going to regret this." I draw in a sharp breath, and the scent of her arousal—hot, pungent, with the lingering scent of strawberries, blurring with the faint hint of copper—fuck—it crowds in on me, pushes down on my chest. Shoves at me, urges me on... Further, further. "Fuck you, Gigi; and fuck me." Oh, wait. I'd been fucked since the day the Seven and I had had our lives irreversibly changed by the incident.

I plunge into her with such force, my balls slap against her skin. Lower my head kiss her. The taste of copper, mixed with strawberries and her inherent sweetness—all of it goes to my head. I pull back, then push into her, burying myself inside her to the hilt, impaling her with such force that the entire bed shakes. The headboard thuds against the wall; a crash sounds somewhere in the distance. *Fuck that.* A grown boils up her throat. I swallow it, then I begin to fuck her in earnest. I thrust into her again and again. Angle my hips, propel forward. I push into her. I want to tear into her pussy, mark her as mine. *Mine.* The word echoes in my ears, thrums in my veins. I tear my mouth from hers, peer into her face.

"Look at me," I snarl.

Her eyelids flutter.

I click my tongue, "Eyes on me, Gigi."

She snaps her eyelids open. Her gaze locks with mine—pupils blown, the darkness so wide, it overwhelms her eyes. I see myself in them—a frenzied, pushed-to-the-edge, out-of-control male whose only goal in life is to fuck this woman. To make her come. To ensure that her first time is so fucking mind-blowing, that she'll never glance at another man again.

"You're mine, Victoria."

Her breath hitches.

"Mine! You feel me?"

She nods

"Say it."

"I am yours."

"To take and to pleasure…"

She swallows.

"Repeat after me," I growl.

"To take and to pleasure." Her chin wobbles.

"To use…"

"To use."

"To rip apart."

She hiccups.

I glare at her.

She pales. "To rip apart." Her lips glisten.

"To piece back together." I scan her features.

A tear slides down her cheek, I lick it up. "Don't stop, Gigi."

"To piece back together," she whispers.

I lower my forehead to hers, "So help me, God."

"So help me…"

I thrust forward and she screams, "God!"

I close my mouth over hers, absorb the sound. I fuck her, with more intensity than I've done anything else before in my life. I pull her close enough that her breasts are flattened against my chest, her nipples hard enough to imprint themselves into my skin.

My balls draw up; the pressure builds at the base of my spine.

I pull back, gaze into her eyes. "Come for me, Gigi," I growl.

Her body bucks, her eyes roll back in her head, her spine arches, the trembling sweeps up her legs, her breasts thrust up, and her mouth opens. She shatters, and so do I. I come, shooting hot gusts of cum inside of her, watching her, matching her, taking her with me, over the edge. Sparks of white flash behind my eyes. My knees seem to buckle under me. I stagger back, still inside of her, holding her to me. Make it around to the bed and sink down on my back, pulling her to me.

Tension drains from my limbs. I cuddle her and she turns her head into my chest. I tuck her head under my chin. Her muscles twitch, her breathing evens out.

I let sleep pull me under, making sure to keep her plastered to me.

The images swamp me. I know I'm dreaming but I can't stop myself.

"Don't go, Mom."

My mother grips my arms, " I wanted to stay for you, but I can't. I can't do this, Saint. I'm sorry."

"So that's it?" Anger suffuses my chest, " You're leaving?" I take a step forward. At thirteen I already tower over her.

Her lips firm. "I tried, Saint, I really did. But it's too hard. You know what they say about ensuring you have your oxygen mask on before you fit it over your child, during turbulence on a flight—?

"What's that got to do with anything?"

"This is my version of it, Saint." Her lips twist "I need to breathe. I need to make sure I survive, else I'll be of no use to anyone else."

She turns away, wheels her suitcase along as she heads for the door.

"Jasmine," my father calls after her, "if you leave, you'll never get another penny from me."

She pauses at the door. "You think I married you for your money, William? You are wrong. All I wanted was you, a home for us that I could fill with love. But that wasn't enough for you. You wanted more power, more money…more everything. It's why your son was kidnapped, and even then, you didn't have the time to negotiate for his release."

"I paid up, didn't I?"

She whirls around. "Open your eyes, William. Money doesn't buy everything."

My father prowls forward. "It bought his freedom," he nods at me.

"At what cost?" She asks.

"He's free, isn't he?" my father huffs.

"Is he?" Her eyebrows knit. "Look around yourself, William, you've created a space which suffocates me."

"And whose fault is that?" My father prowls forward. "You couldn't cope with the fallout of his kidnapping. You couldn't be strong enough for him. Don't push your shortcomings on me, woman."

"Oh, so you want to talk about my shortcomings, do you?" The skin around my mother's lips whitens. "And you think you're perfect, you—"

"Stop!" I bunch my fists at my side, "Both of you, shut up."

Silence, a beat. My mother flips her hair over her shoulder. "This is why I need to leave." She waves a hand in the air. "If I stay, it's only going to get worse, and that's not helping any of us."

Her fingers tighten on her suitcase. "I'm sorry, Killian. I truly am. But you are strong, you'll get through this."

I won't.

I love you, Ma. Please, don't leave me, is what I want to say. Instead I press my lips together, force myself to swallow the scream that bubbles up inside. My throat hurts, my head feels like it's going to burst. What's wrong with me? Couples divorced all the time, and it happens to be my turn to face the shitstorm. Big fucking deal.

So why the hell do I want to bawl my eyes out right now?

"Let her go." My father prowls forward.

I glare at him, "You could at least pretend to care."

"It's no use." He drags his fingers through his hair. "People fall out of love, Saint."

The band around my chest tightens. "That's a bloody lousy excuse and you know that."

My ma wipes the tear that's rolled down my cheek. "You're hurting, Saint, but this too shall pass."

"What-fucking-ever," I growl.

She frowns at me. *Sure, rebuke me for my bad language. Like you actually care.* If she did, she'd stay, wouldn't she? I fold my arms over my chest.

She scrutinizes my features.

"What gets broken without being held?" she asks.

What's the answer? What is it? I cast around in my mind...come up blank.

"Well?" She tilts her head.

My heart begins to race. "I... I don't know." I force the words out. Sweat beads my palm.

"A promise." Her lips twist. "Imagine you are in a dark room. How do you get out?" Her chin wobbles.

I swallow, my fingers tremble and I shove them into the pockets of my pants, "I...I don't know the answer to that either."

"Stop imagining." She draws in a breath, "You get to imagine your life anyway you want it to be, so stop imagining what you don't want. Get out of the dark room. Face your fears. You, and only you, have the power to save yourself. Remember that, Saint."

She grimaces, then pulls off her ring, hands it over to me.

I stare at it. *The fuck am I going to do with that?*

She grabs my hand, pries open my fingers and closes them around her ring. "This is for you, Saint."

She brushes past me, down the steps.

My father draws abreast. He places his hand on my shoulder; I shake it off.

"She knew what she was getting into when she married me." His voice is hard, "She knew my business would always come first. She wanted more, and that wasn't part of our bargain."

He meets my gaze, unflinching. His blue eyes, so like mine, are cold. Calculating. A shiver runs down my spine.

"So this was all a...transaction?"

"You could call it that." His jaw hardens.

"And what about me?" My heart begins to thud.

His expressions forms into a mask. "You were a mistake."

"A mistake; it's all a mistake." I snap open my eyes. It's that same familiar nightmare that has haunted me for so long. Why has it surfaced now? I glance around the room; it's empty.

30

Victoria

"Fuck, fuck, fuck."

I hunch into the corner of the shower stall. What did I do? Why did I do it? I'd taunted him, until he'd lost control. Oh, he'd called me out on that, all right. He'd known I was manipulating him. Well, to the extent that someone like Saint could be, that is. He hadn't reached his level of success without learning how to manage his impulses, how to gauge his opponents and move in for the kill when they least expected it.

Bet he hadn't been expecting the surprise I'd pulled on him.

My sobs well up, the tears flowing down my cheeks. I pull my knees into my naked body as the water pours over me. My hair sticks to my face, my shoulders. I fold my arms over my knees, drop my head onto them, and allow myself to cry. *Shit. Why am I falling apart now? Why are my arms and legs shaking?* Goosebumps flare on my skin. My heart slams against my ribcage. A ball of emotion chokes my throat. I try to breathe, but my lungs burn. *The hell is happening? Am I having a nervous breakdown? And about what? Finally losing my virginity?* It's not a big thing… Not a milestone. *Why had it even hurt?* Hadn't I read somewhere that the hymen has been bred out of us?

It was stupid of me to have held onto it so far. Not that I had tried too hard to lose it. I had been too busy working toward a scholarship, and in university I'd focused on my studies. Been too much of a bookworm, and far happier to spend my time with fictional characters than in the real world. If it hadn't been for Nina, her… I'd have never seen much outside of the class room, either.

I hope she's okay. She has to be… It's the only thing that makes all this worthwhile… Except, when he'd taken me with that ferocity, it had completely floored me.

When he'd stared into my eyes and made me repeat those words… My sobs intensify. It had felt… Real. Like I was truly wedded to him, joined to him. He'd marked me, the asshole. He'd fucked me with a determination that had cast aside everything else that had happened in my life. It felt like I was starting with a fresh slate…

I left Victoria behind. All that remains is Gigi. *His Gigi. Hell, this is insane.* The thoughts whirl around in my head and my arms and legs seem to go numb. *What is wrong with me? I have to get out of here. Away from him.* Before he realizes the extent to which he's already imprinted on my cells. I draw in a ragged breath, then lurch up to my feet. My legs prickle with pins and needles, then crumple. The ground comes up to meet me. *Shit!* I brace for impact, and hit something hard… solid…warm…vertical.

"Victoria."

His voice curls around me. His grip on my shoulders is reassuring, familiar… His slippery skin under my cheek…too inviting. I can't afford to be drawn to him, can't have him finding out what I am going to do to him. Can't allow him to realize how our entire encounter has affected me. I shove at his shoulders, "Let me go."

"Not a chance."

He wraps his big arms around me, pulls me into him. One big palm rubs across my back. "Cry as much as you want. I won't judge."

His voice is soft…so unlike how he's ever spoken to me before. A fresh burst of sobs wells up. *Shit, it's like everything pent-up inside of me has been building up, waiting until I couldn't hold it in anymore.* A spark to dry wood and it had flared out of control. The tears don't seem to stop. My cheeks heat, my eyes burn, and I try to pull away from him. He cups the back of my head, presses my face into his shoulder. Then he sinks down onto the bench in the shower stall and pulls me onto his lap, the water flowing over both of us.

Damn it, I don't want to lose it like this with him. It's exactly the kind of weakness he'll exploit to his advantage. I try to speak and hiccup instead. Try to pull away again. He tightens his grip even further.

He cuddles me close enough for his shoulders to block out most of the water. A safe haven in the center of a storm. A shield against the worst that life had thrown at me. *Why do I want to believe that he can protect me from what is to come? Why do I want to sink into him, forget about everything that has happened to me and conspired to bring me here, in this shower, in his hotel suite, wrapped around him, crying my eyes out?* It makes me sob harder…as if that were possible.

He holds me tightly. Vibrations rumble up his massive chest. I press my ear closer against his ribcage. I sense him move, rock me to and fro. I listen to the purr that thrums up his throat—a low humming, subvocal I recognize. I pick up the notes of a tune that had wafted up the stairs when my mother had played it at night, in our home in LA. I had often fallen asleep to it.

Now I focus on the words of *Hey Jude,* tune into it, use the familiar melody to ground me. I swallow down my tears. He continues to rock me, singing the words under his breath.

"This is getting to be a habit," my voice cracks. I swallow, "You singing to me."

I sense his lips curve against my hair.

"You seriously do suck at it though," I mumble.

He chuckles. "Should I stop?"

I shake my head, nuzzle into his chest, "It's curiously loveable…" I hesitate, "or maybe I should say loveably curious."

"That's a first," he laughs. "No one's ever called me either one of those. But then I've never acted so out of character as when I am with you."

Wait, what? Every time I want to hate him, he has to go and do something which destroys that resting dick face persona he's cultivated.

He runs his fingers down my arm. Goosebumps flare on my skin and I shiver.

"You're cold." He shifts his weight under me, and I shake my head. "Don't go."

"I wasn't..." he hesitates. "I was going to run you a bath."

"A bath?" I swallow to clear the scratchiness in my throat.

"Thought that would help ease the soreness."

"Soreness?" *Oh, he means…. Right.* My cheeks heat, which is stupid, considering everything he's done to my body already. I've never felt this naked, and not just in the physical sense.

I bury my face deeper into his chest.

He chuckles, "Don't go all shy on me now."

I shake my head. I will not speak. If I do, it will only reveal how, embarrassed I am by my outburst. He rises to his feet, steps out of the shower stall, and walks over to the sunken bath tub. He lowers me to the edge of the tub, keeps a hold of me. Then bends down to open the faucets. Water pours into the tub and steam rises, warm against my back. He wraps my arms around his waist and his thick dick nudges against my neck. If I turn my head, I can open my mouth and take him in, and— He cups my cheek, "There's time for that later."

Jesus. What? He can read my mind now? Heat flushes my cheeks again. This is not me...really—blushing, crying, collapsing at his feet like a complete idiot. *God! The hell is wrong with me?* I tip my chin up, "Don't think that you have broken me."

His lips curve, "Oh! Trust me, you will, and when you do." He kisses my forehead, "I'm going to enjoy building you up again."

I swallow. The warmth in his gaze, OMG... my heart stutters, my core pulses. All the pores on my skin seem to pop.

He whispers his knuckles across my jawline, "You're one heck of a woman. Has anyone told you that, Gigi?"

I flush even more. My cheeks must be scarlet by now. He has a habit of reducing me to a puddle of gooiness, a trembling mess who has no idea whether she is coming or going, or what the hell her life is all about. Before I met him, it had been easy. I mean, besides losing my best friend to the Mafia.

I had set out to save my friend and had landed directly in his grasp; one I am in no hurry to evade. Not yet. Just for a few hours, a few days, can't I pretend that all this is real? The way he regards me with tenderness in his eyes, how he scans my features as if to make sure that I am okay. How he rubs his thumb across my lower lip, then bends to kiss me. A brush of his lips—soft, barely there, a feather-light whisper of emotion that dances over my skin, sinks into my blood, warms the space around my heart, melting the barriers I'd built up against him, against the world, against anything that could hurt me. "Saint... I need to tell you something."

"Shh!" He deepens the kiss. Nips on my lower lip, swipes his tongue across my mouth with such intensity that I melt... I ooze into a puddle at his feet.

He leans back and I sway toward him.

"Later," he chuckles. Then leans past me to empty a bottle of something into the tub. The scent of roses, lavender, and something spicy fills the air. I sniff it.

"That's a very feminine bath product you have there."

"It's for you."

"Oh?" I squint up at him. "Were you that sure that I'd end up here in your suite?'

He hesitates, then reaches for my left hand. He twines his fingers with mine, rubs his thumb across the wedding ring...*my* wedding ring, the one he gave me. Which belonged to his mother. My heart stutters. A warmth coils against my rib cage. The pressure builds again behind my eyes and I sniffle.

"Hey." He places his other knuckle under my chin. "Waterworks again?"

"No one's more surprised about this than me." I swallow down the lump that crowds my throat. "I've never once, not in the past many years, broken down like this."

Silence descends. I glance up, survey his features. His face is expressionless.

"You don't believe me?" I wipe the back of my hand over my nose.

"Oh, but I do." He frowns. "You have a strong will behind that fragile exterior. It's what attracted me to you from the beginning."

"Because I was a challenge?"

"Not only." He scans my flushed face, my hard nipples, down to the triangle between my legs. "You were a riddle I wanted to solve. Tough, yet hurting; sensitive, yet so prickly. Soft skin that hides a myriad of conflicting emotions." He places his hand over my heart. "That push-pull inside of you, Gigi, it's a fucking potent force. It makes me want to pull you apart, piece by fucking piece to find out everything about you… Taking my time over it as I tease multiple orgasms out of you, and have you trembling, shivering, pleading with me to stop, and even then I won't…not until you forget about everything except us; except for the lust that strums between us, the sensations that spark between us when we are together, the pull that ties us when we are apart— when—"

I place my hand on his mouth. "Stop," I whisper, "I can't…take more of this; it's…too soon, Saint."

He takes in my features, peers into my eyes, then nods.

"Later, then." He lowers his head and brushes his lips over my fore-head. "For now, let's enjoy our bath, shall we?"

He holds out his hand, so gentlemanly, the gesture so different from how he's acted so far with me that I blink. And, hold on, had he kissed me earlier, on my forehead? A peck, with something resembling affec-tion? My head spins. I grab at his hip.

"You okay?" He scoops me up in his arms again, bridal style. "Gigi?"

I blink, stare as his features fade in and out in front of my eyes.

"Victoria." His voice snaps through my head.

I jerk my chin. "I… I'm a little befuddled."

"Tell me about it," he chuckles. "It's not like me, to fall asleep so soon after making love."

"What do you mean?" I squeeze my eyebrows together.

He steps into the bath tub—still wearing his socks, huh?—then lowers himself into the massive tub that's big enough for five people. He settles me on his chest.

"I hadn't intended to black out that quickly after our love-making."

"That…" I stab a finger in his direction. "Why do you insist on using that phrase?"

"Which one."

"Don't pretend."

"No, really." He scoops up some water, pours it over my shoulders. "Please do clarify what seems so wrong with what I said."

"You said love-making, not fucking, or shagging, or screwing or any of the other ways you could have expressed yourself.

He raises his shoulders and lets them drop. "Semantics, my lovely girl." He pours out some shampoo and proceeds to work it through my tresses, "If you prefer it though, I could say fucking."

My belly flips-flops.

"Or shagging."

I wriggle my hips.

"Or screwing," his voice lowers to a hush.

My nerve endings spark. My sex clenches, the emptiness inside of me yawning, stretching and coming back to life. *Why is it that the filthiest words from his mouth turn into weapons of seduction? Why does it sound so damn hot coming from him?* On the other hand, it is a relief. This alphaholish behavior? That's the side of Saint that is familiar, the one I can handle.

"Not fair," I huff. "With that voice of yours, you could literally talk me into an orgasm."

His eyes gleam.

I wave my hand in the air, "Can't believe I said that. Like your ego needs any more stroking."

He pushes up his pelvis and his dick throbs against my hip.

"That's not what needs stroking."

"Oh, my God!" I push up, or try to—for he simply wraps his large arms around my waist, and holds me in place.

"Where do you think you're you going?"

"To get dressed."

"Not happening."

"Why…?"

"Why not?"

"I… I need some space."

"Not happening either."

I exhale a breath, then turn to scowl at him, "Saint, really, you are a confusing man. Has anyone told you that?"

"Me?" He leans back against the bath tub. His biceps bulge with the motion. Hard, thick, ropey…like other parts of him. *Jeez, get your brain out of the gutter. You're accusing him of having a one-track mind?*

"Is there anyone else here with us?" I ask.

"You tell me." His features form into that mask I am coming to hate. The one that says: gone is the warm, caring, easy-to-get-along-with man I'd briefly witnessed, leaving behind the one I hate… And lust after, since the moment I'd met him. No… Not true, I'd lust after him in any…and every form.

Goosebumps dot on my skin. I fold my arms around my waist. "What's that supposed to mean?" My words stay suspended between us for a second.

He holds my gaze, peruses my features, then runs a hand through his hair. "Adam Rhodes."

Of course. I glance away.

He reaches down, runs his big hand across the flesh of my upper arms. Warmth seeps into my blood instantly—insidious, seductive, pulling me, grounding me, anchoring me to him. *Shit.* I pull away. He releases me.

"You were married to him, but…" He seems to hesitate. Huh, Saint? Uncertain about something? I tilt my head.

"You want to know why I was a virgin?" I ask.

A nerve throbs at his temple. He doesn't reply. Doesn't say a word. Watches me intently. Waiting…waiting… The silence stretches for a beat. A bead of sweat crawls down my temple.

His jaw tics.

My nerves stretch, my belly trembles, and I firm my lips, "It wasn't a marriage at all, we were each playing a role."

"Clearly."

I wince at the bite in his voice.

"He…he wasn't a bad man," I say.

"And there was no sexual relationship between the two of you?"

"He... I... We agreed to keep it platonic. He needed a woman on his arm. I needed..." I bite my lip. I turn away.

This time he reaches out and pinches my chin, "Tell me. Don't hold back now." His jaw tics. A dense wave of anger spools off of him.

"Security. It was an arrangement, that's all." My nerve endings crackle. "You have nothing to be jealous of," I mumble. "We were only married for a month."

"You didn't love him, yet you married him. Makes me wonder what hold he had on you." His grip turns punishing.

I wince, but don't pull away. The pain he inflicts is a reminder that I am alive... So is he. There is hope for both of us... I just need to make it right by him...while figuring out how to also rescue Nina.

This is the perfect moment to tell him why you are here. Confess it. Win his trust... And what if he hates me for it?

Worse, what if the Mafia finds out?

There is no telling what they'd do to Nina if that happened. I bite the inside of my cheek. I can't betray her. I have to keep up the pretense. "No hold, Saint," I lie, "other than the kind a man with money has over a woman who needs security."

"Is that important to you, Gigi? Security?" He drags his hand down my arm, until his fingers brush the ring on my left hand.

I glance down at the emerald winking against the bubbles.

"Sure," I swallow. "You've always had money. You didn't have to scrimp and save for small treats, or watch your mother work two jobs to support you, or work your butt off to win a scholarship to college. You're not the one who was left alone when your mother died, then meeting the one person who became your best friend only to lose her; you aren't at the mercy of—" I twist my lips. *Shit, what is wrong with me? Why does he always catch me unawares? I almost blurted out everything that happened to Nina...to me. Dammit.*

"Mercy of...? he tilts his head.

"Mercy of fate, of course. We can plan all we want, but life takes us in directions we'd never intended to go."

He lifts his other hand in the air, twirls his finger, "You mean like this."

I glance around the massive bathroom that is three times the size of the room in which I had grown up. "Exactly." I turn to glance at him.

He lowers his arm, slides his hand between my legs, inserts two fingers inside of me.

I shudder.

He hooks his fingers, and I can't stop my internal muscles from clamping down on him. A shiver of lust crawls up my spine and my breathing goes ragged. I half close my eyes, take in his features. He watches me with curiosity, a hunger in his eyes, his lips pressed together as if intent on the task at hand. He twists my arm around my back, so my chest is pushed forward. My breath trembles and my nipples pucker to hard points. I wiggle, lean in, needing him to close his mouth around them. He holds me in place.

"You still sore?"

His voice fades in and out of my hearing. I focus on his fingers sliding in and out of me—soft, gentle. *Christ, he doesn't have a tender bone in his entire body, yet there is no mistaking the barely imperceptible movements of his digits inside of me.* I draw in a breath, and his scent, dark and edgy—now laced with roses, which only heightens the pheromone-laced impact of his essence—goes straight to my head. My head spins. My eyelids flutter shut.

"Victoria?" His voice seems to come from far away. "Gigi?" His breath whispers over my cheek.

"You okay?" His lips quirk.

I nod.

"Are you sore?"

I nod again. He ceases that beautiful friction, withdraws his hand.

"No." I force my eyelids open, "I mean, I am sore, but not tha-a-t sore."

"Ah," his lips twitch.

A flush creeps up my throat, but damn that. I want his fingers back inside of me. Want him to do all of those things he's been hinting at over the past few weeks.

"You asked what I needed, Saint?"

His gaze narrows. He looks down his patrician nose, the skin stretching tight over his cheekbones. He jerks his chin.

I raise my head, "I want you to fuck me like you don't care about me. Can you do that? Can you screw me without mercy?"

31

Saint

Fuck, bloody, fuck. She is hiding something from me. It's there in the curve of her cheek, the angle of her chin, in how she lowers her eyelids to stop me from reading the emotions that claw at her. In how she wraps her hand around my neck and leans in close enough for our eyelashes to tangle. In what she asks me to do, "Will you do this for me, Saint?"

"No." I reply.

She pales. Her chin wobbles. Then she firms her lips and retreats. I swoop out my hand, grab the back of her neck. "I am going to make love to you instead."

Her gaze widens. Her pupils dilate. She opens and closes her mouth, "I… I…don't think you should do that."

"Why not?"

"It could…uh…lead to complications."

"This is already far from simple." Her neck is so fragile that my fingers meet around the front of her neck.

"It's not what I want."

"You lying to me?"

She chews on the inside of her cheek. "I am not going to admit the truth to you."

"I'll get it out of you yet." I haul her close. Graze the heel of my palm over her pussy. *Gently, gently. Don't want to hurt her more than I already have now. F-u-c-k. This entire emo mindset is going to take some getting used to.*

She whines, and I can't stop my lips from curving.

"You like that, hmm?"

She opens and shuts her mouth, "Saint."

My name from her lips sounds like a whispered prayer. I close the distance between us, "You wanna come for me, Gigi?"

She nods. I swipe my thumb between her lower lips and her body shudders. Her hand on my shoulder spasms, she digs her fingers into my skin, attempts to pull herself closer, to impale herself on my fingers.

"First, answer this riddle."

"What?" she blinks.

"Would you rather have a hamster or a cat?"

"Is that a trick question?"

"Answer me, Gigi."

"A cat."

"What would you call him or her?"

"You're asking me this…now?"

"No better time to get to know you than when I have my fingers inside of you, hmm?" I press my thumb into the bud of her clit. She stutters.

"What's that?" I slide my finger in and out of her again; she groans.

"What's the name you'd choose?"

"Cats," she gasps. "I've always wanted to own two cats. I'd call them Salt and Pepper."

I frown, "Like that crazy cat-obsessed fucker Lennon did?"

She blinks. "How the hell do you know that? Have you been reading up on The Beatles?"

"You know what they say—nothing like knowing everything about your enemy to get the better of them. Knowledge is power, and all that."

"And you, have you ever had a pet?"

"You don't get to ask the questions."

She pouts, "That's not an answer."

"It's the only one you're getting." I twist my fingers inside of her and her entire body bucks. "Oh… Saint… Oh, I'm…"

"Come for me, Gigi."

She opens her mouth and a low wail keens from her.

I withdraw my fingers, bring my mouth to hers, "How do you feel?"

"Knackered," she whispers, then yawns.

"Good."

Keeping her in my arms, I rise up and step out of the bath tub. Walking over to where the towels are stacked on a shelf, I lower her to her feet. She winds her fingers around my waist as I pull out a large towel and dry her off first, then myself. I scoop her up and march over to the bed, lower her to the mattress. Sinking down next to her, I draw the sheets over us, before tucking her into my chest.

When was the last time I spooned someone this way? Never… Yeah, that's the honest answer. So why her? Why this woman who holds a piece of the puzzle of who was behind the incident that turned the lives of the seven of us upside down?

Why her?

Why me?

Why this strange obsession with her that is quickly turning out to be a fixation?

"Saint?" her husky voice reaches me.

"Hmm?"

"Can I ask you a riddle of my own?"

Nope. Never. I'd sworn never to allow another to question me. To trick me again. To trap me into revealing more than I should, to step-ping into a situation which could lead to my demise. Perhaps it is the sex… Or the fact that she has crept under my skin, or that the fucking has completely undermined my barriers…but hell… Answering one question wouldn't matter, right? I mean, what do I have to lose, hmm?

Maybe it is the false sense of security that having my wife in my arms seems to envelop me in, which allows me to comply with her wishes. This once.

"What do you want to know?"

She remains silent for so long, I am certain she's fallen sleep. Her breathing grows steady, her muscles relax, her body twitches as she settles into me.

I tuck her head under my chin, wrap my hand around her waist, my palm coming to rest over her pussy…my favorite place. *Yeah, that's how much of a goner I am. Maybe there is something in this marriage thing, after all? Something like, announcing your intention to the world ensures that you follow through on your word…or…the fact that I had been her first. Her fucking first. I shouldn't care, but fuck… How could she have been a virgin?* Surely, she would have had partners before me? Not that she was inexperienced either. She'd enjoyed the sex, hadn't shied away from it… *So what is she hiding from me?*

I wind my fingers across her now-drying hair, and smooth it about her shoulders.

"My question is…"

I pause.

"Would you rather have a baby of your own or would you baby-sit?"

My heartbeat ratchets up, "The fuck kind of question is that?"

"Forget it," she mumbles. "I have no idea what prompted that question anyway. It's not like it matters. Not like this…thing between us is real or anything. It's a means for you to get what you want, right?"

"The man who came to see you earlier… He wasn't your lover?"

"No," she shakes her head.

"So he was…"

"My contact with the Mafia... My handler."

I still my hand.

"The Mafia planted me to play the role of Adam's wife." She turns in my arms, her lips swollen from my kisses, her cheeks flushed from the hot bath. "But you knew that already."

I tilt my head. *Should I reveal how much I know? Has she guessed how much I've already uncovered about her past?* "Go on." I pull back my arm. She shivers and I pull the blanket up to her ears.

"They…they wanted me to keep an eye on him."

"Adam knew about it?"

She nods, "He had no choice, but to accept that I was reporting on his activities back to the Mafia."

"And you, Gigi? Did you have a choice?"

"It…it isn't that simple." She licks her lips, brings her hand up to chew on her nails. I weave my fingers with hers, pull it down between us.

"It really is. Tell me what they have on you and let me help you."

"Is saving damsels in distress your specialty?" she asks.

"I'm no fucking white knight, and you know it."

"You're also not as much of an asshole as you make yourself out to be," she muses.

"Each of us have the stories we tell ourselves, and the masks we put on to face the world," I answer.

"And you, Saint, what's the persona you've bought into?"

I allow my lips to kick up, "I am not the one with the agenda here." She pales, turns away from me. I tug on her hand so she has no choice but to stay facing me. "Don't push me away, Victoria. This is our chance to come clean so we can make a fresh start of it."

"Is that what you're offering?"

I hold up her hand with the emerald ring glittering on it. "Isn't this proof enough?"

"Is that why you gave me your mother's ring?"

"Not only." I run my thumb across the smooth surface. "It felt right. When my instinct points me in a particular direction, I follow it."

"What does your instinct say about me?" She lowers her chin, peers up at me from under her eyelashes. That green gaze of hers deepens, stormy emotions caught in their depths.

"My head says that I shouldn't trust you."

The remaining color leaches from her cheeks.

"Let me go." She yanks at her hand, but I don't release it. I use the leverage to haul her into my chest. "My instinct says to ignore what my logical mind is pointing out to me—that you are dangerous, that for both of our sakes, I should walk away from you, that if I were a betting man, I should cash in my chips and leave, that you are a riddle with more than one answer as a solution. Too bad, when it comes to you..." I search her features, take in the hollows under her eyes, the sharp jut of her cheeks, "I have no choice but to follow my heart, Gigi."

She bites on her lower lip, "I... I am not sure what that means."

"It means..." I cup her chin, "why don't we trade secrets, hmm? Hell, I'll even start with answering your question..." *The fuck. Am I actually going to do this?*

"What's your answer?" The skin around her eyes creases.

"That I want neither." I set my jaw. "I don't intend to have children, and hell, I'm definitely not qualified to be a babysitter."

She pales.

"Does that disappoint you?" I search her features.

Her lips turn down, then she tips up her chin. "It's what I expected. Besides, it was a hypothetical question."

"Good, then you won't mind if I ask you another."

Her eyebrows knit together, "What?"

"Why did you ask to become my sub? You could have approached me with another proposition. So why this?"

She draws in a breath, "I researched you, found out about your tastes, about some of the other women." She flushes.

Something hot blooms in my chest, "Does that make you jealous, Gigi, imagining me with another woman?"

She tips her chin up, "You know it does." She places her hand over my cock, "And if you dare look at any of them again, I'll..." She squeezes my balls.

I groan...then wince. Her jealousy is a fucking turn on. Does she realize that? Sweat beads my forehead. Heat swarms in a knotted coil at the base of my belly, "What else did you like about what you saw?"

"You ..." she swallows, "You had what I was looking for."

"What is that?"

"You are the kind of man who'd know what his woman needs when she doesn't. You wouldn't allow her pleas to get in the way and that... It's not easy."

"That's an awful lot you are supposing," I smirk.

"I followed my instincts." Her lips quirk.

The band around my chest tightens. This woman... She is fucking strong... That sassy side of her? Surely, it will be my downfall.

"And what do your instincts say now?" I tilt my head.

"That you know what's best for me." She squeezes her hand around my erect cock and blood rushes to my groin.

"The things you do to me when you say that." I groan. My heart begins to race. "But, you need to recover first."

She shakes her head. "Later. I need this Saint. I do."

I draw in a breath, "One more question, then."

"But..."

"You ask."

She rubs her cheek into the pillow, her fingers rubbing across the swollen head of my shaft.

"Gigi."

"Saint?"

"Ask your question."

"Why do you live in hotels? Why doesn't a man like you not have a mansion of your own?"

"You heard about that?"

"Summer may have mentioned it." She flushes but doesn't back down, "Will you answer that?"

I raise my shoulders, "It's too much of a commitment to have a place of my own. Besides, given the hotel chains I run, it seems like a waste not to use the facilities they afford me." I twist my lips. "Nothing like keeping the staff on their toes… Every time I stay in a hotel, I force the management to up their game."

Will she believe me? Can she look past the obvious to what I'm not saying?

She frowns, then jerks her chin, "Guess it makes sense."

My ribcage feels too tight. *Can't she look past the front I am putting up?* Fuck that. I had been happy this far, had figured out how to make the most of the cards I had been handed. Had even managed to find a balance of sorts, thanks to my more extreme tastes. *Why did she have to come along and disturb that? Why does she make me yearn for more? Bloody hell.* I shake my head.

One more chance. Give her one more chance to reveal the truth. Say it, Gigi. Tell me why you're really here. Confess it and I'll do what is needed to keep you safe. I'll do anything to extricate you from whatever situation you've found yourself in.

She twists her fingers around my cock.

I place my hand over hers, "My turn to ask a question."

"Right." She blinks, squares her shoulders.

"You ready, Gigi?"

She nods.

"Why did you agree to marry me?"

32

Victoria

"It's not like you gave me a choice?" I set my jaw.

"You could have left," he retorts. "It's not like I was holding you captive."

"Weren't you?" I massage his balls, squeeze the base of his cock at the same time.

"F-u-c-k." Color flushes his cheeks. His blue eyes deepen into the color of azure.

His fingers spasm over mine.

He wraps the fingers of his other hand around my neck in that possessive grasp I'm coming to recognize.

"Who's holding who captive here, hmm?" His gaze intensifies. He releases his grip on my hand, only to cup my pussy. "Tell me why you agreed to marry me."

I shake my head; he slips three fingers inside my cunt at the same time. *Omigod!* My eyes roll back in my head; my grasp on his cock tightens.

He circles his thumb around the swollen bud of my clit, and my entire body bucks. A trembling sweeps up from my toes, surges toward my womb.

He pulls out his fingers from my pussy and I whine, "No, goddam you, don't do this."

"Your answer, Gigi, why did you marry me?"

"Because I wanted to, you asshole." I tip up my chin, "Is that enough for your ego?

"No."

My jaw falls open, "You can't be serious."

"Oh, but I am, my darling." His lips twist, "Tell me the real reason, and I promise I'll let you come."

"You're an unfeeling brute." Anger tunnels my vision.

"And you're a cunt."

My pussy instantly clenches. Hell, why do these filthy insults from him resonate with that secret part of me? "Fuck you, Saint," I snarl.

"With pleasure Gigi, but first, your answer."

I swallow; a flush steals up my throat. Goddam him for forcing me to bare the part I hate to him. "After we met, I began to fantasize about you." I glower at him, "Once I realized the kind of kink you indulged in...it became worse. My dreams became steamier. Then I stumbled across that woman giving you head in your office...and..."

His breathing heightens, "It turned you on?"

I nod. "When she blew you, and you threw your head back, the chords of your neck stood out in relief, your beautiful chest bathed in sweat, as you gripped her hair and held her in place. You fucked her face and all I could think was... I am going to kill that bitch," I swallow, then whisper, "and..."

"And?" His nostrils flare.

"And that I want that." I swallow.

His biceps bulge. This was turning him on even more, huh? I tilt my chin up, push my breasts into his chest.

"I knew then that I needed you. I yearned for you to break me, to make me forget about everything else, to force me to remember only the shape of your face, the fullness of your dick down my throat, the imprint of your fingers in my cunt as you made me come. The—"

He lowers his head, blots out the world, then closes his mouth over mine. He robs me of my breath, my words, my will to live without him. He simply takes it all from me. He fucking absorbs every last thought from me. In that moment, he makes me his. He flips me on my back, notches his dick at the entrance to my pussy, then cups the top of my head. Huh?

He plunges forward, burying himself to the hilt with such force that my entire body moves up. My head hits his palm— *Huh*. Even in the midst of passion, he remembers to stop me from hurting myself— That's so unlike what I've come to expect from this complex male.

He tangles his tongue with mine, brings his other hand down to grip my butt. He slides his thumb into my back hole, pulls out and thrusts back inside of me. His balls slap against my tender flesh as he fills me. He impales me, fills me up, joins me to him with such intensity that tears spring to my eyes. The pressure radiates out from my core, up my body, toward my extremities. Every inch of my skin seems to flare with a strange iridescent glow. My scalp tingles, my toes curl, and I arch my back, knowing I am going to—

He releases my mouth, glares into my face, "Come for me, wife." His command rips through me, hurtling me up, up, over the edge. The pressure in my chest explodes out; flashes of white blind me.

When I come to, he's poised in exactly the same position.

"Jesus," I croak.

"You do know that's also the name Lennon gave one of his cats, right?"

"What?"

"Face it," he rubs his nose with mine. "Your hero, John L, was a cat lady in disguise."

A giggle bubbles up my throat, "I can't believe you're telling me this…now…when…" I glance down, "when you're inside of me."

His dick lengthens, pushing against my inner walls. Another trembling spirals up from where he's sheathed inside of me. "What the—?"

"You keeping count this time?" He tilts his hips and the head of his dick brushes against my cervix.

"Saint!'

"Gigi," he leans down and licks my lips. "Are you keeping count?"

"Of what?"

He pulls back, then pounds into me, and ohmigod, the climax crashes over me. I throw back my head and a keening cry emerges from my lips. Another shudder rolls over me, I pull back my shoulders, thrust my pelvis up as liquid heat pools between my legs.

"How many was that Gigi?"

"What?"

"How many orgasms so far?"

"Two?"

He clicks his tongue. "Let's make that three."

His dick thickens inside of me. Holy shit, no way is he still erect. I force myself to focus on his face, his deepening gaze, the dark hair stuck to his forehead, the sheen of sweat that covers his shoulders. I dig my heels into the backs of his thighs, push myself up, and wind my arms around his neck.

His big body trembles, and he braces his weight on his elbow, then slides a second finger inside my back hole. The tension coiled in his muscles vibrates out, the heat from his body intensifies, and his heart beat ratchets up. I turn my head into the crook of his shoulder, bite down on his skin, and his cock jumps. A shudder grips his body and his hoarse cry fills my ears, "Fuck, Gigi." His entire body stiffens, then he comes, shooting hot streams of cum inside of me.

He collapses onto me, his weight pressing me down into the bed. I wind my limbs around him, lick the blood from the broken skin on his neck.

The muscles on his back ripple. He turns and brushes my lips with his, "You're full of surprises, Gigi."

He begins to pull out and I shake my head. "Stay," I whisper against his lips.

He hesitates, then flips us over, so I am once more on his chest, with him inside of me. I snuggle into him, the warmth of his body a contrast to the air hitting my back. I shiver.

"You cold?"

"A little." I rub my cheek against the fine hair that peppers his chest. He reaches out behind me, the muscles of his body rippling as he pulls the sheet over both of us.

He folds an arm around my back, tucks my head under his chin.

"I have another question for you," I venture.

He stills. "I hate answering questions."

"No shit," I slip out my tongue and lick his skin.

His cock instantly jumps inside of me. I chuckle, "Where do you get this stamina from?"

He folds an arm behind his head, "I learnt a long time ago, that I had better make the most of the moment at hand. You never know what's going to happen next, you get me?"

I press my chin into his chest, peer up at him. "Does this have to do with the incident?"

"The girls have been gossiping, huh?"

"Summer may have mentioned it in passing."

"What did she say?"

"That it was up to each of the Seven to talk about what happened to them."

His brow clears.

"What was your question?"

"You changing the topic?" I frown.

He draws the hair away from my face, "When it suits me."

I snicker, "Do you always get your way?"

He smirks, "Is that the question?"

"Did it matter to you so much that I was a virgin?"

"Why do you say that?" he asks.

"Because," I run my tongue over my teeth, "since you discovered that you were my first, you've forgotten to be as much of a douchebag to me."

He gazes off into the distance, "You're right." He scratches his chin. "I never expect any of the women I sleep with to be virgins… Certainly, never expected to marry one." He lowers his gaze to my face.

"So it was a big deal for you?"

He cups my cheek, "If you mean, does it appeal to the primal, chauvinistic man in me that no one has been inside of you before me, that I was the first to make love to you? Then, yes. I'd never thought it would be important…and it isn't… And it is."

I lower my brows, "What do you mean?" He runs his fingers

though my hair. His fingertips drag across my scalp. Tendrils of heat ripple from the contact. I turn my head and lean into the touch. "You were saying…?" I prompt.

"That making love to you was more significant than I thought it would be. My being your first was a bonus, but even if I hadn't been, it wouldn't have mattered… But you were… And it makes me wonder, why the hell you didn't sleep with anyone before me?"

"Because I was saving myself for the right man…?"

"Who is probably not me."

"My," I blink, "what's prompting this soul searching?"

"Let's see… Was it the strawberries dipped in your cum which may have become my favorite food of all time? Or the mind-blowing sex after? Or the fact that you've been so receptive, so responsive to my touch?" He trails his hand down my spine.

I shiver.

He pinches my chin, tips my head up, presses his lips to mine and kisses me. Gently. Softly. Slowly. So bloody thoroughly. My heart begins to race all over again. Wetness pools between my legs.

"Being inside you is my favorite place in the entire world." His dick thickens, punctuating his words.

"Saint," I whisper.

"Let me, Gigi." He nibbles on my lower lip, and pushes up and into me. He makes love to me gently, barely a thrust in his every move, he propels his hips up with enough torque for his hardness to chafe the inside of my channel. He brings his other hand between us and cups my breast, the calluses on his fingers setting off pinpricks of pleasure that travel straight to the space between my legs.

He holds my head in place, then places his other big hand on my butt. "Hold on, sweetheart," his whisper curls around me, sinks into my blood, wafts over, encouraging me to give in, sink in, to open myself up completely, irrevocably to him. His gentleness is so firm, yet so demanding, it's a complete contrast to the sadistic part of him.

Both sides of his personality are the same, yet different. Both authoritative in their own way. He pistons his hips up and down again and again, hitting that space deep inside of me that he seems to always find with such precision—that sends pleasure shooting up my nerve endings to my extremities. My toes curl, I dig my fingers into his hair, and hold onto his shoulders. "Saint… I'm… I'm..."

"Come with me," his voice ripples across my skin and I shatter, my entire body trembling, melting, spiraling down a tunnel at the end of which is him. Only him. His hoarse cry threads through my subconscious mind, and he comes inside of me. Sleep tugs at the edges of my vision. My muscles relax. He pushes my head down into his chest. His heart beat thuds in my ears. Reassuring. Hypnotic.

"Sleep, Gigi, I'll keep you safe. "

33

Victoria

Over the next three weeks Saint is true to his word.

He takes care of my every need. He is attentive to me, from the moment we wake up in the morning, when he insists on ordering and eating breakfast with me, often joining me for a quick shower before he sets off for work. So we haven't had a honeymoon, not that I expected it, but this is close. He doesn't want me to worry about anything. He insists I stay in, make full use of the hotel's facilities—the pool, the sauna, the daily appointment with the masseuse, not to mention the access to the best beauticians in the city in the in-house salon.

I can't remember the last time I felt this pampered.

In the evenings, Saint frequently texts me from the office, commanding me to be naked and ready for him, usually arriving within twenty minutes of the message. And then he'll tease me, often spank me up against the post, arousing me before fucking me with that intensity and the hint of cruelty which characterizes his every move. A few times we've indulged in more of the games where he tests my taste in alcohol. I admit, I had more luck with that than with the food. What can I say? Clearly, I am a closet alcohol slut.

He's taken me on the bed, of course... And on the table by the window, on the carpet, in the walk-in closet, where we'd ended the night tangled up in clothes—his and mine.

One night, he'd met me in the restaurant downstairs as I had been finishing dinner. He'd had a drink, then waited until I'd finished dessert. After that, he'd been in such a hurry, he'd hustled me into the ladies' restroom and proceeded to fingerfuck me against the door. The fear of being caught had been enough to make me orgasm within the first five minutes. Then again, when he'd ripped off my panties and stuffed his dick inside of me. And a third time, when he'd thrust into me again and again with such force that my body had bucked into the door, and he'd commanded me to come in that authoritative voice— the one which has me rushing to obey him. I'd slumped against him after that. He'd stuffed my knickers into his pocket, scooped me up and carried me off to his private elevator, and then upstairs to his bed, where he'd proceeded to tie me spread-eagled to the bedposts, and then... Worshipped my body. There is really no other way to describe it.

He had touched every part of me, kissed every nook and cranny, massaged every curve, rubbed my breasts, nibbled on my nipples, my fingers, my toes—all with that same single-minded intensity, as if he had a point to prove... To himself? To me? He had wrung two more orgasms out of me that night...until I had begged him, pleaded with him, cajoled with him to take me and put an end to my agony... He had finally relented then—turned me around on my arms and knees and thrust into me with such force that the entire bed had jolted. Then he'd proceeded to take me again and again until he'd come deep inside of me. He'd touched a part of that I hadn't even known existed. Perhaps it had affected him too, for he'd been gone the next morning.

I'd spent most of the day recovering.

That was two days ago. He hasn't touched me since, which is strange... considering we've had sex every night for almost three weeks... He has an insatiable appetite, and enough stamina to make my knees go weak thinking about how he's marked me each time.

Tonight is the first time since we got married that he is running late at the office. A meeting of FOK Media with all the Seven—well, minus Baron, he'd said. I glance at the clock: midnight. Shit. Where is he? Is he really at work?

Why hasn't he called or texted me?

I sit up in the bed, where I have been tossing and turning over the last hour, trying to sleep. Damn it. I have no intention of keeping his bed warm, like a good little wife, waiting for him. *And isn't that exactly what you've done over the last 3 weeks?* Yeah. I haven't left the hotel, content to hide myself away here. Have turned down invitations to meet the girls, even an invitation to tea with Meredith.

Amelie had called me a few times, to check that I was okay. We'd chatted and I'd reassured her I was fine, just coming to terms with my newly married status. She'd made me promise that I'd call her if I needed anything; I hadn't, of course.

Fact is, I don't want to break this pattern of marital bliss we seem to be indulging in. It sure feels like marital bliss.

Or perhaps it's the calm before the storm? I shake off the hardness that coils in my chest. I need to keep busy...while I waited for my 'lord and master' to turn up.

Thankfully, he has stopped insisting I call him Sir, which is a relief. What caused him to change his mind? Not that it has stopped him from being as demanding in his needs toward me. All of which I have been happy to comply with.

Our time together is almost up. Was it wrong of me to not try to get the information needed before this? Had it been foolish of me to try to make the most of the time Antonio had granted me? He'd assured me he'd keep Nina safe during this time. Had I been mistaken in trusting him on that? He won't hurt Nina, I am sure of that. If anything, his expression had indicated that he has feelings for her, but that's my intuition. What if I'm wrong?

What if I had been stupid to allow Saint to lull me into a false sense of security? I haven't wanted to do anything to upset the balance of sorts that we seem to have established. Where the hell is he, anyway?

I shove the covers off of my body, then forgo my clothes in favor of a bathrobe. This late, there won't be many hotel guests around. I take the elevator down to the heated indoor swimming pool on the first level. Draping my bathrobe over a lounge chair, I dive in, begin to swim laps. The rhythmic ebb and flow of the water over me, the burn in my arms, the power of my body pitted against the resistance provided by my headlong rush—all of it sinks into my blood, calms me. I reach the far end of the pool for the fourth time, when an electric current runs up my spine. I thrust an arm out, push forward, raise my eyes and spot the figure at the head of the pool. My muscles bunch, I miss a stroke, go under, then come up gasping. My heart begins to thud, my pulse beating at my temples as adrenaline laces my blood. I propel through the water, toward the man who stands motionless. Waiting...waiting for me. I reach the edge of the pool, hold onto the rim.

Run my gaze up those beat up cowboy boots, the tailored slacks that outline those powerful legs, to the tent of fabric at his crotch. My throat dries. Of course, he's aroused. He hasn't had sex for...three nights now. Unless, he'd sought out someone else before coming here?

Ask him, damn it. And what? Sound like a nagging wife? I toss my head. No way. Besides, that would be a dead giveaway that I've been thinking of him all day. And no way, am I giving away what little power I am clinging to in this relationship

I tip my chin up, meet that searing blue gaze.

"How did you find me?

"Very little happens here without my being aware of it."

I glance up at the corners of the ceiling. "The cameras?"

He nods. "I switched them off, by the way." His lips kick up.

My throat closes. He reaches down, unbuckles his belt. The sound of leather against his buckle rasps across my sensitized nerve endings. He lowers his zipper and my pulse rate ratchets up. His thick shaft spills out. He widens his stance, grabs his cock and pumps himself hard once. A bead of precum appears at the tip of the angry head. My mouth dries.

I can't take my gaze off of his swollen dick as he proceeds to massage himself. His strokes are ferocious, punishing. His breathing grows shallow; my chest rises and falls in tandem. His shaft thickens, and even with the distance between us, I can see the veins along the underside pulsing, throbbing. My sex clenches, my nipples tighten, and goosebumps pop over my skin. I lick my lips, gulp down my anticipation. Don't move. Don't say anything. Wait... *Wait.* He massages himself once more, then stops.

What the—?

As I watch, he toes off his shoes. Letting go of his dick—which stands erect without any help from his hands, thank you very much—he shrugs off his expensive jacket, drops it to the chair, followed by his shirt. His tanned skin gleams in the warm ceiling lights; his eight pack abs flex as he proceeds to pull off his socks.

He shucks off his pants, along with his boxers, then poses in place for a second. Enough for me to take in the awesome sight of that naked expanse of 100% masculine alpha male who belongs to me. He is mine, from the moment I'd laid eyes on him. Why had I ever thought I'd be able to avoid his charisma, his power, the raw animal magnetism that emanates from his sexy-as-fuck presence?

I gulp, my hand slips, and I slide back into the pool, only he's already there. He dives into the water, arcing up to close his arms around me. His lips find mine and he plants his bulk between my thighs, so I have no choice but to part them. Then he thrusts inside me, instantly filling me as he impales me completely. All I can do is grab onto his shoulders and hold on, as he pushes forward, pins me against the side of the pool, and proceeds to fuck every thought out of my head.

He swipes his tongue across my lower lip, brings his hand down to cup my butt as he slides his finger inside my puckered back hole. My entire body bucks. He winds his fingers around my neck, holding me in place, before ripping his mouth from mine. He peers deeply into my eyes, holds my gaze, urging me with his expression to strain against him, push my pelvis forward, match him thrust for thrust. He kicks his hips forward one last time, bottoming out inside of me, then whispers, "Come."

The climax instantly crashes over me as he comes inside of me, his body spasming along with mine. I sag against him, all thoughts fucked out of me as I float in that strange after-space that comes from being completely and utterly spent.

The world tilts. I sense him tugging me along to the steps at the side of the pool. He scoops me up in his arms, then walks out of the water. He snatches up one of the towels piled by a lounge chair and dries me off, then himself. He picks up my bathrobe and places it around my shoulders. He helps me into the robe then ties it around me with great care. He fetches his pants and steps into them. Carrying me in his arms he takes the private elevator up to his suite. Once inside the room, he strips us both, then carries me into the shower.

He proceeds to shampoo my hair, then seats himself on the stone bench in the shower before washing every inch of my body. He begins to soap himself, and I catch his wrist.

"Let me," I clear my throat, realizing those are the first words I have spoken since I saw him at the pool.

He nods, then leans back, spreading his arms across the back of the bench. I reach around to shut off the shower, then pour out the liquid soap. I work it in across his biceps, down his corded chest, digging into the dips between his pecs. He makes a noise of satisfaction, then sinks back, widening his stance. I massage down his belly, to his thigh, then sink my knuckles into the tense backs of his calves. Sitting cross legged on the floor, I place his large foot on my lap, brush my fingers between his toes. Then hold up his foot to massage the underside and gasp, "Saint."

He instantly tugs on my grip. I let go of his foot and he stamps it flat onto the floor.

"What happened?" I ask.

His jaw tenses.

"Those scars, Saint..."

He sets his jaw, "What about them?"

"Did you get them when you were kidnapped?" I swallow, "Did they do this to you?"

"What's it to you?"

"Not all of the scars are old."

"What do you mean?" He lowers his arms to his lap, his movements deliberate, "What are you trying to say, Victoria?"

Shit. When he calls me by my full name, it's never a good sign.

"Just that, if you're trying to hurt yourself..."

He rises to his feet and my heart thuds in my chest. I have to look up, have to sweep my gaze up every ripped inch of him to meet his gaze.

His eyes blaze, then a shutter comes over his face. "I'm not." He steps around me and heads for the shower door.

"Saint," I jump to my feet, turn toward him, "you can talk to me."

"Oh?" He straightens. "And why would I do that?"

"I'm your wife."

He turns then and his lips curve in a smile that doesn't reach his eyes, "Fake wife, darling."

I wring my fingers together, "You don't mean it, you are simply lashing out at me because you are confused inside."

"We spent some time together; the sex was okay," he tilts his head, "sometimes."

Bastard.

"Don't go mistaking the last few days for some kind of intimacy between us." His lips twist, "It was a transaction, make no mistake."

I swallow. My throat hurts and my eyes burn. Was I wrong to imagine that the last few weeks had shifted the tone of the relationship between us? No, it *can't* be. I tip up my chin, "You're lying."

"And you..." He looks me up and down, "You are replaceable." Turning he grabs a towel, and leaves.

34

Saint

No one can replace her and that is the problem.

I dry myself with the towel, then toss it aside.

She has crawled under my skin, sunk into my blood and I can't get enough of her. I'd been heading to work the last three weeks every day —including weekends—because hell, I had to make a point to her, and to myself, that I'm not dependent on her. This entire sham of a relationship will be over soon enough. She is going to trip up and expose the real reason she propositioned me. I'll walk away from her then, and what... Find another? I ball my fists at my sides. What will happen to her once I find out her secret? Where will she go? If she thinks the Mafia will let her walk away, she is being awfully naïve. They'll kill her. My heart begins to thud and a cold sensation coils in my chest. I can't let that happen. I'll figure out a way to extricate her from whatever mess she is in...regardless of whether there is a chance for us together. Fuck. I pace the carpeted floor the water drying on my skin.

What *is* wrong with me? Why *can't I* fight this need to... What? Take care of her?

I'd let down my guard enough to take off my socks today. That...has never happened before. Not when I'm in the dressing room of the gym, nor with any other woman. The socks stay on, always. I am not hiding the scars... It's more that I don't want to answer any questions about them.

Have I become so relaxed in her presence that I had not only taken off my socks, but also had allowed her to wash me? A first. No one had been given that privilege...before her. I had begun to look forward to coming home to her— Home? Did I call this hotel suite—which is a transient place to stay, at best—home? Is it home because she is here? Why do I enjoy waking up with her coiled into my side? What is Gigi doing to me? Whatever it is, it has to stop.

The bathroom door opens, a cloud of steam wafts out, and from it, she steps forward into the room.

I draw in a breath.

She's naked.

Not that I hadn't seen her without clothes earlier. But the sheer impudence with which she glides forward—head high, spine straight, perky breasts thrust up, breasts that tremble with every step she takes —that's different. She hasn't shown that fighting spirit of hers over the last few weeks. Perhaps I've been too busy taking what she offers, I haven't challenged her recently, and damn, if I haven't missed the thrust and parry between us. She walks around the bed to her side.

I twist my lips. Step forward. "Stop," I growl.

She ignores me, pulls back the covers, no doubt preparing to slide in and fall asleep. And leave me tossing and turning next to her? No way.

"Do as I say, or I swear, you'll regret it," I stalk to her.

She turns her back on me... *Big* mistake. I reach her, and she stiffens, pulls her shoulders back. I swoop down to grab her around the waist and she swerves to the side. What the hell?

I angle toward her; she brushes past me. I pivot, turn to face her as she backs away.

I lower my voice to a hush, "You don't want to do this."

She pales, then tips up her chin, "I am doing this. I'm not playing your games anymore"

"You'll regret this." The pulse thuds at my temple.

She tosses her head, "So, what's new?"

I take a step forward.

She skitters back, "Afraid you'll lose the chase?"

My heartbeat ratchets up.

"Is the big bad billionaire worried that his wife will be able to outrun him?"

My vision tunnels. The hair on the nape of my neck prickles. I drum my fingers on my chest. "Be careful what you wish for, sweetheart, for when I catch you this time, I won't' show any mercy."

She throws back her head and laughs. She fucking laughs. "You're funny, Saint, you know that?" she wheezes. "I have news for you, asshole."

I growl.

"—Oh, you don't deserve the title of alphahole yet. All you've done so far is threaten me and use your wealth and so-called power to keep me under your control. Well, let me tell you, that's not gonna work anymore."

"Oh?" I bare my teeth.

She winces, then pulls herself up to her full height, "It's true. Anyone can be a bully... But to use your wealth to actually make a difference in the world? To use your power to help those less fortunate? To bare your heart and show your feelings? To make yourself vulnerable enough to be hurt? That's true strength."

I roll my shoulders. "You done?"

"No." Color suffuses her cheeks. She closes the distance between us, thrusts her finger into my chest. "I thought you were different, that behind that obnoxious persona is someone who—"

"Cares? Who feels? Who had fallen in love with you? Who would change his life for you? Who would reform for you and help you in whatever little plan you have going here?"

She pales.

"I have news for you, doll. Your cunt is no magic pussy, that one taste of it, and poof, I turn over a new leaf."

She swallows.

"You...you're hurting, Saint. That's why you are trying to hurt me."

I laugh, "What a crock." A bead of sweat slides down my back.

"You're afraid." She leans in and her scent envelops me.

My groin tightens; my gut churns.

"That's why you're lashing out at me. I understand, Saint. Let me help." She raises her hand toward my face, "You're—"

"Bored," I yawn, then step back. "Save your insights, my sweet fake wife, for I couldn't give a fuck about your thoughts."

A lone tear squeezes out of the corner of her eye.

A hot sensation stabs at my chest.

"Take a good look, sweetheart," I spread my arms, "cause I am not changing."

She searches my features with an intensity that borders on hate... *Love?* Nah! Not that. *Never* that. Everything between us has been a charade... *Well,* except that she'd been a virgin. Fuck, what *does* it mean that she came to me untouched? Sweat beads my palms. Nothing. *It means* nothing. Another maneuver in this scheme of hers to catch me off kilter. If she'd intended to get close to me... Well, she has succeeded. And it stops here. Now.

"Get out," I jerk my chin toward the door.

"What?"

"Out of my bedroom," I growl.

"No."

I blink. "Excuse me?"

She ducks under my arm, then slides into the bed and pulls up the covers to her chin. "I am sleeping here. You take the couch."

35

Saint

"What the fuck?" I glance up at the ceiling.

My wife had thrown me out of our bedroom and I had taken it. The fuck had happened there? Had I actually dragged my sorry arse out of there and retreated to the living room...like a loser? My present condition certainly seems to indicate so.

I shift my frame on the couch in the living room, which had seemed comfortable enough on the face of it, but try squeezing a six-feet-four-inch frame onto the bloody thing for the night...and fuck, it isn't a laughing matter. How the hell had everything gone so tits up? How had I allowed that tiny woman to get the better of me? Had I actually agreed to turn the marital bed over to her for the night? And why hadn't I simply checked into another hotel room for the night? Why can't I bear to leave her alone, even for one night? Because she is my asset and I can't leave her unguarded. Bull-fucking-shit, what a crock that is. All the time I'd been away at the office, she'd been on her own. Okay not quite. I'd had my people tailing her, yes, even in the hotel. So what? It's the only way to find out what the hell her endgame is in all of this.

I fold my arm over my eyes, stretch myself, and my bloody legs hang over the side. Shit. Clearly, I am too large for this space. I turn over, punch the cushion under my head. How the hell had it come to this? I am in the most expensive suite, in an iconic hotel owned by me, in a city where I am—okay was— the most eligible bachelor—in a country where I am consistently among the top five richest men. And here I am, spending the night on a couch? Fuck. I turn over and slide off of the couch. Hit the floor on my arse. Insane. This is beyond ridiculous. This is a clear sign that I am pussywhipped.

If I told any of the Seven about this... Well, outside of Sinner—bet that fucker would empathize with what it is to be faced with an angry wife. Jesus, that's the second time in a row I've referred to her as my wife. She's your fake wife, you wanker. *As you've reminded her over and over again. And broken her heart. You hurt her, you bloody reprobate.*

I drag my fingers through my hair.

But hell, if her words hadn't hit home. She'd struck a nerve—more than a nerve. She'd pushed herself into my deepest darkest space, the place I'd vowed never to let anyone into. She'd insisting on unearthing my secrets, bared my insecurities and held up a mirror to my flaws. Of which I have many. I've never hidden them. And I'm not starting now. I've never denied that I am callous. What was it she called me? A brute. Yep, that's what I am. Someone who doesn't give a fuck about others. Who goes after what he wants and takes it, damn the consequences. So, what am I doing, skulking around in the dark, on my arse in my hotel suite? This space is mine. I push up to my feet. And she is mine—for the duration of this sham marriage. At least. And no one keeps me away from what I own, least of all my sassy, devious, spitfire of a wife.

I stalk to the door of the bedroom—how dare she shut it on me?— and shove it open. I step into the semi-darkness. The curtains are pulled back and the brightness of the streetlights pours in through the window, illuminating the figure on the bed. I prowl over to her, rake my gaze over the figure tucked in, looking quite comfortable. Her fingers are tucked under her cheek, her lips slightly parted. Her chest rises and falls; her cheeks are flushed. No doubt she'd fallen asleep as soon as I had left, while I had tossed and turned in my make-shift bed.

I grab the sheets and pull them off.

"What the—?" She sits up with a little scream, breasts heaving, naked body glimmering in the moonlight. My throat closes. The blood rushes to my dick. Fuck. I don't have any clothes on either. Good. This should make it convenient.

"Move over," I snarl.

She blinks up at me. "Saint?"

"Who the fuck else?" I growl. Of course, *it's* me. Who had she expected? Her late-husband? That fucker, Antonio? I bunch my fists at my side.

She glances down, takes in my stance, then brings up her hands to cover her breasts. Anger thrums at my temples. I am her bloody husband. She doesn't get to hide her gorgeous body from me. And why the hell is she staring at me with fear in her eyes? I wouldn't hurt her. Well, not physically at least— Okay, well...only when it is required. Then, I'll do what's needed to her body, to give her the most pleasure I can. What is wrong with that? It is for her own good, isn't it?

And the way you hurt her with your words... *Is* that for her own good too?

I bunch my shoulders, glare at her features.

"Wh...what's wrong?" she stutters.

Nothing. Everything. "You're on my side of the bed."

"Oh," she glances around, then scoots over.

"Not so fast." I swoop down. Another scream leaves her lips. I scoop her up, then plonk down on the bed, with her spread across my lap.

She wriggles. I lean my weight on the small of her back.

"Let me go."

"No."

"What are you doing?" she huffs.

"You were in the wrong."

"Why? Because I slept on your side?" Her tone is incredulous.

"Yes."

"That's preposterous," she tosses her head.

"No, that's cause for punishment."

Her entire body stills, then a shudder crawls up her spine.

"You like that, don't ya?" I palm her butt.

She bucks again and I lean more of my weight on her. I am using my superior strength to overpower her, exactly what she'd accused me of doing earlier. Well, good. I *am confirming* her already-low opinion of me, right? I snicker.

She turns to glare at me, "You're looking for an excuse to spank me."

"Oh?"

She nods, "Couldn't bear the idea that a woman had gotten the better of you."

I squeeze her butt cheek and she shudders.

"Go on," I bare my teeth, "why did you stop?"

"If you wanted to touch me, you only had to—"

I raise my hand and she winces.

"You were saying?" I ask.

"That...that...if you wanted to make love to me, you only had to ask —ow!"

My palm connects with her backside and she huffs.

I raise my hand, slap her other butt cheek.

She cries out, "It hurts, you oaf."

"Good." I spank her first butt cheek again and the other, and the first, then the other.

"Ow, ow," she screams again, aaaand my cock engorges. She wriggles her body, tries to pull away, and the friction against my shaft is so fucking sweet. A groan rips out of me. I increase the intensity of my spanking, alternating between her arse cheeks.

She grabs hold of my leg, grinds her clit into my thigh. The blood drains to my groin and all of my senses hone in on her.

"Fuck, Gigi, I want you."

I stop, and her entire body quivers. The redness of my palm prints stands out against the curve of her butt. I bend, kiss the wounded skin. She moans, and my heart stutters.

I stand up with her in my arms, then turn and lower her to her arms and knees onto the bed.

"Hold on."

36

Victoria

That's all the warning he gives me, before he lines up his dick against the entrance to my soaking wet channel.

"Saint."

He pistons his hips and slams his cock all the way inside of me.

His balls slaps against my tender flesh; pin pricks of pain dance up my spine. My thighs tremble; his grip on me tightens. Vibrations radiate from the point of contact. A melting sensation coils deep inside of me.

"Saint," I groan.

"I know." The words are strained. He stays there, with me impaled on his shaft. A second. Another. His cock throbs, stretching me, as my pussy adjusts to the intrusion.

"You ready, Gigi?"

Even before I can nod, he pulls out, then thrusts forward. My entire body jerks.

A tingling sensation sweeps up my legs. I curve my back, thrust back, trying to take more of him inside. More. I need more.

"P-please," I stutter.

"What?"

"Please take me, Saint."

A growl rips from him. He begins to fuck me in earnest, and I meet his every thrust, pushing back with my hips, digging my knees into the bed for purchase.

"You're so damn tight. Even after all these weeks, I can't get enough of you. You're a witch, Gigi. You've completely undone me."

His words send vibrations of heat swirling in my belly. Everything in me is focused on him, on how he's buried inside of me. On the pulsing, seething, aching hollow that he leaves inside of me each time he pulls back. "It's not enough," I gasp. "I want..."

"Tell me." he growls. "Tell me what you need."

"I need—" I widen my knees, then reach back between my legs and squeeze his balls.

His dick jumps inside me, lengthening even further. He groans, then pulls out completely.

I whine, "What are you doing—?"

He flips me over, plants himself between my thighs. The bed dips, as he plants one knee, then the other, on the bed.

I open my mouth to demand what he's doing, and squeak when he guides his cock to my trembling opening.

I glance down at the sight of his shaft poised to enter me... *Holy* shit! It's the hottest thing I have ever seen. I gasp, draw in a breath, then scream as he buries himself inside of me—full, complete. The trembling screeches up my spine. the blood drums in my temples, and my vision wavers. "Saint," I whisper, "I am going to come."

"Don't you dare, Gigi."

His voice is fierce.

He drags his hands up the backs of my thighs, loops my ankles over his shoulders.

He pulls back, then slams inside me again, and the sensation of his gorgeous thickness filling me, stretching me... *My* God! I'll never be the same after this. Fucking, love-making... Whatever name I may give it... It's a primal meeting of our flesh, our souls. Something knotted inside of me dissolves. The climax bubbles up, waves of tension ebbing, then flowing forward. "Saint," I choke, "I can't..."

"You can," he growls.

The fullness inside me pushes up, needing wanting, demanding that I give in to it.

"Saint," I whisper.

"Eyes on me," he snaps. I jerk my gaze up to his, and the force of those blue eyes pins me in place. My chest hurts and a pressure builds at the backs of my eyes.

His lips kick up, a fierce smile lighting up his face.

"You're beautiful," the words spill out of me.

His smile widens and his gaze intensifies. "And you're mine."

"Yours." I nod.

"Come with me." He thrust forward and my orgasm overpowers me. I arch my back, open my mouth, and hear the sound of someone wailing. That's me, I know, but I can't stop myself. Tears blur my vision and I collapse, as he comes inside of me. I hear his harsh groan from somewhere above me. He slips down to cover my shaking body with his, his face nestled against my breast.

We stay in that position for a few seconds...maybe minutes. He anchors me as my body quakes and tears stream down my cheeks. Finally, my breathing steadies, mirrors his. I sense his heart thudding against my chest. His weight on me grows heavy, my limbs protest, but I don't say anything. This...whatever this is...it's different.

Does he realize how things have subtly shifted between us?

He stirs, then moves onto his back, pulling me on top—and wow, he's still inside of me. I mean, that's not easy to achieve, I'm sure, but he pulls it off without missing a beat.

He drags his palm across my hair and his fingers snag on a knot.

I wince.

"Sorry." He plays with my hair, undoing the knot with the same intense precision that he seems to bring to so much in his life.

"I began self-harming not long after my mother died, " his voice rumbles against my ear. "So much was not in control, then. I had no idea how to cope with the anger inside of me, which was already building after the incident. And when she died, my world fell apart. She was the only one who understood the level of PTSD I had from the incident, the only one who indulged my compulsion to speak in riddles."

He pauses, his throat moving as he swallows.

"But the strain of it all became too much for my parents. They broke up. She left home. Right after she left, my father told me I was the reason for the change in their relationship. I was a mistake, you see? There was no space in their marriage for me. He blamed me for what had gone wrong."

"Oh my god." I stare at him horrified. *Why the hell would his father say that? And his mother? How could she have left Saint, when he needed her the most?*

His features tense. "A month later, she died in an accident. I'm afraid I didn't take it well."

"I'm so sorry," I whisper.

"You have a knack for getting to the truth, don't you?"

I glance up at him, "Only with you, Saint." I rub my cheek against his chest. "Only you."

He pulls me close, tucks my head under his chin. "Sleep." His voice is soft, but my body seems to obey his command on instinct. Darkness closes over me.

"What? When did it happen?"

Saint's voice filters into my sleep-addled brain.

I come awake slowly, tuning into his words.

"I can't come right now, I'm…" He stops speaking. Guess he's on the phone? Who is he talking to? The same person who'd called him the last few times when he'd left me?

I hear his footsteps thud as he walks away.

I crack my eyelids open, glance down to find I'm sprawled on my front…on Saint's side of the bed. I'd gone to sleep on him… Had he woken up to find me coiled into him? Had he thought me weak? Because I'd submitted to him? I'd trusted him. Had I been wrong to do so? I glance over my shoulder to the open doorway of the bedroom and spot Saint. He's naked... Of course, he is. The man doesn't have an unconfident bone in his body.

He holds his phone to his ear, bends his other arm and runs his fingers through his hair. His biceps bulge, the planes of his back undulating. My mouth dries. I swallow.

He glances back toward me. I clamp my eyelids shut.

His voice filters through to me, "Are you sure the information is accurate?"

He listens. "The pickup is going to take place in an hour?"

Footsteps approach the doorway.

"Right."

I crack my eyelids open, enough to watch him lean against the doorjamb.

"I'll make it."

What the fuck—? He's leaving me after what took place between us?

His gaze roves over my shoulders, across my body wreathed in his sheets. Can he tell that I'm awake?

He glances away. I relax into the sheets. His scent is all around me; the heat of his body warms the bedclothes, tempting me to roll over and wallow in the remnants of his essence. Shit. I am getting addicted to him. Why does he have to be so...so...irresistible. So damn tempting. A 100% masculine hunk who has no idea how lethal his charm can be... And he isn't even trying.

"I know..." his tone lowers. "I am well aware that I got married three weeks ago, but this... What we do together is important."

Well, shit. Of course, whoever is on the other side of the phone takes precedence. My stomach churns and my breathing goes shallow.

Don't let him see how pissed off you are. And I have every right. That last time together, it went beyond the realm of fucking. Besides, isn't he the one who'd said he was making love to me on our wedding night? His actions of last night—especially the way he'd lashed out at my asking about the scars, only to return to our bed and confess that he self-harms—it backs up his words.

So who is he talking to now?

He widens his stance, giving me a full-frontal view of his cock.

I swallow.

"Got it," His voice dips, "I'll be at Mill Hill East Broadway in half an hour." He disconnects the call then crosses the floor toward the walk-in closet. I hear the sound of clothes rustling.

He's doing it then? He's leaving?

I sit up in bed. "Saint," I call out.

He steps into the room, dressed in sneakers, jeans and a sweatshirt that stretches across his chest. My breath catches. Saint in casual wear is even more potent than Saint in office clothes.

I clear my throat, tip up my chin, "Where are you going?

His shoulders bunch.

"It's a business meeting." His glance flickers away then back to me.

My heart begins to race. He's lying; I know he is.

"In the middle of the night?" I ask. "And dressed like that?"

He raises his shoulders, then sighs, "It's a work emergency." He heads for the door.

"Don't leave."

He turns to look at me and his expressions softens, "I'll be back soon."

I straighten my shoulders and the sheet falls to my waist. "You're leaving me?" I pout.

His gaze falls to my breasts; his chest rises and falls. "Not of my own volition." His voice is husky.

He tears his gaze off of my body, "You keep the bed warm, babe. I'll be back before you know it."

He crosses the living room to the front door. I hear the sound of the main door to the suite snick shut.

I jump out of bed, then race to the front door. I press my ear to it, hear the sound of the elevator door closing.

Where the hell is he going so early in the morning?

I walk back into the bedroom, take in the messed-up sheets, a pillow thrown to the floor. There's a dent in the pillow on his side of the bed, where we'd both slept. A shiver works its way up my spine.

I'd thought…that he had feelings for me… *Love?* Nah, that's too strong a word. Possession. The marriage is a bullshit fake to end all fakes…but perhaps it had elicited some primal feeling in him? Something that made him want to exert his ownership over me…because in some way, he's made me his.

Am I his?

Is he mine?

Sure, he'd shared more of himself with me. That doesn't mean anything; not when he'd lied to me about the call and left. I chew on my fingernail. There must be a good reason for his actions; there has to be. So why couldn't he tell me?

For that matter, why haven't I revealed the reason I am here?

Why haven't I told him about the hold the Mafia has on me? I could use his help. The thought has crossed my mind. But… I chew on my lower lip… What if I told him and the Mafia found out about it? They'd hurt him…and Nina. Sure, Saint has resources at his disposal…but the Mafia… They're everywhere, and they are ruthless. I can't play with both of their lives; I can't take the risk of something happening to them.

I curl my fists into my sides. I can't endanger the lives of both of the people I've come to care about.

No, the only way to protect both Saint and Nina is to complete what I came to do. But first, I have to find out why he lied to me.

I need to catch up with him, and find out why or who he keeps rushing off to see.

Walking to the closet door, I wrench it open. Ignoring the clothes he bought me, I cross the floor to my bag on the far end. Strange. I can't find any of my underclothes in the bag. Well, I am not going to wear the lingerie that he bought for me, it doesn't seem right to do so, not when he could be cheating on me as we speak… shit, don't do that, don't make assumptions, not until you find out the truth for yourself.

I forgo the underwear and pull on my jeans and a top; then tug on ballet pumps.

My heart begins to race. Adrenaline fills my blood. I grab my handbag from where I'd dropped it on the table near the door, then race out.

I punch the button to the elevator and the doors slide open. I step in, take it to the ground floor. Moderating my pace, I reach the guard by the door. It's the same guy who'd come toward us the day Saint and I had had our altercation on the sidewalk.

"Ma'am." He touches his finger to his forehead, in a semi-salute, "Can I help you?"

I bite my lips, "Uh… Actually, yes." I tip up my chin, "Can you get me a rental car or a taxi, please?"

He frowns.

"Saint told me I should ask you for help if I need anything." I add.

He stills, then nods. "I won't be a minute, Ma'am, if you'd wait here?" He disappears out the front doors. I shift my weight from foot to foot. A group walks in, and I shuffle aside.

I wring my fingers together; sweat slides down my back. What am I doing? Will I be too late to catch him?

The doorman walks in. He extends his arm and I take the key fob from him.

"It's the red Maserati parked right in front."

"A Maserati?" I blink, "Oh, but I don't need anything that flashy—" Not to mention that it'd stand out on the road. "Isn't there any other car, a little less…uh... Expensive?"

"Mr. Caldwell specifically allocated this one for you."

"Right."

Had he remembered my tastes from our conversation a few weeks ago? That must be it. What does it mean that he did? And when had he indicated to the doorman to direct me to this, if I asked? Had he guessed that I might want to drive my own car at some point?

"Ma'am?" the doorman prompts me.

I curl my fingers around the key fob, then eye his name tag. "Thank you, Dorian."

He nods, "No problem." He holds the door open for me.

I walk down the steps, press down on the key fob to unlock the car doors. I slip into the driver's seat, then program the way to Mill Hill East on the GPS.

It takes me 30 minutes to get there on the highway. I ease into a parking lot on the main street, then walk up the sidewalk. I spot Saint's Jaguar almost immediately. It's parked outside a coffeeshop.

Is he meeting someone here? I peek in through the glass wall, but can't see him. I turn to go…then glance back. There, at the far end, are the unmistakable broad shoulders which could only belong to one guy. His dark hair curls at his collar. He's facing away, talking to someone. I try to peer past him. *Damn* it. I can't see who's in the seat opposite him. *Show me your face. Go on. Do it.*

As if she hears me, the woman in the seat rises to her feet. She's tiny, perfectly curved and wearing black skintight jeans. Her blonde hair flows to her waist. I can't make out the color of her eyes, but no doubt, they are as stunning as the rest of her. She blows out a breath, folds her arms over her waist.

She hauls her handbag over her shoulder, then throws her hands in the air. Her slim, tight-fitting shirt rides up, revealing a smooth flat stomach. I ball my fists at my sides. Of course, she's model perfect. Is she his ex-girlfriend? Ex-something? Or maybe…current?

Her gestures are heated as she talks to him.

He leans back, runs his fingers through his hair.

She stabs a finger at him. He squares his shoulders.

She turns to leave, takes a step away, only for him to jump to his feet. He grabs her wrist. His face is in profile, but there's no mistaking the anguish in his features. I've never seen him this…disturbed. Not in all the time that I've known him. Nothing I've said to him has ever made him this overcome with emotions… Well okay, almost. The only time I've seen him this overcome is when we made love—no, fucked. That's all it was. He'd fucked me, and that last time, I was sure I'd broken through to him, just as he had shattered all of my defenses. I'd been sure it was the beginning of… Trust? Love? Whatever. Doesn't matter.

The woman he's talking to tries to pull away. His lips move, and her features crumple.

He pulls her to him and she buries her face in his shoulder.

He holds her close… My guts churn. *Fuck you, Saint.* Fuck you for making me want to…believe. Moisture streaks my cheek. I dash away the tears. I will not cry over this…two-timing, conniving jerk. I step away, retrace my steps back to my car. The red Maserati gleams in the dawn light.

Why did he have to remember my preferences and then go and do this? Damn it, I want to give him the benefit of doubt. But hell, if that scene didn't indicate there is a relationship between them.

I stomp over to the car, open it and throw myself inside. Smash the door closed with enough force that the entire vehicle shudders. I cringe. The car is new… And I am not jaded enough to not appreciate the power under my hands. I grip the steering wheel, press my forehead to it. "Bloody hell." *Why did you have to do this, Saint?*

I slap my hand against the steering wheel. Pain sweeps up my arm. It helps center me. I focus on the vibrating threads that sink into my nerves, follow them to where they disappear. Draw in a breath, allow the calm to steal over me. Somewhere along the line, I've become a masochist. When I inflict pain on myself, it helps me feel alive. It's something I can control. My response to it… To him. Why is it that I had felt compelled to hand that power over to him? Asking him to take me on as a sub had been…unplanned. It wasn't until I'd seen him that day, sprawled back in his chair, his glorious cock in his hand, as he'd looked me up and down with the smirk that had dared me to issue the challenge to him. I'd wanted to surprise him, wipe that satisfied smile off of his face. He thought he had me pegged? Well, he has no idea who he is dealing with.

He thinks he can take me for granted? He has another think coming. I am going to teach him not to mess with me. Over the last few weeks, a part of me had felt I was taking advantage of him.

Now, my conscience is clear. I can conclude my mission. I can complete the mission and save Nina. There is no more reason to hesitate. I wipe the tears off of my face, then reverse the car out of the parking lot.

Thirty-five minutes later I pull into the parking space reserved for Saint at the offices of 7A investments. I am his wife, right? What's his is mine, and all that. I can take what rightfully belongs to me. I slam the doors shut, reach the elevators meant for the penthouse where the Seven have their offices. I call for the elevator and it arrives in seconds.

I step inside, press my thumb into the receptacle meant for identification. It lights up green. Of course, it does. Saint has already shared my identifying information with the entire security system.

I tuck my bag into my side, jab at the button for the top floor. The doors close. The numbers above the elevator door increase. They open onto the executive floor. I step out and stride confidently toward the last office on the floor, where this entire bloody saga had begun. *Don't run. Don't hurry. Keep your pace. You are his wife. You have every right to be here, remember?* At least, it's a floor only frequented by the 7 and those to whom they have given clearance. And it's too early for the employees to be around. Not that any of them could come to my aid, if Saint were to catch me. But why would he? He is with his... Girlfriend? Mistress? Whoever it is. I am safe…as safe as could be expected for a woman about to commit a crime—one that will free my friend. I wrench open the door to his office. There's that dark and edgy scent of his—pheromones and leather, laced with a woodsy scent that is uniquely Saint. My belly flip-flops. Hell, the scent of him is enough to turn me on. *Get what you need and get out of here. Do it.*

Rounding the table, I plop my bag on his table then drop into his chair and yank at the top drawer—it's unlocked. My breath catches. I ease it open. There, on top of the papers is…a USB drive? I stare at it. This is too convenient. Did he place it there for me to find it?

I snatch it up and insert it into the laptop.

I place my forefinger on the lock-pad and the screen springs to life.

I freeze. Did he really trust me enough to have my fingerprints recorded onto his every device? Can I access all of his secrets…so easily? The hair on my forearms rises. It's a trap. It has to be. I stare at the screen; but damn it, I have to take this opportunity. I can't not do it.

A window pops onto the screen, prompting me to access the files on the USB stick. There's one file so I click on it and a video begins to play. The image of a boy tied to a chair fills the screen. His face is streaked with dirt, hollows under his cheeks. He's wearing a school uniform, his white shirt streaked with mud…and blood? His breathing is ragged. There's a sound off-camera, then he stirs, looks up and straight into the camera. I gasp. He's blindfolded but that patrician nose... The slant of his jaw? It's Saint. My heart begins to race. A man moves into frame, his back to the camera, he slaps the boy. Saint's body jerks.

The man leaves; Saint slumps back in his chair, blood trickling from a cut in his lips.

My stomach lurches and bile laces my throat. Shit, I can't be sick, not now. I click out of the video, eject the flash drive, then shove it into my handbag.

I turn to leave, then hesitate. I mean, come on, I have access to his computer. Do I dare? I pause. Do I? Fuck it. I swivel to face the screen, open up his email folder and scan through the emails. What am I looking for? Any clue to the woman? Anything to indicate who she is? The subjects of the emails all seem boring...work related. Shit, this is getting me nowhere. I click out of the emails. What now? I open up the pictures folder... Peruse the images. There. I click open pictures of Saint with Sinner, Saint with Weston and the other guy from the Seven... Arpad? Yeah that's his name... Saint with... I pause. It's a picture of Saint with the girl I saw him with earlier. It's taken somewhere in the open, by a river...? The two of them are fishing. Saint's smiling at her—shit, he never smiles like that.

His features are relaxed, his clothes more weather-beaten than anything I've ever seen him wear. My fingers tighten on the mouse. Damn it, this was a mistake. What do I care what the relationship between them is?

I click out of the pictures, scan the names of the other folders...

Anything else? Anything. Come on. There's a folder called "Gigi."

I click it open… then open up the file called 'Beatles.' Beatles, huh? It has files...marked in the order of years. From 1963—the year the first Beatles album came out—to the current year. I open the first file... A page filled with facts… Every single detail of every hit, links to relevant events that happened to the Fab Four in that year—the tours, the albums released, girlfriends at that time, news headlines they made. Wow. *Did* he do all *of* this research? Nah! Probably had some minion pull it up for him… He is thorough, I have to give him that.

I scroll down to the file marked "Gigi." Gigi? I click it open...and it is filled with riddles. Questions about the Beatles… So this is how he prepared for his meetings with me, like I was some kind of acquisition.

It's so very Saint. Being thorough, strategic... He'd been planning on how to converse with me...because he'd realized The Beatles were a pet obsession for me? But why? Why would he go about it in such a methodical fashion... Almost as if he—

"Victoria?"

I jump and the hair on the back of my neck prickles.

I look up to see his familiar features towering in front of me.

"Saint...?"

37

———

Saint

Her features freeze and her gaze widens. I step into my office.

She swallows.

I prowl forward and the color fades from her cheeks.

"What a surprise to find you here, *wife*."

She draws in a breath, then tips her chin in that gesture of defiance I am coming to recognize so well. My woman will never give me an inch; she'll make me fight for it. And fuck, if I don't love that about her.

Love? Fucking love.

There is that word again. A confusing emotion—one which muddles my instincts, clouds my intuition, and causes me to doubt my own judgment.

I reach my desk, pause in front of it with my legs spread wide apart. I prop my hands on my hips, "You have something to tell me?"

She swallows.

"Out with it, Gigi." I glance over the part of her that is visible above the monster hunk of a wood, which— Truth be told, I'd bought the desk in a fit of defiance. I'd wanted it to be the biggest desk among all the Seven. Don't judge. I'm entitled to spend my hard-earned money how I like it, right? Especially on her. I'll shower her with whatever she wants, and stuff she doesn't even know she needs. Hell, I'd trade in all of my riches for one more night of ecstasy with her—under me, in my bed, bent over my desk, ass in the air... Gigi crawling over to me across that wide surface, asking me to punish her for a crime she'd committed. I lower my voice to a hush, "Say the word, sweet thing." She pales. Her chest rises and falls. "Confess to your misdoings and I'll mete out your punishment."

She bites down on her lower lip. I jerk my gaze to that glistening flesh—pouty, full, pink and sensuous. Like the melting triangle of goodness between her legs. My dick lengthens and her gaze drops down to my crotch. I don't need to look down to know the crotch of my pants is tented right then.

"Do it," I growl.

She flinches. Her upper body moves, then she rises to her feet. She grabs the arms of my chair, swings her legs up, and hoists herself onto the chair.

"What the fuck?" I blink.

She's naked from her waist down.

No panties. Nothing except the curve of her hips silhouetted against the light pouring in from the wide windows behind her. Nothing except for the smooth expanse of her creamy thighs marked with reddened scratches. I'd done that, at some point during the last night, when I'd gone down on her. After she'd fallen asleep on my chest, her breathing had deepened. I'd stayed unmoving for an hour… Maybe two? Until I'd been sure I wouldn't wake her. Then I'd slid her onto her back, parted her thighs, settled in between her legs and feasted on her. I'd made sure not to wake her…had been gentle, soft, soothing, slow… I had licked and slurped and eaten her out, until she'd quietly come under me. Then I'd moved up to kiss her, to share our joined taste with her. She'd sucked on my tongue as I had eased into her; I'd finished myself off with a few thrusts. Hell, I'd been so turned on by the act of tonguing her cunt that… I hadn't been able to stop myself. I'd left my stamp on her. I'd claimed her over and over again. The phone call had woken me up and I'd left. Saying 'no' hadn't been an option. Some things are too important. Not even my feelings for her could prevent me from acting.

I'd wrapped up my meeting, checked up on her—yeah, I'd bugged her phone. So? Don't judge. Only I can keep her safe… And if that means I am stalking her? Well, it's for her own good, right?

"Gigi," I breathe. "What are you doing?"

"What does it look like?" She grabs the hem of her top and pulls it off. No bra… Fuck… Her pink nipples perk up, inviting me to come closer, closer. I bump into the desk... *Shit*, when had I bridged the distance between us?

"Victoria, have you forgotten the rules?"

"On the contrary, Saint." She climbs up onto the desk on all fours. "I'm submitting to you completely. This is what you want, right? Me… begging for you?" She crawls toward me, her breasts jiggling; her beautiful shoulders arch with each forward motion.

"You don't know what you are doing."

"Don't I?" Half-way over, she stops. Dropping down, she picks up a riding crop with her mouth.

She glances up, the strip of leather caught between her pearly white teeth. Fuck, fucking fuck. My groin hardens and a pulse flares to life at my temples, behind my eyelids, even in my fucking balls. "You're playing a dangerous game," I growl.

She glides forward, head held up, green gaze daring me to inch forward, to bend from my waist, to take the offered object of punishment from her. I shake out the modified whip. It whistles through the air. She flinches and a bead of sweat dots her upper lip.

"I know what you're doing, Gigi." She's trying to distract me. I drag the switch between my fingers. Her gaze drops to my hands. I slap the crop on my outstretched palm. Her shoulders shudder and her breathing grows erratic.

"You want this?"

She touches her tongue to her lips. My hand shakes. It fucking shakes as I hold it up.

"Say it."

"I…I…"

"Now."

"I want it, please. Saint. Use it on me. Make it hurt enough that I forget everything else that came before it. Own me, Saint. Hit me on my behind, then fuck me in the arse."

"Bloody fuck." My vision tunnels, and my cock insists on springing forward—ready, impatient to be done with all of the preliminaries. To simply bury my aching self inside her welcoming heat, to finally come home. "Jesus, Mary and Joseph," I snarl.

"Those… Those were the names of the three cats Lennon had at one point," she answers.

I laugh, "You're perfect, you know that? The answer to my twisted prayers." I push the tip of the crop under her chin.

She stills.

Drag the leather down her throat, between her breasts, down the concave of her stomach to where the bud of her clit peers out.

She shudders. "Saint…"

I withdraw the crop the same way, drag it under my nose, "Your scent, Gigi." I glare at her. "The sweetness of your arousal is more potent that honey." I swipe my tongue up the strip of hide.

A whine bleeds from her lips.

I swipe the crop through the air. "Turn around."

She instantly complies. The creamy mounds of her arse thrust out at me.

"Fucking gorgeous."

She swivels her head.

"Don't," I admonish her.

She faces forward.

I drag my crop across her buttcheeks and her entire body trembles.

"Which Beatles album spent the longest consecutive time at number one?"

"Their debut album… *Please, Please Me*."

"You bet." I bring the crop down on her arse.

She screams, "Bu…but I got the answer right."

"So?"

"Sadist."

I chuckle, "Now you recognize my true nature." I tilt my head, "Which song by the Beatles features only thirteen different words in the lyrics?"

"It's a love song recorded by John for Yoko," She bites her lower lip.

"Tell me Gigi." I prompt.

"I want you..." she huffs.

I bring the cane down on her backside.

She cries out, "I hate you."

"I don't." I slap the whip across her backside. She chokes. "In fact, I think I may even be falling in lust with you."

I lower the crop again and again. She cries out, wriggles her hips, throws her head back. The skin of her arse cheeks blooms red. The tracks stand out against the creaminess of her skin. "Fuck, Gigi. I need you now."

I loosen my grip and the switch slips from my hand. I drag my knuckles up her pussy. "You're soaking, babe.'

"Saint, please," her voice is strangled.

"You ready for me?"

"I've been waiting for you since before I knew who you were," she whispers, "when all I had was a hope and a wish for someone to push away all the memories that hold me back."

"What's holding you back, Gigi?"

"I...I can't tell you."

"You will."

"I... I..." she huffs.

I lower my face, press my cheek to hers, "Say it... Say what's on your mind."

"They... The Mafia... They kidnapped my friend, Saint." Her voice trembles, "They're holding Nina hostage. They...forced me to play the role of Adam's wife."

"Why you?" I cup her pussy. Her thighs clench.

"Why did they contact you?"

"Nina was my roommate at UCLA." She swallows.

"You were close?" I strum her pussy lips.

"Very." She shudders. "My parents moved from London to LA when I was twelve. My father left us shortly afterward." Her lips twist. "My mother ended up having to work two, sometimes three, jobs to make ends meet. Her focus was to put me through college so I could find a good job and carve a better future for myself."

She blinks; her chin wobbles.

I drag the wetness from her cunt to her back hole. "You got a scholarship to UCLA," I prompt.

Shit, why had I said that? Me, the cold-hearted bastard who could string out an entire business discussion without showing mercy... The slightest hint of uncertainty from her and I can't stop myself from reaching out to help. This has got to stop.

I smear her wetness into the valley between her butt cheeks. She shudders. "That's where I met Nina," her voice quavers. "After my mother died, she was there for me; she pulled me out of the emotional hole I'd dug myself into. Clearly, the Mafia knew how close we were."

I dip a finger inside her back hole. Her butt clenches and her entire body jerks.

"Saint," she protests.

"Complete what you were saying," I instruct.

She swallows "There was no way I could abandon her." She tips up her chin, "But you know all this already, don't you?"

I grunt.

"Yet you married me?" she asks.

I tilt my head.

"Why?" Her chest rises and falls. "Why would you do that?"

"To keep you close…" I draw in a breath, "Not only that, though. It may have started out that way, but I fell for you somewhere along the way. You understand that, right?"

I slip another finger inside her back hole and she groans. I pause, giving her time to adjust to the intrusion.

"Oh, my god, Saint…" she mewls. "Please, it's not enough."

"Soon, darling." I pull out my fingers, then grip her hips to hold her in place. "What hold do they have on you, Gigi?"

"I… I told you everything already." Her shoulders stiffen, her spine ramrod straight.

Why is she not telling me everything?

"What have they asked of you?" I lean over, kiss the shell of her ear.

She moans.

"You have to tell me if you want me to help you."

I position my dick between her arsecheeks and she shivers.

"Let me take some of the burden off of you, Gigi. Tell me why you're running scared? You're my wife, sweetheart. I'll do anything for you. You know that, right?"

"Will you, Saint?" She thrusts out her hips and my dick nudges the opening of her puckered hole. Lust spirals up my spine and tension winds tight in my groin. I need to be inside of her. Need to take her again. "Anything," I force out the words through clenched teeth, "Anything for you."

"Then tell me who the phone calls are from? The woman for whom you'll leave your wife and go running? Who is she, Saint?"

I dig my fingertips into her hips and she winces. I loosen my grip, slightly. It'll leave marks on her there. *Good.* If this is the only way I can assert my ownership on her, then so be it.

"You…saw us?"

She nods. "I…followed you."

"That's why you came to the office?"

"I came here because… I couldn't bear to return to the bed we'd shared, after… You left to meet another woman."

"You have no idea what you're talking about," I growl.

"Then tell me, Saint." She turns to glance at me.

"I… I can't; not without putting you in danger."

"Me?" She blinks.

"It's the kind of thing you want no part of."

"Why can't you let me be the judge of that?" she scowls.

Fuck, fucking fuck. She has no idea what she's asking of me.

"Why can't you trust me to decide what's best for you?"

"Is it?" She swallows. "Or is this more convenient for you?"

"There you go, doubting me again." I blow out a breath. "Besides, I am sworn to secrecy. I made a promise to her."

She winces; her face pales. "What about the promise you made to me? You swore to take me as your wife, to cherish and to protect me."

"All of which I intend to do."

"Then start with this. If there's even a small chance for us to be together, then tell me what it is you're hiding?"

"I…" I lower my chin to my chest, "I can't, Gigi. It's not my secret to tell," I hold her gaze, "but I can show you how much I want you."

"It's not enough." She tosses her head, "You can take your dick and stuff it—"

"Oh, I am going to stuff it all right." I bare my teeth, "Inside you, where it belongs."

"No," she tries to pull away.

I hold her in place, "Yes."

"I don't want this."

I shove my hand around and between her legs, "You do." I slide my fingers inside her soaking cunt. "Whatever our differences may be, however divisive the secrets between us, there's one place where we can't hide from each other, and that's when we fuck."

"Fuck off."

"I intend to, only I am going to take you with me, sweetheart."

I shove my fingers in and out of her and she whines. I grind the heel of my palm into her clit; she throws back her head. She snaps back her shoulders, thrusts up her hips. My dick stabs into her backhole, and she groans.

"Damn you, Saint. Damn you for the responses you wring from my body."

"Good, the feeling's mutual then."

I pinch the swollen nub of her clit and she screams. Her body bucks and her knees part further. She lowers her cheek to the desk, shoves her trembling butt toward my face.

"Fuck, Gigi, I have to take you." I release her pussy, squeeze her arse cheeks, holding them apart. "Now." I kick my hips forward, and my dick slips inside her puckered hole.

38

Too much. Too full. Three weeks of Saint owning my body and I haven't adjusted to his size.

My knees shake and my nipples pucker. The flash of pain settles into a dull throb. Something inside of me gives, eases open, and he slips inside further. A groan rumbles from him. I open my mouth, wanting, needing to scream out my surprise. Of how it's strange and yet…real. How he's pinning me here, to the present, with his massive cock that throbs, lengthens, pushes at my boundaries.

"Saint," I choke out his name.

"Killian."

"What?"

"Call me Killian."

"You're fucking killing me with your cock." A giggle wells up my throat, "Your timing…is just…"

"Impeccable?" He chuckles.

"Ridiculous." I mumble.

"I prefer quirky. Admit it, Gigi, if nothing else, we're well matched. You, with your weird obsession with that ancient boy band…"

"And you, with your strange affliction for riddles," I choke out.

He stays still, his length embedded inside of me.

"Why do you like to ask questions?" I force myself to ask, to think about something. Anything other than how weirdly arousing it is to have Saint stick his cock inside the most forbidden part of me. A tremor spirals out from where we are connected. "Shit." I dig my palms into the smooth surface of the desk, force myself to breathe, "You going to share a little more, Saint, or is this off limits—?"

"It forces me to think rationally," he replies.

"Rationally?"

I sense him nod.

"Every time my emotions threaten to get the better of me, the questions help me find my balance."

"So, it's a coping device?"

His grip on my hips tightens. He bends forward and the heat of his body sears my back. The hard jut of his pubic bone digs into the curve of my butt. "You trying to analyze me?"

"Uh...understand you," I stutter.

"What if I don't want you to?" He swipes my hair off of my neck, presses his lips to my nape. I can't stop the moan that tumbles from my lips. The intensity of his touch, the intimacy with which he handles my body...it's...mind boggling. He's crawling his way inside of me, imprinting himself into every hidden part of me... Soon, there'll be nothing left but to open myself completely, to offer up the last unseen parts of me... Soon. Not yet. I can't. Not if I want my friend to survive. That's why I am here, remember? To get the information from Saint and hand it over. I 'm so close...so damn close. "Saint," I whine.

"Easy, Gigi." He slides his palm between my legs and cups my pussy. "My beautiful..." he strums my pussy. "Responsive..." he pinches my clit. "Soaking wet..." he slides three fingers inside my melting core, brings his other hand around to grip my neck. He squeezes and a heat sears up my spine, the pressure at my temples growing. Spots of blackness weave in front of my eyes. I need, I want... I must have.

"I know."

He pulls out, only to push my legs apart. His dick nudges my pussy, then he pushes forward and impales me. His thick length slams home, filling me, stretching me, holding me in place—immovable, unshakeable. The only man who truly gets me.

He thrusts forward again and again. Tilts his hips and pushes into me. He bloody owns me. This man. He's imprinted himself on my soul.

He pushes his cheek into mine. "Come for me, wife." His possessive whisper sweeps through my mind. The trembling sweeps up my back. Pauses. Waits.

"You're mine, Gigi, you feel me?"

Was there ever any question?

He releases his hold on my neck and the climax smashes into me. I hear the sound of a distant screaming…recognize it as me. Flashes of white overwhelm me as he empties himself inside me. My knees give way, but he's there. He wraps his big arm around my waist, secures me to him. My head lolls, I allow my hands to flop by my side. I am one big oozing gooey mess. At his mercy. His to command. To hold and to piece together any which way he deems fit.

He pulls out of me and I can't stop the groan that leaves my lips. He pulls me up, cradles me close, then carries me in his arms bridal style. "Where…" I swallow, "Where are we going?"

"Shh, babe, let me take care of you."

He cuddles me and I allow myself to curl into his chest. Coil my fingers in his shirt. "You didn't get undressed."

"I was in a hurry," he chuckles. "Next time."

Will there be another time? I have what I came for. Once I hand it over… I'll be far away from here…from his friends…from the girl friends I made here... What then? Nina will be free and everything can return to the way it was.

Will it? My throat closes. Will anything be the same without him? What am I going to do when I can't see him, feel his skin on mine, his rough fingers between my legs, his presence, his dominance, him. How am I going to live without him?

I turn my face into his chest, inhale his dark scent.

"Did you sniff me?"

His voice sounds from above me.

"Don't tell me you don't smell me?" I huff.

"Roses and something tart."

"Huh?"

"That's your scent, Gigi."

He shoulders open the door of the ensuite, walks toward the counter next to the basin. He lowers me on my back.

I wince.

"Hurts, huh?"

"You don't have to sound so pleased."

He laughs, "I didn't spank you half as much as I wanted to."

I peer up at him from under my eyelashes. "Oh, please. You went for it, all right. I was counting.'

"Oh?" He snatches up a wash cloth, moistens it under the running water.

"What are you doing?" I frown. He rummages in the cabinet below the basin, pulls out a tube of what looks like ointment. "What's that?"

"You don't get to ask the questions, remember?" He picks me up in his arms again. "Can't you simply enjoy your man taking care of you?"

Is he my man?

Am I his?

What's next?

Shit, my mind's going into overdrive. All of my nerve endings seem to be firing at once. Far from being exhausted by the happenings of the past half hour… His spanking, and then his fucking, seems to have awakened me completely. I've never felt this alive, this… Open to him. It feels like we've turned a corner. I shake my head. I must be hallucinating from all of the hormones in my blood stream that his fucking must have released.

He approaches a chair I hadn't noticed in the corner of the spacious bathroom.

He places me over his lap, baring my arse to his gaze.

"I'm convinced you have a fetish for backsides," I grumble.

"Only yours." He presses the cool cloth to my hurting skin. I moan.

"Good?" he asks.

"Very."

He holds the fabric there a little longer, then drops it to the side. I sense him opening the tube he'd pulled out earlier, then coolness laces my burning backside. The hurt instantly recedes.

"Oh," I snuggle into his lap. "That feels amazing."

"Enjoy it, Gigi." He continues to lather on more of the—antiseptic I assume? Then caps the container and drops it to the floor at the side. He runs his fingers up my spine, to my nape, digs his fingertips into my scalp.

I arch into his touch, "That's so good."

"Hmm."

He leans over; I hear the tap run. He parts my legs, drags a wet cloth across my core.

I tremble. This...caring version of him? I know he has it hidden behind all that grumpy alpha-maleness, but it always takes me by surprise.

He flips me up, taking care not to abrade my backside, then carries me back into his office. He crosses the floor to a large armchair and sinks into it, holding me.

"Let me know if it hurts."

He lowers me into his lap.

I wince, then settle in.

"Okay?" He asks.

"Yeah." I coil into his chest.

He plays with my hair, strokes my shoulders, runs his fingers down the side of my arm. With long masterful strokes he massages my aching limbs, my thighs, my calves.

The tension drains from me. I yawn suddenly, then shake my head, "I think I'm falling asleep."

"You're coming down from the high."

"Right... The spanking?" I mumble. "But a few seconds ago, I was sure I had never felt more alive."

"You enjoyed it?"

"Of course." It's an admission of how only he can pleasure me. So what? It's not like I have anything more to hide from him. Well, nothing more than the biggest secret of all. I yawn again and tears streak my cheeks. "I think I need to take a nap."

"You do that." He strokes my hair. "It'll refresh you for the party tonight."

"Party?"

"Oh, yeah. Sorry I forgot to mention it to you." His fingers still, then he wraps them around my neck. His grip tightens. I grip his wrist and he releases me, only to cup my cheek. So possessive. So nice?

"One of the things that the Seven insisted upon." A whisper touches my forehead. Did he kiss me? "They took the last few weeks to organize a proper party to celebrate our wedding. Can't be helped. A man of my status needs to use this occasion to his advantage."

I frown. Status? Saint doesn't care about that. He makes his own status, as far I know. What is he not telling me? What is he hiding from me? I open my mouth to ask, but he pulls me in closer. "That okay by you?" His scent intensifies around me.

My head spins. "Sure, why not?" Everything is okay, so long as he keeps me wrapped up in him. I crack open one eye. "Will I need a dress?"

"It's taken care of." He chuckles, " You grab 40 winks, while I get us home."

I snuggle in, then mumble, "Don't forget my bag from your desk."

39
____

Saint

"What do you think?"

I glance up from where I'd been pacing in the living room of the suite. She stands framed in the doorway to the bedroom. The green gown clings to her breasts, seeming to be kept up by nothing except their perkiness. It cinches in at her impossibly tiny waist, only to flare around her hips, and flow down in straight lines, to her toes. She props a palm on her waist, thrusts out a leg through the slit that rides all the way up to the waist.

My hand tightens on the glass of whiskey I hold. "The fuck are you wearing?"

Her eyebrows lower, "Have you forgotten that you picked out this dress?"

So what? She has no business looking that beautiful, that over-the-top seductive in that outfit. When I'd seen it in the store…all I had thought of was how well it would match her eyes. I'd imagined her wearing the gown, and fuck, if I hadn't come right then. Of course, I had picked it out for her. Had wanted her to wear a dress that was revealing enough to make her uncomfortable. One of my crazy-ass ideas that had seemed brilliant at the time. Why does she have to look so delectable in that? Why the hell does it matter to me that men will eat her up with their eyes? I toss back the rest of the whiskey, place it on the counter of the bar I had been leaning against.

"Turn around."

"What?"

I circle the air with my finger.

She frowns.

I jerk my chin. She draws in a breath, then does a slow turn for me.

"The fuck?" The back of the dress is far, far worse. It dips in a V that plunges down all the way to the top of her arse crack. The shadowed cleavage between her ass cheeks mocks me. I was inside of her not a few hours ago.

I'd carried her into the private elevator at the office—it was too early for any of the other Seven to be around—then to the top floor, where I had directed my helicopter back to my hotel suite. That way, there had been no chance of anyone seeing her in her undressed state. I'd let her sleep in my bed, watching her as she'd not stirred... Not until I'd woken her up an hour ago to get dressed. I'd left the outfit for her, needing to see her wear my choice. It is perfect for her. It brings out all of her best attributes, the silver-tipped heels on her feet giving her a few added inches that accentuate the jut of her butt, the proud thrust of her cleavage.

I prowl toward her, place my palm flat in the middle of her bare back.

She shudders, "Saint."

"Get out of this dress."

"I will not." She turns to glare at me, "I put a lot of effort into looking good."

"Is that what you call this?" I step back, look her up and down,

My heart stutters; she so fucking beautiful. And yet... She still hasn't revealed the real reason she came to me.

I draw myself up to my full height. "Step out of it, Gigi, or I'll make you do it."

"Try me," she juts out her lower lip, then turns away.

I push her up against the wall, hook my finger in the 'V' of her dress and tug. The delicate fabric rips.

She gasps and the sound coils in my belly. I'm instantly hard.

She looks over her shoulder. "What are you doing?" her voice is breathless.

I yank at the cloth and it parts all the way down to the hem. I let go and it pools to the floor.

"Jesus," I take in the silver thong that rides the top of her butt.

"The fuck are you wearing?"

She wriggles her feet, tries to angle her body. I apply more pressure to her back. She arches up.

"Answer me," I growl.

"What does it look like?" The anger in her voice slices straight to my gut. My belly tightens. My cock tents my pants.

I run a finger down the silvery thread caught between her arse cheeks.

Her thigh muscles ripple.

"Saint," her voice hitches, "please."

"Please what, Gigi?" I plant my thigh between her legs, pushing them apart.

She shudders, "Why…why are you doing this?"

I dip a finger inside her pussy. The melting heat clings to my skin. "That's why," I growl. "Because I only have to glare at you, and your body instantly responds." I yank on the thin silver fabric and it snaps.

A small scream leaves her lips, "You…you don't want to do this."

I laugh, "Don't you realize? In no way, can you tell me what to do."

I unbuckle my belt, lower my zipper.

"Stop," she snarls.

I yank her butt toward me, position her right, shove her legs apart further, and—

"Don't—" her voice breaks.

I pull out my dick, position it at the opening of her melting pussy. Drag my hand up and around to cup her breast, "I want you," I growl.

"Not yet."

I squeeze her nipple, run my tongue up the curve of her ear, "Yes, yet."

"First answer my riddle."

"Huh?" I pause, "What did you say?"

"Answer my questions. If you get it right, you can have me… Else…"

"Else?"

"You have to wait until I am ready."

"You know I don't allow anyone else to question me."

"Why not?" She frowns at me, her cheek flat against the wall. "What are you afraid of Saint?"

"Nothing."

I roll her nipple between my fingers. Her mouth parts.

"See, your body can't deny me."

"That's true," she swallows, "but you relish challenges, Saint, and I'm challenging you to own my mind."

"What does that mean?"

"Answer my question…and I promise, I'll never stop you again."

The familiar fear bursts through my mind. My heart begins to race. Sweat beads my temple.

Fact is that I'd take her anyway I can get her…but… I also can't deny her. My dick nudges the soft opening of her pussy, and I force myself to stay there. Stay.

"What is always too late?" Her voice slices through the lust in my head.

Don't answer. *Don't*. Damn her, she is the only person I'll always answer. Fuck her for exploiting that, and fuck me for answering.

"Regret," I snarl.

She tips up her head, "Some try to hide, some try to cheat, but time will show, we always will meet."

I pause, my pulse rate ratchets up. "Death," I grind out.

"When I sneak up on you, you'll never be the same again." She smiles, "What am I?" A tear slides down her cheek.

I bend into her, lick it up. "Betrayal," I growl.

She swallows.

"You going to betray me, Gigi?"

"What do you think?" She tips up her chin, her gaze challenging. "The mighty Saint, who's never had the courage to lose his heart ever before... You think I have the guts to betray you?"

"I think," I grip her hips, position her just right, "that you already have." I propel my hips forward and enter her.

Her head falls back against my shoulder. She brings up her hand and I grab her palm, flatten it against the wall, pressing my fingers in between hers.

"My God, Gigi, you're..." My cock lengthens inside of her. She thrusts back, grinds her butt into the hard wall of my pelvis. "Please." The word spills from her lips.

A groan rips out of me. I grind my teeth so hard, pain rips up my jaw. I lower my head to the curve between her neck and shoulder, "Fuck you for getting to me. Fuck me for not being able to resist you. Fuck us both for what we are doing to each other." I bite down on her neck.

She screams.

Her pussy clamps down on my cock. I pull out, and the friction of my dick against the melting walls of her channel is too much. More blood rushes to my groin. I drag my fingers up to her breasts, squeeze her nipple.

Her body bucks. I rip my teeth from her shoulder, turn her head to mine. "Open your eyes," I growl.

Her eyelids flutter open, her pupils so big in her eyes, they seem to swallow up most of her iris, leaving only a ring of green at the circumference.

"Saint," she whispers.

"I fucking love you," I snarl.

Her face whitens. "You can't."

"Too late," I bare my teeth. "Congratulations, you got what you set out to do."

I propel my hips forward, bury myself inside her with such force that my balls slap against her skin.

Her mouth opens and her throat moves as she tries to speak. I shake my head, "Save it for later, babe, cause both you and I are going to pay for this." I pull out and thrust back in, impaling her again and again. Her body jerks and spasms grip her body, sweep up her hips, her breasts.

Her gaze widens, "Omigod," she gasps, "I'm going to…"

I pull out, and come on her back.

"What the—?" She blinks.

I step back, survey the white ribbons of my cum that crisscross her curves. Pulling out my handkerchief—monogrammed because, what the fuck? I gotta play the part of gazillionaire dickhead with no details spared—I throw it at her. "Clean yourself up."

I tuck myself back in, turn and stride to the lift.

"Oh, and Gigi," I glance at where she hasn't moved from against the wall, "don't be late."

40

Victoria

I pause outside the entrance to the ballroom of the Claridge's—the same one where, only a few weeks ago, I'd wed Saint. Wed him? Ha, that has to be a euphemism for... The most mind-blowing sex ever... Okay, so I don't have experience to compare it to; but hell, if that matters.

I've seen enough porn online, heard enough from friends in university, swapped enough secret fantasies with Nina to know... What I had with Saint was exceptional.

I shudder, nervously toy with the ring he gave me. The emerald warms against my skin. *Stay strong, you can do this Victoria. You only have the next few hours to get through... And* then what?

Escape? Get out of here, away from the Mafia... At what cost? You'll give up the man who'd professes to love you? He may as well hate me. That's what his tone had implied. No, Saint doesn't understand the meaning of the word love. He is obsessed...fixated, maybe... Sure, he finds me attractive, but he'll forget me. He'll move on quickly.

To another hotel suite, another lay, another woman to take and conquer. My heart stutters. He'll forget about me soon enough…and I… I will be free.

Still tethered to the thought of him—his touch, his feel, the crude way he'd taken me earlier, how he'd torn off my gown, not caring for the fact that it was new and expensive. It shouldn't màtter to me. That flaunting of his wealth had been a crude gesture… One meant to put me in my place. And I had found it hot. I had been instantly wet and throbbing and aching for him. My nipples tighten against the short black sheath. I run my hands down the fabric that clings to my thighs.

This isn't one of Saint's purchases. It had been in the bag I'd packed before leaving Amelie's. No way, am I wearing anything else bought by him. Not after how he'd reacted to my wearing the previous one. What the hell had come over him? He'd been like a man possessed. He'd fucked me, then not allowed me to climax. Just like he'd refused to tell me who that woman is. There has to be a simple explanation to it… So why won't he reveal it? How can it be for my safety when it is tearing me apart from inside?

And all that, after he'd professed his love. *Hell!* I clutch my hands around the simple silver purse that dangles from my hand.

Why did he have to go and do that?

Almost as if he'd known that it was his last chance to tell me his true feelings. And he'd meant it. I squeeze my eyes shut. *Deny it as much as you want…but there had been a hint of desperation in his tone, a dangerous glint in his eyes.* And the way he'd fucked me…as if it was our last time.

He is no fool… He knows something is going to happen… So he'd played his last card. He'd…hit me where it hurts—hoping it would hold me back from what I have to do.

If he thinks his declaration is going to stop me… Well, he has misjudged me. He isn't the only one who plays with people's feelings, who can set their eyes on a goal and use anything and everything…and anyone, to get to it.

Sweat beads my palm; I wipe it on the silky fabric of my dress. My knees knock together and my throat dries.

"Victoria, honey, are you okay?"

Amelie grips my shoulder.

"Why don't you sit down?" She leads me to an armchair pushed up into an alcove of the hallway a few feet away.

I sink into it. She keeps her hand on mine, and takes the seat next to me.

I draw in a breath, then another.

She grabs a bottle of water from the antique table in front of us, unscrews the cap, and hands it to me. I take a grateful sip.

"Better?"

I nod, then lower the bottle. "Is my make-up okay?"

She surveys my face, "You're always perfect, V."

I shake my head. If she only knew.

I reach over, place the bottle on the table.

She squeezes my hand, "Now, tell me why you were having that panic attack."

"I wasn't."

She stares at me. "Is this to do with Saint?"

A giggle bubbles up, "What in my life isn't to do with him right now?"

"It's normal for newly-weds to feel overwhelmed."

Not like this, it's not. I squeeze my fingers together around the bag in my lap.

"When are you guys going on your honeymoon?"

"There's not going to be any honeymoon."

She frowns. "Of course, there is. Saint asked Meredith to book tickets to—" she snaps her mouth shut. "Ugh, sorry. Did I give away a secret?"

I toss my head, "Doesn't matter. Saint's good at putting on a show."

She peers up at me from under her eyelashes. "You know that's not true… I mean, all the Seven are consummate actors and jerks—"

"And a-holes of the first order."

She nods, "But you saw how hard Sin fell for Summer and see how devoted Jace is to Sienna. When they fall, they fall hard. They don't stop until they've swept their women off their feet."

I shift in my seat. "It's really, really not like that. All this…" I wave a hand in the air, "is an act.'

"Saint said you'd say that," she nods.

"When did you talk to him?" I stare at her.

"Umm." She changes position, "I wasn't going to tell you, but—"

"But?"

"—seeing as how much of a tizzy you've got yourself into, you should know—"

"What?" *Don't tell me, don't. Please.* "What is it?" I scowl.

"Remember when I ran into you outside the 7A offices that night?"

"Yeah…" my voice trails off. *Shit. I don't want to hear this, I don't.* I grip the arm of my chair.

"What do you think I was doing there at that time of the evening?"

"I thought that…" my voice trails off, "…that you'd come to meet Weston?"

"That ridiculous, selfish, no-good reprobate?"

Uh, oh. "Strike that." I wave my hand in the air.

"Why would you even think I'd arrived for a rendezvous with Weston?" she grumbles.

Nice, one. I've put my foot in my mouth now, haven't I? "Forget it," I mumble.

She glares at me.

"Honestly, Amelie," I lean forward, take her hand in mine, "I didn't mean to piss you off, but there's chemistry between you two…" And that's putting it mildly.

"I've barely had a single conversation with the man, and anyway," she sniffs, "this isn't about me and Weston."

"Right," I snatch up another bottle of water and hand it to her.

She uncaps it, drinks from it, then sighs, "So, as I was saying… I was there that night because Saint called me and asked me to come by. He thought you could do with some company."

"Hold on…" I reach for my bottle of water, press it to my aching temples. "He asked you run into me?"

She twists her mouth, "He told me to pretend it was a chance meeting."

After he'd told me he didn't want me and allowed me to assume that he wasn't accepting my proposition… My head spins. I squint at her, "You're not making any sense."

"You're telling me?" She chugs down more water. "He swore me to secrecy."

"And you agreed?"

She reddens, "Hey, I thought it was romantic. Besides, he told me that he'd—" she chews on her lower lip.

"What?" I peruse her features. "He made you a deal?"

"He said," her gaze flicks away, then back to my face, "that I'd get to make the wedding cake, and take credit for it. He said he'd ensure all the media would cover the event and my name would be mentioned."

"But the wedding ceremony was impromptu…"

"Not the one that's about to take place."

"Oh?" I frown, then stiffen, "Oh."

She nods and her features scrunch up, "He's been...uh... planning this for a few weeks. He—ah!—" She shuffles her feet. "He wanted to surprise you with a society wedding that'd get a lot of attention."

"Oh, he did, did he?" I growl. The nerve of the man. *How dare he take me for granted?* There's a bitterness to my voice that I can't disguise when I ask her, "Did he also pay you to friend me?"

"Of course, not." She sits up straight. "Look V, I swear, he only wanted to make it special for you."

I snort.

"Besides," she wriggles around trying to find a more comfortable position. "I could hardly turn him down."

"Of course, not," I echo her.

She stiffens, "It's not easy, trying to make it on your own."

"You bet, it isn't."

She scowls, "It's cut-throat out there." She waves her hand in the air, "Think of what this kind of exposure could do for my business."

I stare at her, "I'm thinking a lot of things, all right."

She reddens. "Please try to understand, V. I mean, if you guys were going to get married, then why not keep the catering for the wedding in the family, huh?"

"I suppose Isla's doing the wedding planning?" I ask.

She glances away, then back at me.

"Of course, she is," I scowl.

I suppose that makes sense too. I mean why look outside when the talent is in your circle of friends? So why does it feel like a bloody betrayal? I place the cap on the bottle, screw it back in place with deliberate precision. "So, the time when Meredith met me outside Self-ridges…" I glance up at her, "She brought me here to meet all of you. Did Saint put her up to that as well?"

"You'll have to ask Meredith about that." She swipes the hair back from her face.

"Did he ask you to round up all the women so you all could keep an eye on me?"

"It…it wasn't like that." She leans forward to take my arm.

I shake it off, "All this time, I thought, perhaps, I had a support circle here, that perhaps I had a chance of finding a place where I belonged… I should have known that asshole would set me up. It was all about making sure that he was informed of my movements."

"He wanted to keep you safe."

"Bullshit," my voice echoes around the space.

A couple speaking at the far end of the corridor looks our way. Like I care? I glare at Amelie, "It was a way of controlling me, making sure he could monitor everything I did. He wanted to see if I'd give myself away."

"Give yourself away?" She frowns, "What are you talking about? Saint wanted to ensure that you didn't feel lonely, that's all."

"You believe that?"

She holds my gaze, "I do, Victoria. Saint's madly in love with you. I've never seen a man more besotted. Sure, he may be unorthodox in the way he shows it, but you have to admit, it's romantic that he's been so… Forceful."

I throw back my head and laugh.

The couple glances at me again, then move away, putting more distance between us. Good.

Too bad, Saint hadn't gotten the memo as well.

"Keep kidding yourself that way, girlfriend— Oh, I forgot, you're not really my friend, are you?" I rise to my feet.

"Please, V, don't be like that."

I turn to leave.

"I admit Saint prompted us to befriend you. Our friendship may have started out that way, but we've all grown to like you... Hell, you've become my BFF so damn quickly..."

I pause, then turn to glance at her, "BFF?" I chew on my lower lip.

"I swear." She holds up her hand.

"I want to believe you; I do." I shift my weight from foot to foot. "But imagine if you were in my place and you found that your... Uh... The man you're interested in goes behind your back and gets to the women you think are your friends. What would you think of it?"

"I..." she blinks rapidly, "I'd think he cares for me... A lot."

I scoff, "Wait until it's your turn and one of those alphaholes sets his sights on you. I'll be sure to ask you then, how it feels... Then again, I probably won't be around."

"Oh, pfft," she waves a hand in the air. "Of course, you'll be around. And I'm not the settling type. I intend to focus on myself. I've planned a retreat to rediscover myself," she beams.

I squint at her, "What do you mean?"

"I am going to take a few weeks off over Christmas. I'm going away to an isolated cabin in the countryside. It's owned by the Seven, and it's one of the things Saint promised me in return for..."

I throw up my hands, "Jesus, I can't believe you agreed to that."

"I knew I shouldn't have taken him up on that offer." She blinks, "I'll refuse him; I won't go to the cabin. In fact, I'll tell him I don't want any credit on the cakes and desserts I provided for the wedding party."

I scan her features.

She wrings her fingers together, "Shit, I'm sorry, V... I really didn't think it would upset you this much."

Maybe it's me. Maybe I am overreacting. Everything is running away from me, this entire sequence of events moving too fast for me. I hunch my shoulders. I feel so alone—so damn on my own. Nina has always been there for me. And she isn't here... and I have to go through with this sham of a fake wedding. It is the only way to keep on track, and complete what I came here to do. She'd be free and it would all have been worth it. It would, right?

"V," Isla approaches me. "I'm sorry."

I draw in a breath.

"Please tell me that you're not angry with us."

I sigh.

"Please... p-l-eee-ase," Amelie singsongs.

This woman! I may not have known her long, but her happy-go-lucky nature is a thing of beauty. She wears her heart on her sleeve, hadn't blinked an eye before inviting me into her home. If there is one thing I know, it's that when I need her most, Amelia will be there to help me, just like Nina had been.

"Fine," I mutter.

She whoops and throws her arms around me. "OMG! Thank you, V. Thank you. Everything is going to work out now. I promise you. Saint loves you. He really does."

Hell, he's fooled all of them; but I can see through him.

I pat her back, then straighten my shoulders. "Guess I'd better get this over with, huh?"

41

Saint

She had to do it, huh? She had to take the goddamn USB. I'd checked the drawer after she'd fallen asleep, when I'd gone to grab her purse, and it was gone. Then because, apparently, I have a hidden masochistic side, I had checked her purse...and spotted the fucking thing. *Fuck.* So this is how it feels to have your life go tits up.

I toss back the whiskey, then place the empty glass back on the bar counter. The bartender tops it off. I lift the glass to my lips, take a healthy sip.

"Living the dream, I see?" Weston slaps me on the back.

I chug down the rest of the amber liquid, slap the glass back on the bar.

"Easy, ol' chap." Weston leans his hip against the bar, watches as I reach across and grab the bottle from the bartender. I tilt the bottle of Macallan's Single Malt to my mouth, swig from it.

"As classy as your shoes," he clicks his tongue.

"What's fucking wrong with my shoes?"

"A bit worn out for the rest of your suit... How much did that set you back by? £10,000?"

"£20,000," I toss back more of the whiskey. It burns a path down my gullet, and sets off a burn in my stomach, "but who's counting?"

"Trouble in paradise, I take it?"

"Fuck off," I growl.

"It's only your goddamn wedding we're here to celebrate," he smirks.

"Fake wedding, douchebag."

"This is exactly how Sinner started out... Now look at him," he jerks his chin.

I follow his gaze to where the wanker stands in a corner, arms around Summer. The two are engaged in intense eye-fucking... The kind I indulged in with Gigi. No, that was real fucking... *Fuck* that... It was some intense shit. The harder I took her, the more she gave me. The more I pushed her, the deeper her resistance grew. Hell, I'd intended to punish her...maybe myself, when I'd taken her against the wall. Couldn't stop myself from tearing the dress off of her—the beautiful dress I'd imagined her in when I'd bought it.

I should have blown off this entire fucking party and simply stayed in my suite with her. Hell, she deserves more than this impersonal hotel space. She deserves a home... A real one, with furniture and curtains that she's picked out, and all that shit that women seem to thrive on. Not that Gigi is like other females. She is fucking stronger than she seems. A sultry seductress whose call I can't resist. One glance at her and I lose myself. She only has to be in my vicinity for my dick to take notice...and other parts of me...especially that offending feeling in my chest that has assailed me since the first time I'd kissed her, "Fuck."

I raise the bottle to my lips and glug down some more of the liquid.

"That's the economy of a third world country you're drinking down, by the way."

I wipe the back of my hand over my lips, "I am not going to apologize for being born into wealth." I slap the bottle back on the corner, "Not that it helped when we were kidnapped."

"Money's overrated," he rubs the back of his neck.

"But it's a necessary evil," I counter.

"Sometimes I do wonder what would have happened if I'd stayed with Doctors without Borders… Would I have been less of a douche then?"

"No," I shake my head.

"Touché." He frowns, "And your glowering Romeo mood is catching."

"Not glowering," I growl, "not a Romeo." The hair at the nape of my neck rises; electricity flickers across my nerves. She's here.

"Here comes your Juliet," Weston confirms.

I brace my shoulders. Since when *have* I needed Dutch courage to face a woman? Since when have I made a habit of drinking enough to layer on a veneer of indifference before facing a room full of people? Since that bloody beautiful, dark-haired witch had gotten under my skin.

"She still in mourning?" Weston frowns.

"What? Of course, not," I shake my head. "That piece of shit husband of hers was one only in name."

"Sure doesn't look that way, given what she's wearing."

"She didn't…" I pivot, take in her slender figure poised at the entrance. She's draped in black. The dress clings to her curves, covers every inch of her torso, and ends above her knees. It is far from the seductive gown she'd worn earlier… Just the opposite.

The high collar grazes the tip of her chin—not a sliver of skin on show. The full-length sleeves drape over her wrists to cover her palms, leaving only her fingertips exposed. She's wearing high, over-the-knee boots that come to mid-thigh.

The six—or is that eight?—inch heels boost her legs so they seemed to go on and on. Slender yet muscled, perfect to coil around my waist. She takes a step forward and a slim band of skin peeks out between her dress and boots. I'm instantly hard—Okay, harder. By any standards, her dress is more than demure… And that's the issue, because the flash of skin is almost obscene, given every other inch of her is covered in black. She raises a hand to flip down the veil attached to the jaunty hair accessory attached to her sleek hair. The thick strands are caught up and tied at the nape of her neck in a demure bun—that screams for a man's hands to rip out the pins and drape the waterfall of dark desire about her shoulders. The slash of red across her lips highlights her full, pouty lips. The overall effect is part widow-part slut.

"Fuck," I squeeze my fingers into fists.

Next to me, Weston grimaces, "She's doing it on purpose, to get a response out of you."

"No shit," I growl.

"She wants you to lose your shit in front of all of the guests," he warns.

"The fuck I care?"

"She's baiting you, Saint."

"She fucking succeeded." I take a step toward her.

"You don't want to do this," he grips my shoulder.

I shake him off, "Oh, but I do." I pause, shoot him a sideways glance, "Can you ensure that all the paparazzi have their cameras on us?"

He frowns, "You sure about this?"

"A hundred fucking percent." I stalk toward her.

A guest steps in my path. "Fuck off," I growl at the man clad in an ill-fitted suit.

He pales, then draws himself up, "I didn't come here to be insulted."

"Too fucking bad, you just were."

"You'll pay for this." He holds up his phone, snaps what is, no doubt, a shot that's going to be all over the internet.

"Knock yourself out, tosser." He's confirmed that it had been the right decision to invite every piece of shit news reporter and key influencer in town.

I walk toward her as men and women step aside, their gazes tracking my progress. Good. She takes a few steps forward, her gaze fixed on me.

I thrust out my chest.

She tips up her chin.

I look her up and down. She props a palm on her hip, angles her body. She strikes a pose, ensuring I take in every detail of how the fabric clings to the slope of her shoulders, the thrust of her breasts, the tiny waist ensconced in lace. She leans her weight to the side and the dress pulls tightly on her thigh. My cock twitches. I hasten my pace.

She stays rooted, her chest visibly rising and falling. I near her and the color from her already pale cheeks leeches out.

"You going to faint?" I curl my lips, "Not had your orange juice or whatever it is you need to stave of the shakes?"

She firms her jaw, "Your concern is touching." She pretends to flick a tear from her cheek, "Went straight to my heart."

My lips twitch, "And I wasn't even trying." I come to a halt so close that she has to tilt her head right back to keep her gaze locked with mine. A single strand escapes from the hairdo and floats across her cheek.

"You've made your choice, hmm?" I raise a hand.

She flinches.

I twine the hair around my finger, then tuck it back behind her ear.

She swallows, "It seems that way, doesn't it?" Her voice is firm, "You do you, Saint."

She bites down on her lower lip and my gaze drops there.

"Oh, I plan to do you first, darling wife." I swoop out my arm, wind it around her waist, and haul her to me with such force, she crashes into me—from breasts to waist to hips, she's plastered to me.

Her gaze widens and fear trembles off of her.

"Don't disappoint me now, my love. This is what you wanted—an open spectacle in front of the world, with every eye on us. A signal to those you work for that you've accomplished what you set out to do."

Her throat moves; she wets her lips and lowers her gaze to my mouth. "Yes…" she whispers. "It's what I need. I want you to hate me, Saint. Everything I've done is so you abhor me—so you forget me when I leave."

"Where are you going?"

"Somewhere you won't be able to find me," her smile twists. A single tear rolls down her cheek.

"Save the fucking histrionics," I snarl. "I love you, doesn't mean I am going to let you get away with this."

She stares, then chuckles, and a giggle spills from her. She begins to laugh.

"The fuck is wrong with you?"

She glances past me, pales.

"What is it?" I frown.

"Kiss me."

"What?"

She throws her arms around my neck, raises her chin, presses her lips to mine.

"Don't—"

She bites on my lips, digs her fingertips into my hair and drags them across my scalp. My groin hardens and my vision tunnels. A groan tears out of me. Fucking fuck, I can't refuse her, I can't resist her. Fuck her for rendering me so helpless.

I drag her up to tiptoe, deepen the kiss.

She sucks on my tongue, kisses me back with a fervor that borders on desperation. The hair on my nape rises. My heart twists in my chest.

This entire sequence of events, starting with her walking into that office and asking me for help… Was any of it real? A hollow sensation roils in my stomach. A bead of sweat slides down my back. I tear my mouth from hers. "The fuck is happening?"

She swallows, peers into my eyes.

"Tell me, Gigi, I can help you." I scan her anguished features.

"I can't let you," she whispers.

"No," my pulse begins to race, "don't do this."

She cups my cheek. "Promise me, you'll put this behind you, and move on."

"The fuck you talking about, woman. If you think I am going to let you put yourself in danger, you've got another think coming. I won't allow it, Gigi, I—"

"You ready to leave, Victoria?" a new voice booms.

My heart slams into my chest. I swing around to face a familiar face.

"You?" I snarl, "The fuck you doing here?"

42

Victoria

"Hello, Antonio."

He comes forward, arm outstretched.

Beside me, Saint stiffens, "Get the fuck away from her."

"Afraid it doesn't work quite that way, old sport." Antonio turns to me, "You going to tell your new husband, or should I?"

I tip up my chin, "I need a second."

"You've run out of time." Antonio smiles, white teeth flashing against tanned skin. He prowls toward me.

I shudder, take a step back. Saint's warmth envelopes me; he wraps an arm around my waist. "You don't have to do this," he whispers in my ear.

I do. I don't have a choice. If I don't do as he says, he'll kill the friend who's meant more to me than any family. No, I have to do this, with no help from anyone else.

I yank at Saint's arm. His muscles flex, "I am not letting you go."

"I was never yours to begin with."

"The fuck?" he explodes.

I elbow him in the waist. He huffs and his grip loosens enough for me to pull away. I turn on him, "I'm leaving you."

"What?" He frowns, scans my features then chuckles, "You're getting back at me for my asshole attitude, huh?" He lowers his voice, "You know that's because I can't help myself. It's in my blood, I'm a born wanker." He raises his shoulders, "but for you, Gigi... For you, I'd change."

I swallow, then shake my head. "You...won't." *I don't want you to.* "Your uncompromising meanness is too much a part of you. Besides… this entire arrangement between us was a farce."

"Not for me." He takes a step forward, "It may have started off that way, but I developed feelings for you."

"Like I care?"

"Of course, you do," he growls. "You love me, Gigi."

"No," I back away from him.

"Yes. You do. You're too frightened to admit it." He glares past me. "What does he have on you?"

"Nothing." I retreat another step.

Antonio's heat assails me. My skin crawls. My fingers jerk. Don't shrink back; don't show how afraid you are right now. His massive hand descends on my shoulder. The blood drains from my face.

"Don't fucking touch her," Saint's feet don't seem to touch the ground as he crosses the distance between us.

"Don't come closer," I swallow.

"Stop right there," Antonio snaps.

Saint's jaw tics. A vein throbs at his temple. He folds his fingers into fists, and his entire body tenses.

A woman screams. People scramble back.

I glance sideways and freeze. Antonio holds a gun, its barrel trained on Saint. My heart jackknifes in my chest. "You promised," I whisper. "You said you wouldn't hurt him. You promised that if I gave you what you needed, you'd release my friend."

"Maybe I lied," Antonio smiles, his thin upper lip a slash across his face, "maybe I didn't. It's up to you how this plays out."

I swallow.

"Tell him to stand back."

"Stop hiding behind her, you coward," Saint growls. "Let her go and fight me."

Shit, shit, shit. The hell is he doing? "Shut up, Saint," I huff.

He glares at me, the skin around his eyes crinkling.

"Don't tell me what to do," he pulls back his shoulders.

"This once, will you listen to me?" I whisper-shout.

"She has a point," Weston walks forward.

Antonio points the gun at him, but he raises his hands, "Easy there."

Antonio turns back to Saint. "For someone who was kidnapped and tortured, you turned out well."

"Tortured?" I blink.

Saint's jaw hardens, "Let her go, and you and I can talk this out."

"Oh?"

Saint nods. "What do you want? Money? Fame?" He glances around at the assembled paparazzi. "Though why you'd want every single camera in the country on your back—"

"Not mine. Yours."

"What?"

Antonio turns to me, "Hand it over."

"What's he talking about?" Saint growls.

I nudge my fingers into my purse, pull out the flash drive.

"I believe this is what you are looking for," I hold it out to him.

He turns the gun on me. "Don't attempt anything funny."

There's an indrawn breath from Saint. Tension screams off of him. Does he recognize it? Does he realize it's the USB from his desk? Will he ever forgive me?

"No, tricks." I raise the device, "Take it. Everything you want is on that."

He holds out his palm and I drop the device onto it. He pockets it, then grabs me and holds the gun to my temple. Sweat beads my upper lip.

My heart races so fast, I am sure it's going to break out of my ribcage. My knees buckle and the world tilts around me. Antonio tightens his hold on my waist, yanking me closer. I flinch, hunch my shoulders.

"Let go of my wife," Saint growls.

"Wife?" Antonio laughs, "Is that what you call this relationship?"

Saint's shoulders bunch, "Shut the fuck up."

"Have you told her what they did to you when you were kidnapped?"

I half angle my body, glance from Saint to Antonio. "Of course, I know about the incident," I force my voice to stay steady.

"Oh?" Antonio begins to inch back. "Has he told you what they did to him in that cell? How they tortured him and his friends? How they systematically broke him?"

Saint growls low in his throat. The fine hair on the nape of my neck rise. "Of course, he did. We…we have no secrets."

Shit, what am I saying? What does it matter that Antonio is trying to push Saint until he loses control? Why can I not allow that? I straighten my shoulders. I need to deflect Antonio' attention for as long as I can.

"You told him your secrets, Victoria?"

I pale. "I… Have none."

Antonio grins, "You'll have to do better than that." He jerks his chin toward Saint, "Even your husband doesn't believe you."

Don't look, don't. I swing my head in Saint' direction. He's glaring at me, his features contorted. His blue eyes blaze with… Anger? Hate?

My pulse rate kicks up. Shit, why *does* his opinion of me matter? "I never withheld anything from you." I glance away, "Not out of choice, at least."

"I believe you."

I whip my gaze to his face, "You do?"

"Of course. All of your actions have a reason."

"Oh!" My heart stutters and warmth coils in my chest. "You believe me?"

"Always." Saint's lips twist, "Even your lies tell me a story."

"Saint, I—" I step forward.

Antonio pulls me back.

I cry out.

Saint jumps forward.

"Stop right there," Antonio aims his pistol at my husband.

"I… I'm fine," I choke out. "Don't come close."

Saint's throat moves as he swallows. "Get away from her," he growls.

"Get back." Antonio, waves his gun and the crowd scrambles away. "The rest of you too."

I survey the room and find Sinclair—with Summer behind him—Weston, Damian and Edward standing in a semicircle.

Amelie and the girls are clustered in a corner away from the action.

Antonio jerks his chin, "I won't warn you again."

"Get back, you guys," Saint growls.

Weston hesitates. Damian and Edward stay unmoving. Sinclair balls his fists at his sides.

"She's my wife," Saint's shoulders bunch, "I take the risks."

"Fuck that," Weston scowls. "We have each other's backs."

"So what if we don't always like each other," Sinclair mutters.

"Except Baron." Damian glowers. "He prefers to keep his shit separate."

"Fucking Baron," Edward agrees.

Antonio glances between them, "You guys are insane."

"Am I late…?" Arpad walks in with a blonde on his arm. She screams.

There's a soft pop. I blink at the gun in Saint's hand. Where the hell had he kept it hidden?

Antonio staggers. "Fuck," he swears aloud, takes another step back.

"Let her go," Saint growls.

Antonio retreats toward the door, keeping me between him and Saint.

"Ask your husband to put down his weapon, or you're going to be widowed twice over," Antonio growls.

"No, don't hurt him." My pulse rate goes through the roof. "Saint," I swallow, "do as he says. Please."

Saint doesn't move. His gaze is fixed on my face. His features are hard, his eyes glaring pools of blue. Is he angry at me?

Why is he angry at me?

Antonio reaches the door. "Say goodbye."

"No," I snarl, helplessness filling me. "You can't do this. I did every-thing you asked me to do."

"Too bad I never keep my word." Antonio raises his gun toward me. Flashes light up around me, then everything goes dark.

43

Saint

"Fuck, fuck, fuck." I pace the floor in the waiting room in the hospital. "I am her husband. I should be in there with her."

Damian watches me from the chair he's sprawled in. "You did a good enough job convincing the doctor in charge to allow Weston to be present."

"He's a doctor, isn't he?"

"A surgeon… A heart surgeon, no less." Arpad straightens from the window, where'd he'd taken up position since we'd arrived at the hospital.

"So? He's the only medical professional I'll trust her with."

"Saint, you're being unreasonable." Damian frowns, "This is the best hospital in the city, and the doctor you have attending is a specialist."

"Fuck that. Can't trust anyone, and you know that."

Damian draws in a breath, "Can't say I disagree with you, but has it occurred to you that you're not helping things with your crazy, possessive streak.

I turn on him. "Wait until you fall in love and it's your wife in there fighting for her life—"

He raises a hand, "Shit's not for me. You and Sinner, collapsing one after the other… Nah, seeing what you two went through is more than enough to put me off any kind of relationship, let alone marriage."

"Famous last words," Sinner walks in, his arm around Summer.

Summer breaks away and stops in front of me. "How is she?"

I drag my fingers through my hair, try to speak but the words stick in my throat. I turn and begin to pace again.

Damian replies, "She's in surgery; Weston is in with her."

"The doctor allowed him in?" Sinclair frowns.

"Romeo here didn't give him a choice," Damian mutters.

"He nearly decked the paramedic who asked him to release her into their care," Arpad grimaces.

"Asshole dared to ask me to stand back from her," I growl.

"Only because they needed to check her vitals. You understand that, don't you?" Damian straightens. "Honestly, you needed to take a chill pill, and let the professionals get on with their work. You were only getting in their way."

I take a step toward him. Arpad and Sinclair both step in front of me.

Edward ignores the proceedings, his face buried in a book, in the chair he's occupied since we'd arrived here.

"Hold on," Sinclair reaches for me.

I sidestep him, "Don't fucking touch me, man."

"Sure," Sinclair rocks back on his heels, "It's understandable you're feeling on edge and all. I get it."

"Oh, do you now?" I smirk. "Just because you're married and all that shit, you think you understand how it feels to have the woman you wronged take a fucking bullet for you?"

"Jesus, Saint, you're living up to your name."

"The fuck you mean?"

"You're taking the sins of the entire world on yourself. See what I did there?" Sin raises an eyebrow and smirks.

"You douche, this is not the time to indulge in fucking word play."

"Says the man who has a riddle to suit every occasion," Arpad mutters.

"Not this one." I dig my fingers through my hair, tug on the strands. "My mind's a fucking blank." Also, not true. All I can think of is her pale face, her limp figure crumpling to the floor. I'd raced toward her and caught her before she had hurt herself further, thank fuck. I'd carried her out and to the ambulance, I'd refused to let go of her hand on the ride here.

I flex my fingers. Blood stains my palm; I stare at it. My heart begins to race. The scars on my soles itch. *Whack-whack-whack.* I flinch.

"Answer this, boy, and you go free."

It's a trick, always a trick. He asks me questions to which I never have the answers. This is how he plays with me. Traps me in my mind, trying to crack the puzzles. I've never gotten an answer right so far. Goddamn him. It's a sure way to mess with my head. He'll never let me go free, not even if I get it right. Damn him, he's screwing with me. If I get out of here alive, I'll never be caught unaware.

"Saint."

I'll read up until I know the answer to every fucking question ever. No one will ever ask me a riddle again. I'll be the one in control. Always.

"Saint!"

There's a touch on my shoulder, I pivot around, fists raised in front.

"Easy," Sinner steps back, putting distance between us.

Damian and Arpad freeze.

Edward slaps his book shut, "The answer's a minute at a time."

"What?" I frown.

He places his book on the seat next to him, then leans forward, "The answer to the question that's on your mind."

"You a mind reader now, along with being a priest?" I glower.

"If the occasion demands." Edward places his elbows on his knees, "You're wondering how you're going to get through the time she's in there?"

"Fuck off."

Edward winces, "I'll let that pass, this time." He raises his hand. "Your turn to ask a riddle."

I glare at him, "Fuck that."

"Fine, I'll go then." He smiles, "A prison you feel safe in, yet never quite happy. Whenever you try to leave, it only grows bigger."

He glances around the space, "Anyone get it?"

"Comfort Zone?" Arpad ventures.

Edward nods, "Very good."

"Here's another." IIe taps his fingers together, "If you break me, I do not stop working; if you touch me, I may be snared; if you lose me, nothing will matter. What am I?"

"Your heart?" Damian asks, then stares at Edward, "Shit, there's a parable hidden somewhere in that, isn't there?"

"Of course, there is," I growl. "Edward here, is a cheeky bugger. He leverages his status as a priest to get away with sin."

Edward loses some of his color. He straightens, then shakes his finger, "Not gonna distract me there, Saint."

I snarl.

His grin widens. He lowers his hands, "The more you carry it with you, the heavier a burden it becomes. What is it?"

Silence.

He scans the faces of the group assembled, "No one?"

"Go on, Father, tell us," Arpad drums his fingers on his chest.

"A guilty conscience." Edward's lips kick up in a smile.

"Enough," I snarl. "Spit out whatever it is you are trying to say."

"Do you have one?" Edward asks me.

"Mine's bigger than yours, Father."

"Not getting into that argument with you." Edward's grin widens, "I mean, do you have a guilty conscience?"

I run a finger under my collar. "Of course, not."

"You could have fooled me," Edward's eyes twinkle.

"Okay… So I owe her an apology." Fucking more than an apology, actually. "I owe her my life." I rake my fingers through my hair. "I was careless; I panicked when that fucker restrained her. He touched her and I couldn't do anything about it." I crack my neck from side to side, "I won't let that bastard live."

"He let her live." Weston enters the room, wearing his surgical garb.

"What?" I turn around, "What do you mean? How is she…?"

He watches me with a considering gaze.

My throat closes. "Is she?" my voice cracks. Jesus, fuck. I curl my fingers into fists, "Tell me Weston, or so help me I'll—"

"He could have shot her in the chest or in the head, but he didn't." Weston rubs the back of his neck."

"He shot her," I growl. "She was bleeding."

"It was a flesh wound."

I blink.

"What?" Damian straightens.

Edward rises to his feet.

Arpad, Sinclair and Summer move in closer.

"So… She's fine…?"

"The doc stitched her up, but she's okay."

"Right." The knot in my chest eases. I head for the entrance when a nurse enters. "The patient is asking for—"

"Me," I step forward, "I'm her husband."

She glances past me, "Dr Weston, she wants to see you."

"There's a mistake." I frown, "She must have asked for me. Saint? She's my wife."

The nurse's features taken on an expression of pity. I stiffen. I hate that look, have seen enough of it.

"Let me through," I growl.

I brush past her and she touches my arm, "I'm sorry, but she doesn't want to see you."

44

Victoria

I dig my fingers into the hospital bed. My shoulder throbs. The pain from the gunshot wound matches the throbbing sensation in my chest. At least they pulse in synchrony. That has to count for something, huh? A giggle bubbles up my throat.

Hell, don't lose your shit now. Deep breath, stay calm. You've come this far; you can see it through to the end.

I shut my eyes and see Saint's face—his concern, the way he'd seemed to appear from out of nowhere and catch me as I fell. The last thing I remember is the fear in his eyes, the paleness of his beautiful features, the vein throbbing at his temple. Then his arms had closed around me, he'd cradled me to his chest, and I had felt safe... Safe, despite the fact that I'd been shot.

I'd known then that he'd do anything to protect me. He really did mean what he'd said. He cared for me... As for love? Perhaps he does love me, but will he accept this child...? Will he want to participate in bringing up this child, when he'd told me in no uncertain terms that he doesn't want children.

Weston walks into the hospital room, "You okay?"

I nod, try to swallow, but my throat is dry. I glance toward the side table. He walks to it, pours out some water and hands me a glass. I accept it and take a few sips.

"He wants to see you."

My fingers tremble. The glass tips and water splashes onto my hospital gown.

My heart hammers in my chest. "I don't… I can't…"

He leans forward, rescues the glass and places it back on the table.

"Does he know?" Weston pulls up a chair and drops into it.

"No," I twist my fingers together. "Did you tell him?"

He shakes his head, "But Saint has a right to know."

I tip up my chin, "That's for me to decide. He won't want it."

"Whatever is between the two of you, that's your business." He leans forward, "But I am his friend, and I owe it to him to let him know."

"I'm his wife." I set my jaw, "It's my decision when I decide to share this with him."

"So you will tell him?" He frowns.

I twist my fingers together, "When it's the right time."

His jaw tics, "You want this child?"

I nod, "More than anything else in the world."

"How long have you known?"

"I… I guessed…when my period didn't arrive on time." I raise my shoulders. "But I put it down to the stress of the last few weeks."

"Did you plan this?" He frowns.

"No," I swallow.

He sets his jaw.

"Really." I hasten to add, "I understood how precarious my situation with Saint was… I even started taking the pill. No way, would I have been this irresponsible."

Yet here I am, pregnant.

Weston raises an eyebrow. "When you say you 'even started taking the pill,' do you mean you just started when you and Saint got together?

I nod.

He shakes his head, "Victoria, it can take up to seven days for birth control to become effective."

My mouth drops open.

"The doctor must have told you..."

"Oh, my god," I whisper, "I must not have heard her."

Had I planned this subconsciously? I've always wanted a child of my own... No, I wanted Saint's child. I admit it, but I didn't consciously plan for it to turn out like this. I hunch my shoulders.

"I... I wouldn't hurt Saint." I swallow, "Not on purpose."

He changes position, surveys me for another beat. "I believe you," he says, then places the tips of his fingers together. "As your doctor and your friend, I'd advise that you allow him to share the load. This is when you need him the most."

"I don't need anyone."

He scowls ,"Victoria."

"Swear it," I sit up and hold out my hand, "Swear you will not tell him yet, that you'll give me the chance to break the news to him."

"Fuck." He jumps up. "This is why I steer clear of all entanglements. It's a bloody minefield. I don't want to get dragged into this."

"Promise me, " I plead.

"I can't not tell him. However," he turns to me, "I'll delay it on one condition."

"Of course," I huff. "You Seven know how to haggle. Everything is a negotiation for you guys."

"Maybe," he raises his shoulders, "if it gets me what I want..."

"What?" I meet his gaze, "What do you want from me?"

"Meet him, once."

I shake my head, "No, no, that's not happening."

There's a commotion at the door, then Saint stalks in.

"Don't think he's leaving you a choice." Weston's face softens, "Let him help you, Victoria."

"Keep your promise," I implore him. "That's all I want."

Saint draws abreast with Weston, "What are the two of you talking about?"

"The Doctor was just leaving," I look pointedly at Weston.

He turns to go.

"You should join him," I turn my head to the side, study the view from the window—a road, a building across the street. Rain patters down the window pane. Bleak. Miserable. Just like my life is going to be without him. *Shit. Stop it.* This is the right thing to do...for him...for me...for the child I'm carrying. Saint isn't ready to have children and I'd never force that on him.

His father had called him an intrusion... A mistake. And mine? Well, mine had checked out, leaving us to cope on our own. The track record for fathers being present and engaged in both of our lives is not reassuring, to say the least. I bite the inside of my cheek. I won't let my child go through the same experience. It would be better for my child to never know a father, than to be rejected by one. If that means giving up the man who's come to mean so much to me, then so be it.

"Gigi."

I bite my lips. "Don't call me that, please."

He hesitates, then lowers himself into the chair. "How are you?" he asks.

"I'll be better once you're gone."

He makes a low noise in his throat, "If anything had happened to you—"

"I'm fine."

"He shot you."

"Antonio didn't intend to hurt me."

"Except he did," his voice cracks.

I turn to face him, and flinch. His hair is mussed, his face unshaven. Redness rims his eyes... And his gaze. Oh my God! His blue gaze burns into me with an intensity that makes my heart lurch. "Saint," I say his name before I can stop myself.

"I have my guys on him. He's revealed himself and I am not letting him go until I take him and everyone associated with him down.

"You can't," I bite the inside of my cheek.

"What? Why not?"

"If you do, he'll kill my best friend. The deal was for me to win your trust, to find the evidence you had on the Mafia and return it, in exchange for—"

"Your friend's life?" He snarls. "And what about your life, Gigi, your safety is my priority. You, are my priority. Nothing is more important than you. And that fucker dare pull out a fucking gun and threaten you, in front of me?" His nostrils flare. His biceps bulge, his shoulders seem to grow in size. Hell, Saint in full blown protective alpha mode is... bloody hot. I am going to miss that... so bloody much.

"I won't let him get away with it." He glares at me.

"I hadn't expected him to pull that stunt, Saint. Honestly. If I'd known he was going to hijack your event and ruin your reputation…"

"Fuck that," he swears.

"But…but he made you look like a loser." I protest.

"You're still here, aren't you?" He scowls.

"I can't stay, Saint."

His jaw tics, "If you think I am going to let you walk, with that man loose out there…"

"If he'd wanted to kill me, he'd already have done it. He wanted to cause a diversion to escape. He won't reveal himself again. His face is too well known. Besides, I am of no use to him anymore."

He frowns, "So stay with me. I thought I was in control, but all along, it was you who was leading me on. You were always one step ahead, Gigi—"

"Victoria," I correct him.

"Fuck that," he growls. He widens his stance, and damn him, but my gaze drops right to the tented fabric between his legs. Surely not. He can't be aroused. Is that Saint's resting position? It has to be. That's how big, how thick… How bloody massive his larger-than-average dick is. I'd felt it inside of me, curled my fingers around it and squeezed him, massaged him and made him come, had taken him down my throat and swallowed his cum, had shattered all over his fingers, ridden his dick as he'd brought me to climax. My thighs clench. My stomach flutters, I press my hand to my belly.

"What's wrong?" He frowns.

"Nothing." I bite the inside of my cheek.

"Stop lying."

"Fine," I glower at him. "You want to hear why I don't want anything to do with you? Why I know there's no future for us?"

"Tell me," he leans forward, his fists balled between his knees. "Tell me why you want to leave me."

I stare into his face and my heart begins to pump hard enough to pound in my throat. My palms begin to sweat. *Do it; tell him.* I brace my shoulders, "I don't want you."

45

Saint

"What?" I blink.

"I hate what you do to me."

"You don't." I scan her features.

"I loathe that we can't be honest with each other." She meets my gaze unblinking, "I despise how you bring out the part of me that I have hidden from for so long."

She pulls off my ring from her finger; holds it up. The stone glistens in her palm. I stare at it, my heart pounding erratically.

"Take the ring, Saint."

I hold out my hand and she drops the piece of jewelry into it.

"What gets broken without being held?" I close my fingers around it.

She blinks, chews on her lower lip, "Is it…a promise?"

My lips twist.

Her face pales further.

"Imagine you are in a dark room..." I peer into her face, "How do you get out?"

She curls her fingers at her sides, "Stop imagining," she whispers.

"When my mother asked me the same questions, I didn't have an answer for her. For a long time I was convinced that it's why she left me."

"Oh, Saint," her features twist. She half sits up, reaches for me.

I pull away, "I don't want your pity."

She half smiles, "Pity is the last thing on my mind where you are concerned."

I straighten.

She lowers her brows, "How old were you when she left?"

"Thirteen." I shuffle my feet. "A year after the incident."

"When you and the Seven were kidnapped?"

I nod. *Shit, it never gets easier to talk about this.* I square my shoulders. "They held up the car I was in, knocked my driver unconscious, and abducted me on the way home from football practice."

"Is that why you prefer to drive yourself around?"

I nod, "And why I keep a gun on hand." I raise my shoulders, "No way, will I be so vulnerable again."

"And the riddles?"

"What about them?"

"What got you so dependent on them?"

I lean forward, squeezing the ring in my palm with such force that the emerald cuts into my skin. The soles of my feet burn; I press my heels into the ground. "I can't talk about that," I straighten.

"Can't or won't?"

I rise to my feet, "Does it matter?'

"And the woman?" She asks.

I scowl. "It's not what you think it is." I stare into her face.

She scoffs. "You expect me to believe that?"

"Believe it..." I raise my shoulders, "or not."

She stiffens, "Is she your sister? Your cousin? Hell a blood relation of some kind?"

I shake my head.

"So who is she?" Her eyebrows knit.

"She's a... friend."

"A friend?" She glowers at me.

"Also a business associate." I crack my neck. "There's uh! Nothing between us."

"Fine, say I believe you." She wrings her fingers together, "What were you talking about with her?" She sets her jaw. "Why do you go running every time she calls?"

Shit, I'd done no wrong so why the hell am I feeling defensive?

I draw in a breath, "I can't tell you. I told you, I won't put you in danger."

She throws up her hands. "And you want me to stay? When there are so many secrets between us?"

"When I make a promise, I keep it, Gigi. Unlike you."

She pales.

"Shit." I drag my fingers thought my hair, "I didn't mean it."

"Sure you did."

We glare at each other. She's right. She brings out the worst in me. She makes me feel things I never have... She makes me hurt. *Fuck! Why is this thing between us so complicated?* Sweat trickles down my back. "You're right." I glance away. "Whatever was between us, it's over."

I turn to leave.

"And you say you love me?" she huffs.

I walk toward the exit.

"I can be a game, but there are no winners, what am I?" her voice stops me.

I pause, then because I can't fucking resist, I answer, "Blame."

"What's another name for Saint?" she asks.

I grip the door frame, "Don't do this, Gigi."

"Answer me," she snarls.

I step through the doorway.

"Coward," her voice follows me out.

I freeze.

"You heard me," she huffs, "You don't have the courage to face up to what's between us."

"And you do?"

"Yes." She presses her hand to her belly, "Everything I am doing is out of love."

"For whom, Gigi? Everything you're doing is to punish me."

"There are some things bigger than you and me."

"Like what? Lies? Betrayal? Your affliction for that…man who shot you? He's taking advantage of you. He's using you Gigi."

"So be it."

"He'll never let your friend go."

"He will."

"It was all a farce. If you leave here, you'll never be safe."

"We'll see, shall we?" She sets her jaw.

I glare at her, "Why do you have to be so stubborn?"

"Why do you have to be so…blinded by your own ego?"

"It's the only thing that's kept me alive so far."

"What kind of living is it, if you can't even come clean to your own wife?"

"Oh, so *now* you are my wife?" I thrust out my chest.

She throws up her hands, "Just leave Saint, please."

"I intend to." I turn to go, when the phone in my pocket vibrates. I slide it out of my pocket, see the message from an unknown number. I swipe open the screen, play the message. A video flickers to life.

A woman speaks into the screen, "This message is for Victoria." She swallows, "V? This is Nina. I am fine." She glances at someone off-screen. "Antonio has promised not to hurt me as long as no one comes after him." She firms her lips, stares at the screen, "I am fine V, really. Call off whoever is shadowing Antonio. He'll take care of me." A smile curls her lips. "I believe him, V." She pauses, then adds, "Take care of yourself." The message switches off.

"What is it?"

I walk over to her, hand her the phone.

She glances at me, then back at the screen. I play the message for her. She pales, replays the message once again, then hands the phone back to me.

"You believe her?"

She nods. "No reason for Nina to lie."

"Yet, you kept the truth from me. Why didn't you tell me what the Mafia wanted from you?"

She pales.

"Why, Gigi?"

"Because...I had to protect you Saint. I couldn't...risk the Mafia finding out. What if they did something to you? I could have never lived with myself," she draws in a breath.

"You wanted to protect *me*?" I scowl.

"Why not?" She sets her jaw, "Is that so difficult to understand?"

"Yes," I growl, "because you don't get to put yourself in danger for me... You never get to endanger yourself for anyone else—especially not for me. I can take care of myself, you feel me, Gigi?"

"Oh, spare me the macho bullshit," she mutters.

The fuck is she talking about? Of course, I am macho. I was born this way... No excuses there. I can't stop myself from taking care of her, any more than I could stop myself from breathing. I glare at her; she glowers back. Stubborn woman.

Why can't she understand that if something were to happen to her I'd never survive it? *Fuck.* I rake my fingers through my hair. "You make me a little crazy, Gigi, you know that? You make me do things that I can't explain. You fucking tie me up in knots, and that makes me desperate. It makes me miss things I didn't know I wanted in the first place."

"Like?" She stares at me, "Like what?"

"Like, being married to you, for one. I had no idea that I needed you—your touch, a glance, the whisper of your voice to infiltrate the recesses of my mind."

"What else?" she whispers.

"I want you, isn't that enough?"

"I want more." She swallows, "Can you give me that, I wonder?"

My heart begins to race. "What is it?" I ask. "What more do you want?" *Do I want to hear it? Do I?*

"Will you answer my riddle?" A small smile curves her lips.

"You know I only ask, but never answer," I scowl.

"Just this once, Saint." She squares her shoulders, tips up her chin and holds my gaze, "Please."

My pulse thunders at my temples; my palms grow cold. *Shit, why am I nervous about agreeing to this? Don't do it, don't.* I jerk my chin, "Fine then."

Her lips twist. "What's easy to make, but impossible to keep forever?"

I peruse her features. *What is it? What could it be?* A glimmer of a thought brushes against the edges of my mind. *Nah, it can't be. Not that.* I glance around the room, drag my fingers through my hair, "I...can't guess what it is."

"I'll give you a clue." Her chest rises and falls. "You'll see me soon but you can't see me yet."

I frown; my heart begins to race. *What the hell is she hinting at?* "I..." I swallow. "That sounds implausible."

Her lips curve in a small smile, "Here's another hint." She leans forward, "The more you give up, the more it gives back to you."

My pulse rate ratchets up. *She isn't saying what I think she is, is she? Nah. Not possible...* I widen my stance. "That defies the laws of physics," I say. "I don't think I like the sound of it," I laugh, the sound nervous. *Bloody hell! What's wrong with me?* My palms begin to sweat. The ring slips from between my fingers, clatters to the floor, rolls toward the bed. I swoop down and grab it.

Her gaze falls to my hand, "You can guess it."

"I can't." I rise to my feet, clutching at the ring like it's a bloody lifeline. "Besides, whatever it is," my voice cracks; I clear my throat, "I don't think there's space in my life for it."

I pivot, head for the door.

"So, this is it then?"

Her voice brings me up short.

I pause, slide the ring into my pocket.

"How can you say you love me, when you don't want to fight for us?" she cries out.

"There is no us. Not anymore." I stalk forward. "You were right. There are too many secrets between us, Gigi. That's no way to start a relationship."

I reach the exit.

"Saint?"

I don't turn around. "Goodbye, Victoria."

46

What did the cat say to her Valentine?
Answer: You are purr-fect for me

Victoria

I tear open the envelope, pull out the papers. "No." They slide from my fingers, hit the floor in a cloud of white and black. Like my life. I thought it would get easier with time, but every passing minute of every hour of every day, the hollowness in my chest grows bigger, more turbulent, louder, pressing outward, making my heart race, filling me with panic, telling me I was wrong. I should have given him a chance. A choice. Another opportunity to rip me apart, tear out my heart and trample it to pieces under his size 13, dusty cowboy boots.

Yeah, I know his shoe size.

No thanks to that weird-as-shit, eccentric taste in shoes he has. Who remembers the shoe size of a man who broke her heart? Correction: Okay, I left him, so technically I broke my own heart. I've been numb since I left the hotel, my life an endless cycle of days and nights.

The nights… They are the worst. The darkness taunts me. The cold sheets wind around my limbs, weighing me down, pulling me into a restless sleep filled with images of him, our time together, how he'd kissed me, how he'd wrenched orgasms from me. How he'd run his fingers over my skin, thrust them into my pussy, taken me, curled me into him, spooned me as we'd fallen asleep. Hell. The only way to escape is to wake up, make myself chamomile tea, and watch mindless television. Shit. I am turning into a hermit, never leaving the house, except for the checkup at the hospital, that had confirmed that my pregnancy is progressing well.

I massage my stomach—my child… Saint's child. Had I subconsciously planned this all along?

Is that why I'd asked for contraceptive pills instead of the injection?

Had I hoped that I would fall pregnant?

Had I wanted it all along?

I had been on a mission for the Mafia, for hell's sake. And my subconscious thought was that *this* was the time to bring a child into the world? How irresponsible could I be? Am I such a dreamer that I'd hoped, somehow, everything would work out? That I'd get together with him and we'd live happily ever after? The band around my chest tightens. I'd been incredibly stupid... And lucky that, somehow, I'd managed to avoid being hurt so far. If you don't count the emotional hurt, of course.

I stare at the fallen sheafs of papers. Lucky, huh? I burst into tears. Damn hormones. And damn Saint, for allowing me to fool myself into hoping for a more permanent relationship.

I stumble over to the settee in the tiny living room and bury my face in my hands. I had spoilt my life…and his or hers—this little one who will never know a father. The bloody asinine man has haunted my every waking thought, has crawled into my dreams, has me second-guessing myself every time I am at the supermarket, sure that I'll see him in the next aisle. As if he would be shopping in the supermarket. Shit. I *am* losing it, I *am*.

The sound of a light knock at the door has me wiping my tears. By the time I open it, I've composed myself.

"Victoria?" Amelie frowns, "Have you been crying again?"

"Moi?" I press a hand to my chest. "Why would I?"

"Don't lie." She steps forward and her foot brushes the papers on the floor. "What's this?" She bends to pick them up.

The pressure builds behind my eyes. *I will not cry, will not.*

"Divorce papers?" She glances up at me.

"Read it." I bite on my lower lip, "The asshole is making sure I have nothing to do with him."

"That's what you said you want, right?" She walks across to the coffee table and places the papers there. Then straightens, "It is, isn't it?"

"Yeah." I bring up my legs, to sit cross-legged on the sofa. Somehow this is the only position that feels comfortable nowadays. Don't ask.

"You don't sound convinced."

"What do you want me to say?" I shove a cushion behind me.

"That you want him to come after you, discover that you are pregnant, and then fall to his knees and apologize for being a bloody idiot."

"Right," I laugh. "You obviously don't know Saint."

"Not as well as you." She glances pointedly at my belly, "What are you going to do about it?"

I swallow, then place my palms over my belly. "I want this child. It's just, I'd thought, I'd hoped…" My face crumples. "It's hard, Amelie. I knew it wasn't going to be easy to do this on my own...but I hadn't realized how daunting it would be."

"Oh, V." She rounds the table, sinks down next to me and pulls me close. I bury my face in her shoulder and allow the tears to come.

She pats my head, holds me close, "Let it out, V. You've been through so bloody much. I don't know of anyone who could have come out of it still standing."

"And pregnant," I mutter through my tears. "Not that I'm complaining. I mean, it's the one good thing to have come from all this mess." I wipe my tears, and sit back, "Do I look terrible?"

She looks me up and down, "Yes."

I chuckle, "Gee, thanks. I can always count on you sugar-coating reality, huh?"

"That's my specialty. Comes with being an expert pastry chef."

I snicker, "That's a terrible joke."

"You smiled, didn't you?" She leans across, and snatches up the tissue box. "What are you wearing anyway?"

I pull out a few of the tissues, blow my nose. "An old shirt I'd forgotten I own." It's one of Saint's. I packed it by mistake. Okay, so it wasn't a mistake. I wad the tissues in my hand and hunch my shoulders. "What the hell am I going to do, Amelie?"

I stare at the advertisement on the television screen, showing a family sitting down to Christmas dinner.

"If there's anyone who can cope with this, it's you." She rubs circles on my back.

I snort, "I'm not feeling capable of much at the moment, I can tell you that."

Another image flashes on screen, this time showing the opening credits of "The Grinch Who Stole Christmas."

"Bloody depressing." She picks up the remote control and switches off the TV.

I chuckle, "I thought you like Christmas."

"I do." She links her fingers together, "But I've been overworked filling up orders for Christmas parties since—" she reddens. "Sorry didn't mean to bring up the... Uh! ...wedding party."

"It's fine." I pick up a cushion and hug it, "I 'm glad at least you and Isla benefitted from all that publicity."

"More like notoriety," she snorts. "But really, it seems whoever said that all PR is good PR, has it right. Isla's booked up into late next year and I have more orders than I can fulfill for the foreseeable feature. "

The paparazzi had blown up the internet with accounts of how a mystery man had held the wedding celebration hostage, then escaped without taking anything. People had taken to calling it a prank pulled by one of the Seven.

Saint had encouraged it by releasing a short statement to the media clarifying that no one had been hurt by the escapade. He hadn't answered any further questions from the media—who had speculated for days, before one journalist had concluded that it had been a giant waste of time—except for the desserts served at the party, which had been incredible. One thing had led to another, and the internet had blown up with people wanting to find out who had planned the wedding and what the guests had been enjoying; so Isla's wedding planning venture and Amelie's catering business had boomed in its wake.

All's well that ends well... Everyone got what they wanted, including Antonio. A shiver runs down my spine. He seems to be sticking to his promise of leaving me alone...so far. If he'd wanted to kill me, he could have when he'd shot at me. He seemed to have purposely missed at that close range. Well, I guess that means he is letting me get on with my life... Such as it is.

"What are you going to do for Christmas?" Amelie asks.

"I haven't given it much thought." I glance around the flat. "Maybe I'll stay in here, get some rest," I say.

"You mean stay in and get depressed?"

"I won't." I hunch my shoulders, negating my own claim, "I'm trying, Amelie." I stare at the blank television screen.

"Why don't you come up to the cabin with me?"

"Cabin?" I frown.

"The one that Saint said I could borrow for the holidays?" She flushes, "Shit, I can't say anything without putting my foot in my mouth."

"It's okay." I force out a laugh, "It's not like I can go through life being upset every time his name is mentioned."

"I... I won't go, if that helps. I can stay here and keep you company?"

"Nonsense." I frown, "You deserve this time to rest and rejuvenate."

She turns to me, "I don't want you to be on your own."

"I've survived the last few weeks, haven't I?"

"Have you?" She looks me up and down.

I flush, "Do I look that bad?"

"Worse."

I yank my hair back from my face, "I...haven't felt motivated."

"It's understandable. It's why I'd rather you not stay on your own through the holiday season."

"And I'm not coming with you, to the cabin."

"Why don't you stay with Summer and Sinclair—?" she asks.

"And risk running into him?" I straighten my shoulders, "Okay, I know that's being a coward, but right now, I'd rather stay as far away from him as possible.'

"You mean cooped up inside here, drowning in your own thoughts?"

"What would you have me do?"

"Let me help you," she glares at me.

"You have." I sag against the sofa, "You know, I couldn't have come this far without you. It's thanks to you that I found this apartment to house-sit for the next year... and within walking distance of the hospital too.

She shuffles her feet, "Seriously, it's not a big deal." She waves a hand in the air, "I wish you could tell Saint about the child."

"You haven't heard him speak about how much he hates kids."

"That's only until he realizes you are about to have his." She plonks her palms on her hips. "A man like him will do anything to protect his own flesh and blood."

"He sure did a slap-up job of taking care of me."

"Only because you hid things from him."

"What about the secrets he held back from me?"

"Did you ask him about it?"

"I did," I swallow. "He didn't want to reveal them to me. We have no common meeting ground."

"Except one," she, once more, looks down at my belly.

I redden, "Seriously?"

"Marriages have been built on less, and the sexual chemistry between the two of you is clearly off the charts. I mean, you're pregnant with his child."

"No kidding."

"So, you're going to give up on the two of you?"

"He's the one who gave up on me."

"Give him one last chance?"

"No."

She throws her hands up in the air, "You're so stubborn."

"Guess that's how I've gotten through the shit life has thrown at me, huh?"

"You sure you won't let me come to the hospital with you?"

I shake my head. "It's a routine check-up, I'll be fine."

47

Saint

"You're a dickhead."

Weston's voice comes through loud and clear over the phone.

"Why you had to break up with her and then send her divorce papers, without trying to at least make up with her one last time..."

"Look who's giving me relationship advice," I snicker. "The man who can't hold down a single woman for more than week."

"Out of choice, bitch. The more the merrier, as they say," Weston retorts. "More than what I can say for you. Did you manage to, at least, get to the office today?"

I take a sip of the whiskey, then wince at the taste. Shit, not even good old Macallan fine malt *seems* the same. Face it, nothing *compares* to the taste of her cunt, her mouth, her lips… *Fuck,* fucking fuck?

"You okay, ol' chap?"

"Why the fuck are you calling me anyway?"

"Why do you think?"

"I think I am going to hang up, dickwad—"

"Hold on, I'm getting another call."

"Don't you fucking put me on hold, Weston—"

The call goes silent. Then classical music drifts over the line. "The fuck?" He has Mozart playing while he puts me on hold? I hang up, then begin to pace. Is he right, should I have tried harder? But this is what she wants, right? A clean break. Neither of us needs to look back. I had made sure she came out of the entire incident with her identity concealed. It had cost me thousands to track down every single paparazzi in that room, and pay them off enough that they would leave out all mention of her. I may have had to lean on one or two of the errant ones to ensure they destroyed all evidence of that day. But it had been worth it. The event had faded away from public memory. The next scandal had surfaced and we were yesterdays' news.

Like me and her—

Fuck. I rub the ache in my chest. —Except for the emptiness that crawls in my guts and the thoughts that crowd my mind. Not to mention the nightmares that seem to be never too far away when I sleep—the voice asking me questions, demanding that I answer them. Fuck. I rub at my temples. This is insane.

I had let her get under my skin... That's the only reason I am beginning to unravel this way.

Once she signs the divorce papers, I can walk away, and have nothing more to do with her.

So, we are no closer to finding out who was behind our kidnappings. Antonio? Well, the man had disappeared. I'd had my PI on his tail and Antonio had given her the slip. He hadn't been seen or heard of in the last three weeks since the party…

And that message. Why doesn't that reassure me in the least? The hair on the nape of my neck rises. Shit, I am simply imagining things. The man is long gone. He'd gotten what he wanted—the USB which had been sent to me.

He can keep it, for all I care.

If it leaks on the internet… Well, it would only lead to more speculation—not that I care—but it would be easy enough to suppress it.

If it were to happen, which it won't. Clearly, the man had wanted to get his hands on it. For what, though? Why was it so important to get a hold of it?

The phone buzzes in my hand. Fucking Weston. I silence it. It rings again, I switch it off. The phone on my desk rings. I walk to it and snatch it up, "What?"

"It's Weston."

"Tell him to fuck off."

"He says it's urgent." Meredith's voice is patient, "I think you should take this call."

"Fine," I glower at the receiver.

"Asswipe," Weston drawls back.

"Jesus, can't you fucking go away to a place where there are no phones—preferably no means of communication—so I don't have to hear from you?"

"Same to you, with knobs on," he snickers. "Listen," his voice turns serious, " I called you because I've gotta come clean to you about something."

"What?"

"Promise you won't go all apeshit when I tell you."

"Shit." My heart begins to thud, "Just say it."

"I don't know, I promised her I wouldn't."

"Who?"

"Victoria."

"You and she spoke?"

"At the hospital that day, and I'd been hoping for the two of you to come to your senses. Hell, I'd hoped she would tell you herself. Not that I should be breaking doctor-patient confidentiality... But I warned her."

"Fuck that. If you don't tell me right now—"

The sound of honking reaches me over the line.

"Bloody cunt," he swears.

"What?"

"Not you. This fucker who's trying to overtake me—what the hell —?" he swears aloud again. There's more honking, the sound of brakes screeching.

"Weston, what the fuck—?"

The sound of metal scraping against metal, then Weston's voice comes on the phone again, "Shit, Saint, this is not over not by a long shot. She's preg—"

The line goes dead.

"The fuck?"

I glare at the receiver. My fingers tremble and my knuckles are white. How strange. I place the phone back in the cradle. Then reach for my phone. She's what? She's…fine. She has to be. And Weston? Shit, my heart begins to race. The noise in my head clears. He was in an accident. I need to get to him. I reach for the phone and dial my operative.

Half an hour later, I race up the corridor of the Whittington hospital. My investigator had tracked down Weston with a speed that had impressed even me. Well, I owe her a small fortune—but she'd delivered. This time, I barrel into the private room, and swerve. A jug of water misses me narrowly and crashes to the floor behind me.

"The fuck?"

I glance at Weston, sprawled on the hospital bed. His arm is in a sling, cuts and bruises mar his face, and his shirt is torn… Other than that, he seems fine. Which is more than I can say about the white-faced nurse who turns to me.

She throws up her hands, "Are you family?"

"A friend."

"Fine. Then," she thrusts a small plastic cap filled with pills at me, "you make him take those."

She brushes past me.

"Hold on, is he okay?"

"He won't be able to use his arm for a little while." She raises her shoulders.

"The fuck?" He snarls, "I am a surgeon. I need to use my hands."

She winces, then turns and scurries from the room.

I turn to face my friend. Sweat beads his forehead and dirt smudges his face.

"You okay?"

He sets his jaw, "Totally."

I glance at the pills.

"You're not going to make me take those," he growls.

"Nah, man." I set them down on the table next to the bed, "I am not your nurse. Besides, you're funny about painkillers, right?"

"Yeah," he scowls at his injured arm. "The fuckers say I need to rest my hand," he growls.

"What happened?" I ask.

His face reddens, "I fractured my finger, apparently."

"Finger?" I clear my throat, "Don't tell me... It's..."

"My fucking middle finger." He holds up his hand with the sling, showing me the bird... Or rather, his middle finger in a splint.

He winces, then lowers his hand. "Hurts like a bitch, too," he grumbles.

A chuckle bubbles up; I change it to a snort.

"You think this is a joke, Caldwell?"

"Of course, not." I keep the grin on my face though. "You're a doctor. Can't you make them change the diagnosis?"

He glowers back, "Funny. Should I laugh at that?"

"Don't care, ol' chap, just don't cry on my shoulder."

He pushes into the bed, "Why are you here, you dickhead?"

I stop laughing. "What happened?" I lean forward.

"This car came out of nowhere and forced me off the road."

"You sure?" I steeple my fingers together.

"Do I look like I am kidding?"

"No," I drag my fingers through my hair. "Well, the good news is, it's only a fracture."

"To my hand. My right hand. My fucking dominant hand. You know what this means, right?"

I straighten, "You'll be out of commission for a little time?"

"I am a surgeon, asshole. If the arm doesn't mend properly, I'll never be able to operate again."

"Shit," I pale. "I'm sorry man."

"Fuck." He bangs his head back against the headboard, "Fucking, fuck."

"Easy." I frown down at my friend, "At least, you're alive."

"They weren't trying to kill me, just put me out of commission."

"By causing you to fracture your middle finger?"

He scoffs, "It wasn't an accident, man, I'll tell you that."

"So, you think this was done on purpose?" I frown.

"Sure seems that way to me?"

"Why would anyone want you out of commission?"

"Beats the hell out of me." He straightens his shoulders, "One thing is for sure, we need to double the security on all of the Seven and those who matter to us."

A frisson runs down my spine, "Before the accident, you said something, before you got cut off..."

"That I was being forced off the road?" His forehead crinkles.

"No at the end, you said Victoria was…"

"Pregnant."

"Shit." The world sways around me. I sink into the chair, "That's what she was trying to tell me."

"She told you and you let her go?" he snaps.

"Not exactly..." I stab the heel of my shoe into the floor. "She asked me a riddle, which I couldn't solve—"

"Hold on." He leans forward, "*She* asked *you* a riddle."

"Yeah."

His gaze widens, "You never allow anyone to challenge you."

"I let her, okay?" I squeeze my eyes shut. "Only her," I swallow. "It's complicated."

"No shit."

I hear the smile in his voice, crack my eyelids open. "Don't feed me a line about sentimentalism and all that shit."

"You're doing that, all by yourself."

I sink back in my chair, massage my chest, "I think I'm going to have a cardiac."

"Handy I'm right here, then, isn't it?"

"Har, har," I snarl. " You're fucking annoying, man. "

"Speak for yourself."

"Fuck this shit." I dig my fingers into my hair and pull at it, "Why couldn't she tell me?"

"It sounds like she did," he says. "You simply didn't want to answer the riddle."

"She could have simply told me, you know?"

"And then what? Would you have accepted her and the child?"

"Maybe. I don't know." I lower my chin to my chest, mumble, "This is bloody complicated."

"Tell me about it."

I glance up to find him staring at the sling.

"I'm sorry about your finger."

He sighs, "Me too." He grabs another pillow and props it behind his shoulder, "What are you going to do now—?"

My phone buzzes.

I pull it out. It's a message from an unknown number. *Huh?* I swipe open the message.

Come and get her. She's in East London. You know where to look.

I pale.

"What's wrong?" Weston frowns.

"You were right; this is not over yet." I jump to my feet, race for the door.

"Where are you going?"

"To rescue my family."

48

Victoria

I had been stupid, so stupid. I try to swallow and my throat hurts. A drumming sensation presses in at my temples.

I yank at the ropes that tie my wrists behind my back. I try to open my eyes, but the darkness presses down against my eyelids. Shit, had he also blindfolded me? I feel along the floor with my feet... At least, I still have my boots on. Good thing I'd opted for them over ballet pumps. I'd been half way to the hospital, crossing the garden that bordered the side of the building, when someone had grabbed me from behind. I'd opened my mouth to scream and a soft cloth had been thrust into my face. I'd drawn in a whiff of a sweet, cloying scent, and had begun to black out. I'd been drugged, there was no doubt about that.

My guts churn and bile rushes up my throat. The baby... My heartbeat ratchets up. This can't be good for the baby, surely? I draw in a breath, another. *Take it easy. It's going to be fine.* I swallow down the nervousness that clogs my throat. Who could have done this? Antonio? What does he want now? Where am I?

Footsteps sound; I freeze. Who can it be? Will they hurt me?

Silence for a few moments. I hunch my shoulders, hold my breath. *Go away, please don't come close.* There's a sound of shuffling so close. A bead of sweat runs down my spine. Who is out there? My captor? What is he going to do next?

I hear a click and the hair on the back of my neck rise.

"Come out of there." A familiar voice rips through the silence, "I know you're in there. I'm giving you five seconds to reveal yourself before I start shooting."

"No," I try to say the word out loud but my voice is muffled. "Saint, it's me," my words are garbled. I can barely speak through the gag in my mouth. I shuffle forward, my feet thumping against a barrier.

"Who's there?" His voice is tense. The sense of danger ratchets up. Shit, he can't shoot. I won't let him hurt me... Us. *Worse* than what might happen to me and the baby, it would destroy him. I wriggle forward, kick out again and slam into a barrier.

The next instant, there's a creak of a door being opened and the air shifts. The darkness lightens by several shades. Had I been thrust into a closet? An electric current runs up my spine. It's Saint. He's here. I try to speak again, my voice muffled.

"Victoria." My blindfold is pulled off. I blink against the brightness. Arms wind around me. He scoops me up, restraints and all, and places me on the ground.

He pulls off the gag; the bindings around my wrists loosen. I crack open my eyelids to find him kneeling over me. There's a flash of steel, then the ropes around my ankles give away. I collapse into him. "Saint," my throat hurts and a headache pounds at my temples.

"Jesus, Gigi." He pulls me into his lap and cradles me.

I press my ear to his chest, listen to the thundering of his heart. He rocks me back and forth. "You're safe," he mumbles into my hair. His grip tightens around me and pain shivers up my arm. I whimper.

"Are you hurt?"

He pulls back to peer at my arm. I look down to find the sleeve ripped. A thin trickle of blood stains the cloth. A growl rips from him.

I shudder, "I... I'm fine."

"You're bleeding."

"It's a scratch," I insist.

"Who hurt you?" He pinches my chin, so I have to peer up at him, "Did you catch a glimpse of who it was?"

"No," I swallow, "I was walking to the hospital."

"Hospital?"

"For the check-up."

"Check-up—?" His voice trails off. A strange look comes into his eyes. Fear? Anger? Then his features close. "Is everything okay? Are you—?"

"I'm fine." My chest hurts; the back of my throat burns. Shit, why should it matter to me that he doesn't want kids? This entire thing had gone wrong. He was supposed to have guessed my riddle, then embraced me, kissed me, and taken me home. To his hotel room, I mean, because of course, the man doesn't have a place to call his own. He prefers the transience that being in a hotel room gives him. The freedom from relationships, from someone like me.

I push at his chest.

His grip tightens. "Victoria.'

"Saint."

We speak at the same time.

"I…"

"You…" I swallow, "you were saying?"

A dull thud echoes around the space. I stare at him and his gaze widens. "We need to get out of here." He rises, carrying me.

"I can walk," I protest.

He ignores me and heads for the doorway. For the first time, I glance around, taking in the space. It's an empty room with a closet in the corner, the one I had been locked in. I shudder.

He holds me closer, "You're safe."

His voice rumbles in his chest. I shouldn't feel the need to lean on him, to thrust my nose into the strip of flesh that peeks out from between his lapels, and inhale his scent. My lungs fill with his essence and my heart rate stabilizes. Shit, why do I feel so secure, so protected when I'm with him? For so long, I had depended on myself—my instincts, my ability to withstand anything thrown my way. And how had that worked out, huh? I'd done a slap-up job of it—negotiating

Nina's release, and my continued freedom, by agreeing to play a role in Saint's downfall.

Tears prick at the backs of my eyes. Even my bloody hormones are no longer on my side.

"I'm sorry," I whisper.

"For what?" He prowls down the steps, reaching a landing that opens into another vacant room.

"For everything."

"I should be the one apologizing for being so hardheaded."

"No arguments there," I snicker through the ball of emotion in my throat.

"Guess that's one more thing we agree on."

He walks out onto the landing, glances around, then continues down the dilapidated steps toward his Jaguar, parked outside.

A couple of boys in hoodies mill around nearby. I take in the house next door—paint peeling, garbage cans over-filled, with trash on the pavement outside. Across from us, there's a boarded-up store. The other houses on the street seem as deserted. The electronic lock beeps, then he opens the door on the passenger side and places me in it. "Buckle up."

He leans back, shuts the door, and walks around. One of the boys stops him. They speak, then he pulls out his wallet, pulls out a few notes, and hands them over. He reaches into another pocket to pull out a card. He slips that to the second boy and they fist bump. In seconds, he's in the driver's seat, and starts the car.

"What was that about?" I ask, as he eases the cars from the curb. The boys step back, watch us as we pull away.

"Told them to call me if they see anyone coming in or out of the house."

"How did you find me?"

He pulls out his phone and hands it to me, then focuses on the road ahead.

I read the text. "Who sent it, you think?"

"Antonio?" he growls.

"Perhaps." I lean my head back into the seat. "It's confusing. Why would he ask you to call off those following him, then kidnap me, only to send you my whereabouts? And how did you know exactly where to look?"

His jaw tics. "When we were abducted, that's the house where we were held. I should have bought it and torn it down a long time ago. Guess none of us wanted anything to do with it. After that incident, we simply wanted to put it behind us and move on." His knuckles turn white.

"Saint," I turn to him, "Why...would he send you to the same place?"

"A warning about what would happen if I screwed with the Mafia?" He growls, "He has no idea how personal he's made this. No way, am I letting him go without having my vengeance. He dared touch you, Gigi. He's going to pay for it."

His harsh tone slices down my spine, my nipples bead, and lust curls in my belly. Hell, hearing him all worked up on my behalf is way too much of a turn on to resist.

The phone in my hand—his phone—pings again. I stiffen and my heart begins to thud. I glance down at the screen.

"What does it say?"

I wet my lips. Read, and re-read the message.

"Aloud, Gigi."

Maybe it's the fact that he uses my nickname, or the way his voice stretches with tension, or the command in his tone that whips across my skin and makes my pussy clench. Shit, I want every dirty thing he can do to me again. Is this any way for a pregnant woman to be thinking? Is it the hormones? The fact that I am carrying his baby, that's making me so aware of his nearness.

His voice lowers to a hush, "Don't keep me waiting." That dominant edge of his intent slices through my barriers, reducing me to a trembling mess inside.

I swallow, then scan the words again, "You found her. Don't let her go."

"What?" he snaps.

"That's it." I dig my heels into the floor, "That's all it says."

He stops at a traffic light, then snatches the phone from me. He scans the screen again, then swears under his breath, "The hell does that mean?"

I twist my fingers in my lap, "Apparently, Antonio has a conscience after all."

"What do you mean?" The signal turns green, he presses down on the accelerator, and the car leaps forward. My breath catches; my heart thuds in my chest.

"Sorry," he mutters. "It's just— I don't get it. Did he stage this, to get us to speak again?"

"Seems that way," I huff. "He was never an easy man to comprehend."

"Don't talk about him."

A warm sensation blooms my chest, "You jealous?"

He laughs, the sound bitter, "My wife has a history with another man, a past I don't know anything about. What do you think?"

"I was a virgin."

His knuckles on the wheel tighten. "There are other ways to have a relationship, other than a physical one."

"And you think that's what I had with Antonio?"

"You tell me."

"He was my contact with the Mafia. He's the one who negotiated a deal with them to ensure Nina's release—in return for getting him the USB with the video clip of you being held in that room."

He makes a noise deep in his throat.

I glance sideways at him, "I'm sorry, Saint."

"For what?"

"For giving the media a chance to tear down your reputation."

"I don't give a fuck about that."

"And your company, the losses it suffered because of the ensuing media uproar?"

"I managed to shut down most of the journalists who were there that day."

"How?" I turn to him, "Of course, you paid them to stay quiet."

"Just when you think money doesn't buy everything… It surprises you with how much it does help."

"So, I guess you survived that unscathed then."

"Except for the fact that my wife betrayed me, and handed over the most important piece of evidence of what had turned my life upside down."

I wince, bunching fingers into fists.

"You could have simply asked me. I'd have given the USB to you."

I swing around to face him, "You would have done that?"

"Maybe," he raises a shoulder. "Of course, I'd have extracted my punishment for it."

My toes curl.

"And you'd have loved every minute of it."

His lips twist in that smirk that's hot and mean, and seems to promise more of all the filthy things that he'd ever done to me.

I fold my hands in my lap, "I'm not coming to your hotel."

"I'm not allowing you to return to that apartment."

"You know where…?" I straighten, "Of course, you do. I'm surprised you don't own the entire building."

He stays silent.

I turn sideways in my seat, "You do, don't you? You own the building."

He stays focused on the road.

"What did you offer Amelie this time?"

"Nothing. She refused to help me. I…" he flicks a quick glance, "I used my resources."

"It was too much to hope you'd simply let me leave and get on with my life?"

"What about the life you carry inside of you?"

I pale. "You…you guessed?"

"Weston told me," his features harden.

I stare straight ahead. "You couldn't crack my riddle that day. Imagine that? You, who are able to solve almost any puzzle. You couldn't guess the answer."

"Even I have my shortcomings, it seems," he retorts.

"Or maybe you didn't want to find out what I meant?" I tip up my chin, "Admit it, you don't want this child."

49

Saint

"I want to take care of you, Victoria." I keep my gaze focused on the road. "Since the first time I saw you, it's all I've wanted to do. I can't share you with anyone else."

"Not even our child?"

"I didn't say that." I tighten my jaw.

"What are you saying then?"

Her voice sounds tired, defeated. I glance sideways to find her hunched back into her seat. Dark circles surround her eyes. There are hollows below her cheekbones. Her beautiful hair is disheveled. She looks fragile, exhausted by everything she's faced. I tighten my fingers on the steering wheel. I had failed in my duties as her husband. I had promised to protect her, shield her from the world. I had let my fears, the bad things I'd imagined could happen, get in the way.

Oh, a part of me had guessed what she was trying to say that day.

My subconscious had clocked the way she had placed her palm on her belly, how she'd glanced at me with hope and trepidation. How she'd straightened her shoulders, ready to take on anyone, even me—the man who was hers. I slam my hand against the steering wheel.

She stiffens.

"Sorry," I mutter under my breath. Fuck, for someone who always knows what he wants, I sure am unable to interpret the signals that my brain is trying to send me. "Come back with me, Gigi. Give me a chance to show you how it could be between us."

"You mean, hurt me again? Trample all over my feelings and refuse to acknowledge what's between us?"

"I love you. I've told you that already. Hell, I married you."

"And served me divorce papers."

"I thought that's what you wanted."

Her lips turn down. She glances away.

Anger laces my blood. Frustration twists my guts. "Let's talk about this later, shall we?"

She nods.

That worries me more. Gigi's always been a fighter, feisty to the core, challenging me at every turn. Fuck, that's what had attracted me to her—that core of unshakeable steel inviting me to push her, control her, try to manipulate her to get a response from her. Perhaps the entire ordeal had finally caught up with her. That fucker, Antonio, had accomplished what I hadn't been able to do during the course of our time together. No way, am I letting him get away with this latest attempt at trying to kidnap her. If he thinks simply getting some woman to record a video asking me to keep away was going to cut it, then he is wrong, so wrong.

I pull up at the curb of Claridge's. Jumping out of the car, I walk around to open the door. She steps out. I grab her hand, entangle our fingers, and lead her up the sidewalk.

A gust of wind blows, knocking over the sign the homeless man holds. It falls right in my path. I pause, glance down.

"How should I greet thee?
  With silence and tears."

I swear aloud; she stiffens.

"What's wrong?" she asks.

"Nothing…" I step over the hardboard sign, head for the door of the hotel.

"Thanks for dinner," Homeless guy calls out.

I pause, half turn, to find he's packing up his shit. He places his hat on his head, then rises to his feet.

"You ain't as much of a tosser as you seem," he chuckles.

I blink, watch as he plonks the sign over his shoulder, then marches up the road.

"Is that fucking odd or what?" I pivot, stalk toward the hotel.

"Why did he thank you for dinner?" she queries.

"He probably eats every night at the hotel," I mutter.

"He does?"

I nod, "All of the leftovers of the day are donated every night, in a makeshift soup kitchen we set up in the back."

Her forehead furrows, "You do that?"

"It's economical." Heat suffuses my face, "Don't go making me out to be empathetic or some such shit, because I'm not."

"Of course, not." Her lips curve slightly.

The wind blows again and she shivers. I pull her close, steer her up the steps and through the open door. Bypassing the main elevators in the lobby, I head for the one at the far end of the floor. The doors open almost immediately, and I step inside with her.

I frown, "Did you see his face? The guy who took you?"

She shakes her head, "I only heard him a couple of times through the closed door of my room."

She curls her finger into my shirt and I cuddle her even closer. "You're safe with me, Gigi."

"So you keep saying," she sniffs.

"I mean it."

She peers up at me, "I know."

"I won't let Antonio or anyone else get to you."

"Antonio won't hurt—"

"That's all I am going to say on the topic," I growl.

She purses her lips. For a second, I am sure she's going to counter me, then she draws in a breath and nods. "Truce?"

"For now."

"Jesus," she huffs, "can't you ever let me have the last word?"

"Never," I allow my lips to curl.

She frowns. The doors open, I step onto the penthouse floor, then guide her to my hotel suite. Once inside, I pull her with me, through the living room, into the bedroom, then the ensuite.

"What are you doing?"

I don't answer. If I do, no doubt, my words will hurt her further. I reach the tub and turn on the water. Steam instantly rises in the air. I lift her onto the counter, then undo her buttons.

She tries to pull her shirt off. I catch her hands in mine, "Let me, Gigi, please."

She tips up her chin, searching my features. What is she looking for?

Her green eyes darken and her lips part. Her fingers tremble in mine. I move in closer. She parts her legs and I step into the space between them. "Gigi," my voice comes out harsh.

"I love it when you call me that."

I allow my lips to curl, "Thought you hated my nickname for you."

"I lied," she whispers.

"I know," I lower my head, until our eyelashes tangle.

"I'm sorry," her lips tremble and a tear slides down her cheek. I bend down and lick it up. A sob catches in her throat.

I place my forehead against hers, "Don't cry, Gigi." I swallow down the lump that blocks my throat. Fuck, what is it about this woman that guts me so completely?

"Didn't mean to," her chin wobbles.

"I'd fucking slay anything that causes you misery. I'll drown out the entire fucking world, set fire to the monsters that lurk in the dark around you. I... I'll rip open my chest and show you what it means to be near you."

"Would you accept this child as yours?"

My eyes fly open. "I'll never shirk my responsibilities when it came to the two of you."

"That's not what I asked."

I step back, reach above her to pull out the antiseptic and cotton wads. "It's all I can give you right now."

"It won't be enough."

"Can we take this one day at a time? I am trying Victoria, I promise I am." I place the medicines on the counter next to her, then reach for her shirt. This time she allows me to undo the buttons, help her out of the shirt.

I take in the mark on her shoulder. A growl rips out of me, "Fuck." I reach out to touch the fading scar. She flinches.

"Does it hurt?"

"Not anymore."

"Fuck, this was my fault."

"Stop trying to take responsibility for everything." She squares her shoulders. "I am the one who played ball with the Mafia… Things were bound to get a little crazy. I mean, it's not like they'd have let me walk away without paying a price."

I grit my teeth so hard, my jaw hurts. "I'll ensure they never get to you again."

"I know." She smiles a little, "I always knew you would be my knight in shining armor."

"More like the villain."

"I have a thing for bad guys."

"I noticed." I chuckle, "So long as it's me you're talking about and not that bastard…"

"You really don't have to worry about Antonio."

"How can you be so confident?"

"Nina, the woman in the video?"

I nod.

"He…has a thing for her. It's the only reason I agreed to take on this entire mission, knowing he'd never let anything happen to her. It's why he'll take the evidence I gave him to the Mafia and ensure that they stick to their word."

"I hate it," I growl. "No way, am I going to put your future in the hands of that motherfucker, I am going to track him down and when I do—"

"What?" A new voice rings out. "What will you do?"

I swivel around, ensuring my body is between her and whoever's walked in.

"What the fuck are you doing here?"

50

Victoria

"Antonio," I try to scramble off the counter, only Saint steps back, imprisoning me.

"What game are you trying to play, Victoria?" Antonio's hard voice fills the space.

I shove against Saint; he doesn't move. He may as well have turned into a concrete wall. "I need to talk to him," I mutter, keeping my voice to a whisper.

Saint's shoulders bunch.

"You can talk from where you are."

Right. I glance down at myself, then do up my buttons. I give his back another shove; he still doesn't move. I huff, then peek around him, "What are you doing here?" I scowl at Antonio. "I thought you'd be on your way back to Sicily by now?"

"Sicily?" Saint exclaims.

"Shit." I clap my palm over my mouth.

"The hell?" Antonio looks between us, then folds his arms over his chest. "You bugged the USB drive?" He glowers at me, "You thought I wouldn't find out?"

"Bugged?" I blink, "I didn't."

"That was me," Saint says.

"What?" I exclaim.

Antonio swears under his breath, "I should have trusted my instincts and left when I had a chance."

"That, you should have," says another voice.

Antonio swings around.

Weston stands there, arm in a sling.

Antonio reaches for his gun, but Sinclair steps inside the bathroom door, gun aimed at Antonio, "Don't even think about it."

Antonio freezes.

Sinclair jerks his chin and Antonio walks forward. Weston steps aside, allowing Antonio to walk through.

Sinclair follows.

Weston glances at Saint, "You guys okay?"

Saint nods, "Thanks, man. I owe you."

A look passes between them, then Weston retreats, "We'll be in the living room. Don't take too long; we need to figure out what to do with this mofo."

The door closes.

Saint swings around to face me. "You okay?" he grips my shoulders.

A trembling grips me as adrenaline drains from my blood. "You... you knew that I was going to hand over the evidence to him?"

"You didn't mention that he had connections to Sicily?" He retorts.

"He's part of the Mafia... of course they're connected to Sicily." I mutter, then throw my hands up. "I didn't think it was important okay? I peer up at him, "Guess we still have secrets from each other?"

He peruses my futures, then exhales a breath. "Why the hell can't we trust each other?"

"I'm trying." I mutter.

"Yeah." He rubs the back of his neck. "So am I." His lips quirk, "and to answer your question, I suspected that you might do so."

Oh.

I raise my fingers to my lips, he grabs my wrist. "No biting your fingernails." He admonishes me.

O-k-a-y. I peer up into his face, "So, all this time, when you pretended you wanted nothing to do with me, you—"

He nods. "I had my men follow you. I tracked your movements."

"Even in the apartment?"

He frowns.

"Please don't hold back, Saint."

"There are cameras at the apartment," he finally concedes.

"You spied on me?"

"Not…always."

"But you did."

"On occasion…" He draws himself up to his full height, "I watched you bring yourself to orgasm every night, and wished I was there. It should have been my hands on you, my cock buried inside you, it should have been me wringing those moans from you instead of an inanimate object."

My cheeks burn, "Shit, you saw all that?" It should be creepy and awfully stalkerish, so why do I find it strangely reassuring that he'd had his eye on me all this time?

He tilts his head, "How else do you think I survived the last few weeks?"

I frown, "Yet you didn't guess I was pregnant until Weston told you."

His chest rises and falls, straining against the shirt he wears. "I am a dick. What can I say? The mind recognizes what it wants to."

I chuckle, "Well, we make a fine pair, don't we?" The hair on my forearms rises. "We're so bloody wrong for each other."

"On the contrary, I can't think of anything more right. You bring out the worst…and the best in me. You drive me insane, Gigi. You tie me up in knots, and every time I think I've figured you out, you throw me a surprise."

"Is that good or bad?"

"It's good…and bad." He leans down and licks my lips, "And it's definitely a bloody turn on. Thing is, there is no one for me but you."

"Even though I am pregnant with your child."

"Especially because you are pregnant with my child," his blue eyes deepen with some emotion I can't quite place.

"I don't want you to feel like you have to do the right thing by me."

"I only want to do all the wrong things to you," he smirks.

"You know that's not what I mean."

He pulls away and the cold air swoops over me. Damn it, why do I miss his presence already?

"I swore never to bring any child into the world—to allow myself to become that vulnerable, to imagine what could happen if he or she was kidnapped and kept hostage..." His entire body tightens, "If any child of mine had to go through what I did, I swear, I'd kill anyone and everyone who'd harm a hair on their head."

I stiffen, sweep my gaze over his face, "Is that what you're afraid of? Being vulnerable?"

"Not being able to protect my child from the world. That's my worst nightmare."

"You protected me, didn't you?"

"I allowed you to get kidnapped on my watch." He scowls.

"You found me didn't you?" I half smile. "I bet you watched me every hour of the day and night to ensure I was safe."

"And still, he managed to get his hands on you."

He doesn't deny it then. I am not sure how that makes me feel. Cared for? Creeped out? Both? And turned on? To be the focus of someone's attention to the exclusion of anything else... Is there any other feeling in the world that can equal that absolute single-minded intensity of his gaze?

"You saved me." I grab his hand and press it to my belly, "You saved both of us."

He squeezes his eyes shut, "Stop trying to make me into some kind of hero. I'm the kind of monster you should stay away from!"

"Oh?" I bite the inside of my cheek, "Who would you rather see me with, Saint?"

He growls.

"Who's the man for me? Who do you think can protect me the way you can? Who'd watch over me like my own protective guardian angel, and ensure he was there each and every turn so nothing ever touched me?"

His nostrils flare.

"Tell me, Saint."

"Me," he growls, "Only I can do this. I trust myself for this job, no one else."

I chuckle.

He glowers, "Don't think you've won this argument."

"No?" I tip up my chin.

He shakes his head, "We're just getting started, Gigi."

He grabs up the cotton ball, then helps me out of my shirt and dabs antiseptic on the scratch on my arm. I hiss and he bends his head and blows on the wound.

Goosebumps rise on my skin.

"Cold?"

"No." I watch as he straightens, then tosses the cotton into the dustbin. He rips open a bandage, and sticks it over the wound. "It's the best I can do, until I can get a doctor to come in and check you out."

"I'm fine."

He drops the sticky paper from the bandage into the waste basket then straightens, "Humor me."

"But-"

"If not me, for the baby."

Right. "Fine," I swallow, "but don't think you can always use the baby as an excuse."

"If it gets you to do what I want..."

I frown, "Honestly, Saint, you could at least pretend you aren't trying to get your own way."

"What fun would that be, huh?" he shrugs out of his shirt, then drapes it over my shoulder.

"What are you doing?" I frown.

"Wear this."

I glance at my shirt, which is ripped and dirty. Not that I want to wear it again. It reminds me too much of what had transpired—that feeling of helplessness, of sitting in the dark and waiting for the worst — *No.* I shake my head. *Never again.* I don't want to be in that position ever again.

Saint snatches up my soiled shirt. "I'll get rid of it."

I peer up at him, "Thanks." I pull on his shirt and his scent of dark masculinity instantly cocoons me. My heart skitters and my pussy clenches. *Shit, not the time to think about sex. Not.* I button up the shirt, then fold up the sleeves.

He drops the shirt into the bath tub, "I'll get housekeeping on it."

I nod. Of course, he'd have servants at his beck and call. *Where the hell do I fit in with all of this?*

"Hey," he hooks his knuckles under my chin so I have no choice but to meet his gaze, "everything will be okay, I promise."

A slight pain catches at my lower belly. I rub at it.

"You okay?" he asks.

I nod, then push off the counter, "Let's get this over with."

51

What is mine but only you can have?
Answer: My heart

Saint

I stalk into the living room, making sure to keep myself between her and the guys. Right now, I don't trust any other male around her—definitely, not that bastard Antonio. Is it the fact that she is pregnant? Pregnant. My heart begins to thud. *Shit, what am I going to do about that?* How will it feel to have a child…a fragile life dependent on me? Will I be able to do justice in my role as their father?

Am I good enough for this? Will I be able to fulfill my responsibilities? What if I can't? What if I fail?

Just as I had all that time ago?

When he'd asked me the riddles.

And I hadn't known the answers.

And he'd hurt me. I hadn't been able to defend myself.

Will I be able to protect my family? My palms begin to sweat. The soles of my feet burn. I stumble and someone grasps my elbow. Warm fingers entangle with mine. I glance down to find Gigi holding my hand.

"You okay?" she whispers.

I glance into those green eyes, "Now, I am."

Her lips curve in a slight smile.

"I love you," I keep my voice low enough that the others can't hear me.

She blinks, as if surprised, then her cheeks flush, and she glances away. A hot sensation stabs my chest. Does she have any feelings for me? Will she forgive me for what I did—that I hadn't been able to accept the fact that she was having my child? My flesh and blood. *Mine.* I tighten my grasp on her hand, then step forward. I urge her to sink into an armchair and stand next to her.

Antonio looks up from the settee across the room. Weston is seated in a chair on his left. Sinclair leans a hip against the wall, his gun trained on Antonio.

"Have you explained our plan to him?" I ask.

Weston nods.

I turn to Antonio. "You agree then?"

He lowers his chin, "You mean turn against my people, and lead you to the person responsible for what happened to the Seven of you?" He glances up, "What do I get in return?"

"You get to walk away from this alive."

"And if I don't?"

I lean forward on the balls of my feet, "We'll hand you over to the authorities, and trust me, you'll never get to be a free man again."

He sits up straight, his massive frame taking up a big portion of the settee, "I'm not exactly a free man now."

"You'll have a chance to rescue Nina—"

His jaw hardens.

Ah! Interesting. This is his weak spot. Clearly, the man isn't as smart as I'd given him credit for. If he were, he would never have revealed it to me.

"You'll have the means to leave the Mafia, start a new life with her, if that's what you want..."

The skin around his lips whitens. He squeezes his fingers together, and the skin of his knuckles stretches white.

This is a calculated move, of course. Dangling everything he wants in front of his eyes, only to rip it all away. Unless he cooperates, of course.

I prod him, "What do you say?"

Antonio glances at Gigi.

"Don't look at her, you asshole," I growl, then clamp my lips shut. Apparently, Antonio isn't the only one unable to control himself. This woman has come to mean more than anything in the world to me.

He tilts his head, "You love her?"

I frown, "What's that got to do with anything?"

He levels an intense stare, daring me to answer him.

"Of course, I do, you piece of shit."

"You'll take care of Victoria?" he asks.

I take a step forward and Gigi grabs my hand. I glance down and she shakes her head. *Shit, I'm letting him provoke me. Again.*

"Better than myself," I reply.

"You're aware there's nothing remotely romantic between us, right?" he uncurls his fists.

"The hell are you trying to say?" I growl.

"Nina was my ward, so to speak. I was responsible for her wellbeing. Human relations... They can be complicated, you know?" He drums his fingers on his thigh, "At some point, my feelings for her got more intense. I got personally involved. She'd never forgive me if something were to happen to her friend."

I drag my fingers through my hair, "So why did you shoot at Victoria?"

"It was a flesh wound. It got your attention, made you realize how much you need her in your life."

"You kidnapped her," I thrust out my chest.

"And sent you to her," he tilts his head, "because you still allowed her to walk away, after almost losing her once.

He's right.

"And here you are confronting us again, instead of escaping?" I frown. "Why didn't you ask Victoria about the bug when you took her?"

His jaw hardens, all expression wiped off from his face.

"Well?" I lean forward on the balls of my feet, "What's your play?"

Antonio glances around the room, then turns his gaze back on me. "There's no play."

I straighten, "You're lying."

"I discovered the bug, after you rescued her." He grits his teeth.

"You believe this asshole?" Weston mutters.

"Nah, do you?" I tilt my head.

Antonio's lips quirk, "The one time in my life I do something unselfish..." He shakes his head.

"What the fuck are you talking about?"

He sighs, "You had your head so far up your ass, you couldn't see how important she was to you. I wanted to push you along, make you come to your senses and own up to your feelings." He cups his chin in his hand. "It's what Nina would have wanted."

"That doesn't explain why you came storming into the hotel," I retort.

His features stay impassive.

"Well?" I growl. "Now is your chance to come clean, you bastard."

"When I discovered the bug, I got pissed off. By putting me at risk, you put Nina in danger and that sent me off the deep end." He draws in a breath. "I wasn't thinking clearly... I charged back to challenge Victoria on it," he says. "By the time I came to my senses, I was already here in your hotel..." His voice tapers off. "I knew it could be a mistake, but I thought I might be able to turn the situation to my advantage."

"You wanted to be found out by us?" I scowl before another thought occurs to me, "You hoped we'd make you an offer to work with us?"

"That's what I had calculated," he nods.

"You took a risk." I rub the back of my neck. Should I believe him? Is he telling the truth? "You willingly put yourself in danger. Why?"

"It seemed like my best shot," Antonio says simply.

I glare at him, "That's not the only reason, is it?"

He hesitates.

"I am calling the cops," I threaten.

"You wouldn't," Antonio growls. For the first time, he seems shaken. Good.

"Try me," I drawl.

He glances at Gigi, then back at me.

Anger crowds my mind. "That's it," I snap, reach for my phone.

"Wait," he mutters.

I keep my fingers poised over the keypad.

He sits up straight, places the fingertips of his hands together. "Nina," he says, his voice shorn of all emotion, "I did it for her."

"For Nina?" I frown, "Explain."

"I promised Nina that her friend would be taken care of, and I thought you would do that, but you're an idiot—"

I growl.

He holds up his hands in supplication, "The point is, you weren't taking care of her, and I needed to make sure that you did. That's what triggered the idea of Victoria's kidnapping..." He shrugs, "You went through a similar experience," he meets my gaze—the fucker actually looks me in the eye—and says, "and you needed something drastic to —I don't know—make you realize that you were fucking things up."

My vision tunnels; the blood pounds in my temples. Only when my fist connects with the side of his face do I realize that I have closed the distance between us. His head snaps back and blood erupts from his mouth.

"That's for putting Victoria's life in danger, you bastard."

He chuckles, wipes the blood from his face and looks around the room, a satisfied gleam in his eyes.

The fuck? I raise my fist again.

Weston grabs my shoulder. "Let him be."

"No," I growl. "You heard what he said. Asshole's fucking with me."

"He's illustrating how emotions can make you lose your cool to the point that they trip you up," Weston cautions.

"Weston's right," Sinner adds.

"The fuck I care about that?" I snarl.

"Fucker's methods are unconventional," Weston agrees, "but damn , if it didn't work, right?"

Gigi makes a sound somewhere between a cry and a laugh. "He got through to you, Saint. I was never in any danger, and besides," she steps forward, "he did it for Nina."

I straighten, make to swing at Antonio again, but Gigi grabs my arm. "Please, Saint, he put his life at risk for Nina, and that has to mean something."

Fuck, if that negates how he'd threatened Gigi's life, but if she says... Well, then... I draw in a breath. "This Nina," I say, trying to piece things together, "she's important to you?"

"I already told you she is." His dark gaze grows inscrutable. "It's why I'll take this deal with you."

"So, you're agreeing to spy on the Mafia and help us track down who was responsible for the kidnapping when we were kids?"

He nods, "It won't be easy, but I have some ideas."

"Life's not easy," I glower.

"If something goes wrong..." he glances at the other two, then at me, "If they discover I've turned on them, I need you to promise get Nina out."

Victoria squeezes my hand.

"For my wife," I growl, "I'll do it for her."

He jerks his chin, "Guess we have an agreement then."

"What about the USB you appropriated?"

"The Mafia wants it back." He tucks his elbows into his side.

"The fuck would they want that for?" I rub the back of my neck.

He raises his shoulders, "My guess is that the USB is marked in some form that can help them trace it back to its owner. They want it to help track down the snitch who sent it to you." He cracks his neck. "I'm only the messenger in this. Suffice to say, it's my ticket to get back in with them."

I scowl.

Antonio continues, "As for Victoria..."

I growl.

He raises his hands, "I let her go—doesn't mean the Mafia won't change their mind and come after her."

"You focus on your mission," I lean forward on the balls of my feet, "I'll take care of what's mine."

Victoria tugs on my sleeve.

I turn to her. Her face is pale.

"You okay?"

She presses a hand to her belly; sweat beads her upper lip,

"Victoria!" My heart begins to thud, "What's wrong?"

"I...I'm not sure." She pitches forward.

Saint

"It's my fault." I drag my fingers through my hair, "I didn't get to her in time, and now she's in there struggling for her life."

I dig the heels of my boots into the carpet, survey the bland surroundings of the waiting room in the hospital—the same hospital where Weston had been admitted earlier.

"Now, let's not jump to conclusions," Sinclair squeezes my shoulder. "Let's wait for the doc's verdict." He continues, "By the way, in case you were wondering, I cleared things up with Antonio—"

"I wasn't."

"Nevertheless, I removed the bug on the USB and sent him on his way."

I ignore him, "What's taking them so long in there?"

"Uh, the fact that you insisted Weston be present as they examine her?"

"They should be used to it by now," I mutter. "Besides, it's Weston's hospital, isn't it? And he was already with us. They can damn well do as he says...and me, for that matter."

"Not that I don't understand the sentiment," Sinclair sprawls in his seat, his suit none the worse for wear. "But...even I know better than to get in the way of doctors and such fine professionals who are specialists in their field."

"Easy for you to say." I squeeze my fingers into my sides, "If that had been Summer in there..."

His jaw flexes. "Fine," he purses is lips, "what's your point?"

"My point is..." I draw a blank. Run my finger around the sleeve of my shirt. "It's...shit..." I squeeze the bridge of my nose. "I don't know, what it is." *What's wrong with me?* My wife had collapsed, and this time I hadn't acted quickly enough. I had watched, rooted to the spot, as she had slumped forward, collapsed to the floor. I'd rushed to her, pulled her into my arms, watched as her body had bucked in my arms. Her eyes had rolled back in her head, and all color had leached from her face.

My hands and feet had gone numb, I could barely move, and couldn't string two thoughts together. Me, the man who always has an answer to every question. I couldn't do anything but hold her in my arms... And pray.

Fuck! I've never been religious, never been to a church in my life. But if there is a power larger than all of us, then I had appealed to it for help. I had sworn that if she was okay, I'd contribute a good chunk of my assets to FOK Media—that's short for *Full of Kindness,* nope I kid you not—the non-profit that the Seven of us had founded. I'll use the money to do good... In my own way.

I'd held her hand all the way to the hospital in the ambulance. She'd regained consciousness en route and had cried. She'd been out of her head with panic that she was losing the baby—our baby, fuck! The little being whose presence was only beginning to take shape in my life... Had it been snatched away before it had materialized?

I hadn't wanted the baby... But if anything happens to either of them, I'll never forgive myself... My heart begins to race and a hollow sensation roils in the pit of my stomach. Bile laces my tongue and I swallow it back. No, I am not going to lose her or the child. I want both of them. I need them in my life—to anchor me, to love, and to be loved. Is this what it means to love and to be loved? To rip out my guts, expose myself to the world, to share my deepest weaknesses and invite the possibility that I'll never recover from the sucker punch?

I jump up from the chair and begin to pace. *One foot in front of the other, don't lose it. You owe it to her to keep it together. You need to be strong.*

But if I had been better at taking care of her, she wouldn't have landed here in the first place.

If I hadn't taken her up on the offer in the beginning, it would have never come to this. I ball my fingers at my sides. I couldn't have resisted her. No way, would I have turned her away. The thought of her with any other man...having anyone else's child? I dig my fingernails into the palms of my hands with such force that pain shoots up my arm. She is mine. This child is mine. Everything I want is in that room, waiting for me to acknowledge it, to accept it. Am I too late? Have I missed what was right in front of me all along? I want this child, need her in my life more than anything else in this world.

If something were to happen to her or to the child, I'd... I drag in a sharp breath.

Footsteps sound.

I swivel around as Weston walks in the door. He pauses inside, leans his shoulder against the door frame. Whiskers darken his cheeks and his eyes are bloodshot.

He hadn't been in there long...maybe an hour or less. Had he given up hope so quickly? Was there nothing that could be done?

His gaze meets mine; he shakes his head.

"No," my knees buckle.

Sinclair grips my shoulder, "Steady, ol' chap." He turns to Weston, "Stop dicking around, you prick. What's the prognosis?"

Weston looks me up and down, "Now you understand how it feels."

"What... ?" my voice cracks. My vision tunnels as specks of black pull at my subconscious mind.

He tilts his head, "Do you see how it could be if you lost her?"

"You...you bastard." I stalk forward, covering the distance between us. "How dare you play with my feelings?" I roar.

"Thought you didn't have any..."

"Shut your trap, motherfucker. Tell me how she is."

"You sure you want to know?"

I grab my wanker of a friend by his collar, yank him to his toes.

"Hey," he winces, "I'm already wounded."

"Your hand won't be the only thing you can't use, if you don't answer my question."

"They are fine." He breaks into a wide grin, "Mother and baby are doing fine."

Adrenaline laces my blood. A pulse pound at my temples. I pull back my fist and let it fly at him.

53

Victoria

"It may only be given, not taken or bought. It's what the sinner desires, but the saint does not. What is it?" Saint pauses inside the doorway of the room.

I peer up at him from the bed.

He prowls inside, drops into the chair next to me, then takes my hand, "That was the question I was asked, by my kidnapper."

"The one you couldn't answer?"

He nods, weaves his fingers with mine. "I'd answered each of his riddles until then, but this one... It evaded me. Perhaps it was because I was exhausted by then. Maybe I had given up hope somewhere inside. Each time he took me out of the room where I was being held with the other boys, I was sure I would never return.

Each time, he would hang me upside down and throw questions at me. Anytime I couldn't answer, I was flogged on my feet until I managed to come up with the right answer. That day, I knew I was close to my breaking point. My brain was fogged. I had used up all of my reserves of energy. When he asked me the question, I barely heard it." His throat moves as he swallows.

"What happened then?"

"He whipped my feet. Every time he stopped and asked me if I knew the answer, I couldn't form the words. The blood flowed down my legs, along with it my life. The beating went on longer than any time before. Until I couldn't feel my feet anymore. Until the fire from the wounds ran down my legs, down my spine, slammed into the back of my head. Until some of the capillaries in my eyes broke, and blood ran down my cheeks. Darkness crowded in on me. I thought I was going to die... I never did guess the answer that day. He left me hanging there for hours... Days... Who knows?" He shrugs, "That's how the cops found me when they rescued me. I woke up in a hospital, wondering what the answer was. I couldn't guess it all this time... Then the answer came to me as I paced the floor of the waiting room outside, appealing to whichever higher power might hear me that you'd be okay."

"Oh," I swallow and a hot sensation grips my chest. "What was the answer?"

"Forgiveness," he peers into my face.

"That was the solution to the riddle?" My heart begins to race.

He nods, "Will you forgive me for everything I put you through, Victoria?"

I try to pull my hand away, but he holds on.

"Why?" I purse my lips.

He frowns.

"Why should I forgive you, Saint?" I ask. "You refused to accept our child."

"The one you didn't tell me about?" he retorts.

"I all but revealed it to you in the form of a puzzle."

"You could have come outright and told me," he scolds.

"To you? The master riddler?" I throw up my hands. "You who can crack almost any puzzle?"

His jaw tics. He shuffles his feet.

"You tested me again and again with your games. Yet the one time I asked you the one question, the answer to which mattered so much to me, you pretended not to know the answer."

He squeezes the bridge of his nose, "I think I knew what you were trying tell me. I guessed it, my subconscious alerted me it, but I didn't want to accept it." He winces. "I made a mistake."

"Wow," I blink, "You're actually acknowledging that you're not perfect."

"Seems today is a day of many firsts." He rubs his thumb over the pulse on my wrist, "Including my telling you that I want you, Gigi." He leans over and cups my belly.

A shiver runs up my spine.

"And I want this child more than anything in the world. If anything had happened to the two of you, I wouldn't have been able to live with myself."

He whispers his knuckles across my jaw, "Promise you'll never scare me like that again."

"I scared myself." Tears prick my eyes.

"Hey, don't." He wipes away the moisture that trickles down my cheek, "I am here, and I'm not going anywhere."

"Never?"

"I plan to be by your side. Through sickness and through health. Through ups and downs. Even when the children we have together are grown up and have left home, I'll be there taking care of you, protecting you, providing for you."

"Saint," I whisper. A ball of emotions chokes my throat. *Is he saying what I think he is?* My heart stutters and a warmth fills my chest.

"It's true," he nods. "I was too afraid to acknowledge what the thought of becoming a father does to me."

"What is that?"

"It makes me feel as vulnerable, as out of control, as I had been all that time ago when I was kidnapped and held captive. When I had no idea if it was day or night, where I was, whether I would survive to the next hour. I swore then, I'd never allow myself to lose control."

"And having a child is exactly that." I bring my other hand up to cup his face, "To cede power. Children bring their own brand of energy, and will create their own futures. You'll never be able to completely control the circumstances around them."

"I am going to try my damnedest," he growls.

"And I am going to call you out when you get too overbearing," I trace my thumb over his pouty lower lip.

"I can't change." He glowers, "It's what I am."

"Won't stop me from chipping away at your grumpy-pants ego." I set my jaw.

"Won't stop me from trying to fuck the sass out of you." He smirks, and damn him, but I'm instantly wet.

"You can try," I pout.

"I love that you can stand up to me." His features soften, "I might even let you get your way."

I blink.

"Sometimes," his lips curl.

"Well thank you so much," I grouse.

"If you behave."

I resist the urge to roll my eyes.

"There's one more thing."

Of course, there is.

He slides his hand into his pocket, pulls out the ring, then slips it onto my finger, "Never take it off again."

54

Two days later

Victoria

I glance through the window of the townhouse on Primrose Hill. The beautiful back garden rolls down from the residence at a gentle slope. There's an infinity pool in the middle of the garden and beyond that the view of the city stretches out.

Heat sears my back, a tingle runs up my spine, then Saint steps up, boxing me in with his arms on either side.

"Like it?"

"The view, you mean?"

"Also, the view." He chuckles, "You love the house, admit it."

I turn in the circle of his arms, "Cocky much?"

"That's my middle name, baby," he smirks.

"Will I never learn not to feed your massive ego?" I huff.

He leans in close enough for his hardness to brush against my waist, "Not the only thing that's massive."

I laugh, "Not that I am complaining, but I think we should wait."

His face pales, "Shit, are you feeling okay? No pain or anything... Should I call the air ambulance?" He reaches for his phone, swipes the screen and presses a number.

I grab his wrist. "I'm fine, really. I meant, wait until we return to the bedroom."

"Oh," he breathes out a sigh of relief, then hangs up.

Then I frown, "Hold on a minute, did you say, air ambulance?"

He reddens. "I didn't want to be caught unawares again. And no way, can my heart survive another ambulance ride to the hospital, so..." He cracks his neck, looks past me, "Uh, the infinity pool is wicked, huh?"

"Don't change the topic."

"Would I dare?" He glances down at me.

"Yes, you very much would dare." I frown, "What have you done Saint?"

"Nothing," he purses his lips, looking for all the world like an errant child. Why do I get the feeling my hands are going to be full with not one but two kids? The man in front of me often acts like one.

"Tell me," I scowl. "Remember what you said: no secrets."

He blows out a breath, "Why the hell did I promise you that, remind me?"

"Because you love me?"

He squares his shoulders. "Exactly. Which is why I had to do it."

"Do what?"

He tilts his head, "Don't freak out when you find out."

"What?" My heart begins to thud. "Out with it, Saint."

He rubs the back of his neck, a sure sign that whatever he's done is going to freak me out.

"It's only an air–ambulance," he mutters.

There's a *whomp-whomp* sound behind us and a breeze blows in through the open window.

I turn, and my jaw drops, "No."

He moves in, places his chin on my head, "I had to, babe."

I stare as an honest-to-goodness helicopter rises up beyond the infinity pool. I spot the sign of a red cross on the side that indicates it's used for medical purposes. It whirs over us, followed by a slight thump as vibrations roll down the walls. Did it land on the terrace of the townhouse? "Oh, my God," I turn to face him, "I can't believe you have a helicopter on stand-by."

"Maybe I can't control everything, but hell if I can't try to bring down the risk. This way, if there's an emergency, we can get to the closest hospital in under five minutes."

"I... I..." I open and close my mouth, "Only you'd do something so audacious."

"You're worth it, babe."

"You sound like a cheesy commercial."

He blinks, then chuckles, "I do, huh?" He lowers his forehead to mine, "That's what you do to me, darling. You've turned me into a blubbering shell of my former self."

"Hey," I swipe at his shoulder, "don't blame me for that. It's been barely twenty-four hours since you accepted your role as a father-to-be, and I can't believe you've already... Done all this."

"What?"

I wave my hand in the air, "You bought this townhouse on Primrose Hill—"

"I've had my eye on it."

"You had it furnished enough that we could move in right away."

He leans back, "Feel free to change anything you want."

"That's not the point."

"Then what is?"

"It's you." The waterworks threaten again. Shit, is it the hormones? Or is it the fact that, with Saint there to lean on, I finally feel secure enough to let go of all of my fears? In its place, there's a vulnerability that is new, that threatens to overwhelm me. That seduces me to simply melt into him and let him make all of the decisions. Hell! Is this what it means to be a real submissive? To have the onus of decision-making taken away from me? And why do I like that so much?

"Hey," he tips my chin up, "what is it?"

"You're overwhelming me, Saint."

"Ah," his lips quirk. He wipes away my tears, "And?"

" I like it.

"So?"

"I'm not sure if I want to."

"But you do," he smirks.

"I do?" I frown.

"Of course, my lovely Gigi. If you'd allow yourself to relax into the moment, you'd see that this is exactly what you need."

"B...but."

"Trust me, babe."

I peer up into his eyes. Do I dare put my faith in this alphahole of a dominant male, the father of my unborn child, who's changed his entire life for me overnight?

"I do," I whisper.

"Excuse me?" he frowns.

"I do trust you, more than myself. I believe in you so much that it hurts," my voice cracks.

His nostrils flare, "Do you have any idea what it does to me to hear that from you?"

He bends in close enough for our breaths to mingle, "You're mine, Gigi." He touches his lips to mine.

His touch sinks into my blood, coils in my belly.

"Promise me one more thing?" I whisper.

"Anything." He kisses me again.

"Promise you'll see a psychologist for the flashbacks and for the...scars?"

"You mean for my self-harming?" his voice is wry.

I peer up into his face. Hope blooms in my chest. The fact that he had called it by that term... That is the first step to recovery. It won't be easy, but as long as we are together, we can overcome any challenge.

"Will you?" I prompt him.

"For you," he searches my face, "if it makes you happy."

My heart does a little lurch, "It does." I smile up at him.

"And you make me happy, Gigi. Very happy." He crashes his lips to mine. I gasp and he swipes his tongue inside of my mouth—owning me, dominating me. I shiver, and his grasp tightens. He nibbles on my lower lip, and heat suffuses my skin. He rains kisses down my chin, my throat, down to the hollow between my breasts, on each nipple.

My scalp tingles and my toes curl. He drops to his knees in front of me, places a soft kiss on my belly. "Mine," he growls. A melting sensation pulls at my core. He drags his hard fingers down my thighs, coaxing them apart. My knees weaken; he grips my hips, holding me up. Then, through my dress, he nuzzles the triangle between my legs.

"Oh." Goosebumps dot my skin.

He inhales deeply and the sound is so erotic, so right, blood rushes to my lower belly. My pussy trembles. I dig my fingers into his hair and tug.

A low growl rumbles up his throat. The vibrations sink through the fabric of my outfit and warm my blood. I shiver, "Saint."

He presses his face into my pussy and a throbbing flares to life—hot, aching. My bones seem to melt all at once.

"Saint," I plead.

He slips his fingers under my dress, traces the backs of my knees. Sensations radiate from his touch. Every part of me that he touches seems to turn into an erotic zone.

"Saint!' I whine.

I sense his lips curve against my melting core. He slides both of his palms up the backs of my thighs, leaving pinpricks of pure lust in their wake. He cups my butt cheeks, squeezes gently. I draw in a sharp breath, grab the back of his head and urge him closer, closer.

He slides those wicked fingers under my panties, grazes the crevasse between my arse cheeks.

I shudder. Memories of how he'd taken me there swamp me. "Please," I gasp out.

"You like that, hmm?"

I nod.

He pushes aside the fabric of my dress, then buries his face in between my legs. The hot, aching tension inside of me winds up tighter—begging, needing more, so much more. I thrust my pelvis forward, but his grip stops me. He peers up at me from under those thick eyelashes; I take in the sight of his handsome face framed between my thighs and moisture pools between my legs. "Saint," I pant, "don't stop."

"You aren't completely recovered from your episode," he replies.

"Fuck that." I toss my head.

He chuckles, " I am proving to be a bad influence on you."

"Oh, please," I frown, "I was swearing long before I met you."

"Oh?" He tilts his head and his eyes gleam. "And this?" He slips his finger up to brush my pussy.

A moan spills from my lips.

"Were you doing this as well?"

"You know I wasn't. You are well aware that you're my first."

"And your only." His gaze intensifies, "I plan to keep you so happy, so satisfied, that you'll never want for anything..."

My panties grow damper. Damn it, how can he bring me so close to the edge with simply a glance?

"Except for your orgasms, of course." His lips twist in that sneer-smirk that is so very Saint.

"Stop that," I huff.

He chuckles, "What's life without a few games between us, hmm?" He rubs his nose up my pussy lips, and even through the double layers of fabrics, his hot breath sears my delicate skin.

"Oh," I gasp, "please come inside me. I need you inside of me."

He pauses, leans back on his haunches, "I don't want to hurt you."

"What happened was a fluke," I reassure him.

"I don't want it to happen again. If something goes wrong, I swear..."

"That's why you have a helicopter stationed above, ready to rush me to a hospital, huh?" I jerk my chin upwards.

He frowns, rolls his shoulders, "Still."

"No," I shake my head. "No excuses. Please, can you make love to me?"

His blue eyes turn that dark turquoise I am beginning to recognize as the first sign when he is out of control. He firms his jaw, "You sure?"

I scowl, then release him, to shove my fingers under my dress and drag down my panties. They catch on his hands as I tug, and he releases his grip on me. I angle sideways, then shimmy the fabric down to my ankles, straighten and kick it off.

"That clear enough for you?" I ask.

A low chuckle rolls from his lips. He rises to his feet, scoops me up in his arms. Turning, he walks out of the living room and up the steps. "I never did give you the grand tour," he rasps.

"I've seen enough to know the house is beautiful."

He takes the steps two at a time. When we reach the landing, he turns into a hallway, heads toward the double doors at the end. He carries me into a large room, with a familiar four poster bed mounted on a platform.

To the right, a bank of floor to ceiling windows open out onto the sprawling slope of Primrose Hill.

"Wow," I take in the room, "You had the bed moved from the suite?"

He shuffles his feet, "It's where we first made love. I couldn't leave it behind, could I?"

OMG! That is...hot and romantic and sentimental. This man is a teddy bear inside. "I thought it came with the hotel room?"

He scrutinizes my features, "I ordered it the day after I met you at Sterling's wedding."

"Oh?" My heart stutters, "You were so confident that you were going to have me?"

"You bet," his lips curl.

And that arrogance of his? Honestly, I can't make up my mind whether to slap him or kiss him. "Guess I don't get a say in whether we're keeping it?" I pout.

"Nope." He heads for the bed, steps up on the platform, "And not in how I take you once we are in it either."

He lowers me onto the mattress—slowly, gently, his every move such a contrast to the fierceness of how we'd fucked before that I can't stop the moan that escapes me.

"Shh," he places his finger on my lips, "let me take care of you."

He steps back, unties the sash on my wraparound dress. It parts in the front. He eases it off of one shoulder, then the other. Pulls me up into sitting position, to take it off of me completely then unhooks my bra and pulls that off.

I shiver.

"You cold?"

"No... It's how you look at me...like...like..."

He steps back, rakes his gaze down my chest, to the hollow between my legs. "Like?" he prompts.

"Like you want to own me."

Color smears his cheeks, "I thought that's what I wanted too, but I was wrong."

"I don't understand."

"I want to imprint myself into every part of you, sink into you, until it's impossible to tell where you begin and where I end. I want you to think of me even when you're not aware of it. Turn to me before you have a rational thought, coil into my memories as you drift off to sleep, dream of me when you are awake..." He frowns, "I want you to be me. That makes no sense, does it?"

My lips tremble, "I think I understand."

"You do?" His eyebrows knit.

I nod, "You want to love me like you've never loved anyone before?"

"More than I love myself." He brings his lips to mine, kisses me sweetly—a touch, a nibble, a deep drinking from my lips that sets my head reeling. The world tilts.

I look up to find he's stepped back.

He strips off his shirt and my throat closes. The light pours in through the open windows, highlighting the dips and hollows between that eight pack. My belly quivers and my sex clenches. I'll never get enough of his gorgeous body...or the raging intensity of the feelings he manages to cloak so well with it.

He toes off those ancient cowboy boots, shoves down his pants and his boxers, along with his socks. He straightens and his dick springs out—thick, heavy, the head swollen and weeping with need. I hold out my arms. He sinks down to join me. I wrap my legs around his waist, loving the feel of his hard planes biting into my flesh, his thick thighs a heavy comfort between mine. I trace the planes of his back and his muscles coil—so vital, so real, and all mine. His shoulders blot out the world and his face fills my line of sight. He lowers his head so our noses bump. A giggle tumbles from my lips.

"You're gorgeous, Gigi."

Heat sears my cheeks.

His lips kick up. Then he bends his head and captures my lips with his. His touch sinks all the way to my bones; heat tugs low in my belly and my pussy clenches. I tip up my chin, meeting his tongue with mine. A groan rips from him. He drags his palm down my side, settles it on my hip in a gesture that's possessive and intimate.

His cock nudges my opening. I tilt my hips up. "Please," I mumble in my throat.

He slides his dick into my melting pussy. So good, so full, so heavy, and so right. A groan rips from him, or was that me? He stills as I adjust to his size. I dig my heels into his back, wrap my arms around his breadth, and urge him on. He slides in further, his shoulders bunching, the muscles in his back flexing with tension. He's holding back, not allowing himself to give in completely. A smile curves my lips. I drag my fingers down the length of his spine, tracing each contour, each dip and crevasse. He shivers. Oh, this is different. A rush of power engulfs me. I reach his taut butt, dig my fingertips into the tight flesh. His entire body shudders. "I don't want to hurt you," he whispers against my lips.

"You're hurting me now."

He pulls back, "What?"

I smirk, "Unless you complete what you set out to do."

His lips twist. He eases himself inside of me—gently, slowly, his weight stretching my super-sensitive channel. Every ridge of his shaft slides, chafes against my flesh, sending pulsing, coiling, roiling sensations up my back, toward my extremities. The climax builds almost instantly, swelling from the point where we are joined.

He tilts his hips and his cock dips inside further, until he bottoms out. "You're my other half, Gigi," he whispers. "You're the better half of my conscience, the edge to my sense of humor, the lightbulb in my creativity, you're my heart," he whispers.

I swallow down the lump in my throat. Hell, I'd been wrong. He could simply tell me what was on his mind and I'd come with the intensity of his true self.

"Saint?" I clear my throat.

"Hmm?"

"I love you too, but... Would you please just shut up and fuck me now."

He chuckles, then rocks his pelvis again and again, each thrust sending waves of pleasure shooting out from the contact. The orgasm whips up my spine. I strain up and into him, plastering my breasts against him. He holds my gaze with his, scrutinizes my every response, searches my features with an intensity that pierces my heart. My pussy clamps down on his dick and his cock pulses. The climax swells and pauses, waits. I open my mouth and the cry sticks in my throat. I swallow, moan, plead with him silently.

His gaze intensifies; those blue eyes sparkle, glow with that cold heat that calls to me, beckons to me. "Come," he whispers.

I splinter into little pieces. He closes his mouth over mine—soft, searching—drawing another moan from somewhere deep inside of me that he swallows. Another low groan from him, his shoulders shudder, and he comes, filling all of the empty places inside of me. His muscles bunch, then he flips me over and onto him, without pulling out.

I coil into his broad chest, wrapping my fingers around his biceps, or trying to—considering their width.

He draws his warm palm across my back, from nape to arse and back again. There's a whisper against my hair.

I turn my head, place my chin on his chest, "You're a hidden romantic, Saint Jordan Killian Caldwell."

"I actually did miss one," he drawls.

"What?"

"When we first met, you asked if I'd missed a name." He flexes his shoulders, "Turns out, I did."

"What is it?" I rest my chin on his chest. "No, let me guess."

He raises his eyebrow, "Do I want to know?"

I snicker, "Is it, insensitive wart?"

He smirks.

"Giant squid?"

He chuckles, "It is giant, though I'd rather liken it to an octopus than a squid."

I choke, "You're a mugglepuff, you know that?"

He blinks, "I have no idea what you're talking about."

"You don't?" I sit up.

"Nope."

I gape, "You've never read Harry Potter?"

"What does that have to do with anything?" he glowers.

"You hate The Beatles..." I count off on my fingers, "You've never read a Harry Potter novel," I shake my head. "Next you'll tell me you've never seen, *When Harry met Sally*."

He reddens.

I throw up my hands, "What the hell am I doing with you?"

"Does it help that the missing name is Harry?" he drawls.

I pout, "You're kidding me."

"Believe it," he raises his shoulders, "or not."

I peer into his face, "That's such a typical Saint-Douchebag-Caldwell retort."

"And it turns you on," his lips curl.

"Now hold on a second—"

His phone buzzes.

I freeze.

His jaw tics.

It buzzes again.

"Let it go," I whisper.

He searches my features and swallows, "I can't."

He sets me aside on the bed, then straightens. He reaches for the phone from his pants pocket, checks the message and silences it, then proceeds to get dressed.

I watch the play of muscles on his back, the coil of power in his thighs as he stalks to the door.

A hollow sensation smolders in the pit of my stomach. *He dare walk out on me again?* I stiffen, curl my fingers into fists.

This time I won't let him leave. This time I am going to fight for what's mine.

"Saint," I yell after him. "Where the hell are you going?

He pauses, turns around. "Aren't you coming with me?"

55

What did the bee say to the flower?
Answer: Hello, Honey!

Victoria

An hour later, I watch as Saint eases his Jeep into the deserted parking lot.

I'd dressed quickly and followed him out earlier. He'd led me to the garage in the basement, which had been a surprise, considering I'd never seen him drive anything but the Jaguar. I'd been shocked to find that, in addition, he has a Jeep, a Harley—of course he has a Harley. What billionaire doesn't huh? More surprising, had been the SUV—a Mercedes SUV.

I'd paused in front of it and he'd simply tilted his head in that manner which is meant to convey, *Of course, I have a car which can be fitted with a baby seat.*

I'd stared at it and he'd said, if I didn't like it, he could get me another. I'd simply shaken my head, too bemused to say anything. I'd followed him into his Jeep, stared around at the simple interior. With his jeans, black sweatshirt and beat up cowboy boots, this vehicle feels more like him than anything else. Is the obnoxious billionaire persona an act then? I frown. Will my alphahole ever stop surprising me?

"You okay?" his voice slithers down my spine, coils in my gut. Now that smoky, sensuous burr of his tone... I'll never get used to that.

"I'm good."

"So why are you biting your nails?"

Oh. I pull my hand back, then shove it under my thigh, for good measure.

"Something on your mind, babe?"

Hell, why does he have to be so intuitive when it came to me, huh? I flip my hair back, then mutter, "You taking me to meet that woman?"

He nods.

'Is she like, your ex?' is what I want to ask, but he'd denied anything between them, and damn him, but I want to believe him. Besides, I am not going to turn into a nagging shrew, not when he's taking me to meet her. I'll find out soon enough, what this is all about, huh?

His gaze stays focused on the road.

I glance sideways at him, and my stomach does that little flip-flop at the sight of his patrician nose, that mean upper lip, the pouty lower lip—moisture beads my core. Shit, I am pregnant and he'd made love to me—in the sweetest way possible—just before we left the house, so why am I already turned on by taking in the profile of his face?

I turn to stare ahead as he veers off of the main road. The narrow road he's turned onto winds its way through a heavily-shaded strip of trees. He takes another turn, then pulls into a driveaway.

He switches off the ignition and silence descends.

I peer through the windshield at the field in front of us, "Are we still in London?"

"We're in Zone 4 of the city, so on the outskirts."

He reaches to the dash, pockets a small paper bag, then opens his door. I open my door and step out. He comes around the vehicle, holds out his hand. I take it. He weaves his fingers with mine, "Ready?"

No, I'm not. I take in a breath and nod. He leads me toward the small two-floor cottage. I sniff the air, assailed by the scent of dried hay and huh, is that the manure I smell? The pounding of hooves splits the air. I glance up as a horse gallops over from the edge of the field to the wooden stile.

His dark black coat glints in the sunlight. He tosses his head, snorts.

Saint, lowers the zipper of his sweatshirt, then pulls out the packet and empties out a couple of sugar lumps.

"Is that for the horse?"

He smiles, walks toward the fence, "Devil here, is a pure-bred Arabian. I couldn't pass up the opportunity to sneak him a treat, could I?"

He holds out his palm and the horse moseys over and licks up the cubes. Devil snorts again. Saint reaches up to run his fingers over his long nose. The horse, whines, stamps his feet. The horse lowers his head and Saint scratches him behind his ears until a rumbling sound emerges from him.

What the—? I blink.

"He sometimes behaves more like a dog than a horse," a voice explains.

I whip around to see a woman walking toward us. She's the one Saint met the other day. Tiny, exquisitely curved, her legs are enclosed in boots and slim jeans. Her plaid shirt is tucked into her hourglass waist. Her hair flows around her shoulders. Behind her, the door to the house stands open. Guess I'd missed that, entranced by the ease with which Saint had petted the horse.

She walks up and holds out her hand, "I'm Tink."

"Tink?" I frown.

She sighs, "Yeah, I was named Tinkerbell. I do prefer Tink, though."

"Don't blame you," I mutter. "I'm Victoria." I take her hand.

"Your name suits you." She looks me up and down, "You do bear a resemblance to Posh—"

"Don't say it, please. I don't know her, have never met her. She is no relation to me..."

"—Spice," she completes her statement. "Sorry, bet you've heard that a million times and hate it as much as I do my name."

"Hate to say it, but yours suits you, too," I bite my lips.

"Well, guess we are kindred, huh?" She drops my hand, turns to Saint.

"You made it," she jerks her chin.

"It sounded urgent."

"Sorry, but I think you need to see this one," she replies.

Saint pulls away from the horse, dusts his palms on his jeans, then reaches for mine, "Shall we?"

Tink leads the way inside, past a small living room, to another room that's furnished like an office. A bank of computer screens fills most of one wall. There are more screens sitting on the desk, each showing different images, two of them have maps with dots blinking on them. Whoa, someone loves their technology.

She slips into the chair, pulls up surveillance footage.

The screen shows a group of girls in a room which looks like a dormitory. Some of them are lying down, some sitting. One of them paces back and forth. She pauses, glances round the room, looks straight at the camera. Her desperate eyes seem to fill the screen, as she begins to weep.

The other women in the room sit up. One of them gets out of her bed to approach her... One of the others gestures to her. She hesitates, then falls back.

Tink shuts it off. "Sorry," she apologies, "it's hard to watch."

Saint wraps his arm around me and pulls me into his side. I rub my cheek against his sleeve.

He kisses the top of my head, "Shouldn't have allowed you to see that... But I wanted you to meet Tink and find out about the work we do together."

I look up at him, "So, you and she..."

"She runs an initiative that helps rescue those kidnapped or those who go missing." His lips stiffen. "No one should go through what I went through; nor the kind of mental trauma..." he peruses my features, "inflicted on Nina, and then on you."

What I'd been through couldn't begin to compare with his experience; but we'd both survived the challenges thrown at us.

Is that why we're attracted to each other, because we are survivors? No, it's more than that. We could have met anywhere, in other circumstances, and yet, the connection between us would have been there.

"This is why you respond so quickly every time she calls?"

He nods, "It normally means she's tracked down the whereabouts of a victim or victims," he nods toward the screen "and needs my help."

"Saint finances the efforts." Tink glances between us, "I'm sorry if I've called him at inopportune times. Sometimes I've needed backup, and since the operations are kept secret, I can't risk calling in anyone else."

I tighten my grip around Saint's waist. "So this is what you were doing?" My cheeks heat.

"You didn't think..." Tink glances up at Saint, then makes a face.

"Ugh, I wouldn't date him. He's waay too up his own arse." She laughs, "Besides, he's more like a brother to me."

Saint tugs on her hair, in a decidedly sibling-like gesture.

"When did you two decide to start this?" I ask.

Saint shuffles his feet, "I've already told you that I took my mother's death hard." He rubs the back of his neck, "Let's just say, I was out of control for a while."

"That's putting things mildly," Tink snorts. "He opened fire in his house when his father was away."

"O-k-a-y." I peer up at Saint, "Did you hurt anyone?"

He shakes his head, "But I destroyed the place. My father packed me off to go work with his friend."

"That's my father," Tink clarifies.

"He was an urban Cowboy, you could say." Saint rolls his shoulders, "He and his friends ran the adjacent farms. They trained and sold horses, and ran a riding school specializing in equine therapy."

"In the middle of London?"

"Zone 4; it's on the outskirts," he reminds me. "But yeah, they are technically in London."

"Wow," I glance around the space, "This place is something..."

Tink nods, "After my father died, Saint became my defacto guardian."

"The stint with Tink and her father saved me. Her father was more a parent to me than my own. If it were not for Tink's dad... I would have ended up shooting myself."

I glance down at the faded Cowboy boots.

"Those are—"

"My father's," Tink completes the sentence.

"I borrowed them from him," Saint says, "when I lived here on the ranch. It's where I was reborn a second time, in a way. Since then—"

"You wear them because they help you remember to stay sane?"

He nods.

Tears prick my eyes. I turn my face into Saint's arm. "I'm sorry that I doubted you," I whisper.

Saint wraps his arm even closer around me, "You couldn't have known, and I should have told you about this earlier."

I shake my head. "It would have been too dangerous."

Tink smiles, "She's a keeper, Killian."

He drums his fingers on his chest, "I have good taste, huh?"

I swipe at his shoulder, "So that's why you had the riding crop on your desk?"

"Want me to use it again on you?" he smirks.

"Ugh," Tink grimaces, "TMI, you guys."

"Sorry," he snickers, "couldn't resist."

His phone pings. He slides it out of his pocket and his lips curl.

"What are you up to?" I huff.

"Weston's on his way to the cabin in the countryside to get some alone time over Christmas." He pockets his phone.

There's silence for a minute.

"Holdonasecond." I scowl, "Isn't Amelie headed there as well?"

"Is she?" His lips twitch.

"Saint Jordan Killian *Harry* Caldwell," I grumble.

"Uh-oh," he drawls, "am I in trouble?

"You set this up?"

"Me?" His gaze widens.

I stare, "You sent them both up there?"

"Oops." He smirks.

TO FIND OUT WHAT HAPPENS NEXT READ WESTON AND AMELIE'S STORY IN THE BILLIONAIRE'S CHRISTMAS BRIDE HERE

READ AN EXCERPT FROM WESTON AND AMELIE'S STORY...

I stalk toward the door at the far end, take a breath.

The sounds of water splashing, then a male voice breaks into a rendition of *Nothing Else Matters* by Metallica. Huh? The singing's not bad, actually. My thief, apparently, has a thing for classic rock, and can carry a tune. I hum the lyrics in sync with him... *The hell?* I pause, draw in another breath. *Now or never. Do it, Amelie. Go for it.* Whoever it is, he has no right to be here. *Shit, should I have called the cops?*

The singing stops abruptly. *What the—? Did I give myself away?* I half angle my body; the door flies open. Offense is the best form of defense, and all that. I pivot around, raise my weapon, and find I am confronted with a wall of muscle. Naked chest, water running in rivulets down those sculpted abs that narrow into a concave belly which points to his thick, long—

"My face is up here," he drawls.

Heat flushes my cheeks; I jerk my gaze up. Grey eyes clash with mine—stormy clouds that boil in a sky which hints at oncoming snow. Sleet. Hail. An uncompromising will to get his way no matter what. A shiver runs down my spine and moisture pools between my legs.

The skin between his eyebrows crinkles and his nostrils flare. *No way.* He can't smell my arousal, can he?

That mean upper lip thins further. His pouty lower lip juts out above a chin that wears days' old growth of beard. Thick dark hair covers his jaw. How would it feel to have him draw those rough whiskers across my inner thigh? Right before he dips his head, darts out his tongue, and licks my innermost secret place. Goosebumps dot my skin. *Shit, what's wrong with me? Why did my mind go there? You know why… Because this handsome piece of 100% male goodness is, quite simply, the most wickedly delicious piece of dessert I've ever laid my eyes on.* My throat dries. Also, I happen to know him.

"You?" my voice comes out breathless.

"What are you doing here?" he snaps at the same time.

"I asked the question first," I huff.

"I am not in the habit of answering queries posited by women who look like they've been dragged in from a storm."

"What?" My jaw drops. I am gaping, and it's not only because the words complete the image of the man I've loathed from the moment I first saw him at the wedding of one of my best friends. "Dr. f'ing Weston," I snarl.

"That's Doc Kincaid to you." He yawns.

Of course, his surname would have to have the word kink in it in some form. "And are you?" I scowl.

"What?"

"A real doctor?"

He raises his hand, stabs the cigar I only now realize he holds between his fingers between his lips. "Do you want to find out?" He looks me up and down, "I could give you a thorough examination." His gaze settles on my breasts, slides down to my core. "Make sure everything is in working order." He snickers.

Heat fizzes low in my belly. Hell, with that kind of hotness, this man could clearly get my cake batter to rise in seconds… *Wait, did I just think that?*

I make a gagging noise in my throat, "Does that line actually work?"

"You'd be surprised." His lips curl.

Oh, that smirk. My stomach seems to bottom out… Or maybe that's because I haven't eaten since lunch time.

He draws on his cigar, cheeks hollowing for an instant, before he puffs out smoke. Cherries, cloves…cinnamon. Yum. My mouth waters, "How would it be to bake a cigar dessert?"

"What?" He frowns.

Shit, did I just say that aloud?

"Nothing," I mumble, "and you haven't answered my question."

His voice lowers to a hush, "I'll answer yours if you answer mine." Another shiver ladders up my spine. How *did he manage to make that seem like an innuendo?*

"Is everything a trade to you?"

"You should try it." He smiles, a full-blown grin that highlights the laughter lines that stretch from the corners of his eyes. I mean, could this guy be any more perfect? I allow my gaze to take in the breadth of his shoulders, that gorgeous neck, the swell of those hard biceps, the smattering of hair on those forearms—*No, do not look lower; don't do it—* to the splint that he sports around middle finger of his right hand.

"What happened to you?" I scowl.

"This?" He raises his middle finger to show me the bird by default, "I fractured my middle finger a car accident."

"How convenient," I scoff. "You can announce your jerk-face nature without speaking a word."

He chuckles, "You always this nice to injured men?"

"You always go around flashing women?"

"You enjoyed the view." He raises that goddam cigar again to his mouth, wraps those beautiful lips around the smoke stick. And I'd love to get my mouth around his fat, juicy cigar too.

No, no. Enough with the terrible metaphors. But, hello, can you blame me? I am only a woman standing in front of a man—a naked, gorgeous as hell, stud muffin of a male who pulls the cigar from his mouth, and blows out a cloud of fragrant smoke from between pursed lips.

Moisture melts my core. My toes curl.

Jesus, there should be a law against him using his mouth like that. Of course, I could find other uses for that mouth of his too… *No, no no, why are you insisting on going back down that route?*

"Nothing I haven't seen," I toss my head.

"Unlikely." He lowers his right hand—the one with the splint and the default flip-me-off-bird to his crotch.

What the—? Don't look there, bitch— Don't bloody watch him grasp himself and squeeze.

I gulp, the sound audible in the small space. And damn him, but I can't take my gaze off of that gorgeous part of his anatomy.

He lowers his hand to his side, "I rest my case."

Hell, but a certain part of him is far from being in resting position. Gulp. *Did I just word play on his dick play?* Clearly his proximity is rubbing off if all I can think of are these poor jokes.

"By the way," his tone is conversational, "you planning on defending yourself with that?" He jerks his chin.

I tighten my grasp around the spatula and raise it. "This has been known to strike fear in the heart of burglars and those who've tried to break in on me before," I snap.

"Have you been burgled before?" His jaw hardens.

"None of your business."

"Have you?" He takes a step forward. I scoot back. My leg brushes something warm, which moves. A scream spills from my lips, then, for the second time in ten minutes, the world tilts, and I find myself falling… Falling. The spatula slips from my grasp. I squeeze my eyes shut, waiting for my butt to connect with the hard ground, only I'm yanked upright. Heat envelops me and my breasts flatten against something unyielding. I don't need to open my eyelids to know it's his chest, the one with the cut planes, the eight pack abs. I slap my palm against that wall of muscles which coil, move, and writhe under my fingertips. I gulp and my legs threaten to give way under me, but his hold around my shoulders tightens. I spot the smoldering smoke stick of his on the ground.

"Your…cigar," I stutter.

"Fuck that." His breath feathers over my hair and liquid lust shoots up my veins. The scent of cherries and cloves mixes with that edgy darkness that is purely Weston. Speaking of—something hard stabs into my waist. A groan boils up my throat. Not fair—this crazy attraction to someone I'd barely met a couple of times. Why does he have to smell so delicious? Bet if I licked his chest, he'd taste more decadent that the chocolate mud pie cake recipe I've been wanting to bake. I'll lick the frosting off his cupcake any time. *Nooooo.* Not again. Enough with comparing his unmentionables with my favorited stuffed good-ies. OMG, how would it feel to have him stuff his goodies in my cannoli? Wait, did that even make sense?

His voice dips, "You haven't answered my question."

"What?" I blink.

"Did he hurt you?" He enunciates his words at a slow pace as if I am slow of mind… Which, I admit, at the moment, I seem to be. His larger-than-life charisma has turned my brain cells to mush. "Tell me," he coaxes. Is he using the same tone he used with the puppy to make him obey? Well, hell, if it isn't working on me as well.

My stomach stutters. "Once…." I force out the word.

His muscles coil; tension radiates off of his body. "You were burgled before?" he snaps.

"Yeah," I hunch my shoulders, "it happened a week ago… No biggie." I swallow as my heart begins to race. It hadn't been pleasant, that almost encounter. I had been alone in the kitchen of my bakery at 4 am… Hell, it had been horrible, actually. The guy had thrown a fright into me and I had thrown this spatula at him. " I chased off the guy."

His grip tightens, "Did he hurt you?" His jaw tics.

I stare up into his tight features. You'd think Mr. Jerkass here is all concerned about my safety.

"Did he?" his voice snaps through the noise in my head.

"N…no," I shake my head.

"No, what?"

No, I will not give in to this insane chemistry between us. I didn't come all this way to run slap-bang into a man who is, surely, far worse than the one who recently broke my heart. "No, he didn't do any harm." I tip up my chin. "Though I can't promise the same to you."

He chuckles, "I love a good fight, don't you?"

Jackass.

A whine sounds behind me.

I shoot a sideways glance to spot a puppy plant his behind on the ground…exactly the kind of position I'd have been, if 'Mr. Overbearing Brute' here hadn't grabbed me first. Oh, so that's what I'd brushed against earlier and almost fallen over.

"Max," Weston talks to the dog, "you hungry, buddy?"

The puppy whines again.

"I'll be right there, little man." His voice takes on a cajoling tone, and damn him, but my ovaries seem to spasm. *The hell is he doing to me?* Before this, I've never thought about kids… Hell, I've barely managed to embark on a halfway decent career, and I've never thought of myself as someone who'd want a family. But Weston, with his smoldering glare, his hard face, his harder—um—body, and that coaxing manner with which he talks to Max… I can see him with a child tucked under one arm, and me under his other… Heck, I can see me under him, period. My mouth waters. My panties dampen further. *Get your mind out of the gutter, you slut.*

"Isn't he Sinclair and Summer's pet?" I frown. My friend Summer had married Sinclair Sterling, one of the seven billionaire co-owners of 7A investments, not long ago. She'd found the love of her life, that lucky bitch. Not that I begrudge her her happiness. What I wouldn't give for some of that moon and stars glitter to rub off on me as well…

"They're away on an extended honeymoon," Weston grunts.

"Aww. So you decided to puppy-sit?" I breathe. A warm glowing ball lights up inside of me.

He glowers, "Don't gush any sweet icky stuff now—uh, what's your name again?"

Poof—that warm feeling I mentioned? Forget about it. The hell is wrong with this man? "You know my name all right, you ass." I stab my finger in his chest, "So why are you pretending otherwise?"

"Me?" He blinks, "Do I?" He tilts his head, pretending to think, "Is it Lily?"

A slow burn starts up my spine.

"No… No." He cracks his neck, "It will come to me, it will… It's Malia, right?"

Anger laces the edges of my vision. I draw in a breath, then another. *Stay calm, he can only get so much more obnoxious, right?*

"Wait, let me try, one more time…" He pats his temple with the palm of his injured hand. "It's…something French, isn't it? Like… Valerie, Malory, maybe? No, I have it." He snaps his fingers, "It's Celine. I got that right, didn't I?" He chuckles.

I clench my fists, then raise my hand toward his face.

He catches my wrist. "Tsk, tsk," he clicks his tongue. "What a temper you have, little one."

"Don't 'little one' me... You... You wanker."

"Finally," his eyes gleam, "here kitty, kitty, show me your claws."

"I'll do better than that," I hiss, "I'll show you how it is to see the sun at night time."

I bring up my knee, aim for his groin.

TO FIND OUT WHAT HAPPENS NEXT READ WESTON AND AMELIE'S STORY IN THE BILLIONAIRE'S CHRISTMAS BRIDE HERE

Read an excerpt from Mafia King - Karma and Michael Byron's story...

Karma

"Morn came and went—and came, and brought no day..."

Tears prick the backs of my eyes. Goddamn Byron. Always creeps up on me when I am at my weakest. Not that I am a poetry addict, by any measure, but words are my jam.

The one consolation I have, that when everything else in the world is wrong, I can turn to them, and they'll be there—friendly steady, waiting with open arms. And this particular poem had laced my blood and crawled into my gut when I'd first read it. Darkness had folded into me like an insidious snake that raises its head when I least expect it. Like now. I'd managed to give my bodyguard the slip and veered off my usual running route to reach *Waterlow Park*.

I look out on the still-sleeping city of London, from the grassy slope of the expanse. Somewhere out there, the Mafia is hunting me, apparently.

I purse my lips, close my eyes. Silence. The rustle of the wind between the leaves. The faint tinkle of the water from the nearby spring.

I could be the last person on this planet, alone, unsung, bound for the grave.

Ugh! Stop. Right there. I drag the back of my hand across my nose.

Try it again, focus, get the words out, one after the other, like the steps of my sorry life.

"Morn came and went—and came, and brought no day..." My voice breaks. "Bloody, asinine, hell." I dig my fingers into the grass and grab a handful and fling it out. *Again. From the top.* I open my eyes, focus on a spot in the distance.

"Morn came and went—and came, and...."

"...brought no day."

I whip my head around. His profile fills my line of sight. Dark hair combed back by a ruthless hand that brooks no opposition.

My throat dries.

Hooked nose, thin upper lip, a fleshy lower lip, that hints at hidden desires. Heat. Lust. The sensuous scrape of that whiskered jaw over my innermost places. Across my inner thigh, reaching toward that core of me that throbs, clenches, melts to feel the stab of his tongue, the thrust of his hardness as he impales me, takes me, makes me his.

"And men forgot their passions in the dread
Of this their desolation; and all hearts
Were chill'd into a selfish prayer for light.."

Sweat beads my palm; the hairs on my nape rise. "Who are you?"

He stares ahead, his lips moving,

"Forests were set on fire—but hour by hour
They fell and faded—and the crackling trunks
Extinguish'd with a crash—and all was black."

I swallow, squeeze my thighs together. Moisture gathers in my core. How can I be wet by the mere cadence of this stranger's voice?

I spring up to my feet.

"Sit down."

His voice is unhurried, lazy even, his spine erect. The cut of his black jacket stretches across the width of his massive shoulders. His hair... I was mistaken. There are strands of dark gold woven between the darkness that pours down to brush the nape of his neck. My fingers tingle. My scalp itches.

I take in a breath and my lungs burn.

This man, he's sucked all the oxygen in this open space, as if he owns it, the master of all he surveys. The master of me. My death. My life. A shiver ladders its way up my spine. *Get away, get away now, while you still can.*

I take a step back.

"I won't ask again."

Ask. Command. Force me to do as he wants. He'll have me on my back, bent over, on the side, over him, under him, he'll surround me, overwhelm me, pin me down with the force of his personality. His charisma, his larger-than-life essence that will crush everything else out of me and I… I'll love it.

"No."

"Yes."

A fact. A statement of intent, spoken aloud. So true. So real. Too real. Too much. Too fast. All of my nightmares…my dreams come to life. Everything I've wanted is here in front of me. I'll die a thousand deaths before he'll be done with me… And then, will I be reborn? For him. For me. For myself. I live first and foremost to be the woman I am…am meant to be.

"You want to run?"

No.

No.

I nod my head

He turns his head and all of the breath leaves my lungs. Blue eyes —cerulean, dark like the morning skies, deep like the nighttime, hidden corners, secrets that I don't dare uncover. He'll destroy me, have my heart, and break it so casually.

My throat burns. A boiling sensation squeezes my chest.

"Go then, my beauty, fly. You have until I count to five. If I catch you, you are mine."

"If you don't?"

"Then I'll come after you, stalk your every living moment, possess your nightmares, and steal you away in the dead of midnight, and then…"

I draw in a shuddering breath; liquid heat drips from between my legs. "Then?" I whisper.

"Then, I'll ensure you'll never belong to anyone else, you'll never see the light of day again, for your every breath, your every waking second, your thoughts, your actions…and all of your words, every single last one, will belong to me." He peels back his lips, and his teeth glint in the first rays of the morning light. "Only me." He straightens to his feet, and rises, and rises.

He is massive. A beast. A monster who always gets his way. My guts churn. My toes curl. Something primal inside of me insists I hold my own. I cannot give in to him. Cannot let him win whatever this is. I need to stake my claim in some form. *Say something. Anything. Show him you're not afraid of him.*

"Why?" I tilt my head back, all the way back. "Why are you doing this?"

He tilts his head, his ears almost canine in the way they are silhouetted against his profile.

"Is it because you can? Is it a…a…" I blink, "a debt of some kind?"

He stills.

"My father. This is about how he betrayed the Mafia, right? You're one of them?"

All expression is wiped clean of his face, and I know then I am right. My past… Why does it always catch up with me? *You can run, but you can never hide.*

"Tick-tock, Beauty." He angles his body and his shoulders shut out the sight of the sun, the dawn skies, the horizon, the city in the distance, the whisper of the grass, the trees, the rustle of the leaves... All of it fades, and leaves me and him. Us. *Run.*

"Five," he jerks his chin, straightens the cuffs of his sleeves.

My knees wobble.

"Four."

My heart hammers in my chest. I should go. Leave. But my feet are welded to this earth. This piece of land where we first met. What am I, but a speck in the larger scheme of things? To be hurt. To be forgotten. To be brought to the edge of climax and taken without an ounce of retribution. To be punished... By him.

"Three." He thrusts out his chest, widens his stance, every muscle in his body relaxed. "Two."

I swallow. The pulse beats at my temples. My blood thrums.

"One."

Michael

"Go."

She pivots and races down the slope. The fabric of her dress streams behind her, scarlet in the blue morning. Her scent, lushly feminine with silver moonflowers, clings to my nose, then recedes. I reach forward, thrust out my chin, sniff the air, but there's only the green scent of dawn. She stumbles and I jump forward. Pause when she straightens. *Wait. Wait. Give her a lead. Let her think she has almost escaped, that she's gotten the better of me... As if.* I clench my fists at my sides, force myself to relax. *Wait. Wait.* She reaches the bottom of the incline, turns. I surge forward. One foot in front of the other, my heels dig into the grassy surface as mud flies up, clinging to the edges of my £4000 Italian pants. Like I care? Plenty more where that came from. An entire walk-in closet full of tailor-made clothes, to suit every occasion, with every possible accessory needed by a man in my position to impress... Everything, except the one thing that I have coveted from the first time I had laid eyes on her. Sitting there on the grassy slope, unshed tears in her eyes, and reciting... Byron? For hell's sake. Of all the poet's in the world, she had to choose the Lord of Darkness.

I huff. All a ploy. Clearly, she'd known I was sitting near her... No, not possible. I had walked toward her and she hadn't stirred, hadn't been aware. Yeah, I am that good. I've been known to slice a man from ear to ear while he was awake and fully aware. Alive one second, dead the next. That's how it is in my world. You want it, you take it. And I... I want her.

I increase my pace, eat up the distance between myself and the girl... That's all she is. A slip of a thing, a slim blur of motion. Beauty in hiding. A diamond in the rough, waiting for me to get my hands on her, polish her, show her what it means to be...dead. She is dead. That's why I am here.

Her skirts flash behind her, exposing a creamy length of thigh. My groin hardens; my legs wobble. I lurch over a bump in the ground. *The hell?* I right myself, leap forward, inching closer, closer. She reaches a curve in the path, disappears out of sight. My heart hammers in my chest. I will not lose her, will not. *Here, Beauty, come to Daddy.* The wind whistles past my ears. I pump my legs, lengthen my strides, turn the corner. There's no one there, huh?

My heart hammers, the blood pounds at my wrists and my temples, and adrenaline thrums through my veins. I slow down, come to a stop. Scan the clearing.

The hairs on my forearms prickle. She's here. Not far. Where? *Where is she?* I prowl across, to the edge of the clearing, under the tree with its spreading branches. *When I get my hands on you, Beauty, I'll spread your legs like the pages of a poem. Dip into your honeyed sweetness, like a quill into an inkwell; drag my aching shaft across that melting, weeping entrance.* My balls throb. My groin tightens. The crack of a branch above shivers across my stretched nerve endings. Instinctively, I swoop forward, hold out my arms. A blur of red, dark blonde hair, skirt swept up in a gust of breeze. She drops into my arms and I close my grasp around the trembling, squirming mass of precious humanity. I cradle her close to my chest, heart beating thud-thud-thud, overwhelming any other thought.

Mine. All mine. The hell is wrong with me? She wriggles her little body, and her curves slide across my forearms. My shoulders bunch and my fingers tingle. She kicks out with her legs and arches her back. Her breasts thrust up, the nipples outlined against the fabric of her jogging vest. *She'd dared come out dressed like that…? In that scrap of fabric that barely covered her luscious flesh?*

"Let me go." She whips her head toward me, her hair flowing around her shoulders, across her face. She blows it out of the way, "You monster, get away from me."

Anger drums at the backs of my eyes; desire tugs at my groin. The scent of her is sheer torture, something that I had dreamed of in the wee hours of twilight when dusk turned into night. She's not real. Not the woman I think she is. She is my downfall. My sweet poison. The bitter medicine I must imbibe to cure the ills that plague my company.

"Fine." I lower my arms and she hits the ground butt first.

"How dare you?" she huffs out a breath, her hair messily arranged across her face.

I shove my hands into the pockets of my fitted pants, knees slightly bent, legs apart. Tip my chin down and watch her as she sprawls at my feet.

"You…dropped me?" She makes a sound deep in her throat.

So damn adorable.

"Your wish is my command," I quirk my lips.

"You don't mean it."

"You're right." I lean my weight forward on the balls of my feet and she flinches.

"What…what do you want?"

"You."

She pales. "You want to…rob me? I have nothing of value. I'm not carrying anything…except." She reaches for her pocket.

"Don't," I growl.

"It's only my phone."

"So you say, hmm?"

"You can…" she swallows, "you can trust me."

I chuckle.

"I mean, it's not like I can deck you with a phone or anything, right?"

I glare at her and she swallows, "Fine… You… You take it."

Interesting.

"Hands behind your neck."

She hesitates.

"Now."

She instantly folds her arms at the elbows, cradles the back of her head with her palms.

I lean down and every muscle in her body tenses. Good. She's wary. She should be. She should have been alert enough to have run as soon as she sensed my presence. But she hadn't. And I'd delayed what was meant to happen long enough.

I pull the gun from my pocket, hold it to her temple. "Goodbye, Beauty."

To find out what happens next read Mafia King - Karma and Michael Byron's story HERE

Want to be the first to find out about L. Steele's new releases? Join her newsletter HERE

Follow **L. Steele** on **AMAZON**

Follow **L. Steele** on **BookBub**

Follow **L. Steele** on **Goodreads**

Follow **L. Steele** on **Facebook**

Follow **L. Steele** on **Instagram**

Join **L. Steele's** secret **Facebook Reader Group**

For more books by **L. Steele** click **HERE**

MARRIAGE OF CONVENIENCE BILLIONAIRE ROMANCE FROM L. STEELE

The Billionaire's Fake Wife - Sinclair and Summer's story that started this universe... with a plot twist you won't see coming!

The Billionaire's Secret - Victoria and Saint's story. Saint is maybe the most alphahole of them all!

Marrying the Billionaire Single Dad - Damian and Julia's story, watch out for the plot twist!

The Proposal - Liam and Isla's story. What's a wedding planner to do when you tell the bride not to go through with the wedding and the groom demands you take her place and give him a heir? And yes plot twist!

CHRISTMAS ROMANCE BOOKS BY L. STEELE FOR YOU

Want to find out how Dr. Weston Kincaid and Amelie met? Read The Billionaire's Christmas Bride

Want even more Christmas Romance books? *Read A very Mafia Christmas, Christian and Aurora's story*

Read a marriage of convenience billionaire Christmas romance, Hunter and Zara's story - *The Christmas One Night Stand*

FORBIDDEN BILLIONAIRE ROMANCE BY L. STEELE FOR YOU

Read Daddy JJ's, age-gap romance in Mafia Lust HERE

Read Edward, Baron and Ava's story starting with Billionaire's Sins HERE

ABOUT THE AUTHOR

Hello, I'm L. Steele.

I write romance stories with strong powerful men who meet their match in sassy, curvy, spitfire women.

I love to push myself with each book on both the spice and the angst so I can deliver well rounded, multidimensional characters.

I enjoy trading trivia with my husband, watching lots and lots of movies, and walking nature trails. I live in London.

Follow me:
On Amazon
on BookBub
on Goodreads
on Audible
On TikTok
Join my secret Facebook Reader Group
on Pinterest
My YouTube channel
Read ALL my books
Spotify

ACKNOWLEDGMENTS

Edited by: Elizabeth Connor

Cover Design: Jacqueline Sweet

Huge thank you to Li Iacobacci, Danielle Vale and Rachel Kroeplin, my alpha readers.

Huge shout out to everyone in L. Steele's Team Facebook reader group, you guys are awesome!

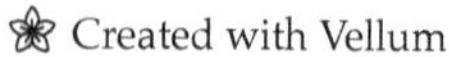 Created with Vellum